The Travels Through England Of Dr. Richard Pococke, Successively Bishop Of Meath And Of Ossory, During 1750, 1751, And Later Years, Volume 44

James Joel Cartwright, Richard Pococke

THE TRAVELS THROUGH ENGLAND

OF

DR. RICHARD POCOCKE,

SUCCESSIVELY BISHOP OF MEATH AND OF OSSORY,
DURING 1750, 1751, AND LATER YEARS.

EDITED BY

JAMES JOEL CARTWRIGHT, M.A., F.S.A.,
TREASURER OF THE SOCIETY.

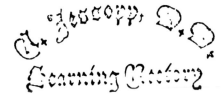

VOLUME II.

PRINTED FOR THE CAMDEN SOCIETY.

M.DCCC.LXXXIX.

WESTMINSTER:
PRINTED BY NICHOLS AND SONS,
25, PARLIAMENT STREET.

[NEW SERIES XLIV.]

PREFACE.

THIS volume continues the narrative of Dr. Pococke's Travels during the years 1754, 1756, and 1757. For some years after the latter date it is probable that the new duties incumbent on his recent elevation to the see of Ossory somewhat interfered with his tastes for wandering. Among the Additional Manuscripts in the British Museum (Nos. 14,256 to 14,261) are to be found accounts of a journey taken by Dr. Pococke round Scotland to the Orkneys, and through parts of England and Ireland in the year 1760; and of further travels in England made in 1764. It may be, however, that portions of the intermediate years were spent in like excursions, of which the manuscript accounts are lost or still remain in private hands. The account of his English journeys in 1760 and 1764 would fill another goodly volume of the Camden Society's publications, but as there is no immediate prospect of the work being continued, the two volumes now issued are made complete in themselves by the addition of an index. Dr. Pococke's " Tours in Scotland, 1747, 1750, and 1760," were printed in 1887 for the Scottish History Society, under the editorship of Mr. Daniel William Kemp, of Edinburgh.

To have annotated these Travels in an entirely satisfactory way would have entailed great labour and research, and would have swelled the work perhaps to double its present size. It seemed to the Editor, therefore, best to leave the learned traveller's text to stand for what it is worth, unincumbered by any comment or cor-

rection. Dr. Pococke's remarks on places and things, based upon
his own observation, are unimpeachable and of high interest; but
none of his statements or theories touching historical, genealogical,
or antiquarian matters should be accepted without careful scrutiny.

In accordance with the usual practice in these publications, the
names of the places visited are printed as they are spelt in the
original manuscript. The identification of many of them without
the aid of a good map will therefore be found difficult. In the
index, however, each locality will be found under its modern form
of spelling, except in a few doubtful instances.

THE TRAVELS THROUGH ENGLAND OF DR. RICHARD POCOCKE.

Wigan, June 2d, 1754.

ON the 25th of May I embarked at Dublin for Flukeborough, near Lancaster, and arrived in the bay on the 27th, about 4 in the afternoon, and went ashore near a small village called Barnsey. We had sail'd by the Pele of Foudrey, an old Castle on a rocky Island at the entrance of the bay of Lancaster ; it was built by an Abbot of Forness Abbey, in the time of Edward the third. The Abbey near it I saw in 1750, in the way to Scotland. A litle within the head of land at the Pele is a small mount call'd Mote Hill. I went two miles to Ulverston, and about half way pass'd by Coningsein, an Ulverstone. old seat formerly of the Doddings now of the Bradeels, from Portfield near Waller, who acquired this estate by an intermarriage. Ulverstone is a small neat market town, but no Corporation, nor is there a justice of Peace in it ; they have a handsome market house built of a reddish freestone brought from near the Abbey or the Mannor as they call it. There is a great trade here in Corn, especially oats, chiefly for exportation, and they weave some Camblets and Serges. On the 28th, crossing the Sands, we went four miles to a small village called Flukeborough, having passed by Holker, a Flukeborough. fine wooded seat of Sr Wm Lowther, who lives there ; it came to him by marriage with an heiress of the Prestons. I went two miles farther to Grange, and crossed the Sands into Westmoreland, and came to the mouth of the River Ken or Kent, on which Kendal stands. In two miles we came to Milthrop, on the small river Milthrop. Bela, where there are paper mills for white and brown paper. A mile above it, at Betham, is a waterfall of about fifteen feet.   In a mile we came to Hirsom, very pleasantly situated ; here I was informed is a Free School, which is a foundation to a College in Cambridge, as are several other schools in this county, the Cumberland men going to Queen's College in Oxford.   We travelled through a very fine country on the Ken, and soon came to Levens, the seat of the Earl of Berkshire, with a pleasant park on the river, which is very beautiful in the views of hanging ground and wood on each side ; a litle above the park there is a fine waterfall of about 10 feet.   I passed in sight of Sisergh on the other side, an old Castle and seat of the Stricklands, who are Roman Catholicks, of which family, if I mistake not, was the remarkable Prelate of that name, who was Bishop of Namure.   I went near Waterbrook, supposed to be the ancient Concangii, which I saw when I travelled last through this country.   We came to Kendal, which I have also described.   On the side of the hill to the South of the town, is a Mount, of which they have a tradition, that it was raised to batter the Castle, which is half a mile to the north-east; the Castle is finely situated on a rising ground, and defended by a deep fossee.   On the west side are some arches, and to the South a tower, with a curious pointed arch in it, which from its shape is call'd the Oven.   They are building a Chapel in the heart of the town, with shops and vaults under it ; and it has more the appearance of a store-room than of a place for Divine worship.   They have a manufactory of a sort of frieze call'd Cotton, at eight pence a yard, sold mostly for the West Indies, for the use of their slaves, and Linsey Woolseys, made of thread and yarn, mostly strip'd, and much used for waistcoats; they have also a manufacture of knit stockings from 2s. 6d. to half a guinea a pair, and lately they weave coarse white silk stockings at 7s. 6d. a pair.   At Black Barton they have a marble like that of Kilkenny, but not altogether so black.   On the 29th I turned Southward, and went over the hills called Kendal Fells, passing near Sisergh, and leaving it on the left, descended into a fine Valley between the hills, in which the small river Winster runs;

Levens.

Kendal.

it is beautifully improved, and the rocks on the top of the hills and the wood have a fine effect. Two miles from Kendal is a small estate of towards two hundred pounds a year, call'd Conswick, which belonged to the Leybournes, a Roman Catholick family, and was forfeited in the year fifteen, not by actually joyning the Rebels, but by some improper conduct. It was put to publick sale, and as the country favoured the old Proprietor in the purchase, it was understood that a person of the name of Cruel bid for him, who made the purchase very cheap and kept it for himself, and the family now enjoy it. I went along the valley and came to the other side at Crosthwaite Church, from which the hills have the name of Crosthwaite. Crosthwaite Fells, and beyond this they are called Cartmell Fells, and we soon came to a Chapel of that name, where there are remains of some good old painted glass. We then came to a very small town called Cartmell, pleasantly situated on the small river. This place is famous for its Priory, the lands of it having been given by King Egfrid to St. Cuthbert. In 1188 William Mareschall the elder, Earl of Pembroke, founded a Priory here of Regular Canons of St. Austin, dedicated to the Virgin Mary; the present parish Church belonged to it, which is like a Cathedral; the Choir part is Saxon architecture, and was, without doubt, the Church of the old foundation, but has been raised. There are remains of very fine paintings in the East window, the Virgin Mary in the middle and God the Father on the left, represented as in very beautifull niches adorn'd with Gothick ornaments exquisitely fine; there is also a figure of a Bishop, probably St. Cuthbert's. On the South side is an ancient monument with two couchant statues, and another in the Isle as Cartmel. belonging to it; the top is crowned with a very bad and probably a very ancient bas relief, which I conjectured might be the Salutation. On the other side of the Quire on a flat stone is an inscription round a long Cross, part of which I made out in these words—

WILELMVS DE WALTON PRIOR DE CARTMEL

The Stalls of the Quire were adorned with carv'd work about the beginning of the last century, by one of the family of the Prestons of Holker hall near; which estate is now in the Lowther family, by marrying an heiress, and is the seat at present of Sʳ William Lowther. There is a tower in the middle of the Church about fifteen yards square, and another built on it within, the angles of which come to the middle of each side of the other, which is very particular. An old gateway remains, in which is the Free School. This place is two miles from Flukeborough, which I had passed in the way from Ulverston to Kendal. I left that place about a mile to the west, & going to Tempton & Wraysholm tower, I crossed a marsh to the Holy well which they call a Spaw; it is at the end of a point of land called Gowborn head, which is a very fine rocky cliff, out of which many trees grow in a most beautiful & extraordinary manner, & particularly the yew, which are so shorn with the wind that they turn up against the rock and grow like a hedge. This water abounds with a marine Salt, but it is resorted to in the summer by people who lodge at the neighbouring places, and come to it by the Strand, which is the best way. From this place we went a mile and a-half

Grange.

by the Strand to Grange, which place we had passed in the way to Kendal, a most delightfull situation, commanding a view of the Strand, of the country to the north, and of that on the Lancashire side. The hilly part of all this country consists of a sort of rock, which seems to be a limestone marble, but is full of flaws, tho' it rises very large, and is used for small bridges, shambles, and the like. On the 30th we crossed the Sands, and consequently the river Ken, seven miles, having to the north a point of land, which, if I mistake not, extends between the Ken and the Bela, mentioned before, which last river is not marked in Speed's maps. On this land I saw a Castle or Tower, called Arneby Tower, in the map

Wharton.

Arnesyde, and we came to the shoar near Wharton, to which place I went; it is a very small town like a village; the mannor belongs to the King; they are customary tenants, pay a shilling an acre, and double rent on the change of a life. There is nothing remarkable in the Church except the monument of one Cole, who it is said was thought worthy by three successive Kings to be made a justice of the Quorum, and he dyed about the year ninety.[*] There are remains of a Rood loft with some old paintings on the front of it ; there is a Canopy also over the end of one of the Isles, and they talked of a Rood at the end of each Isle.   Opposite to the Church is an old ruin they call a priory ; it is now the vicaridge house, but I can find no mention made of any religious house here. I turned South and went two miles to Bolton, a very small town, where they are almost all Freeholders. A mile before I came to this place I had come into the high turnpike road from Kendal to Lancaster, and in four miles more arrived at Lancaster, of which town I have formerly given an account.   They subsist by a trade by sea, and by being a thorough fare ; the town is very neatly built of free stone, the windows and door cases being hewn stone.   They have lately built a new Chapel near the river, not of the best architecture.   I reviewed Wery wall, and was more confirmed in my opinion that it Lancaster. is not a Roman work, the masonry of it being exceeding bad.   On each side of the Mayor's door is a brass Halbert, placed as a mark of his authority.   The hill to the east of the town produces the fine free stone with which they build.   They are erecting a handsome new tower to the Church.   On the 31st I set out to go round that Head of land which lies to the South west of Lancaster, and in three miles, at Condor Green, crossed the river Condor, and in two miles more came to Cokersand Abbey, situated on the east side of a bay, Cokersand into which the river Coker falls, Piling being on the other side, at Abbey. about two miles distance.   This Abbey was first an Hermitage, and then an Hospital for Sick, under a Prior subject to the Abbey of Leicester ; it was made an Abbey of Premonstratensian Canons, in 1190, by William of Lancaster, to which there seems to have been a design to have united another Abbey of the same order, which Theobald, brother of Hubert Walter, Archbishop of Canterbury, built, or designed to build, at Pyling, probably where St. John's Chapel was, now a great burial place, there being another Chapel,

[*] It is doubted whether this is not in Bolton Church.—*Note in MS.*

new built, at Pyling, to the west of the bay.   There are litle remains of the Abbey, except a beautifull small Chapter house entire, after the model of that at York, being an octagon, and the arch supported by a pillar in the middle ; each side is ten feet long, and the diameter about twenty-six feet ; there-is an arched passage comes out to the sea, now filled up, of which the people talk much, but it seems to have been only a convenient way to land goods from the sea.   I saw Cokeram at a distance, where there was a Priory. This coast is flat, and consists of a red free stone.   From Pyling we passed near Presal, and in about three miles came to Stalmin, having gone on two sides of Pylin Moss or bog, out of which they frequently dig stag horns and bones, and they did find one pair of horns that were about 5 or 6 feet apart, probably the horns of an Elk or Mouse deer.   Three miles farther we came to the river Wyer, on the north east side of the mouth of which are warehouses for landing goods for the merchants of Poulton and Kirkham, it being a very good harbour.   We crossed this river and came to Poulton, a litle neat town built of brick, subsisting by trade and tillage.   They have a new built church, tho' but indifferently contriv'd and executed in free stone.   The Fleetwoods, now Heslots, by marriage of an heiress of the former family, have their tombs here, and are patrons of the Church.   At Blackpool, near the sea, are accommodations for people who come to bathe.   Near this place is Singleton, from which the family of the Singletons come, who are now dispersed. I came from Poulton to Kirkham, where I lay.   The 1st of June I passed through Preston, dined at Charley, and came to this place. This is an exceeding fine country the way I came, consisting of small hills finely improved.

Montgomery, June 7th, 1754.

From Poulton in the way to Kirkham we passed by Mettrop Moss and through a village called Weton.   Kirkham is a small town well situated on a litle heigth in the middle of fine meadows ; to the north there is a Chalybeat water called Humphrey's Spaw : there is

Margin notes:

Pyling.

Poulton.

Kirkham.

another in the parish about two miles distant called White Car, of
which, if I mistake not, Short gives an account in his essay on
mineral waters. They have a yellow slate here which is brought
from Holland near Wigan. In the town is an old Pillar with some
uncommon characters on it which I was to see, but it was forgot.
This town and the tythes belong to Christ Church in Oxford, which
is patron of the Vicaridge ; they hold their lands by prescription at
about five pence an acre; and something more by the acre is paid
on a death. On the first of June I went two miles to Frekleton and
near two more to the river Ribble but the tyde did not serve. I
was to have gone to Hescot bank where the coals are brought from
towards Wigan to supply all the parts about Lancaster, and are
there put on board sloops : I was to have gone to Tarleton where
there is some extraordinary Well and water, and to Croiton, where
one Mr. Mannors lives, formerly a Hamburgh Merchant, who has
greatly beautifyed the Chancel of the Church. And so returning to
Frekleton I went along the marshes near the Ribble five miles to
Preston formerly described. They are now building a fine new
bridge of free stone from Whitle hill, about half a mile below the
other, for a more convenient and shorter communication, as I take it,
to the country towards Ormskirk. There was a College of Grey
Fryers on the north side of the town, founded by Edmund Earl of
Lancaster, son to Henry 3d, and an ancient Hospital to St Mary
Magdalene, the mastership of which was in the gift of the King,
some think it was called Priest-Town from this College. The Duke
of Hamilton was routed here with an army he brought to relieve
King Charles the first. I here saw a manufacture of carpeting
made for chairs, and designed to be improved in imitation of the
Turkey carpets; it was made at Ostwood, near Burnley, to the
North-east. They have a great Market here every Saturday.

We went over the Old Bridge and for some way in the Wigan road,
& passed by Whittle hill which produces the free stone ; and going on
in the Chorley road we passed by a seat of Mr. Crumpton, and came Chorley.
to the town pleasantly situated on a stream which falls into the

Yarrow that joyns the Dugles.   About a mile beyond this place they have coal, at what they call the Birth, and beyond it in many places.   It is a coal that cakes well, but for their rooms they use the Kennel or Candle coal.

We went on and in a mile passed by Teukesbury, the seat of S[r] Thomas Standish, and a litle farther near a very fine situation belonging to M[r] Willis, and beyond it is Show place, the seat of Lord Willoughby of Parham.   Over which is a Landmark on a hill that is called Rivington Pike.   Further on we saw Clayton, M[r] Hedlington's, and beyond that Standish, a very fine situation, where a family of that name resides ;   and near Wigan I observ'd a most charming place, Hayes, belonging to S[r] Roger Bradshaw, who has lately found coal there ;   and within a quarter of a mile of Wigan we passed by a Pillar to the memory of Colonel Tyldesley, who dyed there in battle in   when the King's army under the Earl of Derby was routed and the Earl was taken prisoner and beheaded, and about this place King Arthur routed the Saxons.   I have only to add to what I have formerly said of this place, that the situation is pleasant and it is a very neat town with hanging ground behind the houses down to the river, which might be made very beautiful if the people had any taste that way.   They have here great manufactures in iron, copper, brass, pewter, and in making woollen rugs and blankets.   I observed in the Church a very old monument on the South side under a stair case with two Couchant Statues, which they say belongs to the family of the Bradshaighs, as there is another to the memory of one of them who was a Member of Parliament in the time of King Charles the Second.   On the third I set out from Wigan, and went by the Cannel coal pitts in the road to Bolton (in which I had formerly travell'd) for about three miles, and then came in the road to Legh and struck out of it to see New hall, a fine seat with large offices built by M[r] Atherton, who married his daughter to M[r] Guillaume, of Herefordshire, who lives here, but the house is not entirely finished, nor kept in good order; the front is adorned with Ionick-fluted

Hayes.

Legh.

pillars and pilasters, and there is a handsome avenue to it from Legh. This town is supported by the same kind of cotton manufactures as are made at Manchester. It belongs to Mr Guillaum, who is the patron. In the Church is the neglected monument and vault of the Tildesleys, who lived at Tildesley near this town, before that estate was sold out of the family; and the Colonel I mentioned, who dyed in battle, is buryed here. We went on for some way in the road to Warrington, and left it to go to Hollyn ferry, where there is a boat, but when there are not great floods it is commonly forded. I went near half-a-mile further to Warburton, a small village with a Market Cross in it, and remarkable for nothing but a Church built in frames of timber and a brick tower at the east end of it, and there are some tombstones with Crosses on them. Sr Peter Warburton is proprietor of this place; on the other side is a coarse free stone slaty quarry, which serves both for building and coarse paving; they have very good of that kind for paving at Caridge, near Macclesfield. We went on towards Knottesford, and came into the high road from Manchester to London, at Man mere, a long narrow piece of water, with fine plantations at the further end, all belonging to Mr Brook, of Mere, which is near the Lake; there is also another lake on the East side of the road. I came to Knottesford, Knottesford. said to be originally Canutus's ford; it is situated over a small stream called the Lilie, on which there are pleasant meadows between the high ground on each side. It consists of the nether and further or the upper and lower town; the lower town is one street, about half a measured mile long, the upper about half as long. At the entrance of it is a new-built Session house, and at the end of it a very handsom Church and tower of brick, with galleries in it of the Dorick order; where the Schoolhouse is there was a Chapel just below the Church. They have a manufacture here of Tamies or single-threaded camblets, calimancoes, of hair and woosted shags, and of thread. Mr. Egerton is Lord of the Manor. On the 4th, in a mile, I passed by Tuff, an ancient mansion house of Mr Lester's, and in about three miles came to Cranage, where there is a small

Chapel. We passed over the river on which Congleton stands; the Dove and this river rise out of the same hills. In another mile we came to Holm Chapel ; these two Chapels and a third called Goostry are Chapels of ease to Sandbache. Half a mile further we left the London road and went to the West two miles to Sandbache, a small town supported by a great market for corn. There is a curious old cross with several figures on it, in a very barbarous taste, and there was another close to it on the same pedestal. There is a Chalybeat Spaw near the town and at Lavton, about two miles off, a purging water, from five quarts of which two ounces of salt may be extracted. I was here informed that at Stopford and Congleton great silk works are carried on, and a manufacture of buttons. At the latter, Cambden mentions a raised Roman road from Middlewich to Northwich. I went on and passed by a large Mere near Haslington. There is another above called Algier Mere, out of which the river rises. We then passed by Crow hall, the estate of a Minor of the name. At Haslington is a remarkable Church or Chapel, all built with wooden frame, filled up with lath and plaster. Having travelled four miles farther I came to Nantwiche, where I had often been, and travelled by very bad road and troublesome paved causeway five miles to Cholmondley, where Lord Cholmondley has a large park, good house and offices, and a Chapel, but all going to ruin. In a mile we crossed the great Chester road, and in two miles more came to Malpas, which is finely situated in a red free stone, at the South end of those low hills, which are between Whitchurch and Chester, and commands a very extensive view every way from the top of the tower. It is a poor town, consisting chiefly of farmers, shopkeepers, and inns, having no manufactory, and is not a great thoroughfare. The Lordship formerly of the Breretons, whose monument is in the Church, belongs three parts to the Drakes and one part to Lord Cholmondley, who present accordingly to the Rectory which is in the hands to (*sic*) two Rectors, who keep each of 'em a Curate, and have their respective houses, the Rectory being worth 800*L* a year, and

Sandbache.

Crow hall.

Malpas.

they take the duty each in his week. The only thing worth seeing in Malpas is the Church, which is a fine old Gothick fabrick of the later times. There is a Chapel which was the burial place of the Breretons, and in it a fine Monument of white marble with two Couchant Statues on it and Metzo relievos round it, but it is moved, as well as that of the Cholmondleys, to a corner, in order to have a descent into the vault in the middle, and so two sides of them are hid. Round the partition is this inscription: "Pray good people for the prosperous   of Sʳ Radoulph Brereton, Knight Baronet, of the   with his wyfe, Dame Helenor   and after this life to attayne eternal felicitie, Amen, Amen." The Chapel now belongs to Egerton of Old town. On the other side of the East end is the Cholmondley Chapel, with a litle monument in it, on which is this inscription, as far as I could read it: "Hugo Cholmondley de Cholmondley Senior, Miles de march' Walliæ vice P'ses   vice Comes mortem obiit aº aetatis suae 83 aº Domini 1596 et hac humo sepelitur filiusque heres ejus Hugo Cholmondley de Cholmondley Miles." And round the Chapel is this inscription: "Orate pro bono statu Ricardi Cholmondley et Elizabeth uxoris ejus hujus sacelli factor anno domini millesimo quingentesimo quarto decimo." Near the other is this monumental inscription: "To the memory of the Right Honourable Mary Viscountess Malpas, wife of the Right Honourable the Lord Viscount Malpas, daughter of Sʳ Robert Walpole, Knight of the Garter; she dyed at Aix, in France, Decʳ the 21ˢᵗ, 1731, in the 26ᵗʰ year of her age."

There is an inscription on a Gallery that Sʳ Richard Cholmondley built it in 1612.

I observed this day about Sandbach a great number of grubs or small caterpillars hanging by webs to the trees, which they spin, and it's said, turn to flies. I put some of them in a box to see the process of them.

On the 5ᵗʰ I set out from Malpas, and in three miles beyond Three pond lane came into Flintshire in Wales, and soon came to a large village called Worthingbury, where they have a very handsome new-built Church which they told me cost about £1000; it was built out of a Legacy of £500 given by M^r   of Emeral, about £100 raised by a brief and by the parish.   Two miles more brought us to Bangor on the river Dee, famous for one of the most ancient Monasteries in the world, and those who believe the History of King Lucius suppose it was founded in his time; it was called Bancornaburgh Banchor, or the good Choir, say some, or Bangor Ishocel, *i.e.*, Bangor of the Monks.   It was certainly flourishing in the time of St Austin, and so it must have been if Ethelred, King of the Northumbrian Angles, in his wars with the Britains in the beginning of the 7th Century, murdered 1200 of them, because they prayed for success against the Saxon infidels.   It probably after this fell to decay, for William of Malmsbury a litle after the Con-

quest speaks of it as in ruins.   They say there were 2400 Monks in it, and that 100 attended divine service every hour; and Bede saies they were divided into seven parts, each of about 300, with a ruler over each division, and that they all lived by their own labour. The tradition is that the Abbey was in a field call'd Stanier, but I could not see the least sign even of foundations except a litle Mount running paralel with the river and about 200 yards from it, which probably was the wall of the Precinct, and that it may be of this old Roman town, for Bonicum or Boviam is said to be here, and as they retain the name and scite of four gates to the four Cardinal points after the Roman manner, this makes it seem very probable. Port Hogan was on the other side of the river, probably at the bridge, or, it may be, at the entrance to a peninsula which the river forms, where there is a large dike to the left or south as against the inundation of the river, for the water has been four feet high in the Church.   This was the west gate.   To the north was Dungary or the Dung gate; on the hill to the east of Stanier was High gate— I suppose what Camden calls Cluit, because, asking what was Welch for High gate, they told me Clidich deetch.   The south gate was Braunhover.

Bath, June 15th, 1754.

There is very litle remaining of the old Church of Bangor, which seems to be without the site of the ancient town near the river, for possibly in this course of time the river may have gained to the west, so that this part might then be so over flowed as not to be habitable ; the walls of the town doubtless extending to the Bridge.   There are some remains of the painting of the East window, and there is a Gothick font which may be 3 or 400 years old ; and on the north side of the Chancel, in the Churchyard, is a plain stone which they say was dug up in Stanier together with a bell ; but the greatest curiosities here are two tomb stones, which, if the inscriptions had not been legible, and there had not been a coat of arms on one, I should have thought to have been Roman.   They consist each of a stone of about three feet long with a head cut in Mezzo-relievo into the upper end of the stone, so as not to rise above the surface of the other parts of the stone ; on one is the handle of a sword on one side, and what seems to be part of a truncheon on the other side ; under it is the arms, a Bear rampant, which I saw over the gate of Oswestrey. I could only make out these words of the inscription which are in letters partly Gothick : HIC IACET WILLI . . . . APRANS . . . . The other head is on a cushion, but I could not read any more than the two first words as in the other.   These were found in the foundation of the old wooden tower.

This is all a very rich clay country and abounds in oak, but the roads excessively bad, with a pitch'd causeway on one side about a yard wide on which one is oblig'd to go, and is worse riding than in the streets of a town.   We cross'd over the Dee in Denbighshire and went four long miles to Ruabon, a small town situated on an eminence over a rivlet which falls into the Dee. Sr Watkins William Wynne's park of Winstead comes very near this town, in which he had built a handsome new house of a very good freestone of a greenish cast.   I formerly saw this house in which there is nothing extraordinary.   The late owner, who had the misfortune to dye instantly by a fall from his horse in hunting about four years agoe,

Ruabon.

was a godson of the last proprietor, Sr John Wynne, and a great
favourite, and lived with him in his house; his name was Williams
but no relation, and the whole estate was left to him. He lived at a
great expence to support his interest in the country, and had several
houses in which he kept servants and a table, insomuch that he is
said to have died £80,000 in debt, but his elder son of two being
very young it is snpposed the estate will be cleared when he is of
age, tho' I have been since informed that his debts amounted to no
more than his personal estate; the burial place of this family is in
Ruabon Church.   There is one grand monument, if I mistake not,
with Sr John Wynne on one side and another person on the other.
In another part is a tomb with two Couchant Statues on it of a man
and woman, the head of the former rests on a helmet, and there are
many figures round the tomb, and on the cornish is this inscription:
" Orate pro anima John ap Ehe Eaton Armigeri qui obiit vicesimo
octavo die mensis Septembris an° Dⁿⁱ M D IIII. et Elizabeth Cattley
uxoris ejus quae obiit XI die mensis Junii Anno Dⁿⁱ MDXXVII
animabus propitietur Deus, Amen."   This John ap Ehe Eaton liv'd
at Eaton, which I passed by in the way from Bangor, and was proprietor of all the estate of the Wynnes.   There are remains of some
painted glass on the East window, and of a fine carved Rood loft.
There is a Camp in the way from this place to Chirk Castle.   There
is a freestone quarry just beyond the town, and at some distance are
quarries of lime stone, and three miles off there are lead mines at
Mihene. We went on and came again to the Dee with high beautifull
ground on each side of it cover'd with wood.   We soon came to
Kefen-y-Wern, an old wooden house of the Middletons, and in half

Chirk Castle.   a mile more to Chirk Castle, the mansion seat of that family, situated
on an eminence, and a very noble Castle it is with fine dining-room,
gallery, &c.; but the prospects are much more to be admired of a
most beautiful country.   They say they can see fifteen counties.

Up the Valley near the Dee is an old Castle, called Castle Dynas
Zrane, on a beautiful single hill.   We went through the Park, in
which there is fine hanging ground cover'd with oak.   We had a

view of the town of Chirk at a litle distance, and came in five miles
to Oswestre, which I have mentioned before. At the North end of
the town are remains of the old Castle, with a Mount in it; the old
gates of the town remain entire, and some part of the walls. In the
Church is a stone coffin, which seems to have been taken out of the
ruined tomb of the Yeals of Yeal, one side of which only, with several figures on it in relief, remains. In the Square is a good new
Town house, built of freestone. The chief support of this place is
the market and thorough fare, especially as it is the place to which
they bring all their Welch Webbings, which are loaded here on
wagons and carried to Shrewsbury; 'tis a thick sort of flannel, of
which the Soldiers' clothing is chiefly made; it sells by the ell,
which is two yards and a half and six inches, and they can draw
this measure out to three yards; the coarser was 1s. 6d. an ell, but
now it is all from 2s. to 4s.

On the sixth I left Oswestre, and after travelling four miles came
to Tana Manah, near which village there is a hill called Tana
Manah rock, which is a lime stone, and there are a great number of
lime kilns at this hill, which has a fine appearance, the upper part
being a perpendicular rock. In this country they cultivate hemp
and make linnen of it, chiefly for sheeting, which is very strong. We
went a mile further to the river Verney, and passed over it on a
fine stone bridge of seven arches; it is called Newbridge. In this
part there is a sort of brown alabaster, which is a good lime stone.
Up this river is Mathraval Castle, in Meivod Parish, belonging to
the Powis family, where the Princes of Powis formerly resided; it
is supposed to be old Mediolanum, and antiquities have been found
here. It seems as if it had been out of that family for some time,
and that Robert Vipons, an Englishman, built a Castle there. We
came soon to a long hill, and went on the south side of it; if I mistake not, it is called Brethin Maur, having Brething on the other
side of the Severn, and a large extensive mountain to the left; the
former is a most beautiful hill, extending to Welch pool, to which
town we came. We saw to the left Newkey, where Lord Powis has

a smelting house for lead; near it is 'Street-Marshal, writ Yshal Marchel, and called Strat Marcella and Aba domus de strat margel Vall Crucis or Pola; it lyes betwen Guilsfeld and Pole. Here was a Cistertian Abbey, dedicated in 1170 to God and the Virgin Mary, founded either by Owen Reveling or Madol, son of Griffith, and in time came to be visited by the Abbot and Convent of Bildwaf, in Shropshire. Pole is a pretty well built small town, situated on a rivlet, call'd Claydon, about a mile from the Severne. It is a Corporation governed by a Bayliff and Burgesses, and is supported by a large market, chiefly for flannels. In the Church there is a font adorned with foliage, which seems to have been the capital of a large Gothick pillar, and in the Chancel is this inscription, on a plain neat monument, which I insert at length, as it contains some History of the Pembroke family.

"Sr Edward Herbert, Kt, second son of Sr William Herbert, Knight, Earl of Pembroke, Lord Cardiffe, and Knight of the Most Noble Order of the Garter, and of Anne his wife, sister and sole heir of Sr William Parry, Knight, Lord Parrè of Kirkbye, Kendal, Marmyon, Fitzhugh, and St. Quintin, Earl of Essex, Marquis of Northampton, and Knight of the Most Noble Order of the Garter, which Sr Edward Herbert married Mary, daughter and sole heir of Thomas Stanley, of Standen, in the County of Herts, Esquire, Master of the Mint, Aº 1570, youngest son of Thomas Stanley, of Dalgarth, in the County of Cambridge, Esqre, which Sr Edward Herbert and Dame Mary his wife had yssue four sons and eight daughters, viz., William Herbert, Esqre, his eldest son and heir, who married Lady Elinor, second daughter to Henry, Earl of Northampton; George Herbert, second son; John Herbert, third son; Edward Herbert, fourth son; Elizabeth, first daughter, died young; Anna, second daughter; Joyce, the third daughter; Frances, the fourth daughter; Catherine, the fifth daughter; Jone, the sixth daughter, dyed young; Mary, the seventh daughter; and Winifred, the eighth daughter; which Sr Edward dyed the 23d day of Marche, Anno Dni 1594. And this monument was made at the charge of the said Lady Mary Herbert, the 23ᵈ day of October, 1597."

Powis Castle is just over the town, and about half a mile from Powis Castle. the town is the Park, which consists of part of two long narrow hills with a deep narrow valley between them; the Eastern hill is the less, on the brow of which the Castle is situated; there is a gentle ascent up the other to a heigth beyond the park which commands a most glorious view of the course of the Severn and part of the vale in which the Verney runs, of the hills on both sides of that vale in which Bala stands, and, if I mistake not, Snowdon hills in Carnarvonshire is seen from it, and there is a very extensive prospect into Shropshire. The view even from the Castle 'tho in a gloomy day is very fine, and I believe it may have some peculiar beanties at such a time, for it appeared to me extremely beautifull in a hazy evening. The Castle is built of a red freestone, something of a granite nature, in very small grains, and not unlike the stone of Memnon's Statue at Thebes in Egypt. The Castle also is built or dash'd between the stones with red mortar, so that at a distance it appears like a brick building; and there is a small piece of an old Powis Castle. wall in the inclosure which seems to be of very great antiquity, being built of large stones and levelled with smaller, such as I saw particularly in the walls of the antient Seleuciæ Pieriæ built by Seleucus, King of Syria. Part of the Castle has been burnt down, particularly a long gallery, but notwithstanding, there are two or three grand rooms and a narrow gallery; there are also fine hanging gardens in the old stile, and it was famous for its waterworks. On the whole, for a situation of this kind it is the finest place I ever saw.

From Welsh Poole I went the 7th near the Severne for about a mile, and cross'd that river on a wooden bridge call'd Kilconeh; there is a nearer way to Montgomery by the new ford higher up, but the river was too deep. We cross'd over a hill and came into that vale in which the river Cavilet runs, which we crossed on a bridge. This vale is like an Amphitheatre encompassed with low hills, which are downs, except that there is a valley to the north, which rises gently and is finely planted and cultivated; part of Shropshire is in this valley, and it extends to Hockshow forest, if it is not part of it. On the river I saw Cherbury, which has distinguished the noble family of the title of Ld Herbert, which resided at Liner near or just under Montgomery, situated on a fine piece of natural water. To this family the late Marquis of Powis, who branched out from the Pembroke family (*sic*); his Estate came to Henry Arthur Herbert, Earl of Powis, who married a daughter, the only issue of three coheiresses, daughters of his brother.

Montgomery.   Crossing this vale I came to Montgomery. The Castle is situated in a very extraordinary manner on a high rock. On the side of the hills there are some ruins of it, and the parsonage house is close to it. The town is in a hollow between this hill and a lower, in which the Church stands. There is a handsom new market house in the town. It is a small poor place, and chiefly subsists by its markets. In the Church is a good old monument of Richard Herbert, Esqr, married to Margaret, Daughter of Sir   Thomas, L^d chief justice of England in the time of Henry 8th, their Couchant Statues are on it, and under them another with a beard. The front of the Rood loft is very curiously carved and gilt. I have been inform'd that the people of Montgomery and Cherbury have met in wagons, aud acted play after the antient manner.

Going towards the Severn I saw, in half a mile on the hill, a remarkable old Fort, called Kindummy, defended with three fossees every way except to the South-west, where it is strong by nature; and there it is defended by only one deep fossee. We travelled near the Severn, and passed by the wooden bridge which they cross from Welsch Poole to Newtown. I saw at the hills, on the other side of the river, Castle Verrone, of which there are some ruins, and one part looks like a pillar, but it is only a piece of the wall. Very near Newtown is an old Fort in the valley which they call the Mote, and seemed to me to have the appearance of a Roman work. All this country is most beautifull in hills, which are divided by lawn and wood, and where the river turns and locks in the land there is the most finest group of hills I ever beheld. We came to Newtown, ten miles from Welsch pool.

Bath, June 16th, 1754.

Newtown is a very small neat town, where the Severn windes Newtown. so as to be on three sides of the town. There is nothing remarkable in the Church, except a monument of some of Sr John Price's family, whose eldest son lives here in an old mansion house; there is a pleasant part to it, on the Severn. This town subsists chiefly by its markets of corn to supply the country higher up the Severn.

I left Newtown on the 8th, and soon turned up to the left by a stream to see a waterfall called Graicum Pistil, from which the brook has its name; it falls down a rock between woods about fifty feet, the first and last ten feet being a gentle descent; there is a perpendicular fall of about twenty feet, and then for ten feet a steep descent. We went on in the road to Lanidlos, the valley and lower part of the hills being finely cultivated and adorned with wood; but the tops of the hills are downs, and some of them a litle heathy, with several beautifull valleys on each side, through which the streams come tumbling down into the Severn. In four miles we came to a farmhouse called Mueshurer, there is a way to a ford that leads to Caersous on the other side, which they talk of as an old town, tho' they say there is hardly any thing to be seen, but they have found old money there, and by their talk I imagined it might have been some Roman Settlement; the water was too high to venture over. Just above it is a beautifull large hill, flat at top, which appeared to be a fine natural fortification, it is called Craigeh Curle; to the right of it is a beautifull valley call'd Garsonoul; above this the Severn runs in another direction, and on the left side are fine small hills, which are downs, and above them the hills are less, and cultivated to the top. Indeed this whole valley is most beautifull, and many good old farm houses appear among the fields and wood, and some few Gentlemen's houses. It most resembles Switserland, but I think it is finer, and few rivers can afford finer rides as the Severn for such a number of miles. Eight miles from **Lanidlos.** Newtown we came to Lanidlos on the Severn, a small poor town, in which most of the shops are kept by the trades men of Newtown, and are open'd only on market days, which are kept for the sale of meat, bread and cattle. Veal sells 2s. a quarter, kid six pence, butter 3½d. a pᵈ; mutton is dear, poor small sheep selling for six pound a score; and mutton, when they have it, from 1s. 8d. to four shillings a quarter, and very small. They have a manufacture of flannel here. It is the last town on this side Plimlimmon hill, and is but seventeen computed miles, but thirty measured from the Western Ocean. They have a Mayor and Burgesses put in by the Lord of the Mannor. There are copper mines three miles off in the Parish of Clanillas, at Givron; and a great number of lead mines, particularly on the Brindle, a rivlet near Clinburthin pool, which belong to the Mine adventurers. On the 9th I went up the hill to the North, in order to go to the rise of Severn. I saw to the right, over the river Cluedagn, some lead mines beyond Mʳ Glyn of Glyns, and further a hill called Gaervuckeh, on the top of which is a circular rampart of stones. We went on turning westward, and should have gone over the hill but it was impossible by reason of the late rains, and it is partly boggy ground, so we turn'd down and went along over the Severn, and in about six miles from Lanidlos came to the last house this way, where I hired guides and rid about half a mile, and then walk'd to the rise of the Severn, which rises from a spring out of a very small hole, which is filled by the spring; two streams unite and fall down into it; but as these run only after rains, this is called the rise of the Severn, which is in the middle of a deep bog. We met our horses **Plim Himmon.** and ascended to the heigth of Plimlimmon, the mountain out of which the Severn, Wye, and Ridal rise; on this heighth are two heaps of stones, with a small heap on each, they are sort of Kerni, and they mentioned them as marks of the bounds between Montgomeryshire and Cardiganshire, which is at the top of these hills. We had here a very extensive view of mountains, and indeed of nothing else, except that I thought I saw the sea, which appears very near in a day perfectly clear. We had a view of Cader Idris, in Merionethshire, one of the highest mountains in Wales, and a deep valley in which the Douy runs. We descended to view the rise of the Ridal, which is from a fine pool about half a mile round in a hollow on the side of a hill, which is fed by a stream rising out of the foot of the hill ; another river runs very near it, to the north of it, which seemed to flow out of a litle hollow in the hill. They told me it was the Refgeu. We came up and descended to the left to the rise of the Wye, which comes out of the hollow of the hill from springs, a stream after rain joyning it from above. We saw Llangerig on the Wye, four miles from Reyder, and likewise we saw almost as far as that town. I observed to the South a deep valley under or in the road to Dufrain Castle, which I thought agree'd best with the situation of the Tivy. We had crossed a road that leads into Cardiganshire, and I observed some stones placed in different parts to point out the way to the herdsmen in foggy weather. We descended to the high road to Aberistoith, seven miles from Lanidlos, it goes by the river Hivagirick to the Wye, which they told me bounded between the Counties of Montgomeryshire and Cardiganshire. We came to the Wye and went near it for about a mile and crossed the hills five miles to Lanidlos. There are several rivlets meet above Lanidlos, beginning at the right or north, first the Severn, then Cliniruckhan, Dulas, Bullaganah, Avadbriuth, and Thaleu, all running through beautiful narrow vales. On the mountain at the rise of the Severn I observed the bog was 4 or 5 yards deep, then two yards of a clay slaty ground, in other parts it is from a yard to two yards deep, then two yards of a clay slaty ground, but in many places towards the top it is quite washed off and perpetually falling away, the vegetation on the surface it is true is some supply, but it must be continually lessening as well as the clay slaty soil beneath, which is mixed with some free stone of an ash colour.

The bog as a spunge receives and retains the moisture from the clouds and rain ; if these bogs should continue to be washed away, and by their weight they must be perpetually descending on all declivities, this must make a great alteration in rivers, which on rains would rise more suddenly, like torrents, when this spunge is gone that imbibes the waters, consequently the hills must become lower, and as the weightier particles must subside in the valleys they must be raised higher, and in this sense the mountains shall be made low and all vallies shall become higher.

Crossing a rivlet at the west end of the town, I saw a stone in which I expected to find petrifyed coral, but on breaking it I found it to be composed of beautiful cones indented but irregular, something like screws and very beautifull, from a quarter to half-an-inch in diameter ; examining again I found larger but not so beautifull. I imagined I had found a new fossil, but I do not know but it may be a kind of Micetytes.   On the 10th I left Lanidlos and went up the same hill I had ascended to the lead mines, but cross'd to the left out of that road, and came down into the valley in which the river Tulloh runs already mentioned.   We travelled through a hilly country winding round the valleys, which are mostly downs ; single houses with plantations about them and cultivated land, and came into Radnorshire and to the river Morteague, which runs between high rocky hills out of which some trees grow.   Over it is a pillar about nine feet high, set up probably in memory of some transaction.   We soon came to the Wye, and then went through a very pleasant country one mile to Rhiader, or Rhiader Gouch, a very

Rhiader.   poor town situated on a heigth over the Wye.   They are here mostly farmers and shopkeepers, have a market, and it is a Corporation consisting of Bayliff and Burgesses, and this town, Radnor, Presteign, Knighton and Knutlas, send one member to Parliament and the County of Radnor another.   We set out from this place, went

Landrided.   over a high hill, and came in five miles to Landrided, where there are some medicinal waters ; first the black well, which seems to be a strong sulphureous water and purges much ; a quarter of a mile

from it is the Kings well, which I judg'd to be a Chalybeat, and
lastly a small stream dropping from the rock call'd the rockwater,
which I thought was Chalybeat and salt. They have sometimes
much company here, who diet and lodge for half a guinea a week;
and they have a horse course here. We were now in a kind of
Amphitheatre five or six miles in diameter, encompassed with pleasant hills, the Wye being to the South. It consists very much of
commons, and we went through it five miles to Bualt, or Builth, Bualt.
as the folks pronounce it here in Brecknockshire; it derives its
name from Bualt:—There in the wood, Alt in the old British,
signifying a wood. King Vortigern is said to have retired into
this country on his invasion of the Saxons, and that his son Pas-
centius reign'd here. 'Tis said that he went to a wilderness near
Riader goucy, and having married his own daughter, he built a
City on a mountain called Caer Vortigern. They have a tradition
of a town on the top of Plimlimmon, and I was showed the spot
where they say it was, and the tradition is that he and the City
were destroyed by lightning. It is also said that Lluellyn, last
Prince of Wales, being betrayed, was basely murder'd near Rader
Goucy. Cumhire is mentioned as an Abbey of Cistertians in this
County, founded by Cadwathecan ap Madoc in 1143, which is
farther in this County. Builth is pleasantly situated on the Wye, Builth.
the hills about it being cultivated and adorned with wood; it has
pretty good markets and shops and a Manufacture of stockins;
'tho but a small town it is supposed to be Bulleum Silurum. In
the Church is a monument of Sr John Lloyd, with long spurs,
a double collar and a single ruff, and he is said to have been
the first sheriff in this County. At the east end of the town is
a high Mount on which there was a small Castle; on the south
and west sides of it are large ramparts something like Bastions,
which would contain a good number of people, and the fosse within
them is very deep. Here is a wooden bridge over the Wye, which
river is large, considering it is but twelve computed miles from its
source. From the end of the bridge a wall is built about 177 yards

long and six feet broad, with a wooden frame on the top to keep
out the river.   This town is no Corporation, and they are governed
by a justice of Peace who lives in the town; they have salmon here
which goes four or five miles above Riader.   I saw in the road
near Builth a very beautifull oval Ludus Hetmontii, about a foot
long and eight inches broad, which broke very easily in the sparry
joynts that divided the stone; it was probably among the pebbles
which are in the Slaty rock.   They have a very good stone at
Abber Eddon, something of a Slate kind, which makes fine tombstones, and they have the same kind at Tohillis near Brecknock.
Aber Eddon lyes under a great reproach here at this day, as some
people from that place went to Kevenybeth, near Builth, and
murdered Lluellyn, the last Prince of Wales, and his head was
afterwards carried on a pike to London.   On the 11th, as soon as
we passed the Denerog, we began to ascend to the moors, and in
three miles came to them; they are six miles over, and then we
travelled six miles through a very pleasant country to Brecknock,
passing by Landavelog Church, where there is a barbarous kind of
a monument cut in lines; a man holds a sword in his right hand
over his arm, and in his left a sword held before him, and over the
figure is a Cross, under it this inscription :

ıɒ ẇınɱnıL
FıoＵ

which, I suppose, is only the name of the person, tho' it was
mentioned to me as an inscription in an unknown character.
Brecknock is pleasantly situated on the Usk, and the Horedy
which I had passed over runs through the suburbs, and the hang-
Brecknock.   ing ground on each side of it is adorned with trees, the litle hills
covered with wood, the high mountains at a distance, and the fine
meadows give the place a very agreeable aspect.   The town is
great part of it well built and inhabited by several Gentlemen, and

they have three market days, one being chiefly for Cattle. They have a manufacture of coarse cloth like the Kendal cottons, for the use of slaves in the West Indies; they tann great quantities of leather, and make also white leather to send to different parts, as well as for home consumption. It is said that old coins have been found here, and some think it was the old Loventium. The Church of the Benedictine Priors is on an eminence to the north. It was founded by Bernard de Newmarch, a Norman Lord, called in to help against Rhesus, and took the country to himself. The East part of the Cross Isle are very old, consisting of nine windows on each side, with a lower window on each side of them, and it is divided by three Gothic Pillars. At the East end there are five of these windows; there is some painting in the east window, and the old stalls of the Quire. The rest of the Church is built in the Cathedral style. On each side of the body the Isles are divided into Chapels, which belong to four Companies—the Clothiers, the Tuckers, the Taylors, and the Shoemakers, with their arms and implements cut on them; and here they have burial places, open their Halls and adjourn. They have, both in this Church and St Maries Chapel, the old triangular chests for preserving their vestments. Here is a very good old monument of Sr David Williams, justice of the Common Pleas, and his Lady, with their Couchant Statues. But the most remarkable thing is a monument to the Games, built of wood, in three stages, with their respective Canopies. On the middle stage is a wooden Couchant Statue of a woman. Round two of the Canopies are English verses, but most of them are defaced, being formerly in the middle of the Church. One side is hid by being placed against the wall. I copyed what I could of them, on account of the particularity of the Poetry, viz. : —

O Thomas Games, God grant thee Grace
To judge of good and evil ;
Thye daughters and wyfe to serve God daylye,
To fight against the Devel.

Thy sons as wise as Solomon,
 Thy wyfe to live as long
As Enoch did, and so to flee
 To Heaven with joyfull songe.
I wish thy self as rich to be
 As ever Cressus was ;
In power to pass Ottaeman
 To bring all things to pass,
And so to live here in God's fear,
 And his word so embrace
That mee with thee, and he with us,
 In heaven may have a place.
For here death spareth none,
 The rich nor yet the poor ;
We must leave welthe with child and all
 When he knocks at the dore.
And thowghe the bones, as clod of clay,
 Do rest within this tomb ;
And there shall be, as Scripture saithe,
 Till dreadfull day of Dome ;
Where we shall all appere
 Before his glorious face,
With trembling and with dreadfull fear,
 To have our dwelling place,
In joys Celestial
 With Christ in heaven to be.
Which Jesus Christ grant to us,
 Amen say you with me.

In another part—

Is Samson yet alive,
 For all his mighty strenght ?
Both Solomon and Absa to
 Hath yield to death at length.
And Abraham he is dead,
 As scripture tell hit true.
Old Galen he hath left his books
 And bidden all adieu.

There is an old painting in the church of Adam and Eve, and within one of the Chapels of the companies is a monument a Couchant

Statue of a Lady under a very fine Gothick arch, such as the Founders of Churches and Monasteries are usually deposited in. The Church of St Maries in the town has nothing remarkable in it except some very old capitals, some are fluted and some are composed of half rounds. The Priory is the Parish Church, and the whole town is cess'd for the repair of it, the Chapel is repaired by those within the walls who resort to it. On the other side of the bridge is the College and church which belonged to the black Fryars, which by Henry 8th was made a College and call'd Christ Church, and he joyn'd the College of Aberguilly to it. The Bishop of St Davids who has a large house near it is Dean. There is a Praecentor, Chancellor, Treasurer, and, as the Monasticon informs, nineteen Prebendaries. I observed the names of them on the stalls. In this Church are buried the Bishops Manwaring, Lucy, and Bull. To the Lady also of Lucy there is a monument erected which mentions that she was married to him when he was Rector of Burrowe Clere in Hampshire. There is a magnificent monument to Bishop Lucy's son who was Chancellor of the Church and had the title of Reverend, tho' his Couchant Statue is on the tomb with a full bottom'd wig and a night gown. These three Bishops of St Davids liv'd here, and no Bishop has resided at Brecknock since their time. This town has several good houses and inns in it. The old Gates and part of the walls remain, and there are some ruins of a strong old Castle in which there was a Mount and buildings on it.

Bath, June 19th, 1754.

I left Brecknock on the 13th and turned out of the way to see Langor pool which is about a mile to the north of the road; it is two miles long and one broad, and is in the middle of hills, to the top of which there is a gentle ascent finely cultivated so that it has a most beautifull appearance; we returned to the road five miles from Brecknock at Bulch, a litle beyond which place I dined in a garden on the brow of a hill and had a fine view of the country; this place

Langor pool. There is a tradition that a city was swallow'd up here in an earthquake.

is called Crickadow; the top of the hill is of a freestone and so is the bottom, and about two yards between there is a very hard blewish marble. The hills on the other side of the Lesk are lime stone, and they burn much lime on them. About seven miles to the north east is Lanthony Abbey in Monmouthshire, of which they say there are great remains, and at Tarankilly Hill, two miles north of Crickhowel, is a grotto which is very narrow in many parts and some say it goes a great way in. After rideing a mile we passed by Tritouer, where there is an old Castle with a fine round tower; we came to Crickhowel, a small poor town, very beautifully situated on an eminence over the river. In the Church is a great monument of Sir John Herbert of 1691, and there is a very old monument with a Couchant Statue in wire armour, and a fillet bound round his head which is reposed as on two cushions, his hand is in a very uncommon posture on his broad sword which is before him. The arms are three lions rampant quite plain, so that I imagined it was of the Herbert family before there was any other distinction on the arms. There are some letters on the tomb, but I could make nothing of 'em. There are of this family in the neighbourhood and some of the Harcourts. This place for the richness of views of the hills and County and country seats and water is extremely fine. The common road to Abergavenny is on the north side of the river; but we were directed to the South, a longer way, by a person who I suppose was desirous that we should see the country, and it certainly did appear extremely fine. The wind came down the mountains, the trees bent under it and raised their heads again, they seemed to dance like rams; the gentle breezes on the lower hills blew 'ore the shrubs and younger wood, which seemed to play like lambs; the mountains skip'd like rams and the litle hills like young sheep, and sometimes the shades of flying clouds added to the beauty of the Landskip. I formerly pass'd such vales when the fields were white and ready for harvest; the corn grew close and full; the wind skim'd o're the fields and caused a motion in the corn, something like that of the muscles when we laugh and smile; it whistled through the rustling ears, and sometimes resembled chearful laughter, at other some vocal musick; the valleys stood so thick with corn that they seemed to laugh and sing. I observed here a particular granite in large grains of white and blewish, and I found afterward they made small mill stones of them. We came to Abergaveny, most charminly situated on a point of high land over the Usk. It is esteemed the best town in Wales, in which there are good shops, a manufacture of flanels, and, I think, stockings, and very considerable markets. They say here are 3,000 souls in the town. It was encompassed with a wall, part of which remains, and very good gates, and there are some ruins of the old Castle on a rais'd ground, which, with about £1,000 a year, is the estate of Lord Abergavenny. The old Church belonging to the Priory, founded by Hamelin Balon or Baladun, a Norman, is now the Parish Church. In the South Chapel are several fine monuments, with Couchant Statues on them. Some are of the Herberts and some of the Nevils. They tell a story of a dog under the feet of the former, and of a bull on one of the latter, from which they say the family had the name of Nevil, which signifies a beast. On the tomb in the middle the head dress of the woman somewhat resembles a mitre, like that at Farta, in the Queen's County in Ireland. There is a very particular Colossal Statue set aside in the Isle, which I took for a Christopher. They call it the root of Jesse. The Statue, with a long beard and a cap on, has our Saviour on his shoulder, and a stem as of a tree comes round as from the back of the statue up to the litle statue on the shoulder. It is of wood, whited over. There is a Church in the heart of the town in ruins, and a pretty good Eccho to the west of the Town. To the North East is Michael's Hill, to which the Roman Catholicks go out of devotion on Michaelmas day. There is a small summit, which looks as if it had been separated from the rest of the hill, and they talk of its being divided from it at the time of our Lord's Crucifixion. On the 14th we set out for Monmouth. Our road was through a fine hilly country; and we came to that town, situated on a rising ground at the mouth of the Mynwy or Monno. It is a

Abergaveny.

Monmouth.

good town, and chiefly supported by its markets for corn, and a thoroughfare into Herefordshire, Gloucestershire, and Wales. At the Convent of Black Monks are remains of a square Saxon Chapel, and out of the old Church they have built a very good new one, the roof of which is suported by Dorick pillars near three feet diameter. These Monks were brought from St. Florence, near Saumur in Anjou, by Wikenoe de Monemue, in the time of Henry the first, and were first placed at St. Cadois, near the Castle, probably the old building like a Church called St. Mary's. The Castle belongs to the Duke of Beaufort, by whose family a good house has been built in it, which is now lett. A manufacture of earthen ware was carried on here, and particularly for pipes to lay under ground, which did not answer. The Duke has a large house called Troye, half a mile from this town. At the foot of the bridge over the Monno is the Chapel of St. Bridget, of Saxon Architecture; and there is a large new town house built of freestone, but not of the best architecture. One Jones, a native of this town and a Hamburgh merchant, about the beginning of the last century, founded a free School, an Hospital, and a Lectureship. The Lecturer has 100 guineas a year, the Master 80, and the other 50 or 60 guineas. Admiral Griffith has a fine situation close to the town. From Monmouth I cross'd the Wye over a bridge into Glocestershire; went near the banks of it in the forest of Dean, and ascended the hills to the North East, and came by Colford, a small town. All this way are great iron works for smelting the ore of the forest of Dean, which is very fine. I passed by the Speech house where the business of the forest is done, and came to the small town of Newnham, near which we crossed over the Severn at a ferry, which has its name from the town, and went four miles to Mr Cambridge's, at Whitminster, who was not at home. That place is much improv'd since I saw it, being all lawn, wood, serpentine river, and gravel walks through it for the roads, in the manner of Chantilly. I returned by Frampton Green, which is a very pleasant place, and came to the parting of the Bath and Bristol road, took the former and went to Frocester, a small village, with an exceeding good inn. I went through fine woods of beech trees up Froster hill, where I had a fine view of Glocestershire and Wales, and leaving the Bath road to the west came to Wootten underidge, a good town in a bottom between the hills. It is supported by the cloth manufacture.

Bristol, June 22d, 1754.

From Wootten underedge I went about six miles to the Duke of Beaufort's park and to the Duke's House, which is all wainscoated with oak. In the hall are several hunting pieces, in which the late and present Duke are represented, and a fine Sarcophagus on which there are Alt reliefs, Bacchus, &c.; it was the present of Cardinal Mazarine to a Duke of Beaufort. In the two next rooms are several fine pictures; in another room is a fine Cabinet of what they call Pietre Comesse of Florence, in which birds, beasts, and flowers, as well of precious stones as of what they call the hard stone, inlaid and polished. They say it was the work of twenty-five years, and cost as many hundred pounds; in a gallery called the dining-room are several family pieces, particularly John of Gaunt, from whom they are descended, and his son. In the Duke's dressing-room is an original drawing of Raphael's, which cost seventeen hundred pounds; it is that corner only of the famous piece of the Transfiguration of Raphael as St. Pietro Montorio in Rome, in which the boy possessed with the Devil is represented; and in the Dutchesse's dressing-room are several fine pictures; one bedchamber is finished and furnished very elegantly in the Chinese manner. The Duke has a fine library; the pillars between the presses, if I mistake not, are of the Dorick order, and over the chimney is a good painting of our Saviour teaching the Doctors. There are several beautiful Tables in the rooms, some of Alabastro fioreto, one or two of Porphiry, and one of a beautiful grey granite. At the further end of the Park is Worcester Lodge, on the highest ground in the Park;

it is the design of Kent, and is a grand gateway, one arch in the
middle and one on each side, one leading to the staircase, the other
a room for servants ; over all is a grand room which commands a
most glorious prospect.   It is all built of fine freestone.   Here the
Duke often dines in the summer.   There are in the Park near two
thousand fallow deer, and about two hundred red deer.   The
present Duke's family consists of one son, the Marquis of Worcester,
about ten years old, and three daughters.   We came near seventeen
measured miles from Worcester Lodge to Bath.

Chippenham, June 24th, 1754.

I have formerly given an account of Bath ; this place every
year becomes more frequented, and is a most easy retreat for people
of all conditions, especially for those whose estates lye at a distance
from the Capital, and who can dispose of themselves during the hot
months of summer in some other places ; not to mention that there
is no place in the world so fit for the necessary and honourable
business of making alliances, which causes a great increase of buildings here, and many persons are building houses for themselves,
insomuch that a Circus is begun on the rising ground above Queen's
Square, which is to be a Circle with three openings, and the area
is to be three hundred and   yards in diameter.

When I was at Bath I made some excursions.   On the 18th
I went a mile to Lyncombe, a sweet retirement, where there is
a Chalybeat water, and a very good house for lodgings, &c., on
the same terms as at Bath.   A mile and half farther is South
Stone, and as much farther Combe Hay, on a rivlet which crosses
the road to Wells at Dunkerton, and rises three miles to the
west of it, at Comelye.   Here Mr Smith has a very good house,
and has made a fine serpentine river by stopping the water.   From
this place we cross'd the hill a mile and a half to Wellow, on another
stream which rises at Lytton, near the other, and then both meet at
Lower Midford, and after running about a mile fall into the Avon; the
high ground on each side of the rivlets is very beautifull, and there

are many pleasant villages on them. On the   I took a very
pleasant walk to Triverton, where there is a furnace for making
brass, and mills for beating it into plates. On the 20th I rid out,
went to Batheaston, visited Mrs. Ravoe, who, with Mrs. Riggs, a Batheaston.
widow, has built a very good house, highly finish'd, improved the
side of a hill to the road in beautiful lawn, walks, garden, cascades,
a piece of water and a stream running thro' the garden, and live
there in a very agreeable retirement. I turned up the hill by the
rivlet, called here Boxbrook, and saw Box on the other side of it,
and Colerne on this side; we came on the famous Fossway, and saw
the three stones, call'd the three shire stones, where Somersetshire,
Wiltshire, and Gloucestershire meet, and then crossed the turnpike
road from Chippenham to Bristol, and, missing the way to Castlecomb, we went to Nettleton, where I stopt, and went a mile to
Castlecomb, a small town of about 100 houses, situated between the
hills, on the same rivlet on which Box stands, which rises about a
mile higher, another small stream falling into it a litle above the
town; they are chiefly farmers and clothiers, and here, as in most Castlecomb.
parts, they kill meat twice a week and carry it to Bath; there is a
plain Market Cross, tho' at present they have no markets, and it is
in no road; the ancient town was about half-a-mile higher on an
eminence over the river, the Castle being defended by a deep fossee,
and there is a Mount in it, a fossee extended from it round the town
to the north of it, and two fossees went across the town. The Church
has no appearance on the outside, the tower excepted, which is a very
handsom one, but within it a very light, handsom building, and the
arch between the body and the Chancel is curiously carv'd with
three figures on each side. There is a particular monument under
an arch of a person in armour, with shield in left hand, his leggs
across and his feet on a lyon, and a flowing robe. It is probably
either a Scroop, founder or rebuilder of the Church, or it may be of
the Walters of Danetavil, from whom the Wriothesleys, Earls of
Southampton, are descended, to which ancient family this place belongs. They told me Badminton Park was but three miles from it,

and I saw Nettleton Church half way between. I returned not exactly the same way, but passed thorough North Wraxhall, and came again into the Chippenham road. To the east of the rivlet is Cosham, where King Ethelred had a palace, and afterwards it was the residence of the Earls of Cornwall. We went a mile and half to Marsfield, in Glocestershire, a litle town over Cold Aston rivlet. These rivlets are very beautiful, having high ground on each side of them, mostly covered with wood. I returned by Bath Easton.

On the 22d, I went from Bath to Bristol on the north side of the river, a very pleasant road. A mile beyond Kelwastan is a mineral water with an handsome arch turned over it; it seemed to me a Chalybeat, and runs very slow. Within two miles of Bristol we came to Dungess Cross, where a handsom Church is building, and from this all the way to Bristol are collieries. I went to the Hot well, and thence to the Cathedral, where I saw the monument of the Earls of Berkley, repaired by the late Earl, the first being buryed here in the twelfth Century, since which there have been twenty-two Earls; they are mentioned as descended from the Kings of Danemark. I saw the fine Exchange, the design of the late Mr. Wood, whose architecture so greatly adorns Bath and its environs. From Bristol I went in the road to Wells, within a mile of Paynsford, and turning out of it to the right came in a mile to Stanton Drue, where I went to see a Druid piece of antiquity, mentioned by some writers under the name of the Wedding. The name seems to refer to the Druid worship here; it consists of stones that were set up an end, and seem to be a composition of lime and sand and pebbles, there being no other stones of that kind in the neighbourhood.

The stone is a composition of pebbles, which it is said polishes finely, and is found at Okie hole, and at Stone Easton towards Wales. The larger circle consists of about fourteen stones, at such unequal distances that I imagine that several stones had been taken away, as some of them were about fifteen yards apart; I conclude they were all about that distance from each other. It is remarkable

that one pair are but four yards and another about six apart, the
former to the North. I did not observe the situation of the other,
but I believe it was to the East; the latter might be the altar, and
the other an entrance; there seem to have been about twenty-four
openings besides these, which at fifteen yards each make 360 yards,
and these taking up ten yards on a supposition that the stones were,
one with another, five feet thick, twenty-seven stones make one
hundred and thirty-five feet, or forty-three yards, the exact measure
as I paced it, that is 413 yards. I measured one of the largest of
the stones, and it was about seven feet square; it was not an exact
circle as the stones lay, but they might have faln different ways, or
have been moved. In the second circle, which is near it, the stones
are much larger, and the distances about ten yards. I paced it
round one hundred and four yards; at the East is a stone twelve
feet long, and six others very near it. This I imagine was the altar,
and it takes up by my paceing eleven yards; but I suppose it only
ten; then 94 yards remain, eighty of which for the eight paces
between the stones, and then there remain fourteen yards, which is
two yards each for the 7 stones; one of these is fifteen feet square,
and two others are ten feet high. At a litle distance from the great
circle and from this, having the circles on two sides, are four stones
as it were making a square, which were probably about ten yards
apart, tho', as they now lie, two openings one way are twelve yards,
one nine yards, and another fifteen. At fourteen yards distance is
one stone in a line with one side. In the orchard, near the farmhouse by the Church, are three stones. I observed a hill to the
north-west, which seemed to have an entrenchment on it. We saw
about a mile off the glass houses, if I mistake not, at Stanton wich,
and, leaving them to the left, went two miles to Pensford, a small
market town in a bottom on the rivlet which runs to Canesham;
here, near the Church, are some houses for smelting copper, for
which purpose the water is kept up by locks; leaving Stanton
Bury hills to the right, I could see no sign of the entrenchments on
them, and came into the road from Bristol to Bath. On the 26th I

went to see Mr. Allen's house, before which there is a very grand collonade, and on each side a segment of about a quarter of a circle, which is an open portico to the garden, and a gallery under it with very convenient offices, all of hewn Bath stone inside and out. Going up stairs from these is a grand hall and handsome apartments, and on the middle story is a gallery, which is a secret library, the doors, on which the Philosophers, &c., are painted, opening to the books of the sciences in which they excell'd. Most of the rooms are wainscoated with oak and the pannels hung, and one room is wainscoated with what they call gum wood, which is a close and has something of the look of the pale kind of cedar. Behind the house is a fine rising lawn, where the deer feed, but the great beauty of the place is the lawn and wood below, and prospect of Bath, and the villages round about down that valley, with rising ground on each side, through which a small stream runs into the Avon. To the north of the house is a Gothick building and a small house, which is for the gardiner.

Bath.

Mr. Allen.

Shaftsbury, July 1st, 1754.

On the 28th I left Bath and went by Bath Easton, Bathford, Warley, Corckwell, and Wingley, eight miles to Bradford, coming into Wiltshire at Bathford. I found the country very fine on each side of the river, especially near Warley, opposite to which is Claverton, from which the neighbouring down has its name. Bradford is situated in a very extraordinary manner on the Avon, the hills forming a sort of amphitheatre, and the houses rising up the side of them almost every way; it is in the high road from Bristol and Bath to Salisbury, and twelve miles from the Devizes. The river Were, which rises near Westbury, and on which Trowbridge stands, falls into the Avon a litle above the town, and the Frome two miles below it. There was a Monastery here, built by Aldhelm, and destroyed in the Danish wars. A battle was fought near this place between Kenilwachius, King of the West Saxons, and Cuthred his relation. And a Synod was held here, in which

Bradford.

St. Dunstan was made Bishop of Worcester. They have a great manufacture of the finest cloths, and particularly the best kersies in England, and the water is very good for dyeing; I was assured that the greatest part of the cloth is made entirely of Spanish wool, brought some from Bristol but chiefly from London; but this I find is false, being only mix'd. There are several good old houses in the town, built of free stone, as well as some new ones; and the Duke of Kingston has a large house here. In the Church of Bradford is an old stone put up in the wall, and an ancient monument on each side of the Church in niches, as those of founders of Churches commonly are. The man has a long shield, and holds a sword on his body; the woman on the north side has a dog at her feet. There is a monument of the Methuens here, mentioned of Scotch extraction. This Church belongs to the Chapter of Bristol. I observed, in the bridge here, seven true·arches, and judged they might be old, setting in a foot from the outside, and there are two Gothick arches. On the 29th I went three miles to Trowbridge, on the Were, a small well built clothing town, in which there is nothing remarkable but a good old covered Market Cross and the site of the old Castle with a fossee round it; it lyes on the river, and the town is built on one part of it; it was said there were six towers to it. Horsley places Vertucio about Leckam, others guess it was at Warminster or Westbury; possibly it might be on the site of this old Castle. Going four miles further I passed by Heywood, now the seat of the family of the Phips, who was Governor of Bombay, and is buried in the Church of Westbury; it was the seat and estate of Sr James Ley, first Lord Chief Justice of the King's Bench in Ireland, afterwards in England; preceptor to King James's children, and by King Charles the first made, first, Lord high Treasurer and then President of the Council, and lastly, Earl Westbury. of Marlborough, dying in 1678, if I mistake not, without an heir. This is a poor stragling ill-built town, though a Borough governed by a Mayor and Corporation; there are two old buildings near the Church, one of the Parson or Rector belonging to the Bennets of

Weston, the other of the Vicar. It is a Peculiar belonging to the Church of Salisbury. To the north of the town on the side of the hill, near an old fortification call'd Bratten Castle, is a Horse cut of so large a size that it is seen some miles distance. It is made by cutting in pretty deep a few yards from the top of the hill, and being Chalk it shows to great advantage; they commonly go once a year to it from Westbury, about the 29th of May, and clean it from grass which would otherwise grow over it; but as the hill is very steep it is not very easy to go to it, much less to go into it, the Chalk not being firm to the feet. This is, I suppose, of the same nature as those of the vales in Berkshire, of White horse, and of Red horse in Warwickshire; it is thought to be made by the Danes, who were encamped in what they call the Castle, near which gives occasion to the vulgar to say that it was the Danish arms, for the Danes, after they had been defeated by the English near the strong fortification encompassed with a double ditch, retired to it, and held out fourteen days. I went four miles to Warminster, which is a thoroughfare from Glastonbury and other places in the west to London, which, together with the market and a great trade in malt, is the chief support of the town, which is near a mile long; the Church is half a mile from the Market-place; so that they have a Chapel in the heart of the town. There is a remarkable hill between the town and Salisbury plain, which is very near; it is called in old deeds Rip heap, and now they call it Cop heap. There are two Camps on hills to the east of Warminster, Battlebury, a double trench probably of the Danes, and Scratchbury, a square single trenched fortification. The Willibourne rises near Warminster, and the small river Deverell joyns it about this place, which it is said goes under ground and comes out again at a place which I imagined I saw in the road to Longleat, and it is, if I mistake not, called White Shore hill. This place is very near to Salisbury plain, the only place, I believe, in Great Brittain where there are bustards, except Norfolk and Suffolk; they are of the turkey family, but of a larger size, of a brownish colour, lay an

egg which is blew with brown spots, not quite so large, I think, as
a turkey egg; they make their nests in furz bushes, lay six eggs
and hatch about four; they live much on snails and insects, keep at
certain times in large flocks, and sometimes come down to the corn
fields, but they are very shy, run fast and fly slow, so that they are
easily taken; they have often been kept in enclosures; I could
never hear that they bred, but they commonly dye soon; they feed
'em with snails, boyl'd liver, and the like. I went up the heath
towards Longleat, and left Clay hill or Clee hill, as it is commonly
called, to the right, which being a high ground, tho' not a large hill,
is seen at a great distance; it seems there is a custom for the young
people to go to it on Palm Sunday. From Westbury to Warminster
there is a great variety of soil, bad free stone, sand, and sort of stone
marle of a free stone colour. The heaths are of a gravelly soil, and
at Marston there is a free stone full of shells. I was very agreeably
surprized when I came on the brow of the hill over the vale in which
the river Frome rises, not only to see a very fine rich country well
planted, but also on the grand appearance of Longleat, the house
of Lord Weymouth, which this way shows two fronts. There is a
steep descent from the park, and the situation low, and not the best;
but there is a large piece of water with a vessel on it, and a very
fine serpentine river might be made. The house is built round
a court; it is of free stone brought from near Bradford; there are Longleat.
twelve windows one way and fifteen the other; it is of the Dorick,
Ionick, and Corinthian orders, finished above with battlements of
carved work; within the court there is no regularity or architecture.
In the house is this inscription on a family picture: " Sr John Thynne,
builder of Longleat 1566." It was twelve years in building from
that time, tho' the tradition is, that it was in the time of Henry VII.
It was built to the old Priory, which was a Cell to the Monastery of
Hinton in Somersetshire; one side of it has been burnt down twice,
and is only rebuilt in a rough manner, with a dead wall to the court
for offices for servants. There is a large handsom hall in the house,
but no very grand apartments; in one room are two Chinese figures

above three feet high of a whitish metal; one has a pipe in the hand, the other a stringed instrument. From this place I went 2 miles to the New Church, handsomly built of free stone, and is a chapel of ease to Frome. I crossed some streams that fall into the Frome, and went two miles to Marston, the seat of the Earl of Cork and Orrery, situated on the side of a rising ground on the North side of the valley. It is a large convenient house finished in an elegant manner, and his Lordship has a very noble library of books all collected by himself; in this collection is a jaw of an elk found in the freestone soil some where in the County. The Earl is improving the place in very elegant taste. There is a lawn with a statue of Minerva at the end of it; then to the right another lawn with a plantation of wood adorned with busts, and an open temple with an altar in it, and ancient statues. To the left of the first lawn is a winding walk to the cottage built near the place, where a person lived (in the times of confusion after King Charles the first) in a little house under the park wall. Lord Broghill, the ancestor of Lord Orrery, being at church in those times, and a clergyman not coming, a message was sent to him that there was a person in church who, if he pleased, would perform the service, and he preached such an ingenious sermon that Lord Broghill sent for him, and found he was a deprived clergyman of the name of Ashbury, and that he and his son lived under the park, and maintained themselves by their labour; on which my Lord took them under his protection, and procured him a pension. This cottage is built and furnished as it is supposed a person in his situation might have done it, and there is a window with a wooden shutter to it opening to the road, with this inscription on it: " Sunt quos pulverem collegisse juvat." At the other end of the garden in a corner is a little Hermitage near finished for my Lord's youngest son; there is a deep way cut down to it with wood on each side, a seat or two in it—one is made in the hollow of a tree; it leads to a little irregular court, with a fence of horses' heads and bones. It is a cabin, poorly thatch'd, and a bedstead covered with straw at one end, a chimney

Marston.

at the other, and some beginning made of very poor furniture. In one part of the garden a very fine horse of my Lord's is buryed with a monument—a pedestal, with an urn, I think, on it; on three sides, in English, there is an account of the horse, and on the fourth side is this latin inscription, "Hic sepultus est Rex Nobby Equorum Princeps omnium sui generis longe præstantissimus obiit Feb. 12, 1754, Ætat. 35." Two or three fields below the house is a cold bath, as in an enclosure of an ancient Cemitery, with several old inscriptions made for it, and at the end is a small room very elegantly furnished, this I take to be Lady Orrery's place of retirement. A small mile from Marston is Nonney Castle, called also Nonney de la Mere, which is an octagon, the two long sides being about sixty feet long, and the Castle is thirty feet broad, the three sides at each end being very short. There are towers at each corner, which are a segment of a circle, one of these sides being the basis at the end of the Castle, and these towers on the outside come within five feet and a half of each other. In one or two of these towers was a staircase, and the middle part of the building consisted of a grand room on each floor. The building is very strong, and of excellent masonry of hewn stone on the outside. This Castle was built by the De la Meres. I went two miles to a Mansion house belonging to Lord Orrery, a very beautifull situation over a rivlet which falls into the Frome, the ground being in high cliffs on each side, and beautifully adorn'd with rock and wood, and, if I mistake not, they have a lime stone here. I went on to Frome, which is a large town of about 1000 houses prettily situated on the sides of the hills over the river, and consists of two or three long streets; it has been distinguished by the name of Frome Selwood, from Selwood Forest in which it was situated, the name of all the country formerly called Selwoodshire, *seal wad scire* and *Episcopatus Sciriturnensis*, according to Ethelward. It is a great town for the woollen trade of broad cloths, and it is said they have sent out of it to the value of 6 or £700,000 a year; they are also famous for malt liquor. There are two mannors here; one belongs to

Lord Weymouth, the other to Lord Orrery, and out of the latter
two Constables are chosen by the Court Leat for the government of
the town.   There are a great number of Dissenters here of all sorts.
In the Church yard at the east end of the Church is an iron grate
in shape of a coffin with a mitre on it, over the grave of Bishop
Ken, who lived with Lord Weymouth, and putting seven or eight
hundred pounds into that Lord's hands, the produce of his effects, he
gave him an annuity of eighty pounds a year.   He dyed at Longleat,
dressed up in his shroud, and desired to be buryed at sunrising and
his pall to be borne by poor old men.   The Mendippe hills begin a
litle to the west, and extend to the seaside; Lye, under Mendippe,
being about four or five miles from this place.

Wilton, July 2ᵈ, 1754.

On the first of July I left Lord Orrery's and went three computed miles across the valley to Witham, where there was a
Nunnery founded by Henry 3ᵈ.   It was granted to the family of
that Lord Hopton who is famous in the history of K. Charles 1ˢᵗ,
and afterwards came to the Windhams; and the present proprietor,
Sʳ Charles, marrying a Daughter of   he had granted
him by patent the honour of Earl of Egremont, one of the titles of
the late Duke of Somerset.   It is a large house, but a low situation;
the old chapel and some other parts of the Nunnery remain.   Lord
Egremont has lately removed all his furniture from it, not purposing
to live there any more.   The Park rises up finely, and I saw part
of the old enclosure, and, at a litle distance, the Fairy, probably the
farm house of the Nunnery.   I could not find the least remains at
the place called the Charter house, where it is said the first house of
that order in England was founded.   Almost directly east of this is
Maiden Bradley in Wiltshire, where Manassor Bisset founded a
Priory in the time of King Stephen, and his daughter an Hospital
for Maidens; it is the estate of Sʳ Edward Seymour, now Duke of
Somerset, who has always resided in this place.   Leaving Witham,
we soon came on the estate of Stourehead, formerly Lord Stourton's,

Witham.

Maiden
Bradley.

now Mr. Hoare's. It has its name from being at the Stour head, which they say rises from six springs out of so many valleys, and I saw at Salisbury a tomb of the family, on each side of which are three holes to represent the six springs, and the spaces between 'em the hills which divide the vales; this, they told me, was the family arms. Over the northern vale we went on a very fine terras, which is a lawn; on each side there are plantations, and, passing by an obelisk to which there is a walk from the grounds, came to the house, which is a very handsome building of hewn stone, the design of Campbell. There is a fine hall and saloon beyond it, and a very handsom library, and the whole is finished and furnished in the most elegant manner, and, beside many fine originals, there are some very good copies, especially by Davison, I think his name was, of Frome. To the South of the house is a lawn with a piece of water, and from that is a winding descent over the above-mentioned valley; in the way is a Dorick open Temple, and below, over the water, is an Ionick temple, with a handsom room in it; below this are two large pieces of water, which are to be made into one and much enlarged, for which a head is making at great expence. There are to be three islands in it, with different kinds of buildings Stoureton. in them, one of which is to be a Mosque with a Minaret. On the other side of the water is a very beautiful grotto, with cascades of water at the end falling down in streams about a river God. In this grotto are a great variety of spars and christals, and other curious stones; but the most magnificent building is the Temple of Hercules, not yet finished, with a grand portico of the Corinthian or Composite order. A Colossal Statue of Hercules, which is making in London by Risbrack, is to be placed in the nich opposite to the entrance; in the other niches are to be statues and pulvinars; on each side of the entrance is a small open apartment, to be adorned also with statues. The prospect from this spot is very beautiful of the places I have already described, of the village of Stourton in the bottom, and of the vale in which the Stoure runs from this water. I was shown before the house the hole of the vault into which that person was thrown who was murdered by Lord Stoureton's order by his servants, in the reign of Queen Mary, the particulars of which are in Strype's Annals. He could not obtain of the Queen to be beheaded, nor of the Bishop to be buryed in the Cathedral with his family, unless the halter was hung up over the grave, which was of silk, and is now supplyed by one of wyre. This Lord's descendants have a small estate here of about two hundred pounds a year. I saw to the south in the Church of Pen, where probably the battle of Pen was fought with the Danes. I went two computed miles to Mere, and observed to the left the end of a hill fortifyed just over the town, called, if I mistake not, the Castle of Mere, and seems to be Beacon hill in Speed's map. Mere is a very small town, subsists chiefly by a manufacture of tickin; it stands on a rivlet which falls into the Stoure. The Church within is preserved more in its ancient state than any Church I have seen in England, with the rood lofts and seats. I here saw this inscription round a monument of Brass set in stone:

Hic jacet Johannes Bettesthorne quondam Dominus de Chadialkriche fundator istius Cantarii qui obiit VI. die Februarii Anno Domini M°cccxc. Cujus animæ propitietur Deus. Amen.

On another, in the same manner, is a figure in armour with a sword and dagger, with this inscription :

Tu qui transieris videas sta perlege plora. Es quod eram et eris quod sum pro mihi precor ora.

I came into Dorsetshire and went seven miles to Shaftsbury, passing near Gillingham, which gave name to the Forest formerly here, and going also near Hartgrove hill, a very beautiful spot with two fortifyed mounts on it, very near the one to the other. We began to ascend the hill to Shaftsbury, and passed by the water with which the town is supplied by carriage in pails on horses' backs. They save the rain water (in cisterns made under their courts) which fall from the houses, what wells they have being fourscore yards deep. This extraordinary town is situated towards

Side note: I have been since inform'd that the Ancestor of the Earl of Clarendon married the daughter of the person who was murdered, and that she was Great Grandmother of Queen Anne.

Mere.

the South end of a ridge of hills about four miles in length. It is said to be built in the 8th century, and to have been enlarged by King Alfred, who they say built ten parish churches. There was a Nunnery here founded by Lady Ælgiva, wife to Edmund, great grandson to King Alfred, and there are some remains of what they call the Abbey at the South end of the town, and foundations of buildings extend from it to the terrace over the hanging ground to the east. There are about four Churches remaining, but no appearance of any thing which has marks of great antiquity. They have traditions of other Churches, and there are some remains of them Shaftsbury. in houses, and particularly at the Swan there is seen going up to the roof a painted Glory at the East end. It is mentioned that one of the Saxon Edwards was buryed here, but on what authority I know not. There are several old houses in the town. It is the post road from London to Exeter. They have some trade in malt, and supply many parts round about with all kind of roots, and the country with necessary's which is well inhabited, and no towns of consequence very near. These things are the chief support of the town, in which there are computed to be above 600 houses. Auditor Benson, formerly Member of Parliament here, was at great expence to bring water to the town from that head of the Nadder which is called the Donee, by engines which raised the water 300 feet up to the town, but the people taking umbrage on some particular account, refused to make use of this water, and so all was suffered to run to ruin. There is a most glorious prospect from the end of the hill where there is a small old fortification of which the fossee only is seen. The view beginning at the east is towards Cranbourne Chase, then along the Frome towards Blandford, and where the hills come close to the river; one of them to the South is called Ocford hill, and to the east of that is Hamilton hill, where Oliver's forces had a skirmish with the people of the country. We then saw towards Dorchester and a gap in the hill towards Weymouth, called Dorchester Gap; we saw also the country towards Sherbourn, and the hills that are the bounds between this country and Devonshire, all an exceeding rich and beautifull country.

I left Shaftsbury on the 2^d, and chose to go along the hill to the north, and descended at the end of it into that valley in which the Nadder runs, and saw on it Westhatch, a fine plantation, which they told me did belong to Sr Robert Hyde. I passed by Basley hill, which seemed to have been a fortifyed Mount, and came to Wardour Castle, a fine old ruin of freestone; it was an oblong square building, enlarged on each side by a building of three sides. Over the door, and below a bust, is this inscription :

Sub numine : D M O
Stet Genus et Domus gentis Arundeliæ. Thomas
Lanhernia Proles Junior hoc meruit primo sedere loco
Ut sedit cecidit, sine crimine plectitur ille
Insons insontem Fata sequita probant
Nam quæ Patris erant Matthæus filius emit,
Empta auxit, studio Principis aucta manent
Comprecor aucta diu maneant augenda per ævum
Hæc dedit, eripuit, restituitque Deus
1578.

The garden is made round the Castle, and some of the old enclosure seems to remain. The mansion house is built to it. There is a fine piece of water made in the valley to the west. In 1643 Lady Arundel defended the Castle a week with 25 men against 1,300 Parliamentarians, and she and her children were imprisoned, and great damage done to the estate, in violation of the capitulation. In a mile and half I went a litle out of the way to Tisbury Quarry, which is an excellent freestone, in which there are shells, particularly the heart; and I observed a sort of dendrite. In half a mile I came to Tisbury on the same river. In the Church the Lords of Arundel are buryed, who were made Counts of the Empire for the merit of their ancestor, Thomas Lord Arundel, who, serving under Rudolph the second, took a standard from the Turks at an assault at Gran, in Hungary. There are niches for statues at the end of the North Isle, where there was an altar. I observed here some old enclosure, and enquiring, they told me

Tisbury.

that some land that way was call'd the Abbey land. I went two
miles further to Funthill, on a small rivlet of that name, which falls
into the larger river about Tisbury; here Mr Beckford, a native of
Jamaica, and member of Parliament for London, who has three
brothers in parliament, and his sister married to Lord Effingham
Howard, has a very handsom seat and estate purchased of M^r
Codrington, who resides part of his time at Brewham lodge, which
we saw in Somersetshire in the way from Witham park to Stourehead, and partly at Freemantle park in Hampshire, in a house he
has built on the top of an high hill, the offices for shelter being
under ground, and the apartments he lives in built over them,
where there is a well   deep.   The house here was very
much improved by this gentleman, and fronted in the Italian taste;
to the west it is in two half H^s, one to the South-east, and the other
the grand front to the East, on one side of which there is a large
wing of stable offices.   The house is finished within at much Mr. Beckfords.
expence, and there are many modern paintings all over it as well as
on the cielings, and a handsom library ; but what is most curious
is a very fine large organ in the hall, which playes thirty tunes
without a hand, and cost about £1500.   Beyond the park, and
opposite to the grand front, Mr Beckford has built a Church, on
the plan of Covent garden, which is a good termination of the
prospect.   There is a large lawn that way, and plantations to the
west, an open temple on the side of the hill, and an open rotundo
is building higher up on the hill.   To the east is a broad serpentine
river, with a very handsom bridge of free stone built over it of
three arches, with a stone baluster.   To the north is a grand gateway near the village, from which there is a gravel walk to the
grand front about a furlong in length.   I went on towards Salisbury near the river, passing by several villages, and had to the left,
on a rising ground, Grovely, Lord Castlehaven's ; at the distance
of eight miles we saw Salisbury Steeple, and came to Wilton   In
the parish Church is the monument of the late Lord Pembroke, the
vault in which he was buryed in the churchyard, according to his

will, being taken into the Church ; it is a marble bust as against
a pyramid, and under it this inscription—

Here lyeth
Henry Earl of Pembroke and Montgomery,
Baron Herbert of Cardiff, Ross, of Kendal,
Parr Fitz-Hugh Marmion St Quintin
And Herbert of Shurland,
Who died Jan. IX. MDCCXLIX.
Aged LXI.
These Honours, Herbert, titles of renown,
From thy great Ancestors transmitted down,
Preserved their Lustre while by Thee possess'd,
Rest, happy Spirit, then contented rest.
But the rich blood which in thy veins has run
Descends through Thee untainted to thy Son.

At the entrance of the town is a small Chapel, which belongs to
the Hospital. Wilton is famous for a manufacture of carpets, like
those of Turkey, but narrow—about three-quarters of a yard wide,
which is in the hands of three people. I may, at some time, give
you a farther account of Wilton house, as well as of Salisbury
where I lay. and on the third went two miles on the London road
to that river, which rises at Collingbourne and falls into the Avon
a litle below Salisbury. I went about six miles up the river,
designing to go by Collingborne, but missed my way, and went
near a height on which there seemed to be a rough pillar, and
turning into a road towards Andover came to Quarley hill, in
Hampshire, with a fossee round the top of it, about 842 yards
round, and four entrances to it ; five miles to the east is Dunbury
hill, likewise fortifyed, and supposed to be a camp. I came into a
road from Salisbury, and before had fallen, if I mistake not, into
the Ambresbury road ; and in about two miles I left this road, and
went to the left to Amport, on a rivlet, which rises a litle higher ;
and, as it is laid down in the map, is joyned by the rivlet from
Andover, and falls into the Test at Leckford. Here one of the
Pawlets has a seat. We passed two or three more villages, left the
river, and came to Andover. I had a view in the road of Chute

Wilton.

and Collingborn hills. Andover is said to have its name from the
passage there over the river Ande, probably the old name of that Dour is water
river. Here King Ethelred endeavour'd to establish peace by in British.
adopting Anlaf the Dane. It is a small neat town, with a handsome Town house. I saw, a mile from the town, Bere hill, on
which there is an old Camp, and it is said there is another Camp
half a mile from it. At Whorwell, near, a Monastery was built by
Queen Elfrith to expiate some crime of her relations. At Weyhill,
near Andover, a great fair is held about Michaelmas, for hops,
cheese, sheep, wool, and all sorts of goods. There is a great
manufacture in this town for serges and shaloons. It is said there Andover.
was a Monastery and Chantry here. Andover is the high road
from Kingsclere, Overton, and Whitchurch, as well as from Newbury, to Salisbury and Amesbury.

P.S.—I went from Andover six miles to Uphusborn (the wood
on the river), being on a rivlet that rises a litle higher and falls
into the Teit ; it is call'd the Swift. This is the road for wheel
carriage to Newbury, but the bridle-road, and the nearer, is by
Stoke, both meeting at three leg'd cross, near Cruxeaston. I came
by Hawcleer and Penwood to Newtown.

EXCURSIONS FROM NEWTOWN, 1754.

I left Newtown on the 30th of July, went through Newbury and Aug. 12.
by Speen and Wickham, and came by   seeing   Mr.
Archer's in the vale in which the river Lamborn runs, which passes
by Dennington and falls into the Kennet. About a mile before I
came to Lambourn I observed a valley to the right, which is the
division between the gravelly country and the chalk and down
country we then entered. Lamborne is situated on the river of that
name, which is here very small, and I was told that in some seasons
there is no water at the town. It is a neat small town, in which
there are many farmers and publick-houses, and a good number of

shops.   It is the high road between Oxford and Marlborough; they
have a small market, but sell a large quantity of corn by sample.
It belonged to the Fitzwarrens, and afterward to the Essexes.   In
the church, on a monument, is this epitaph :

" Here lyeth the bodies of Sr Thomas Essex, Knight, who
deceased the 21st day of August, in the year of our Lord God a
thousand five hundred fifty-eight, and Dame Margaret his wife."
On the tomb are their couchant statues.   There is a dolphin at his
feet, and his head rests on a helmet on which is the family crest, and
there is a chain with a cross to it about his neck.   The son of this
gentleman sold the estate to Lord Craven's ancestor and dyed a poor
Knight of Windsor.   The Gothic arches of the Church are on Saxon
pillars.   The ancestor of Mr. Hipperley of this place founded an
almshouse for ten old men, and built a chapel adjoyning to the
church for them to read prayers in morning and evening.   From
this place I went two miles to Baydon, and two more to Auburne, a
large village called a town; they have no market, and it consists of
farmers.   There is an old monument of the Goddards in the church
with five or six statues on it.   Here is a rivlet after great rain, from
which it is called Auborne; it falls into the Kennet below Ramesbury, but at present I could see nothing of it, the constant source of
it being lower.   The downs and warrens called Auborne Chase
belong to this parish.   I came over the downs about seven miles to
Minal or Mildenhall, on the Kennet, a mile and half below Marlborough.   They find here in the fields many flint echini, some rare
rib'd cockle-shells, a great quantity of iron-stone; and I have one
piece of very fine small white coral petrifyed.   There is an old
entrenchment on the river which I imagine might be a summer
station for the horse at Canetio, in order to forage.   In a field on
the side of the hill, on the other side of the river, much Roman coin
has been found.

Above Minal, on the other side of the river, is a large barrow in
a meadow, which from it has the name of Barrow close.   The living
of Minal is in the patronage of the descendant of Dr. Pococke, the

famous Orientalist; his son married into the Monpesson family, from whom a remarkable picture came into the family, which is in the parsonage house. It is of a pike four feet and nine inches long and eleven inches broad, with this inscription, which I have corrected:

"This is the bigness of the pike which the Emperor Frederick the Second, with his own hand, hath put the first time into a poole at Lautern, and hath marked him with this ring in the year 1230; afterwards it was brought to Heydelberg, the 6th of November, 1497, when he had been in the poole 267 years." Marlborough is judged to be the old Canetio, supposed to be the ancient name of the river Kennet, on which it stands. It was a Roman station placed by Antonine 20 miles from Vertucio, supposed by Horsley to be Leckham, near Laycock, where coins are found. There are some remains of the old fossè, and the mount is shaped of late years with a spiral walk out of the keep of the castle; it is in the garden of the house belonging to the late Duke of Somerset, and now to Lord Egremont; it is lett for an inn, and has almost ruined all the good publick-houses in Marlborough and done great prejudice to the town itself, as the turnpike road is carried to it behind the town. Prince John, before he was king, had a castle here, which was taken by Hubert, Archbishop of Canterbury, when he was in rebellion against his brother, King Richard. A Parliament was held here in the 52 of Henry 3d, when the Statute of Marlborough against riots was made. To the church, at the east end of the town, there is a very good Saxon door. Over the north side of the town is a bowling-green, finely situated, given by a gentleman of the the town, and adorned and kept in order by a publick subscription. At Poultons, near the east end of the town, is the remains of a deep fossè and rampart, which seemed to have belonged to a private castle. At Preshut Church, a mile above Marlborough, I saw an Marlborough. ancient round font, made out of touchstone and adorned with several members; they say many Princes have been baptized in it. A litle higher, in Clatford wood, I was informed there are of those stones, called Grey Weathers, bigger than those at Stonehenge. I went on six miles to Kennet, and to the head of the Kennet, directly south of Selbury Hill, at a place called Swallow Head, where, after rains, the Kennet does actually rise, but the constant source is a furlong lower, where it rises out of an ousy ground. I took particular notice of Selbury Hill, said to be the tomb of King Sel or Silver; it may be, say they, of Ceol, King of the West Saxons. It is at the end of an hill, from which it seems plainly to have been cut, and the hill at the end was probably higher than the part which joyned to it, and on the west side it appears plainly that it was shaped from the solid hill, because it is steeper than loose earth would lye, or than it is in other parts, and consequently has broken away. There appear also two settlements above this at the top. A sort of fossè appears all round where the ground was high, but to the north, where it is plain, the ground is level. From this place I went a measured mile northward to Aybury, which is a great piece of antiquity most accurately described by Dr. Stukely. I observed the square enclosure which takes in part of the town, being a large

Aybury. rampart. There are many large stones within it, some up an end, others fallen down, and I saw some heaps of stones for building which they had lately made by blowing up and breaking in pieces these curious monuments of antiquity. I saw here only one stone of the avenue to Kennet, but saw several from Kennet up the hill; and before I came to Kennet I observed three stones, one of which was fallen down, and I suppose were those called the Devil's Coits. I did not see the barrow in Mounkton field with stones round it. I crossed over the downs, and in a valley saw many of the stones called the Grey Weathers, but not very large. A thought came into my mind, that as these stones are commonly found in that situation, that they might be strata of stones on the brow of the hills, which by some accidents might have been loosened, and so by their weight most of them have subsided to the valleys beneath. About four miles to the north-east of Aybury is Barbury Castle, an old entrenchment at the end of a ridge of hills which extend from Marlborough to the south-west of Ogbourne; there is a fortification before the entrance, and on the south-east hill is a deep hole with a large dike round it; this I take to have been the well. I observ'd a small trench at the bottom, which went up the side of the hill so as to encompass the works; this was probably for the advanced guard. This is supposed to be Beranberig, and not Banbury, where Kenrick, King of the West Saxons, and his son Ceaulin, fought against the Britains in 556. Four miles from this, to the north of, is Bradbury Castle, another camp with a single deep trench, both of them being about a quarter of a measured mile in circumference, and both of them fine situations, especially Bradbury, called also Leddington Castle, commanding a view near as far as Oxford and into Gloucestershire, Worcestershire, and Somersetshire, as well as Berkshire and some part of Hampshire. About this place, Ina the West Saxon and Ceolred the Mercian Kings fought a drawn battle; these two were doubtless enemies' camps, and it is probable that the battle was between them, it may be about Draicot. There is a Roman way from Minal towards the castle, and it is said it comes from Winchester, and probably it is the same that is mentioned at Escourt, near Great Bedwin, as a Roman way.[a] I saw the Church of Wanboro, with a spire in the middle and a tower at the west end, about which place Roman coins have been found. I went another day by Ogborne and Barbury Castle, and from the heigth observed Swindon, where there is a quarry of a black slaty stone, which rises large and makes very good tombstones. And when I came towards the foot of the hill, I observed there was a sort of a white stone, approaching very near to the nature of chalk, and so it is all along the foot of the hills, and it is remarkable that the chalk country or the gravelly extends all along by the Thames, and the rivers that fall into it, tho' there is a free stone in some parts, as about Oxford. The chalk country extends from the Isle of Purbeck all the way to Huntingtonshire, with veins of gravel between it; on the Severn,

[a] Though on looking into the Itinerary, Iter xiv. it seems rather to be the road from Caleva Attrebatum, Farnham, by Spinae and Canetio, Marlborough, and from that to Durocorinium, Dobunorum, Cirencester.—*Note in MS.*

and rivers that fall into it, is free stone and other stone, and northward, I believe on most parts of the coast except Wales, which is of
different kinds of rock, it is a free stone, most of which seems to be
a composition of sand.   From Barbury Hill I went down to Uscole
and passed near Wroughton, where lately in digging a well they
found, 100 feet under ground, a curious rib'd cockle, which I have
in my collection; the outer shell is gone off, the inner coat of a
greenish mother-of-pearl is most beautifull.   I passed in sight of
Lediard, the seat of the St. John's, now Lord Bullingbroke, which
Margaret Beauchamp gave to her second son, Oliver St. John.
Three miles more brought me to Wotten Basset, a small town of
one street, where there is some cloth manufacture carried on.
There is a small river near it, which falls into the Avon that runs
by Bath, and so into the Severne, the river Rye rising about four
miles to the north, near Swinton, and falls into the Thames.   The
roads in this country are very bad.   'Tis called Breden Forest,
which in 905 was ravaged by Ethelwold Clito and his auxiliary
Danes.   Ethelwerd saies, that the Avon was for some time the
boundary between the West Saxon and Mercian kingdoms, and is
thought to be the Antona of Tacitus.   I went from Wotten Basset
by Broad Hinton and came down to Rockley, in a valley near which
are several grey weathers; among them, it is said, springs break
out, called hunger borns, because they denote an approaching
scarcity, and I was told that the hoarders of corn rejoyce whenever
they rise.   Passing through Ramesbury, I went to see the Church,
as it was formerly a Bishop's see (quere ?), which seems to have
been first united with Sunning, and then to Shirburne, and lastly to

Ramsbury.   Salisbury.   There is a very large tower to the Church with a basement of free stone, something in the Roman style, and probably is
of great antiquity, as are the pillars in the Church, in which there
is a grand monument, ill executed, with a couchant statue on it of
Sr William Jones, Attorney General to King Charles the Second,
whose descendants have lived in a handsome house near; there is
also an old Chapel, called Dorrels Chapel, in which there are some

old monuments that were adorned with brass plates. A litle lower
I pass'd by Litlecot, the seat of the Pophams, descended from Lord
Chief Justice Popham, whose monument I saw at Wellington, in
Somersetshire. I formerly observed at this place the effects of a
whirlwind, which crossed a wood at some distance, tore off the tops
of the trees about twenty feet above the ground, came to a barn of
Mr. Popham's and took off the thatch, oversett a load of straw, did
some damage to an office beyond, and there it is supposed it stop'd,
no marks of it being seen farther. I passed through Hungerford, a
small town famous for nothing but excellent trouts and eels, caught
in the river about this place. Hungerford Park near it is a very
fine situation, as is an hill about Inkpen, called   ; not far
from that is Mr. Sloper's house, at Westwoodhay, on the foot of the
Comb Hills; it is said to be the architecture of Inigo Jones, but it
was the design of a person who married his daughter. I came by
Kintbury, where there is a Saxon doorcase to the Church, and the
corniche seemed to be very old. Two miles from this place is
Hampstead Marshal, where the fine piers remain of the gates and an
old Dorick porch, to which the late Lord Craven began to build a
good house. In the Church, on a flat stone, is this inscription:
"Here lyeth the body of Sr Balthazer Gerbier, Kt. Arch., who
built a stately pile of building, in the year 1662 to 1665, for the
Hon. William, Earl of Craven, of Hampstead Marshal, part of
which was destroyed by fire in the year 1718. He died in the
year 1667." The park belonging to this seat is a very fine situation
and well timber'd, and the late lord built a house in it all arch'd
over to preserve parchments against fire. A litle lower on the
other side is Speen, a poor village, the ancient Spinæ, but there are
no remains of the old town; here is an eccho at a well to the Church
which repeats seven syllables. Newbury, or the New town, rose out
of this. It is a large town, with one handsome Church in it. Going
to the Wharf is a handsome building called the Hospital, which
they say was Kenrick's Hospital, who left a great benefaction
to the town. They make here serges and druggets, but there was

formerly a much greater manufacture than at present. Along this vale they dig a great quantity of peat, which has much wood in it, mostly birch; below it they frequently find a white marle full of small shells; they find also nuts and a sort of a blew colouring earth, as well as stags' horns, and from their description of large horns found some seem to be the elk; but what is most curious, they have found the skeletons of bevers' heads. The ashes of the peat they sell for 4d., 5d., 6d., nay, sometimes 8d. a bushel for manure; they have great trade for flower and malt for London. Three miles farther is Thatcham, a poor town. In the Church I saw the monuments of Sr Douse Fuller's family, who formerly lived at Chamber House near, which was a religious house; at the other end of the town is an old building which seemed to have been a Chapel, and there is another at Dunslade in Midiam, tho' Thatcham is the mother Church; here is a fine house and estate, the late Mr. Warring's, now Mr. Gore's, by marrying his widow. Greenham also is a Chapel which the vicar of Thatcham supplies.

Going lately to Andover by Husborne, I found the rivlet there, called the Swift, dried up. I went into the Church at Andover and observed that the arches of the tower in the middle of the Church were Saxon, and also the pillars in the Church, and there is a fine

Saxon doorcase. In the chancel are the monuments of the Venables, who had the estate and rectory here before the Pollens. There is an inscription here which mentions George H   as founder of the Free School in 1569.

Going to Salisbury, I passed near the Camp of Beer Hill, and close by another, I was informed of, as half a mile from it. Four or five miles from Salisbury there is a Tuscan pillar on the hill over which the road goes, with such a Mercury on it as is in Christ Church fountain at Oxford. Opposite to it, to the east, are the plantations of Mr. Thistlethwait, at   , the heir of Mr. Norton. Beyond Salisbury three miles we went to Langborough, Lord Folkstone's seat on the Avon, near the conflux of a small river, which rises westward out of Cranborne Chace. This house was built by   , and as I was informed, was bought about 30 or 40 years ago of Lord Colerain. It is a triangular house, with a round tower joyning to each corner; it is built of free stone, and is esteemed as one of the best finish'd and furnished houses in England. The apartments below are exceeding neat and handsom, as those above are very fine and grand. In one apartment the furniture is of mahogany carved and gilt, many fine Japan pieces of furniture. One sleeping apartment is furnished with chintz and Indian paper. Another apartment is hung with fine Flemish tapestry of the design of Tenieres; and in the gallery are some very fine original paintings, marble tables, and bronze groups, and the chimney boards through the house are made of Chinese pictures, which show several of their customs. The rooms in the round towers are very beautifull; one is a chapel, another a library; among the pictures, I saw of Beauverie, the ancestor, who fled in Queen Elizabeth's time for religion from Flanders. The river is on two sides of the fine lawn and plantations, and at the further end is a banquetting house; in the part near the house are knots of flowering shrubs.

We went to Wilton and to Stonehenge, and then to Ambresbury. On the plains near died in battle Ambrosius Aurelianus, supposed by some to be descended from the Emperor Constantine, who in the 4th consulship of Theodosius was chosen emperor in Britain, and murdered at Arles. He took on him the government of Britain, and with the help of King Arthur made a stand against the enemy. From him this place had its name; British kings are mentioned to be buryed here, probably in some of the barrows round Stonehenge. Here was a monastery of 300 monks built to pray for the souls of those who were murdered by Hengist's treachery. Alfritha, wife of King Edgar, founded a monastery, to expiate her crime of murdering her son-in-law King Edward; and in 1177 the abbess and 30 nuns were expell'd for their incontinence, and others brought to it. Mary, daughter of King Edward 1st, and thirteen noblemen's daughters, and Queen Elinor, widow of Henry 3ᵈ. took the veil here.   This inscription is said to have been found in this place, thought to be spurious, R. G. A. G. 1600 (*sic*), supposed by some to be of Guinever, wife of King Arthur, who is said to have been buried at Glassenbury.   In King Edgar's reign in 995 Elfric was elected Archbishop of Canterbury, in a synod which was held here.   The Duke of Queensborough has the estate, on which the mannor was built, which did belong to Lord Carleton. It is a small hunting house, but the garden is laid out on the river and up the side of the hill, in beautiful lawn and plantations; there is an handsome stone bridge over the river, another on which a Chinese house is built, and a third is a wooden arch, which was made as a specimen for a wooden bridge at Westminster.   Going on to Andover, I crossed the valley at a place, if I mistake not, called Sowley, where the river I was tracing when I came before from Salisbury runs when the waters are high, but was not at present to be seen here; it is that river which rises in winter at Collingborne.   We left Quarley hill to the right, and went by Thruxton and Weyhill, where the great fair is annually held at Michaelmas.   I came by Andover and Stoke, which is between Up Husborne and Bourne, and by three leg'd Cross, and Cruxeaston to Newtown.

Ambersbury.   (margin label for paragraph above)

Old Windsor, Aug. 13th, 1754.

Leaving Newtown on the 12th, I came in three miles to Itchings-well, where there is a Chapel and a fine stream of water, not observed in the maps.   In a mile I passed under Freemantle Park, where Mr. Cottington lately built an house of two floors, one of which is all under ground, and he dug a well   feet deep.   Here was a camp, and it is said some remains of a castle.   We soon came to Kingscleer, which was a seat of the Saxon kings, there is another rivlet ; this is a very poor town, they have a small market and sell corn by sample.   In the Church is the monument of Sʳ Henry Kingsmill, who died in 1625.   He was father of Sʳ William and of John Kingsmill, who lived at Sandleford. On it are the couchant statues of Sr Henry and his lady; she erected this monument in the 48th year of her widowhood. The large old tower is built on Saxon arches; and there is a font, the top part of which seems to be an old freize, being carved with roses and pateræ, and is of an uncommon marble, something of the nature of a brown granite; the lower part of it seems also to have been an old capital. I went from this place to Rookley down, within three miles of Basingstoke, and came to West Sherbourn, called also Monks Sherburn, and came a mile farther to East Sherburn. In a Chapel on one side of the Church are the tombs of the Brocas's, one adorned with brass plates is of 1477. There are two couchant statues on another; the inscription on one side is covered by a seat, on the other is this inscription:

" Conditur in hoc tumulo Radolphus I F O I C Rexs al Armiger," and " Simul hic Conjugis ossa jacent Edithæ Hæredis nuper et pulcherrima proles Gulielmi Armigeri Brocas Bellorepairi."

Here also is the monument of Richard Atkins, of 1635, who married one of the family of the Vine, whose name is not mentioned, and also of Mr. Lyons, a French refugee, the vicar, who built the south part of the parsonage-house, and procur'd the vicaridge to be enlarged by Queen Anne's Bounty. A rivlet rises here, called the Wey brook; I came to Chinam, within a mile of Basingstoke, belonging to Lady Nicoles, where there is an old Chapel not in service, and soon came into the turnpike road from Basingstoke to Reading, which towns are seventeen miles apart. I came by Sherfield Tourges and Heckfield Heath, where Mr. Sturt has an house and park, and to Eversley Blackwater, a river which falls into the Loddon, as another we passed half a mile from Hundred Oaks, I suppose, falls into this, which is the bounds both of the forest and of Berkshire. Mr. Cummins has a handsome house at Eversley. Blackwater and the village of Eversley is about a mile to the east. We passed by Finchamsted, a Church on a heigth, seen at a great distance, to which, if I mistake not, there is a semicircular chancel in the old way.   Crossing the heaths, I saw to the right Bigshot Lodge, belonging to Lord George Beauclerc; beyond it is a long hill called Lodge Hill, extending near to Bagshot Heath, to the west of that a small hill called Amborough Hill, and a small round one call'd Edgeborough Hill.

Oakingham.   I came to Oakingham, near which there is a brook that rises in the heath, and, I suppose, falls into the Loddon.   It is a small town, with an handsome square; they have a manufacture of serges, serge denim, and baragons, and send malt to London; this place is about five miles from Twiford and Reading.   In the Church Bishop Godwin is buryed, with this inscription:

> THO. GODWIN,
> Ba. et Wells. Eps
> 15—

It is a good Church, with true Gothick slender pillars; there is an hospital in this parish at Locker's Green, founded in the time of King Charles I. by H. Lucas, Esq. for sixteen pensioners, who have £10 a year, with a chaplain who has £50 a year.

I was informed, in relation to the rivers of the country I passed, that the river near Silchester, which rises at Pamber, and is called the Berville river, runs by Mortimer, and falls into the Kennet at Burville, tho' the maps place it as falling into the Loddon.   The Loddon rises at Newnham, near Basingstoke, and goes by Wildmore, Sherfield, Stafordsea, and Swallowfield into the Thames, running near Twiford.   Weybrook, the rise of which I saw at East Sherborn, runs by Stratfield, and then, as I believe, falls into the Loddon.

Hampton Court, Aug. 15th, 1754.
On the 13th I left Oakingham, and going about a mile in the road to London, which passes near East Hamsted, I turned to the right and came to East Hamsted Heath, having to the right the house of the late Sr Wm. Trumbal, which now belongs to his son.

The father . . . . *(blank in MS.)*
I rid towards Lodgehill, to the east of which there is an irregular
hill fortifyed with a deep trench, and is called by the common
people Cæsar's Camp. I went round it, and found it to be 1912
paces round ; the red deer frequent this place much for shelter in
the fossee. This was probably a camp of the Britains, when the
country was cover'd with wood ; and it is not improbable they had
their camp here when Julius Cæsar approached the Thames, and
that it might have its name from being the camp which they had
formed to oppose him. From this place I passed by Mr. Fisher's,
an improvement on a grant he lately had out of the forest, and
through another of the like nature belonging to Mr. Jenison. I
went by the race-posts of Sunning Hill, and turned to the right to
that place, where I tasted the chalybeat waters, which are of the same
nature, but not so strong as those at Tunbridge. They have a large
room, and company resort to it in the season. To the left of this is
Mr. Fisher's park; beyond that is Cranborn Chace, and the road from
Oakhampton, and further on is St. Leonard's Hill, Mr. Anscomb's
charming seat. But a litle out of this road and nearer Sunning is
Cranborne lodge, formerly Lord Ranelagh's, then the Duke of St.
Albans, and on his death granted to the Duke of Cumberland. It is
not a large house, but a very fine situation, commanding a view to the
west, north, and east as far as the eye can reach, a fine view of Windsor, Harrow-on-the-hill and Hamsted hill, and one can just discern
London, also very plainly Stoke House, now Lady Cobham's, a fine
old structure, in a park, built 1571 by Sr Edw. Hastings, knt. of
the garter, and a temple in Langley park belonging to the Duke of
Marlborough. In the gallery at Cranburn are pictures of soldiers
drawn, about eighteen inches long, in the uniform of every regiment of England and Hanover, with the numbers by which they
are now distinguished. This was done under the Duke's direction.
There are some pictures left by Ld Ranelagh, as a Turkish wedding,
the Siege of Buda, A View of the Seraglio, and a German artificial Boar Hunting, and there is also here the Battle of   in

1702, in which the horse are represented as passing the river. There is lawn and walks through the woods about the place. Two miles from it, near the park wall towards Windsor, is the Duke's Island; it is on a pond, with a cutt made round the island, on which a room is built in the figure of a Greek cross, with a couch on each side of the four parts of the cross ; behind it, covered with trees, is a kitchen, &c. The Duke often comes here and spends an hour or two, and sometimes dines. Two miles from Sunning Hill is the beginning of the Duke's great works; the Oakingham road goes through it. It is a valley between two rising grounds, at the extremity to the south-west; on an eminence the Duke has built a triangular tower, which is hexagon within, with a hexagon tower at each corner, which are round within. In one of the towers is the staircase which leads to the beautifull hexagon room, in which there are in the sides three doors and three windows, two of 'em lead to the round closets; in one are litle shelves hung up for books for the Duke's use; in the other, on such shelves, is china for tea and coffee. The hexagon is most beautiful, the sides are adorned with festoons and flowers and fruits hanging down from them on each side of the doors and windows in stucco, and painted in their natural colours ; over each door is a bass-relief, in white marble, a Sacrifice to Apollo, to Hercules, to Diana ; in the center is a branch adorned with Chelsea china, and a group of small statues in the middle of it of the same ware ; the whole cost £200. Below are closets for the housekeeper, and underground kitchen and offices. The views from the leads are extremely fine to the north, east, and south; we saw Westminster very plain, just discern'd St. Paul's, a view all along the Thames that way, then to Guilford and towards Farnham, and a single beautiful hill is seen between, and still farther, and it commands a fine view of the Serpentine River I am going to describe, to which there is a gentle descent. This river extends two miles in the park, and farther into the forest ; it is made by collecting the waters of the several springs and rivlets round about ; at this end it is, I believe, a quarter of a mile broad, and is kept up

The Duke's Island.

by a head, which is made into a fine terrace; it goes under a bridge, and forming a litle lake, it falls down a cascade, made of great stones thirty feet deep, which shows how great a work it was to make a head that keeps up the water in that manner; here it forms another pool, from which the superfluous water runs off in a stream through the valley. Just above the first-mentioned small lake there is a cave made of the same great stones as the cascade, which seems to be a sandy freestone; but some of it is grown exceeding hard, and it may be would polish; these stones are found about the heath, and there is no quarry of them; they are adorning the inside of the cave with cinder of glass houses or clinkers, shells, stalactites, gypse, &c. On the Serpentine river is a small yatch, which has sailed on the sea, a Chinese ship, the middle of which is high, covered and glazed, a Venetian gondola, and five or six other different kinds of boats; at the other end is a wooden bridge of one arch, which, if I mistake not, I was informed is one hundred and ten feet wide. Going up the hill beyond this, and having a view of the ships and boats, it looks like an arm of the sea. About fifty yards from the pales on each side of this water, the Duke has planted large trees, and small ones between them, with a winding walk thorough, and between this and the walls is to be fine lawn, part of which is made, and more is preparing. Going up from the bridge about half a mile to the right is a large Obelisk, and then we soon came to the woods and plantations about the Duke's Lodge, beyond which is a very fine piece of water, and behind the house lawn, and a round temple over the water. From this house to Windsor there is a grand road three miles long. Twenty men are employed all the summer in mowing the grass in different parts. The Duke has wild beasts here, and I saw an ostrich walking in the lawn near the house. It is incredible how fine a place this is made, from being the most disagreeable and uncultivated, and the whole country round it is in a state of great improvement. In the harvest time the Duke carries on no improvements, but in the winter he has commonly a great number of men at work, and all this is done by his own directions, and shows the great taste his Royal Highness has, as it is acknowledged by foreigners to exceed every thing, and has cost an immense sum of money.

I came down from Bishopsgate two small miles to Old Windsor, passing by the Duke of Roxborough's, and went to Mr. Bateman's adjoyning to the Church yard ; this is a most charming box on the Thames. Old Windsor is said to have been a town, and in William the Conqueror's time there were   houses in it, and they find foundations of houses in the gardens and fields at a litle distance from the river. And on digging near the Church yard they find Mr. Bateman's. that formerly it was of much greater extent. Mr. Bateman's is close to the river, a very small house of four rooms on a floor, but enlargéd by making two bow windows and a Gothick front ; nothing can be imagined more elegant than the finishing and furnishing this house, with painted and gilt ceilings, and the furniture is a collection of curious things. He has made what is called a long gallery of three squares ; there are books on one side in carved and gilt cases, and on the other side they are seen in looking glass set in the like work. The dimensions are three feet by nine feet. Behind the house are offices, and at the back of them a room filled with all sorts of Japan, China, and porcelane wares. Among them are two fine Hetruscan vases, one of Nola, the other of Capua manufacture. This opens to a grove, and there is a grove on each side of the house ; beyond that, to the south, there is a lawn all along to the river. The grove to the north extends to Mrs. Bateman's house to the Church yard and parsonage house ; at the former is a sort of a grotesque shell-work with a summer house over it, and beyond that a Chinese alcove seat, near which there is a Chinese covered bridge to an island, and another uncovered beyond it to another island. This and the swans on the river make it a most delightful piece of scenery. Behind this house, beyond the grove, is a meadow of fourteen acres, with a walk round it of above half a mile, part of which is close, in the wilderness way, and on one side to the road an open summer house with a window looking to the road, and the opening to the meadow is in the form of a Venetian window. At one corner of this meadow is the farm house, with a small garden in parterre and a greenhouse; this is in the Chinese taste; in the room below they commonly breakfast in summer, above is the library and within it a museum, with cabinets of coins and of things relating to natural history. From the field there is a passage across the high road to a large flower and kitchen garden, with a pine house, from which there is a fine view of Windsor Castle.

London, August 17th, 1754.

On the 15th I came from Old Windsor and pass'd near Cowper's Hill, the subject of Sr John Denham's poem, to Egham, where I saw in the Church a monument to two wives and a child of Sr John Denham, Lord Chief Justice of Ireland. The statuary of the faces seem to be very fine. There is also a remarkable monument in which a person is represented in statuary as rising up out of his tomb with a covering over part of his body, the rest being naked; under it is " præterita sperno," below are skeletons and heads, as rising above are two Angels; under them are these words, " Surge a somnis." On it is this inscription: " Futura spero, ut a peccatis in vita, sic a morte post vitam, ut secunda reddat primam et ultimam in Christo resurrectionem ex omni parte perfectam." Round the arch of the monument are these words: "Quia vita et resurrectio est per Jesum Christum ad æternam beatitudinem cum sanctis." On a stone in the Church is this inscription, over General Honeywood's son by a gentlewoman he afterwards married: " To the memory of Philip Wright, a young man of singular virtue, of an unblemished character, an affectionate child, a sincere friend, religious without ostentation tho' young; he lived much beloved, and dyed much lamented, the 12th of August, 1739, in the 16th year of his age. Quis desiderii sit pudor aut modus tam cari capitis." The pillars of the Church are of the old Saxon kind. From this place I went three miles to St. Anne's Hill, the top of which seem'd to have been fortifyed; it commands a very fine view, and a litle below the summit Lord Trevor has a house on the south side of it; from this hill I had a view of Runny Mead, I had formerly passed, in which King John met the Barons and sign'd Magna Charta. At Chertsey, a mile farther, I saw in the Church a monument to the memory of one Thompson, Secretary to Queen Elizabeth, master of twelve languages and a great traveller. There are no remains of the Monastery in which Henry 6th was buryed, but his body was afterwards removed to Windsor by Henry 7th

Weybridge.

Two miles further, at Weybridge, Ld Portmore has a good house, and a fine improvement where the Wey and the Huning water fall into the Thames, on which three rivers his Lordship's gardens and fields are most beautifully situated. There is a fine lawn behind the house, and plantations of cedars and other evergreens to the right, which lead to another lawn and a summer house, and then other plantations brought us to the Wye, over which there is a long swivil bridge which turns with one hand; on the other side of this is a lawn, with a building to the left to which there is a litle spire to make it appear like a Church, the building being hid by trees; beyond this is a handsome gateway, like a triumphal arch, of trellis work, which appears in a better point of view when one is opposite to it; on the other hand, by a plantation of trees, one goes to a farm house on the Thames; the cornfields and meadows are bordered by a walk on the river which leads to the embouchure of the Hunins, and is then the bounds of the farm, and on a mount near it they are finishing a beautiful round Temple. Going round to the same bridge again we returned and saw some hay reeks and a barn in the way, which added to the beauty of the view. I went two miles by Walton Bridge, which consists of a very large wooden arch, and, if I mistake not, one on each side of it, and some stone arches, and they are now building fifteen stone arches over the low ground on the Surrey side, which is overflown. All this is the undertaking of Mr. Dicker, who has a peculiar genius for building bridges; he has the toll of this bridge, and they say has lost money by it. I went by Sunbury to Hampton Court, where another

wooden bridge is built, which has a heavy look by reason of the
four houses built on it, two for gathering the toll, one for Mr.
Onslow, Speaker of the House of Commons, and the other for
another who had a property here. I went to see the palace so well
known to every one to have been built by Cardinal Wolsey, and
improved by a court built by King William ; the two grand suites Hampton
of rooms are wainscoted with Dantzick oak, and are mostly hung Court.
with fine old tapistry, pictures of great persons over the doors and
chimneys, chiefly by Vansomner, Vandyke, and Sr Peter Lilly, with
the marble tables between the windows and a great variety of old
China jars. One of the rooms is hung with satin, embroidered in
different colours by Queen Mary and her maids of honour. The
prospect over the Thames is very rich. The gallery, every one
knows, is hung with the famous Cartoons of Raphael, and one room
with Julius Cæsar's triumphs, by   . The Chapel, with a
fine arch in Gothic compartments gilt, was wainscoated with oak
and adorned with carvings by Queen Anne. From Hampton I
came the same day to London.

Blackheath, Aug. 19th, 1754.

On the   I left London and went to Black heath, to pay my
duty to the Earl of Chesterfield. His Lordship has a house at the
Park wall, to which he has built a fine room about 77 feet long and
twenty-two broad, with a large bow window at each end and one
in the middle ; that towards London commands a fine view of the
city. I went down to see the Chapel lately finished at Greenwich,
which is adorned with gilt carvings and is painted white, and there
is a gallery on each side for the officers; Sacred history painted
over the four doors to them, and 3 stucco reliefs in the semicircle
of the altar. The money which arises from showing this and the
hall is a fund for maintaining and teaching an hundred boys in the
hospital, to be apprenticed out to masters of ships or officers aboard
men-of-war. The north end of the west side of the hospital was
built by King Charles II. as part of a royal palace, but, money

being deficient, it was set apart for an hospital for decayed seamen. Lord Derwentwater's estate from £4,000 has risen to £10,000 a year, so that they have 15,000 seamen in it. If the infirmary was built it would hold 2,000, but they have not a sufficient sum for that number. Each man has his closet and bed in it, and they have such plenty every day of dinner that they lay it by for the other meal, and I think they have as much small beer as they please, and 1s. a week pocket-money; and though it is such a delightfull place, yet the confinement is irksome to persons who have been used to rove about the world. The Dorick Colonade is an alteration of Sr Christopher Wren. The house of the ranger of Greenwich Park, which is in the center towards the park, is the design of Inigo Jones. Toward Charlton is a small house built by the late Lord Pembroke, when Lord Herbert. It now belongs to the Duke of Bolton. Lord Egmont has a good old house at the pleasant village of Charlton, from which I descended to Woolwich, which is a town a mile long, having the dock at one end, the warren at the other, and the rope yard in the middle. In the dock the largest man of war is on the stocks that ever was built in England, and it is a size they cannot exceed, as they are obliged to choose out men six feet high to be able with their arms to encompass the main yards which are necessary for a ship of that size. The warren is the seminary for Engineers and the train of Artillery. They consist of one regiment, of which the master of the Ordinance is the colonel. There are several companies of matrosses, and the 48 cadets answer to the company of the grenadieres, and take place. They are gentlemen's sons put in by the Master of the Ordinance, to learn fortification, engineering, drawing, and military architecture, and every thing to qualifie for a soldier and engineer. They are promoted to be officers in this regiment, and their commissions being signed by the king they rank as other officers, but formerly they did not. They are from these also made engineers at three shillings a day, and if sent on duty at five shillings a day and have an additional pay, the under engineer at   the upper at   ;

and they may have commissions and be promoted in the army. They have a day subsistence and arrears. A house has been built for them, in which there are to be three beds and six persons in a room, which is thought too strait, that it is doubted whether they will be brought into it, tho' their lodging in town is subject to many inconveniences, and then they are to have common table at dinner. The officers inhabit the ends, each having a room here. All canon are prov'd and laid up.

Knole, Aug. 28th, 1754.

On the 20th I rode at the back of Sʳ Gregory Page's, [which] I had formerly seen, one of the best habitable houses in England, with a gallery, &c., and a fine sett of paintings in an apartment by   . The park is very beautiful. I went by Eltham, and about three miles farther to Crayfoot, to a house which is building for Mʳ Cleves, a pewterer on Cornhill, on the design of Palladio, after which my Lord Westmoreland's house is built; but they say it is on a smaller scale, however, by taking in two of the porticos into the house. The two side rooms are larger than his Lordship's; the staircase is taken out of one side of it. This has a very bad effect on the outside, as have four ugly chimneys round the dome; but the water of the Newel made serpentine, and the lawn to it is very fine. This house is built by contract for £8,000, and some thousands more has been laid out on this place. Sʳ William Calvert has a house below this on a fine high situation. I went by this river to Orpington, where it rises from a very fine spring in a meadow called Newell, from which it has its name, and running into the Darent below Dartford, falls into the Thames near Erith. I returned by Chislehurst to Blackheath.

From London I went to see the china and enamel manufactury at York House at Battersea. This house was built by Cardinal Wolsey, and belongs to the archbishops, who have let it out in leases. I saw at Chelsea a house which the Moravians have fitted up in a grand manner for their bishop and patriarch, Count Zinzendorf, who lives in it.

23rd. Passing through Lewisham where Dean Stanhope, minister of this place, is buryed, I came to Bromley, where there is a handsome college with a portico round the court, and a Chapel built, with this inscription over the door:—

> Deo et Ecclesiæ.
> This College for twenty poore
> Widows of Orthodox and Loyal
> Clergymen and a Chaplain, was
> given by John Warner, late Lord
> Bishop of Rochester,
> 1666.

I was informed that this foundation is for the widows of beneficed clergymen. They have twenty pounds a year, and the chaplain has £50. At the Church I imagined I saw the original of the compounded Gothick windows; there are five or six in this manner,

so that by bringing a window-frame round this circular part, and taking in either two or three long windows, leaving open spaces between the round window and the frame, a Gothick window is formed, which in time was made with a greater number of members and divisions. There is a nich in the west side of the chancel, into which they have broke, and the hollow of a skull appears only three inches from the surface. This, they say, is the body of Bishop Vender. The Bishops of Rochester have a country house very near the town. I went by Hayes four miles to Keston, where the river Ravensford rises which falls into the Thames at Deptford; here I am told is a camp, called Cæsar's Camp. Seven miles more brought us to Westram. From the hill over that valley I had a fine view into Surrey, which comes very near to Westram, that place being only 6 or 7 miles from Reygate to the north through the valley in which the river Darent runs, taking that name after two or three brooks meet together a few miles lower; one rising above Westram and another two miles above Valence, I shall have occasion to mention. Westram is a small town; John Frith, the martyr and confessor, was

Westram.

born here, and the Hoadleys were of this place, who have given two prelates to our countries. I came a mile to Valence, the house of my worthy friend Capt⁰ Denis, who went round the world in the "Centurion" with Lord Anson, which place I shall have occasion to describe. On the 21st I went to Knole, the Duke of Dorset's; the entrance to the park is from Sevenoke. It is an exceeding good old house, built round three courts; it belonged to the Archbishops of Canterbury, and was exchanged with Henry 8th. Two grand courts have been built since, the paper building next to the garden having been built by the Archbishops, with the Chapel adjoyning, and some say by Thomas à Becket. There are a great number of apartments in the house, several of them, with a small gallery or two, are finished with carved wainscoats of oak, and furnish'd in the old way, and with old pictures. In one room are pictures painted on board, of the great men in Queen Elizabeth's time, collected I suppose by Earl Thomas. At the middle court is a very grand apartment, consisting of gallery, drawing-room, another large room, and two grand apartments with beds; one is called the King's Bedchamber, in which most of the moveables are of silver, and there are some fine ebony cabinets, with reliefs on one of them. In the gallery are pictures of most of the family from Queen Elizabeth's time, by the best hands, and the arms and alliances of each Earl to about King James's time in painted glass, as the rest are in a gallery below, made out of a portico; and in one gallery is a picture on glass of the head of the house, with this Inscription under it:

Quere, if not built by A⁰ Wareham?

> Herbrannus Sackville.
> Præpotens Normannus,
> Qui Angliam intravit
> Cum Gulielmo Conquestore
> MLX . . .

There is a garden behind the house, with a wilderness of large oaks. The park is very fine ground, with a valley going round part of it, and there is high ground on each side the valley; the park is exceedingly well timbered with a great number of many beautifull trees in it, and kept in great order. From one heigth there is a very rich prospect of the Weald of Kent; we saw Tunbridge and Mount Ephraim at Tunbridge Wells, the hills to the west and over them a high hill, which I took, as some do, for the Isle of Wight, and others for Portsdown. In a shelter'd situation in the park, near the garden, they are making a nonagon building; it is to be a sort of a cottage, where poultry of all kinds are to be kept, in which the Dutchess delights, and there is a beautiful view from it of one part of the park.

At Sevenoke Church I saw the monument of Farnaby, schoolmaster here, who wrote the book of Rhetorick; his descendant, Sr Thomas Farnaby, lives near. I saw also that of Lambord, who published an account of Kent, called the " Perambulator." There is some remarkable poetry in the Church.

A free school was founded here by S^r Wm. Sevenoke, Ld Mayor of London in 1418, and an almeshouse for 32 poor men and women, which have been lately rebuilt in a very handsom manner with the limestone they have near. Mrs. Boswell was a benefactress by giving exhibitions from it to a college in one of the Universities. They have found fuller's-earth and marle near this place. In 1450 John Cade killed Sr Humphry Stafford and his brother, and several gentlemen sent against him by Henry 6th. I went four miles to Otford, passing near Seal, which gave the title to the Lords of Say and Seal. Otford is an old palace of the Archbishop of Canterbury, magnificently rebuilt by Wareham, and given to Henry 8th, or exchanged by Cranmer to avoid envy; there were two hexagon towers, with a portico of entrance between, and on one side of them are some remains of a grand gateway; then there is a court of large buildings beyond it, the ruins of which remain; the enclosure of the court seems to be very old, it may be of the time of Thomas à Becket; the other buildings are of brick and window-cases of stone; at some distance there are fine springs rising between stone walls, which are called Thomas à

Otford.

Becket's well, and here Offa, king of the Mercians, beat Ealthmund in 773, and exempted Litchfield from any subjection to the See of Canterbury, and made it an Archbishoprick, and in 1016 the Danes were defeated here in a bloody battle. I went by Kemseng, the Mother Church of Seal, to St. Clair, where Mr. Glanville, who changed his name from Evelyn, has a good house of Inigo Jones's design, and I came to Igtham, Mr. James's seat, within a mile of Wrotham, this also was a house of the Archbishop of Canterbury. The "Gazeteer" saies that Queen Elizabeth granted the honour of Sevenoke to her kinsman Henry Cary, Ld Hunsdon, whose grandson, the Earl of Dover, alienated it to Richard Sackville, Earl of Dorset, but Knole was given to Henry 8th together with Otford, and was granted by him or Queen Elizabeth to Earl Thomas, Lord High Treasurer.

Tunbridge Wells, Sept. 5th, 1754.

On the 28th of August I returned from Knole to Valence, belonging to Captain Denis. This place is situated on a litle stream which falls into the river that is about a quarter of a mile from the place; there is a beautifull variety of rising ground, vales, and wood, and the most is made of the water, which at present forms canals in one vale of the park, that are to be improved into a serpentine river, a stream is carried from them into a wood opposite to the east front of the house, and falls down from a couchant statue of Neptune feet high, and coming on towards the end of the serpentine river falls again in five breaks into a bason, from which it runs underground before the front of the house and forms a large piece of Valence. water on the other side of it, from which it is to fall into another with an island of alders in it, and terminates with a head at the park wall. On each side of the serpentine river first described is a rising ground, that to the west is a gentle ascent to a heigth on which there is a summer house that commands a fine prospect of the country; behind this the ground rises still higher, and opens a more extensive view towards Wrotham; and beyond it from this hill there is a steep descent to the house covered with timber trees, where it is work'd into winding slopes, and the statue of the gladiator stands a litle elevated in the middle. In a word, the whole is a most delightful spot of ground. From Valence I went a mile and half by Brastell to Combe Bank, the seat of General Campbell, next heir to the title of Earl of Argyle. The General is father of Lady Aylesbury. He showed us his house and garden with great politeness. The house is in the Palladian style, with a square turret for closets at each corner. It is highly finished and furnished with fine pictures and ancient busts, some of which are of bronze, and one with a Greek inscription on it. The situation is bold; there is a fine green terrace walk the whole length, over a hanging ground, which is planted with shrubs, mostly of the flowering kind. There is a lawn on each side of the house, and beautiful plantations of a great variety of the most curious evergreens. To the north-west is a descent formed into a kind of grove, through which you see a large piece of water, that appears like a serpentine river. The most curious trees are the tulip tree, which bears a litle tulip strip'd in different colours, and not all white, as the common tulip tree, the deciduous cedar, or the cedar that drops its leaves and is not evergreen, the Newfoundland pine, and some others that are very curious of that family.

Comebank.

I went also to see Squerries belonging to Mr. Ward, whose grandfather, Sr John Ward, was Lord Mayor of London. There is a very good house finished by the Earl of Jerzey, who sold it to this family; in it is a fine piece of Guido, David with Goliah's head. There is a piece of water near the house which through some wood appears like a large river, and a stream rises from it. On one side of the park there is a rivlet, which is in part kept up in ponds; but the great beauty of the place is the wood through which a broad riding is cut and planted with firrs, that may be about a mile along. There are several other rideings through the wood, and a high turret built in it which commands a fine view, in which there is a handsome room. From the rising ground near one sees all the hills towards Reygate, Box Hill, and Mole Hill, near Dorking, the hills towards Farnham, Petersfield, the downs of Sussex, and near as far as Portsmouth, having to the south such a prospect of the Wealds of Kent as I saw from Knole Park. The commons called Chartes are sandy and gravelly, and there is stone all about this country with shells in it.

Tunbridge has its name from the River Thone, and there are four other streams, it is said, that have bridges over them here, and fall into the Medway. There are ruins here of a large castle, built by Richard Earl of Clare, natural son of King Richard the First. Tunbridge. Richard de Clare, Earl of Hartford and Gloucester in the time of King Henry the III., built a church and founded a priory here. The castle is a large enclosure, with a strong building on one side, to which there are towers at each corner, and the windows are of the large Gothick kind. There is a good Latin school here, founded by Sr Andrew Judd, Lord Mayor of London in the time of Queen Elizabeth. The town is ill built, but it is a great thorough fare to Tunbridge Wells, and now thrives on the account of the navigation of the Medway which goes above Penshurst. Tunbridge Wells is five measured miles from this place. The waters are in a vale between the hills, called Mount Zion, to the south, and on the other side Mount Ephraim and Mount Pleasant, on which there are good houses for lodgers, with courts before them and gardens behind, both planted with trees, few of the houses being contiguous, so that it appears as a delightful village full of good houses, the situation being romantic in the middle of a wild heathy country, and there are rocks on some of the hills which have a beautiful effect. The waters are chalybeat, and I have been told there is something of vitriol in them ; it is said they are rather heavy, but they are good in cold chronical distempers, weak nerves, and bad digestions, operating by perspiration and urine. It is a good air, and they are well supplied with all sorts of provisions, particularly with sea fish, and in the season with wheatears from the Sussex downs. The season for the waters is June, July, and August. Just beyond the

by S[r] Andrew Judd

hill to the west is a pleasant valley, beautifyed with rocks and wood on each side; this leads to what they call the rocks on the south side, which are towards the top of the hill, are perpendicular, and about twenty feet high, with large cracks in them through which one may pass ; there is a walk on them, and seats under the wood, some of which grows out of the rocks, and there is an extensive prospect along this valley into Sussex towards Grinstead, one side of the valley on which the rocks are being in that county, which is divided from Kent by the rivlet that runs through Tunbridge Wells. This is a great place of resort from Tunbridge Wells in a morning, and here they often breakfast. About Tunbridge was the forest of Ashdown, now called the South Frith.

From the wells I went four miles near that stream to Groom Bridge, where there is a Chapel in the parish of Spelshurst with this inscription on it:

D. O. M.
Ob Felicissimum Caroli Principis ex Hispaniis
Reditum, sacellum Hoc D.D. 1625 I.P.

It was built by one of the family of the Packers, who had a house near, and their monuments are in the Chapel. The estate is now to be sold under the title of the descendants of the co-heiresses of this family. Here was a considerable village, with several good houses in it, now running to ruin. Three miles further brought us to Wydiham, the burial place of the family of the Duke of Dorset, where the bodies are deposited in leaden coffins in a fine vault under a Chapel, in which there is a monument of couchant statues of white marble to the memory of Earl Richard. A quarter of a mile from it, over the rivlet, are the foundations of the house of Buckhurst, where the family resided before they acquired Knole. A handsome gatehouse is remaining, with the arms of the family on it, and some remains of a building before it with a bow window at the end, which was probably some office, now converted into a farm house. Half a mile the other way, over another rivlet, is a lodge called Stoneland, with fine ground about it well planted. Here the duke commonly

Buckhurst.

resides during the month of August. It was a purchase of the family of   by   . The duke has built one good room, in which is the picture of the obelisk on the Boyn, presented to his grace as it was erected under his first government in Ireland, from which the copper plate is taken. Here is a chalybeat water, not reckoned quite so strong as those of Tunbridge Wells. About a mile to the west I saw the ruins of Highbrook, an ancient seat of the Earls of Thanet, and about 4 miles off Ld Abergavenny resides. To the south-west is the forest of Ashdown, adjoyning to this parish; it is all granted away without any rent, and is now entirely free in the several proprietors. Four miles brings into the road from Lewes to London, and four more to East Grinsted, nearer to London in that road, being 29 measured miles from it—a town I have formerly seen; it has belong'd to the Duke of Dorset's family ever since the time of Edward III. The roads here are almost impassible in winter, and cannot be mended with the stone, which is soft and sandy, so that it immediatly wears and washes away, and the iron works and hop yards make wood so scarce that they will not afford it to mend the roads.

Canterbury, Sept. 10th, 1754.

I left Tunbridge Wells on the 5th, and came by Woodgate, ten miles to a small town called Yalden on the river where a freestone vein begins, and further there there is a gravel, then sand, and the chalk hills, and which continue to Maidstone; we passed over the hill beyond Hunton, but could find no petrifications among the stones. Maidstone is pleasantly situated on the Medway, and is a town of considerable trade on account of its navigation, as hops and other produce of the country are sent by water to London; and the shops are well stored with all sorts of goods from the capital, they have also a great manufacture of thread brought over by the Flemings. There is a large timber-yard here for the supply of Chatham Dock. This place is thought to be the Vagniala of Antonine and was called in British Caermegvead. The Archbishops

Maidstone.

had a house here which is now alienated, it is near the collegiate church, which together with the college was founded by Archbishop Courtney, who as I understood had prepared his tomb in this church, probably that to the south of the altar with niches behind it, but the king ordered his body to be buryed in the Cathedral of Canterbury. There is a remarkable monument of the Beals in this church. The chantry founded by Archbishop Arundel is a mean building and is now a free-school. I was told the old parish church is turned into an assembly room. On the other side of this river is a church and some ruins, which I was informed was a convent, but possibly it might be the college or hospital founded by Archbishop Boniface. This town held out for King Charles; and General Fairfax stormed it before he could take it. The small river Len rises near Lenham and falls into the Medway here; there are some paper mills on it, and one of them is esteemed the finest in England. From Maidstone I went to   Mr. Chamneys in the parish of Boxley, a litle beyond it is Penenden Heath, commonly called   Here there is a small wooden building which is the county house, where the elections are opened and the candidates named, when they adjourn to Maidstone. This place is famous for a meeting of William Rufus and Odo, Earl of Kent, to settle some differences, and history mentions that a Bishop of Winchester by reason of his great age came in a carriage drawn by horses. Very near this heath is the scite of Boxley Abbey, on

Boxley Abbey. which a large house is built. The Abbey was founded in 1145 by William de Ipre, a Fleming, Earl of Kent, the barn belonging to it remains, roofed with chesnut, 'tis said near 400 years. This is a very useful wood, but they say that it looks fair without when it is become rotten within, and goes all at once. This abbey was famous for a rhood which was burn't at Paul's Cross in London. I was told that there is a memorial on a stone here that Sandys the traveller repaired this place and beautifyed the gardens, but omitted to see it. On the side of the hill and near the turnpike road from Maidstone to London by Rochester is what they call Keith Coty

House, which consists of four such stones as the Grey Weathers, two standing up on end at about ten feet distance, and one across in the middle, and a large stone resting on them all about ten feet every way, except that the large one is fifteen one way. It is said to be the burial-place of Caligern, a British general who was slain in battle near this place.[a] I was told that in a field below there were remains of such another monument, but could not be informed whether it is the place call'd Horseted, where Horsa the Saxon general was buried. A litle above this is a fine prospect of the beautiful vale and of the neighbouring hills. A mile farther on the Medway is Aylesford, pleasantly situated, which gives title to a lord of the Finch family, who has a seat at the Old Priory below the town, founded by Radulphus Friburn under the patronage of Ri : Lord Grey of Codnore with whom he return'd from the Holy war. On the south side of the river the manors of Preston and Milhall were given by Hen. I. to the church of Canterbury. The north side where the church stands on an eminence is an ancient demesne, granted away by the crown and came to the Sidleys, and in 1607 S[r] William built the bridge and an hospital here. There is a fine monument of the Culpepers in this church, and if I mistake not Lord Aylesford came to the estate and house here by marrying an heiress of that family. Sir Paul Rycaut's monument also is in the chancel, whose father was a Fleming, and if I mistake not agent to Lord Aylesford's family. He went Secretary to Constantinople with Lord Winchelsea, became consul at Smyrna, then was Secretary to Lord Clarendon in Ireland, and afterwards Resident at Hamburgh to the Free Cities. Here Guortimer the Britain beat Hengist with his Saxons, who went and recruited at the Isle of Thanet. Two miles to the west is Leybourn, an old castle in ruins; and a mile farther at the town of West Malling are remains of a nunnery, with fine Saxon towers in the front; it was founded by a

Aylesford.

---

[a] It is no other than a cromlech, and certainly antienter than the time of Caligern —that monuments are call'd both in Wales and Cornwall coits or quoits from the upper stone resembling a coit.—*Note in MS.*

East Malling.

Bishop of Rochester in the 11th century, and suffered by fire in the time of Richard the first. A mile to the east is East Malling, where Sʳ Roger Twisden has a seat in a most beautiful park, in which two rivlets meet, that are made into serpentine rivers; one falls down in a fine cascade, and a high island is forming below the meeting of the rivers, which is covered with evergreens and flowering shrubs. The lawn and plantations are beautifully disposed, and it is altogether a most chearful spot.

From Mr. Chamneys I went near the Len five miles, through a sandy country; here they dig out the white sand for glass houses and other uses, making large caves under ground. We came to Leeds Castle, built by the Crevequers. It is said there was an

Leeds Castle.

Abbey and Priory here. They have a tradition that Edward the Second's Queen was denyed entrance by Lord Boddlesmere, and that the king besieged the castle, and hung up the Lord who had been so impolite to his consort. The Dutch prisoners were kept here in King Charles the Second's time, and were starved by the person who contracted to supply them; on which they set fire to the castle, and old Lady Culpeper came and set open the castle gates, and 'tis said that of 1500 there went out no more than 80. This estate came to Lord Fairfax's family by marriage with an heiress of Lord Culpeper's. This Lord has now a great estate in Virginia where he lives, and has given up this estate to a younger brother after the death of Captain Fairfax, elder than the present proprietor, who was a man of great genius, especially in the mechanick way, and with his own hands brought optick glasses to greater perfection than have been known. The park is very fine ground, having a great command of water from the Len, and is beautifully adorned with wood and improved at great expence by the present owner. The castle is moated round, and there are two drawbridges to the strong part, which is about three quarters of a circle in its form, with fine vaults under it. The dwelling-house joyns to it. This family are descendants of General Fairfax. We went on four or five miles and passed by Mr. Best's estate near

Lenham, and a litle to the right of that small town; it is thought by Cambden to be the old Durolenum, which others would place at Bapchild between Sitingbourne and Ospring, near Milton. There is a monument in the church of Robert Thompson, Esq., mentioned as grandson of Mary Honeywood, wife of Richard Honeywood Lenham. of Charing, who at her decease had 367 children lawfully descended from her, sixteen being of her own body, 114 grandchildren, 228 in the third generation, and nine in the fourth. I saw Broughton, which was the estate of the famous S[r] Thomas Wotten, in the time of Hen. VIII. and Edw[d] VI. and Queen Elizabeth; Plukley, S[r] Edward Dering's fine old house, very beautifully situated on an eminence; Litle Chart, a large house building by Mr. Darrel, the first Roman Catholick of his family of late years. It is built of brick with ornaments of a white chalky freestone, from France. There are large offices to it. A litle further is Hothfield, the Earl of Thanet's. This young nobleman was advised by his father not to enter into any opposition to the Government, nor to be too severe in relation to the game, in both which respects he acknowledged himself to be in the wrong; and his son has shown his filial piety to the memory of his father. I came to Ashford, a small town near the Stour, which is said to have its name from a rivlet called the Eshow, on which it stands. In the Church are two very fine monuments of the Smiths, Baronets, and a third, which is very handsome. This family were made Viscounts of Ireland. The first monument is of that gentleman who farmed the Customs in Queen Elizabeth's time; the next is of his son, Receiver of the Dutchy of Cornwal of the revenues of Prince Charles, afterwards King Charles the First. They consist of a cornish, supported with pillars and adorned with very fine reliefs of foliage, &c., especially the first; the third, if I mistake not, is his grandson, and I believe father of the first Lord. The descendant of this family, Lord Strangford, is Dean of Derry in Ireland. His Lordship and Lord Blayney in that kingdom are the only Lords who have gone into Orders in the three Kingdoms since the Reformation, after they came to the title of Peers. 1 was shown some old monuments, which I suppose are of the Baronet family of Fogg; one of them, Sr Robert, is said to be the founder of the Church, and Sr John Fogg, Comptroller of the Household to Edward IV., founded a College here for a Prebendary, Priests, and Choristers. A monument also is mentioned near 400 years old, of a Countess of Athol. Here was also a perpetual Charity. From this place I went three miles to the north-west to Eastwell, the seat of Lord Winchelsea. It is a large old house of indifferent structure, on the east side of the park. On the south side is the parish church. This estate descended through several hands to Mr. Colepeper, who married his daughter to Sr Thomas Moyle, the gentleman who built the greatest part of the present house, and it came to the family of the Earl of Winchelsea and Nottingham by marrying that Baronet's daughter. Part of the genealogy of this family is cut on an old monument of the Moyles. Near it is a tomb in ruins of Moile Finch, stil'd Eques Auratus, and of his Lady with their couchant statues, and the names of their children round; eight pillars supported a canopy, which is now all down. The strong lines of the old lady's face are a very fine piece of statuary. In another part is a small monument to Heneage Finch, the great lawyer, who, I suppose, writ the famous treatise call'd Finches Law. The Park is very fine ground, consisting chiefly of a long hill on which there is a wood cut into eight ridings, and there are fine prospects from the hill. I went three miles to Wye, a poor town pleasantly situated on the Stour, and barges come up to it. Archbishop Kemp founded a Collegiate Church here. The College built round a Court is turned into a school There is a monument in the Chancel to the memory of Lady Juana Thornhill, daughter of Sr Bevil Granville, who was killed at the Battle of Lansdown, and sister of the Earl of Bath, and wife of Richard Thornhill, Esqre, who raised a regiment for King Charles the First. This was a royal mannor given by William the Conqueror to Battel Abbey, and by Queen Elizabeth to her cosin, Henry Cary, Lord Hunsdon, and was conveyed by his

grandson, Lord Dover, to the Winchelsea family, who is styled
lord of the royal manor of Wye, and a litle beyond the Church is
the manor house. Edward 2^d before his coronation kept his
Christmas at this house.

Sandwich, Septr. 11th, 1754.

Following the course of the Stoure from Wye, we passed by a
handsome seat of Mr. Knight at Gilmersham, whose park extends
either to Eastwell Park or very near it, and at Chilham a fine old
round castle, with a mansion house near it, belonging to Mr. Cole-
brook, and was, in the time of King Charles the First, built by S^r
Dudley Diggs, Master of the Rolls, and the architect Inigo Jones. It
is a fine situation, on a high ground ; the name of this place is thought
to be. a corruption from Julham, and there is a tradition that Julius Gilmersham.
Cæsar encamped here on his second expedition into Britain, tho' I
could get no information of any entrenchment. On the east side of Chilham.
the river is a bank, call'd Jul-Laber; it is on the foot of an hill over
a chalk pit, the digging of which has destroyed part of it; the bank
is about ten yards wide, fifty-six long, and it may be fifteen high,
and appears to be a work of art. It is thought to be the tomb of
Laberius Drusus, the Tribune, who was slain by the Britains.
After I left this place I was informed that there is an extraordinary
hollow ground, in a wood near the house, in a circular form, which
it is thought may be some remains of antiquity. The Kings of Kent
resided here. Two miles further, at Chartham, they found in 1668,
in sinking a well, some bones and four teeth of an elephant, supposed to have been one of the Roman elephants, which I was told
are in a gentleman's house in that parish. I came to Canterbury,
which stands likewise on the Stour, and is about three miles in circumference; it is the ancient Durovernum, and is said to have been
built 900 years before Christ, and was the capital of the Kings of
Kent till King Ethelbert gave it to Austin, when he was made
Archbishop of the English nation. There are remains of a citadel
and a mount or keep in it, and near it of a castle, all at the west

end of the town.   The castle was built after the Conquest.   The
walls this way appear, part of them, to be Roman, as well as a gate
or two.   They are built on a rampart, defended by a deep ditch.[*]
The old town seems to have extended to about the High Street and

Canterbury.   Peter's Street.   And when Canterbury was given to St. Austin, it
is probable they built the Cathedral and the houses about it, for the
Church and a Convent near it on this ground without the city,
which they enclos'd with a wall—that is built, if I mistake not, on
level ground—for almost all to the east of these streets is Church
land, and when this addition was made to the city it is probable
that they destroyed the old city wall to the east and only built a
slight one between the city and Church land, which remains in part
with the gates that lead to the Close that are kept shut at night.
Some mention that King Lucius began to build a Church here.   It
is certain there was a Church built and consecrated by Austin,
which, in 1011, was burnt by the Danes, and King Canute repaired
it.   In 1043 it again suffered by fire.   But William the First
settling Lanfrank in the See, he began to build a Church, which
was finished by Corboyl, upon the arches which are now seen, part
of which is the French Church under the choir.   This Church was
burnt again in 1174, and was begun to be rebuilt again in King
Stephen's time, much of the old Church remaining towards the
foundation, which is visible, being the old Saxon architecture, and
the cross isles on the outside are of that kind, they being probably
damaged by the fire within, and were repaired in the Gothick style.
St. Anselm's Chappel is visibly very old, and I thought that possibly
it might be the remains of some additions made to the oldest Church
of all.   The four towers are visibly very old, as likewise the two
which are on each side of the most eastern building called the Crown.
I apprehend the old Church ended at these two towers, this crown
seeming to be a new building, and the arches under it are plainly of
a different architecture from the others, and much finer and lighter,

---

[*] I was informed that Sr Thomas More's head is deposited in St. Dunstan's, near
Canterbury, in the family vault of the Ropers.—*Note in MS.*

so that I imagine the old Church extended from the end of the choir to the crown; and Gervais's saying the whole Church was destroyed must be understood of the inside of it and of the inside pillars, which seem all to be new. The old tower at the west end I take to be an old belfery of Lanfranc's time, built, as was the ancient custom, at some distance from the Church. If I mistake not, the part of the Church west of the choir was finished in the time of Henry VII. The altar piece and the choir have of late years been very improperly adorned with wainscoat of Roman architecture. The mosaic remains that was near the shrine of Thomas à Becket. There is a fine bronze monument over the Black Prince, and couchant statues over the bodies of Henry   and his Queen. The court on the north side of the Church is mostly inhabited by the Dean and the twelve Prebendary's, three of which are in the gift of the Archbishop, the rest in the Crown. The Archbishop's palace was at the west end of it and of the cloysters, and was destroy'd in the time of the Rebellion. The cloysters are very fine. One side is old, with a grand seat to every four and old cisterns opposite to the refectory door. The chapter house is a long building like a Chapel, and is used as such for early prayers. There is some very old building about this part, which is supposed to be destined for strangers, and they have a library belonging to the Church. The south court is mostly inhabited by gentlemen. In this quarter of the town, towards Peter's Gate, was a convent, and the gate remains of fine squared flints. There was another on the other side of the street in that part which is made an island by the river, and a third towards the castle, if I mistake not the Dominicans, the others being the Black and Grey Fryars. But the great glory of the monastick state here was the Abbey of Austin, 'tho the devotion to that saint was ecclipsed by the religion that was paid to the shrine of Thomas à Becket. This Monastery was founded by King Ethelbert. The west end of the Church was adorned with two fine towers of Saxon architecture; under that to the north St. Austin and his six successors were buryed, as it was not the custom then to bury either in cities or within the churches. The grand gateway is of a modern Gothick architecture and very fine. The small Chapel of St. Pancras at the south-east corner of the enclosure of the Convent, said to be old, has no marks of antiquity in the building, 'tho mentioned as before Austin's time, and said to have been King Ethelbert's temple when a pagan. St. Martin's parish Church to the south-east of this was built by Bertha, of the blood royal of the Franks and wife of Ethelbert. The east end of it is of Roman brick, not very well put together. But there is a very ancient font in it, made large as for dipping; the upper part is adorned with reliefs of arches intersecting each other, and the lower part with reliefs of circular knots, the whole font being round and of the same size from top to bottom. There are thirteen parish Churches in Canterbury; one of them, I think at Peter's Gate, is a remarkable long narrow Church built on the town wall. There is a large old wooden house, which was the   Inn mentioned by Chaucer in his Canterbury Tales, to which the pilgrims came who resorted here out of devotion to the famous shrine. There is a great colony of Walloon Protestants, driven out of Artois and other parts of Flanders in Queen Elizabeth's time, and of French who came in the time of Louis XIV. The former brought the silk manufacture here; they now make it in great perfection to a guinea a yard, both plain and flowered, and it is thought there are near 3,000 of these people in the city. It is a great hop country all round this place.

Margate.

On the 10th I left Canterbury, crossed into the Isle of Thanet, and in seventeen miles from this city came to Margate. I saw some old buildings, before I came to the town, which I was told was a Priory. This is a fishing town, and is of late much resorted to by company to drink the sea water, as well as to bathe; for the latter they have the conveniency of cover'd carriages, at the end of which there is a covering that lets down with hoops, so that people can go down a ladder into the water and are not seen, and those who please may jump in and swim. In the way to Margate we saw Reculver, in the Isle of Shepey, which is remarkable for two steeples to the Church. It is the antient   . It is mentioned that the Emperor Severus, about 205, built a castle at this place, that Ethelbert, King of Kent, had a palace here, and that some ruins of the enclosure are visible ; and that 200 years after a Monastery was founded, given by King Eadred with the Manor to the Church of Canterbury. 'Tis said that the fishermen, in drudging for oysters, have met with ships' cisterns, and buildings supposed to be Roman, as well as Roman coins, bracelets, and rings. It was a Collegiate Church. A great quantity of fennel grows about these parts. I went three miles to the North Foreland, where there is a handsom light-house, built of brick, and seems to be the style of Inigo Jones. From this place I went three miles to Ramsgate, a town about a mile in circumference. Ramsgate. They are making an harbour at great expence ; the outside of the piers is of hewn stone of the Isle of Purbeck ; they find that lime, made of cockle-shells, is the strongest of all, for which there is a patent, and they make it near the mouth of the Thames. The first plan has been alter'd which made the opening in the middle, it is now to be more to the south, and the design is contracted on the south side, tho' they had advanced considerably in it, according to the first design ; but they say the ground is shallow that way, and that therefore it would be of litle use, and they would have a greater space to clear out, as they apprehend the harbour will fill from the sea. The great use of this harbour is for merchant ships of 200 tuns and under, which usually lay in the Downs and are drove from their anchors, not only with great danger to themselves, but fall foul of men of war and other light ships that could ride in the Downs, and when they meet, either unmoor or slip their anchors and shift for themselves, or have their cables destroyed, and it may be their ships damag'd. The revenue, if I mistake not, for carrying on this work, arises from the vessels that anchor here, and from six per cent. annuities by Act of Parliament.

Dover, Sept. 12, 1754.

From Ramsgate I went on eight miles to Sandwich, having a

broad gravelly beach to the left most part of the way, and consequently the sea must sometimes overflow in some degree. Near Sandwich we passed by a house called Stonar, where they say there was formerly a town. We crossed it from the Isle of Thanet by a ferry-boat to Sandwich. This Island is about ten miles long and eight broad; there are six parish Churches in it, and a Chapel. Egbert, the eighth King of Kent. granted eight plough lands, which was a third part of the Island, to Lady Domnena, whom it is said he had greatly injured. She built a Nunnery here for seventy Virgins. Mildred, who was canonized, was Prioress of it. I was not informed where the Nunnery was; possibly it might be that building I mentioned near Margate, tho' it had formerly been much damaged, 'tis said, and even destroyed by the Danes, who harassed **The Isle of Thanet.** this Isle in such a manner that it did not recover it self till the time of the Normans. The Tuftons, who were Baronets, are Earls of Thanet. This Island, with the help of sea-weed and other manure, is very fruitful. They plough and manure and sow barley, then wheat, and then beans, and lastly oats, and then let the ground lie still a year, and the tillage much the same about Sandwich. They have a particular way of cleaning the ground sown with beans with a machine call'd a shim, with irons at such a distance that two go between the rows and turn up the earth on each side against the beans. They mow the barley and bind it up in sheaves, and the field is raked clean with a horse-rake. The west part of the Island towards the river is mostly marshy. The Saxons first landed in this Island; here Guortigern permitted them to settle; but Guortimore the Britain routed them at Lapis Tituli, supposed to be Stonar above mentioned, and directed that his body **Wiped fleet.** should be buryed here. And at Wipped fleet Hengist beat the Britains. Austin the monk landed in this Island, as well as Lewis of France, when called over by the Barons against King John. They are esteemed as good fishermen as well as husbandmen, all over this Island. The South foreland is the head of land to the south of Ramsgate, and it is probable that the whole point between the North and South foreland is the Promontory called Cantium by Ptolemy. Sandwich is pleasantly situated on the river, and is about a mile in length. The Stoure, when it comes to Thanet, divides into two parts ; that which runs to the north is called Inlade, and that which runs to the south-east, and passes by Sandwich, is called Want sume. The town of Sandwich was defended on the side of the river, and to the gate at each end by a wall and towers, and at the east end by a large tower called the Bulwark, which is now in ruins. The other parts of the town are fortyfied only by a strong rampart, the town not being above a quarter of a mile broad. There are a great number of old houses in it, mostly Sandwich. built with wooden frames, and a fine stream runs through the town. It rose out of the ruins of Rutupiæ. The harbour is now bad, being choaked up with sands. And a ship of Paul the 4ths, sunk here, has hurt the harbour, I suppose at the time of the Spanish invasion, so that large ships cannot come up to the quay. This town suffered much by the Danes, and here their King Canute slit the noses and cut off the hands of the English hostages, which were sent to his father, Swaine. But he afterwards gave this town to Christ Church, in Canterbury. In 1217 Lewis of France burnt it, and it underwent the same fate from the French in 1457, Edward the Third having, by exchange, re-united it to the Crown. The Wool Staple was removed to this place from Queenborough by Richard II. And in Queen Elizabeth's time some Dutch and Walloons set up a manufacture of cloth, which is now lost. The chief support of the town is an export of malt, and an import of wine and other forreign commodities for the use of Canterbury and other neighbouring towns. They also send a great quantity of garden seeds and carrots to London. Sr Roger Manwood, Chief Baron of the Exchequer, founded a free school here on the spot of the Carmelite Convent, with an endowment of two Scholars to Lincoln College, in Oxford. There are three parish Churches in the town ; that of St. Clement's, at the east end of it, is a very old Saxon building, probably erected soon after the town

was first built.   There are several fine old vaults in the town.   A
mile to the north west of Sandwich is a ruin called Richborough,

Rutupiæ.   which is the remains of the ancient Rutupiæ, where the Romans
often landed.   The legion called Secunda Augusta, which was
brought out of Germany by the Emperor Claudius to Isca Silarum,
now called Caer Leon in Wales, was removed to this place when the
Saxon pyrates infested the coasts, and they had a Præpositus here
under the Count of the Saxon shore.   Clemens Maximus had this
office, who in Britain was proclaimed Emperor by the army, put
the Emperor Gratian to death, and was afterwards killed by Theodosius at Aquileia.   Ethelbert, King of Kent, resided here, and
often confer'd with Austin, who was then at Stonar.   It is said that
the Danes destroyed this city.   There are great remains of a square
enclosure of Roman work, as I judge, above half a mile in circumference on the hanging ground over the river, and it is probable
either that the sea came up to the city or near it, or that the river
was more navigable than it is at present up to the town.   In a
rising ground to the south-west of this enclosure is an hollow which
might be an Amphitheater ; they have found many Roman coins
and utensils here, and there is an exact account of all these antiquities
in Archdeacon Battely's book entitled " Antiquitatus Rutupinæ,"
published by his nephew Mr. Battely, student of Christ Church.
It is supposed Juvenal meant this place as famous for oysters by
this expression,—

> Rhutupinove ædita fundo
> ostrea.

It is mentioned that there were two Roman tumuli before the gates
of Sandwich, and on the south side, on the shore, six large broad
Celtic tumuli.   I saw nothing of the former, nor could I discern any
thing like these except some heaps on the shore, which seemed to
me to be raised by the wind and sea.   About two miles to the south
west of the town is a village on a fine low hill, called Woodens-
borough, but commonly Winsborough, conjectured to be a place of
worship of the God Woden.

On the 11th I left Sandwich, and going about three miles in the road to Deal, I went out of it a mile to the south near to Betts-hanger, where there is a very small and slight entrenchment called Cæsar's Camp, of an irregular figure, about three hundred paces round ; but if it was for any military use it could be only a slight entrenchment, thrown up for a night round the Emperor's tent and baggage, and might be the first day's march from the shore. Two miles further towards Deal is an old ruined Chapel at a farm house called Cottington, which anciently belonged to the Lords of that name. The east end of this building is semicircular. I went by Deal. Old Deal, and in a mile from it came to New Deal, which is a town chiefly supported by the shipping that lye in the Downs. Company also resort to this place to bathe. It is an open sea, with a high gravelly beach. There is a storehouse here for naval stores, with a Clerk of the Cheque to give them out as occasion requires. Here is a castle to defend this coast, and there is another a mile to the south called Sandown. From Deal I saw plainly to Goodwin Sands, which is between the North and South Forelands, runs parallel with the shore for three leagues, at about a league or a league and a half distance. It was the estate of Goodwin, Earl of Kent, and afterwards given to the Abbey of St Austin in Canterbury. The land was defended against the sea by a wall, but an Abbot neglecting the wall whilst he was building Tenterdon Steeple, the sea broke in and overflowed the land. These sands are left dry at low water. They break the force of the sea from the east, south, and south west, and render the Downs a good harbour when those winds blow ; but when the wind blows hard at south east, east and by north, and east north east, the ships are driven from their anchors, either on these sands or into Sandwich Bay or to Ramsgate. A litle beyond Deal are several hollow places in the shoar call'd Romes work, and it is supposed that Cæsar drew up his ships into these places, as it is conjectured that he landed between Deal and Walmer Castle, for, coming to a part which, from his description, answers to Dover, he came to a flat country and landed, and the

Walmer
Castle.

shore at Walmer Castle is the first flat land on this side Dover, and
a quarter of a mile on this side of Walmer Castle I saw the angle
of a rampart.   It is a small part of two sides where they make an
angle close on the shoar, and it is thrown up in the Roman manner,
the sea having gain'd here and carried off the land.   This, I make
no doubt, was Cæsar's camp at his landing, and that the sea has
gained on it.   Walmer Castle, with the other two, were built by
Henry VIII.   It is in the hands of the Duke of Dorset as Lord
Warden of the Cinque Ports, where His Grace passes a few weeks
in the summer.   These Castles mostly consist of a round tower in
the middle and other turrets round them, with two stories, one
of them being under ground, and are defended by a deep fossee.
From this Castle we ascended up to the hills that form the cliffs
from this place to Dover, and came to Dover.

Rumney, Septr 13th, 1754.

Dover.

Dover Castle is a bold situation over the sea cliffs, the circumference of the castle is about three-quarters of a mile, and I believe
must contain more than thirty acres ; it extends to the cliffs.   At a
litle distance from them is the ancient Roman enclosure, a fossee and
a rampart with a wall built on it, now in ruins.   Within this is a
very ancient church, which some say was built by Lucius, the first
Christian king ; in which there is a sepulchral inscription to an
Earl of Northampton, who was Lord Warden of the Cinque Ports
in 1614, and his body was removed to another place.   I saw here
part of a sepulchral inscription with these words on it—

Petrus de Creone.   Orate pro anima ejus.

At the west end of the church is the famous tower of Roman architecture, except a litle of the top of it, in which the Roman brick is
seen, as usual, to bind the building, which I have formerly described,
and there is a print of it in Montfaucon's antiquities.   On the opposite hills on the other side of Dover are some ruins, which they say
are the remains of such another tower, this is called Bredenstone,

and by the common people the Devil's Drop. The old part of the
castle is said to have been begun by Julius Cæsar and finished by
Claudius. The well is 360 feet deep, it is, I am informed, round,
and is said to be cased all the way down with freestone : there is a
tradition also that this was the work of Julius Cæsar. In the part
of the castle between this and the cliff in this part is that famous
brass canon which was presented by the States of Utrecht to Queen
Elizabeth ; it is said to be one of the longest in the world, that is 22
feet in length, it takes fifteen pounds of powder to load it, and it is
said will carry a ball seven miles. Under these cliffs which are about
200 feet high are very fine extensive vaults cut out of the chalk,
which are made use of for wine cellars. The new part of the castle
to the west consists chiefly of a very large square building, like the
Tower of London, and was probably built soon after the Conquest.
There are two large rooms on each floor, to which they go by different staircases of stone ; it consists of two stories besides the ground
floor, which serves for cellars. Here King Charles the first con-
sumated his marriage with the Princess of France, and here also King
Charles the Second had that meeting with the beautiful Dutchess of
Orleans, his sister, which was so fatal to that Princess. Other
buildings here are the apartments for the officers and barracks for
foot soldiers when they are quartered here. The prisoners of war
have usually been kept in this castle. We descended to the town,
which chiefly consists of houses on the quay, the square, and one
narrow street above a mile long. The quays and harbour have
been greatly improved of late years, there being two large basins one
within another ; and the town it self is so much increased in buildings since the late war. An old high fort situated among the
houses towards the entrance of the harbour is now of no use.
There is a large beach of gravel before the harbour almost every
way, which is a defence against any encroachments from the sea.
The chalky rocks hang almost over some of the houses and sometimes tumble down and do mischief. There is a Saxon door to
the church of St. Maries towards the north end of the town, and

they found lately in digging near it an old hippocaust.   The pipes are in a room adjoyning to the church and I measured one fourteen inches and a quarter long, six and a half square, with a hole in the middle of the side two inches wide and three long.   There are also some large Roman bricks, made rough with lines, so as to bind more securely, and some of them are made to fit into one another. On one I saw these letters, LIBR.   Near the square are some ruins, if I mistake not, of a Friery.   The great support of this place is the passage to France, and, in time of war, prizes are often brought into the harbour.   Formerly no person could go out of the kingdom at any other port, and this was looked on as the key to the kingdom, on account of the strength of the castle.   To the west of Dover is a beautifull amphitheater of hills, one of them is called Stependown ; and among these hills lies St. Radigund's Abbey.   I was informed that at Barham down, between this and Canterbury, was Cæsar's Camp, and that there are some lines at Chartham down, which is, I suppose, near the place of that name, through which I passed on the Stoure.   In the way to Folkstone I saw a high cliff a litle beyond Dover, which, being the highest on the coast, is supposed to be the cliff which is so finely describ'd by Shakespear.   The road in many places is so near the cliff as to make it an uneasy passage to some travellors.   I saw two barrows on the hill before we descended to Folkstone, and passed near an old fortress called

Folkstone. Castle hill, almost due north of that town.   Folkstone is curiously situated between two rising grounds and on the side of those hills, and is the nearest land to France, opposite to that part which is between Calais and Bullogne.   The platform near the church commands a view of it, and one can distinguish houses and castles.   In the church is this epitaph over the mother of the famous Harvey who found out the circulation of the blood:

A.D. 1606, Novr. 8th, dyed in the 50th year of her age Joan wife of Tho. Harvey mother of seven sons and two daughters. A goodly harmless woman. A chast loving wife. A charitable quiet Neighbour. A comfortable kindly Matron. A prudent diligent House-wyfe. A careful tender-hearted mother. Dear to her

Husband. Reverensed of her Children. Belover of her Neighbours. Elect of God. Whose Soul rest in Heaven. Her Body in this Grave. To her a happy advantage. To Hers an unhappy Loss.

In the church yard are these remarkable verses on a tomb of the date of 1688:

> A house he hath is made of such good fashion
> The tenant n'ere shall pay for reparation,
> Ne will his landlord ever raise his rent
> Nor turn him out of doors for no payment.
> From chimney-money, too, this place is free
> To such an house who would not tenant be?

The water that supplies the town is brought from a spring to the west of the Castle hill. They have a notion that the hills to the north that way have sunk, and affirm that some people observe they see more of a house behind the lower hills than they did thirty or forty years agoe. About a mile from Folkstone we saw Sandgate Castle, something in the style of those already described, only with this difference--that it appears there was a remarkable trap door to be let down at the entrance. We came in four miles to Hithe, a Hithe. very poor town, but much improved within these seven years. In a vault under the church are a great number of human bones and skulls. Some of them appear to have been wounded, and it is supposed that they are the bones collected together of persons killed in battle. This writing is in the vault relating to it.

I saw a gentleman who, with some others, was waiting in the church porch in order to go up into the tower to take a view. At that time the steeple fell down, and it was concluded by those who knew they were gone to the church for that purpose that they were all lost. The sea, as it is said, did come formerly very near the town. About a mile above it is Salt Wood Castle. It is a large enclosure, and has been a grand building. It belonged to the Archbishop of Canterbury. Courtney enlarged the buildings very much, and his arms are on the grand tower in the front. Near it is an old building called Ostenhanger, a seat of the famous Edward

Baron Poinings.   Three miles farther is Limme Church, just over the hanging ground, from which there is a descent down to the ancient Portus Lemanus.   There are great ruins of an enclosure, probably of a citadel, on this descent.   I could not well make out the figure, but I have since been inform'd that it was judged to be circular.   'Tis plainly a Roman work built of stone, with a binding of brick at certain distances.   It seems very probable, according to the tradition of the country, that the river has alter'd its course, and that it did run at the foot of this hill, and it may be by West Hythe half a mile to the east, which might be the port when the sea, leaving the land, did not come up so far as Portus Lemanus, for the convenient navigation of ships; and Hythe is supposed to have been a port when this was no longer proper for shipping. They showed me a house on the side of the hill towards the top, called the French house, which it is said had settled down some feet in the memory of man, probably occasioned by a settlement on some running of water under ground.   There is an ancient Roman military way from this place to Canterbury.

Winchelsea, Septr. 14, 1754.

From Limme I came down to Romney Marsh, supposed to be all the gift of the sea, both by its retiring and throwing up sand, mud, and gravel.   At what time the sea retired so as to make this marsh we may conclude from the Saxon Annal, which mentions that in 894 Apuldore was at the mouth of the river Limene, from which it is concluded that Romney or at least Walland Marsh was then sea, and if so those who would place Anderida at Newenden infer that the sea 500 years before might come up to Newenden. It is supposed to be the country called Mera Werum by Ethelward. It is surprising to observe how the sea is kept out by what they call walls, which are mounds or ramparts of earth, that are made with a gentle descent to the sea, and are secured with rods of wood fixed down by small timber laid every way, and fasten'd with strong stakes.   This marsh is fourteen, some say twenty miles

long, eight broad, and contains between forty and fifty thousand
acres of land, and is divided into certain levels, as that which is
call'd Romney Marsh in particular is bounded one way by a wall
or dyke, which extends from Appledore to New Romney. This in
the map is call'd Rhee wall, where they have a tradition that
the river Rother did run probably after it left Lime. Another
is   wall and marsh, and a third is the New Level. I observ'd
a great quantity of marsh mallow grows about the dikes here.
There are two towns in the marsh and nineteen parishes, which
were made a corporation by Edward IV., consisting of a bailiff,
twenty-four jurats, and the commonalty of Romney Marsh, and they
can choose four justices every year, who hold courts for all causes.
To encourage people to settle here they have formerly been
exempted from paying subsidies, and the lords of the mannors are
entitled to the wrecks and waste. They sometimes find large trees
in the marsh, I suppose of oak, being as black as ebony, and the
timber is good for building when it is dry; and I have been
inform'd that no worm will enter wood that has laid any time Romney
under ground. I came to the town of New Romney, which was Marsh.
a considerable place about the time of the Conquest, having five
parish churches in it, and a Priory, and was divided into twelve
wards. The church is of Saxon architecture, and the tower, consisting of five stories, is very ancient; to the north of it are
remains of old buildings, which I was informed was the old Priory,
and probably at that time Old Romney, a mile off, included this
place; for in the time of Edward 1st, on the 23d of November,
1334, there was such a storm, that the sea, which had before
retired, overflow'd this country and destroyed many houses and
wind mills, and stoped up the mouth of the Rother, which from
that time took its course by Rye. The town has been decaying
ever since. Three miles further is Lidd, a very small town with a
good church, but not a very ancient building. About half a mile
to the west of the town is a double ring, like a figure of eight, and
a circular cavity with hollow entrances cut in it exactly to the

cardinal points. I should conjecture that they are something relating either to ancient worship or games. There are some works on the hill over Brightelmston a little like them, tho' I suspect they might be only the foundations of some old windmills, being not so exactly regular as these are. From Rumney it is a sort of a flat promontory or cape, call'd the Nesse or Nose; the north-east part of it is called Denge Nosse, where there is a light-house four miles from Lidd, one half of the way good road, the other very heavy over pebbles, with large pools of fresh water to the west. I went to this lighthouse, which is a quarter of a mile both from the eastern and northern shore, and they have a well of good water near it. There is a bank to the west of that which is

Lidd. remarkable for a particular kind of holly, which, from the description, I should imagine to be the hedge hog holly; and a particular kind of pease, the pods of which are in bunches, grow on this shoar, and are good to eat, they are the Pisum Marinum or Maritimum Britanicum, the English sea pease. On this beach, near South end, is a heap of large stones, called the monument of St. Crispin and S. Crispinian, where they say they were shipwreck'd and I suppose buryed. This marsh fattens a great number of sheep and black cattle sent from other parts, and they have a large kind of sheep of their own breed. It is from this place that some people call'd Oulers run so much of our wool to France. From Lidd I went 12 miles over the marsh to the Rother, which we cross'd on a bridge into Sussex; and going two miles further by Blayden and part of it on the turnpike road from London came to Rye, a town

Rye. situated in a very extraordinary manner on a hill, which by the meeting of two rivers and the coming in of the tyde is a peninsula. Tho' the town of Rye owes its flourishing state to the decay of Winchelsea, yet it was a place of some note before, for in king Stephen's time William de Ipres, earl of Kent, built a tower here, which is now call'd Ipres tower, and is the prison at the north-east part of the town. But when Winchelsea was decayed, Edward III. built a wall round this town, and it began to flourish greatly.

I observed at the gate we enter'd, one part which seem'd to be of the time of William of Ipres, and another of the same date probably as the walls, so that the first might be the gate when the town was defended only by ramparts. Rye was burned by the French in the reign of Richard 2d. About the year 1607 a violent storm improved this port, which they say was further opened by another of late years, but still it is but a bad harbour, and only small vessels can come into it. There is a Saxon door to the church, and some Saxon architecture within. At the north-west part of the town are remains of a convent, the church of which is converted into a storehouse. They have a very handsom town house, and the place is supplied with water in pipes, which is preserved in cisterns, but the water has a bad taste, occasion'd it may be by not keeping the cisterns clean. They have a trade in hops, wood-and timber, and iron (as there are iron works near) for all sorts of cast iron, and they are great fishermen, and send off fish every day to London; it is also a great passage into Normandy, being one of the nearest harbours to that part of France. I crossed over Sudbridge river on a drawbridge, which rises at Bockley, where there is an iron work, and there is another at Breeden, near Battle. We cross'd another river and ascended to Winchelsea, where there are remains of a very large town; it was built in the time of Edward 1st, when, in 1250, the old town of Winchelsea was, by a great Winchelsea. storm, swallowed up by the sea, which they say was mostly on the other side of the Rother, and it is probable that this river at that time left Romney and emptyed it self this way, for that tempest made a great alteration in the coast of Kent. On the shoar to the south of the river there are remains of a fort, built by Henry 8th, and it is said there was a monastery on that spot. Winchelsea stands high, it being a hanging ground towards the harbour. It was finely laid out with handsom broad streets, so as to make thirty-two squares or quarters, many of which are hardly visible. Three of the gates only remain, one of which is a mile distant from the others, so that it is probable that this town was a mile in length from east to west, and it may be near half a mile in breadth; it was at first defended by a rampart, and afterwards by stone walls. There were three parish churches in it, but now only part of one remains, that is the chancel and cross isle, and there was a tower near the west end. It is a very handsome building, like a cathedral. There are some old monuments in it of persons unknown, two or three of them are supposed to be Knights of Malta, because their legs are across.[a]   On the outside of the east end is a nich, as if for a statue, with a long inscription under it, which is so defaced that it is hardly visible, except when the sun shines on it.   The Church of the Convent is a handsome building, but in ruins, and there are some remains of the Convent it self, and particularly a nich adorned with Gothick work, which seems to have been a pulpit or sort of reading desk in the refectory.   There are many large vaults in several parts; but at present it is only a village consisting of a very few houses, tho' it is a borough town. This place was sack'd by the French and Spaniard, and before it was finished the sea retired from it, and it began to decay.

Lewis, September 17th, 1754.

Going from Winchelsea I soon cross'd a rivlet; near it is a chalybeat water; there is also such a water at Selscomb, near Battle, and it is said in many other places, which they say are all of the same nature as the waters of Tunbridge.   I ascended a high hill, the top of which commands a very fine prospect, eastwards to the head beyond Folkstone, and to the west almost as far as Chichester, and northward of the hills towards Tunbridge, as well as of the vales on this side of them.   I descended to Hastings, which is very curiously situated between two hills, with a small rivlet running in the bottom. It consists of two streets, one for shops, the other for fishermen; on one side of the latter the houses are built on the side of the hill with a terrace before 'em six or seven feet above the street; there is a

---

[a] Such cross-leg'd figures denote only that the owner went to a Crusade or vow'd to go.—*Note in MS.*

church at each end of the town. There are ruins of a large castle on the hill over the town to the west. Mr. Collier has a house and handsom gardens here. Hastings is said to have its name from Hastings, a pyrate, who built forts on the coast. The town was burnt by the French in 1377, and was afterwards rebuilt in the present form. They have a great trade in sending fish to London, and export iron pigs from the neighbouring forges. It is no harbour, but a gravelly beach, and they draw up vessels of 70 tun on the land. They compute about 2,000 souls in the town, tho' only 500 houses. In King Athelstan's time they had a mint here. William the Con- Hastings. queror mustered his army here after he had burnt his transport ships, and near this place the battle was fought, in 1263, in which Henry III. and his son Edward were taken prisoners by Simon de Montfort, Earl of Leicester. I saw here a large silver vase, with an inscription signifying that it was made of the share out of the silver staves, &c., of the canopy of the underwritten persons, canopy-bearers to King George the II. and Queen Caroline, that is, Sr William Ashburnham, Bart., Thomas Pelham, of Stanmer, Esqr., Edward Dyne, Esq., the Honourable Thomas Townsend, Esqr., and James Pelham, Esqr. In the way to Hastings I had seen Bromham, the seat of Sr William Ashburnham, whose nephew is Bishop of Chichester. I went about two miles from Hastings, cross'd a rivlet, and in half a mile another, and passing by Bulverhyth I saw an old ruined church, and to the north the house of Mr. Cramp. Here William the First landed, and since that time the village has been almost entirely destroyed by the sea. A mile further brought us to Bexhill, where there is a mount which serves for a beacon. I observed near Battel a wood, with ridings cut through it, which belongs to Lord Ashburnham, of Ashburnham. I saw Mr. Cranston's seat to the left, and after travelling fourteen miles from Hastings came to Pevensey; here is a very large enclosure of an ancient castle, containing about eight acres. I observed the walls from the town are built of stone, and a row of brick on the inside and out to bind the building, after the

Roman manner. It is true I did not think it a Roman work, but Mr. Somner judges it to be the ancient Anderida, where the band of the Avulae was quartered; as Gildas saies, "In littore Oceani ad meridiem," the design of them being to watch against any enemy that might land. And Archbishop Usher makes it appear that it is Caer Pensavelcoit of the Britains. But if it was not built by the Romans, it was doubtless a work in imitation of their manner of building. Here some have said William the Conqueror landed and burnt his ships, and vanquished Harold at Battel, where he founded a monastery in memory of his victory. I went four miles to the seahouses near East Bourne, very pleasantly situated on the beach, and people resort here to bathe and drink the sea water. I went to East Bourne, where the Earl of Northampton has a seat, the late Lord Wilmington's. The sea cliffs here are high and make Beachy Head, and very fine springs of water run out of them; there is a cave in one of them called Derby's Hole, from one Mr. Derby, minister of East Dean, who lived in it for some time.

Going on towards Brighthelmston, I passed by a camp called Belfonte, near Burling Gap. It is possible this might be the Conqueror's camp, tho' he afterwards went towards Hastings. The road being over the Downs, where they make holes in shape of a T by cutting out the turf; cover part of it over with the sod, and set up stones before them for the birds called White ears to perch on, and when frightened by clouds passing over, or by any other means, they run into the holes and are caught in a springe laid in them; these birds when fat are very delicate, and sell on the spot for a shilling a dozen. I crossed the river Cruckmore, which makes the haven of that name. On it stands Alfryton, where I was inform'd there is an old church. I went near Seaford, a poor little fishing town, which has suffered much in time of war, and in 1560 the French attack'd it, but were repulsed by Sir Nicholas Pelham. As this is the last of the Cinque Ports I shall just touch on the nature of them.

The original of the Cinque Ports seems to have been to defend the coast against any invasion, and the Constable of Dover Castle and Lord Warden of the Cinque Ports, which offices are united in the same person, seems to have succeeded to the Roman officer called the *Count* of the sea coast and of the Saxon shore. The office of Comes, Constable of Dover Castle was first instituted by the Conqueror, and he made this officer Lord Warden of the Cinque Ports. The Cinque Ports are Hastings, Dover, Hith, Romney, and Sandwich, to which Winchelsea and Rye are added as principals, and some other little towns near them as members only, which are as follows:—

Hastings	Seaford *qu.*	
Dover	{ Margate.	
	{ Folkstone.	
Hith.		
Romney	Lidd.	
Sandwich	{ Ramsgate.	
	{ Deal.	
Winchelsea.		
Rye.		

The people of these places are free from subsidy and wardship, and could not be impleaded but in their own courts. And such of the inhabitants as have the name of Barons support the canopy of the Kings and Queens at their coronation, and have their table at their right hand. On forty daies notice each of the five were to furnish one and twenty ships, with twenty-one men in each, for fifteen days at their own expence, and afterwards to be paid by the king; the captain and constable six pence a day, the others 3^d.

I passed by Bishopstown, a hunting house of the Duke of Newcastle's. We came to Newhaven, a small harbour at the mouth of the Ouse, on which Lewes stands eight miles from it; the river is passed by a ferry. I saw a ship building of 230 ton which was to be Newhaven. lanched at a spring tide, and vessels of 150 ton commonly come into the harbour. Over the small town there are some marks of a building and trenches; this is called the castle. They import coals and timber for Lewes, and export bark, timber, and corn. Two miles beyond it I saw a line carried down to the sea. I came to Brighthelmstone, a long fishing town; it is built with the pebbles of the beach, but greatly improved of late by the concourse of people who come to it to bathe and drink the sea waters, under a perswasion that the water here is better than at other places, concerning which a treatise has been written by Dr. Russel. They have a good coffee house and a large room for company, and carriages for the conveniency of bathing. King Charles the II. after the battle of Worcester in 1651 having wander'd about to several places, came here and got off to France, of which there is this memorial in the churchyard which is finely situated on the hill over the town.

Bright-
elmston.

P. M. S.

*This ought
to be in
parenthesis.

* So in the
original, but
should be left
out.

Captain Nicholas Fettersell *through whose Prudence, Valour and Loyalty Charles the Second King of England, *And* * after he had escaped the Sword of his merciless Rebels and his forces received a fatal overthrow at Worcester, Septr. 3^d, 1651, was faithfully preserved and conveyed into France* Departed this life the 26th day of July, 1674.

At the Restoration the Captain had a pension of £200 a year, which has been continued to his family.

There is nothing remarkable in the Church but an old rood loft that is still remaining. I saw on the hill the remains of some ancient works, a circle something like that near Lid in Kent, a semicircular work before it (which possibly might be the remains of an old windmill), and there is a square trench near it.

Chichester, September 20th, 1754.

From Brighthelmstone I went along the valley three or four miles to Stanmore, Mr. Pelham's, where there is a very good house of hewn stone, fine lawn, and plantations, and a wood cut out into walks. From that place an hour's ride brought me to Lewes, a town most delightfully situated on a rising ground, and consists chiefly of one street which extends for a mile in length to the river, with lanes leading from it on each side down the descents to the valley. Beyond the bridge is a large suburb, called the Cliff. This town had two mints in King Athelstan's time. It is famous for a battle between Henry III. and the Barons, in which Prince Edward was taken prisoner, and the King obliged to make a peace on very hard terms. In the old church of St. John over the Castle is a good Scripture history piece, and the doorway of the church is of old Saxon architecture. But it is most remarkable for an inscription, on the outside of the wall, which I here give more correct than it is in Cambden : Lewes.

> Clauditur hic miles Danorum regia proles
> Mangnus nomen ei, magnae nota progeniei
> Deponens Maugnum, se moribus induit agnum
> Praepete pro vita fit parvulus Anachorita.

On the south side of the town are the remains of a convent of the Order of St. Benedict of Cluny. It was a very large enclosure; there is a pond in it, out of which a fine limpid stream rises and runs through the convent, it is call'd Cockstead pond and stream.; there are considerable ruins of the convent, near it is an old church called Southover, and in the bottom to the north of it are remains of a building which I thought might have been a gateway. As part of this Convent was said to have been the seat of the person to whom the estate was granted after the Reformation, it has obtained the name of the Lords place, and there is a small mount within the enclosure which is called the Lords place mount. The Castle was built by the same William de Warren earl of Surrey who founded the convent. There are two mounts or keeps in it, on one of them which is very high is a building from which there is a most glorious prospect to the sea, of the valley between and of the vale to the north, with the river running through them in most beautiful maeanders, and the hills form a most romantic amphitheater, one about four miles to the south-east appears to have been fortifyed. From the Castle the walls extend round the the town on each side, of which there are some litle remains. This town chiefly subsists by supplying the neighbouring places with the conveniences of life, and by many gentlemen who live in it, as it is a cheap market. They have also a considerable trade in wool, which is esteemed the best in England.

From Lewes I went along the north edge of the Downs over that valley in which stands the small town of Dickleng, and after travelling three miles I passed by an old line, and in two miles more a circle and old barrow, and came to Woodbury Camp, situated where the hills form an angle to the N.W. There is a fine view from it, and it is of considerable extent. We descended to the west to Newtimber, where M[r].   and M[r]. Newnham have houses. The best way to Beeding is by the Downs to the south-west, but we went under the hills and came to Ponings, where there are remains of an old large mansion house called Ponings place. In about five miles we came to Beeding, a large village on the river, which empties it self at Shoreham. There was a Priory here under Saumur in France, in which there are some remains of Saxon

Beeding.

architecture. M[r]. Thomas Newlin, Fellow of Magdalene College in Oxford, an eminent preacher, who published two volumes of sermons, was vicar of this parish, and is buryed here. A small

Bramber Castle.

mile from it and near the river is Bramber Castle situated on an eminence, and there is part of a high tower remaining. It was given to the Braoses of King William the first. The river, it is said, was formerly navigable to this place. This and the neighbouring town Stening joyn, if I mistake not, in sending two members to Parliament. A part of Bramber extends to Stening, a mile beyond the castle, and a mile or two farther is a fine seat of Sir Charles Goreing's. I went to Stening; it is a small town, where there is a Saxon church. From Beeding I ascended the Downs; five miles from it is Finden, a delightful retirement on the Downs; over it is an old camp called Cisbury, of which the common people have a notion that it was Caesar's camp, tho' it is doubtless a British camp. One thing is very particular, that on the west hill are several large holes dug, as if to receive water. To the north of Findon is Montin, where Lord Montacute has built, is making great plantations, and has brought water with great expence. About two miles further is Mitchel Grove, a good old house of Sr John Shelley's, who married a sister of the Duke of Newcastle. A litle beyond it we rode through the very pleasant park which belongs to it; and beyond it passed by what is called a park of the Duke of Norfolk's, which did not seem to be kept in order as a park, and passing by a spaw water we came to Arundel, a small town very pleasantly situated on the side of a hill, consisting of one broad street. Some imágine the Arun was the name of the river, from which the valley below had the name of Arundale. There was a college founded here by the Earls of Arundel; the remains of the cloyster is seen on one side of the church, which is a large building, and the east end and a chapel to the north of it is locked up from the rest of the church, as the burial place of the family of the Lords of Arundel, now in the Duke of Norfolk's. In the north chapel is a tomb of 1400, where there is a monument of Earl Thomas of 1596, and of Fitzalan of this family, who was shot with a poisoned arrow. On the south side is the epitaph of Henry Fitz Alan, the last of the line, which is in Cambden. He was Knight of the Garter, Privy Counsellor to Henry VIII., Edward the VI., Queen Mary and Queen Elizabeth, Governor of Calais, General at the siege of Bologne, Lord Chamberlain to Henry the VIII. and Edward VI., High Constable for Queen Mary's Coronation, Steward of her household, and President of the Council, as he was afterwards to Queen Elizabeth. This monument was erected by his son-in-law, Lord Lumley. The castle here was in being in the time of the Saxons. On the coming in of the Conqueror Roger Montgomery repaired it, and was styled Earl of Arundel. His son Robert Bolesme, who succeeded his brother Hugh, was outlawed for rebellion by Henry I., who gave this castle in dower to his Queen Adeliza, daughter of the Duke of Lorrain. She afterwards married William d'Aubery, who was made Earl of Arundel. In the fifth Earl, the isue male failing, his sister was married to John Fitz Alan, Lord of Clun, in Shropshire, by whom this castle came to him, and it is

Arundel.

determined by Parliament that whoever has this castle is Earl
of Arundel, which, if I mistake not, is the only instance in England
of strict local barony.   Fitz Alan, whose monument I have mentioned, the eleventh Earl, died without isue male, and was succeeded
by Philip Howard, his grandson by his daughter, from whom it
came to the Dukes of Norfolk.   It is a very strong old castle over
the river, and there is a round tower on the keep.   The Duke of
Norfolk has a house in it with a Popish chapel, which is shown to
strangers.   I went about five miles in the Chichester road, and
passed near Slindon, Lord Kinard's, only son of Lady Newburgh
by Mr. Ratcliffe, who was beheaded in the year 1747.   There
are fine woods about it, and it came to him by marrying an
heiress, the daughter of   . We went out of
the road to the left toward Selsey, and passing by several villages,
after eight miles travelling, we came to Pagham, and crossing over
in a boat to the peninsula of Selsey, we sent our horses across the
Selsey.   mouth of the river to meet us, and riding a mile by the shoar, we
crossed into the road and came to the village of Selsey, where we
lay, and went a mile and half the next day to the east to Selsey
Church which is doubtless on the site of the old cathedral of this
See, which was removed to Chichester by Stigand the 22d Bishop.
For Edinwald gave it to Wilfrid Bishop of York, then in exile,
who first preached the Gospel here.   Then Cedwalla who conquered
Edinwaleh founded a Monastery in this place.   There are remains
near the Church of a large tower, which fell down in the memory
of man, and of a fortifyed place, which was probably the Bishop
house.   This peninsula is joyned to the land on the west by a very
small strip of land.   It is famous for good wheat, and for excellent
cockles.   I could not find that there were any signs of an old city
here, and I much doubt whether any ruins have been ever seen in
the sea.   I came by Selscomb Mill, a very great work, the race
being made by letting in the tyde, which turns the mill on its going
out.   From Selscom I came to Chichester.

Portsmouth, September 23rd, 1754.

Chichester, called in Saxon Cissanceaster, had its name from Cissa, the second king of the South Saxons, who resided here. At the time of the Conquest there were an hundred houses in it, tho' it had been in a very low condition. St. Peter's monastery and a nunnery are mentioned before that time. The bishop's see was then moved to it from Selsea, and it began to flourish. A small torrent runs on the east side of it, but is frequently dry for a considerable time, and the town is at a good distance from the Creek formed by the sea, of which there are several on this coast. There is a pleasant walk on the walls of the city. The streets are well laid out, and in the center of the town is a fine cross engraved by the Antiquarys' Society, which I suppose is what is called a piazza, built by Bishop Robert Read. Near the north gate was a castle, the seat of the Earls of Arundel, who called themselves Earls of Chichester. It is now the seat of Sr Hutchin Williams, with a padock belonging to it. This and an Hospital is between the north and east gates. Between the east and south gate is a peculiar of the Archbishop of Canterbury's, which is called the Palat. From the north to the west gate are gardens to the houses of that part of the two principal streets, which divide the town into four parts. The space between the west and south gates is taken up by the cathedral and church houses. The outside of the Cathedral is of Saxon architecture, except the two east windows and the cross isle, which is probably the church built by Bishop Ralph soon after the see was moved to this place, at the time of the Conquest, the cross isle excepted. It was burnt before it was finished, and rebuilt in the time of Henry I. The upper windows within are Gothick, and so are the isles. These were probably additions after the church was burnt down again in the time of King Richard I. It was rebuilt by Sesfrid 2nd, it may be with a cross isle and spire. In the south part of the cross isle the history of the foundation of the church is painted, and the pictures of the kings of England, of the Bishops of Selsea and Chichester, which were done by

Bishop Sherburne, who greatly beautified the church and painted the ceiling. On the north side of the body of the church is a monument with a couchant statue, which 'tis said was of Hugh Montgomery, Earl of Arundel, who they say gave the ground for the site of the church. The Duke of Richmond made a fine vault the summer before he dyed, if I mistake not under the library at the east end of the church. In it are buryed his father, and the late duke and dutchess and some young children. This inscription is at the end:

Sibi et suis
Posterisque Eorum
Hoc Hypogaeum
vivens P. C.
Carolus Richmondiae
Leviniae et
Albiniaci Dux
Anno Ærae Christianae
MDCCL
Haec est Domus Ultima.

In rebuilding the bishop's house they found some Roman coins and ancient pavement, supposed to be the temple of Neptune and Minerva, as they had before found this inscription, that is, of the Duke of Richmond's at Goodwood, which mentions the temples to those deities. It has been engraved:

NEPTVNO ET MINERVAE
TEMPLVM
PRO SALVTE DOMVS DIVINAE
EX AUCTORITATE TIB . . . CLAUD . . .
COGIDVBNI RE . . . . . GAT . . . . BRIT
COLLEGIVM FABROR . . ET QUI IN EO
SODALES D . S . D DONANTE AREAM
PVDENTE PVDENTIN . FIL.

They have some forreign trade, and export meal to London, and timber to several parts. To the north of the town near the gallows is a stone with an inscription on it signifying that several smuglers were hanged in 1749 for a very cruel murder. Near this is the

Brille, the remains of an old camp, which extends to the south, near to the town, and is lost, being there entirely defaced; but I saw another, which extends from west to east that probably joyned it, as it is joyned at the north end by another in that direction. I observed also a line extending from the north east corner northward, and as I was inform'd, goes near to Lavant I found the north west angle and traced it to the south west, and then along the south side for some way, but it is destroyed towards the town. It is said to be four furlongs and two perches in length, I suppose from east to west, and two furlongs broad, and it is with great reason conjectur'd to be the camp of Vespasian on his landing. To the north on St. Rooke's hill (supposed to be St. Roche's hill, probably from a chapel on the top of it, which might be dedicated to him) is a round camp two furlongs in diameter. A mile and half west of it is Gonshil camp, an oblong square, and may be Roman. I have formerly seen the following places in this neighbourhood. Goodwood, the seat of the Duke of Richmond, where there is a fine park, and on a hill in it Goodwood. the Duke built a beautiful room, which commands a fine prospect; the ceiling of it is painted after some old Roman designs in a very beautiful manner. This is called ; near the house is a grotto and an underground passage made from it called the Catacombs. There are walks through woods, in which are gothick and other buildings. But this place is most famous for a great variety of forest trees and shrubs; they have thirty different kinds of oaks, and four hundred different American trees and shrubs, which compose one wilderness. This place was very agreable when it was inhabited by the most amiable couple in the world, the late Duke and Dutchess. From Goodwood I went to Halnaere, an old monastery, where I saw the old Lady Derby, who being the sole heir of Sr William Morley, brought this estate into that family. Beyond Goodwood are several lodges of a Society of Hunters, with a large room in which they dine; and beyond this the Duke of Richmond has a fine wood cut out into rideings, where there is a cover'd place, in which they some times used to dine. A few miles beyond this is

Midhurst, which stands on a river that falls into the Arun. It formerly belonged to the Bohuns, who were the spigarnels or sealers of the king's writs. Near it is Cowdry, the seat of the Viscounts Montacute, of the name of Brown, a Roman Catholick. It is an exceeding good old house, and furnished in a plain grand manner, mostly with scarlet velvet ; it is famous for painting, commonly said to be of Holbens, which serve as the wainscoat of a parlor. They are by a scholar of Holbens, if I mistake not ; his name was De Aquila. On the left is the siege of Bullogne, on the right the entry of Edward the 6th, being his procession from the Tower to Westminster in order to be crown'd. The painting in the south cross isle of Chichester Cathedral, representing the first foundation of the church by Wilfrid and the refounding by K. H. 8th, was done by Holben or his scholar De Aquila, and is a very fine performance, and in good preservation. The pictures of the Saxon kings, &c. on the opposite wall are not done by the same hand. Petworth is near the same river, the seat of the late Duke of Somerset, now of Lord Egremont, at which there is nothing very remarkable, except that, if I mistake not, the Sussex stone that is so full of shells and pollishes well is found about this place.

Alresford, Sept. 25th, 1754.

To the north-west of Chichester is Standsted, the seat of the last Earl of Scarborough except one, and now of his relation, Mr. Lumley ; it is a fine situation and a good house, to which there is a long and beautiful avenue of trees. There is a grand staircase in the house, of Virginia walnut, and some of the rooms are hung wi.h tapistry, in which are represented the Duke of Marlborough's battles. Uppark, Lord Tankerville's, is not far from it ; the park belonging to it is very fine ; it did belong to the Fords, and Sr Edward, the famous mechanic, was born here, who, under Oliver Cromwell, raised the Thames water by a machine of his invention into the highest streets in London, to the heigth of ninety-three feet, and built the water engine near Somerset House. It now belongs to Sr Matthew Fetherstone, Bart. In the way from Chichester to Havant I went out of the road to Bosenham or Boseham ; here was a sort of hermitage, to which King Harold used to retire, and taking his pleasure in a boat was driven into Normandy, where he was detained till he had made over the kingdom of England, after Edward the Confessor, to William Duke of Normandy, who afterwards made a conquest of it. There is also a story of Earl Godwin's getting this estate of an Archbishop of Canterbury. There are some things remarkable in the church, being a mixture of Saxon and Gothick architecture, and there is an arched place under it, which possibly may be the old hermitage. Bosenham. The Parsonage house is an old building. But what is most extraordinary is a head of a colossal statue, much abused, but seems to me to be plainly a Roman work ; it was found in the churchyard. Coming into Hampshire I passed thorough a litle town called Emesworth ; it is said the natives of it are exempt from corporation duties in all the towns in England. I came to Havant, a small town in a bad air, which has flourished lately by an export of meal and malt to Ireland. In the church is the tomb of Thomas Aleward, of 1413, who was rector of this place, and was one of the executors to William of Wickham's will. I had this account given me of the old Roman road, called Stone Street Road, going from Chichester to Halneere, three miles over the Downs to Ertham, three miles then to the north side of Northwood or through it, and by Bigner Park, Waltersfield, and Cold Waltham, and, leaving both to the right, crosses the River Arun to Poulver, where there is a large barrow, to Slingfold, to Rouhook, to Oakwood Bridge, and is lost in the fields ; then it goes by Stan Street Causeway to Stan Street Hatch, then probably to Bristow Causeway and Stretham.

A mile from Havant is Warblington Castle, formerly belonging to the Earls of Salisbury, now to the Cottons ; it was moated round ; part of a grand tower remains, which seems to have been of good architecture. Close to the coast lye the islands of Haleing and Thorney, with each its parish church, and both of them are very rich land.   To the former at low water there is a passage by a rough causeway, and a short way across the island and over a ferry to the Isle of Portsea and to Portsmouth.

On the 23rd I went from Havant to   , lately inhabited by   , and now by Mr. Palmer of Ireland; there is a pleasant park to it.   We went by Chalton and Horn Dean, and came into the road from London to Portsmouth, passing through the forest of   , which belongs   , and going over Portsdown came to the Island of Portsea, to which there is a passage by a bridge, it being an island when the tyde is in: To the east of it is a harbour called Langston Haven; there is a fort to defend it lately built, called Cumberland Fort, and there are works to defend the entrance of the island.   Athelfled, wife of King Edgar, gave this Island to New Minster at Winchester; it is fourteen miles round.   At the south-west part of it is Portsmouth, which was burnt by the French in the time of Richard II.   The fortifications were begun by Edward IV., and improved by Henry VII., King Charles II., King James II., and now of late years brought to much greater perfection by new works, especially in this present reign, which are still carrying on, as it is look'd on as the key to England.   The eastern entrance of the harbour is defended by South Sea Castle, built by Henry VIII., and on Gosport side by four forts and a platform of twenty canons.   It is a fine harbour, and extends almost as far as Porchester, and it's said will hold a thousand men of war.   In the church is a monument for the Duke of Buckingham, who was assassinated here by Felton in the time of K. Charles I.   King Charles II. met the Infanta of Portugal and was married to her here.   The Governor has a handsom house and chapel in the town, and there is a large brewhouse, bakehouse, and cooperidge for the Dock, and barracks for the invalids who are here in garrison.   The town of late has been resorted to for batheing and drinking the sea water, and they have made a very handsome bathing-house of wood, at a great expence, with separate baths and apartments for men and women.   Tho' there is a chapel in the

Portsmouth.

Dock, yet they have built another near it for the large suburb,
which is made by the workmen of the Dock, who pay a chaplain to
officiate; and near it is a handsom musick room for a weekly con-
cert, chiefly performed by gentlemen. They are supplied with
water from pumps about half a mile out of town, which is brought
in hogsheads and never fails; they have a well also in the Dock at
which the ships water. The great curiosity of this place is the
Dock, where first we saw the gun wharf, in which are two Chinese Dock.
Pagods seven feet high, with the heads of lyons, as on a sort of a
pillar, all of one piece of grey granite, brought by Commodore
Anson and placed here.

Most of the Docks are lined with Portland stone, and are staunch'd
with the clay brought from Estamsay near. They have from 1,000
to 1,500 men employed in the yard; it is curious to see them go out
at the toll of a bell at noon and night, when every one may take out
any useless pieces of wood and chips, as much as they can carry
under the arm, and small chips in bags, which are examined with a
wooden crow, and all of them observed to see that they do not take
out any iron, or anything valuable. It is curious also to see the
forges where they make the anchors; the largest weigh about 80
hundred weight, that is four tons, which are work'd with machines
to move them. The ropeyard is 102 fathoms in length; they joyn
three lengths to make the longest cable, which is 306 fathoms, and
23 inches round, consequently about eight inches in diameter, consists of 3,000 threds, and weighs five tons. The main-yard of a
first rate man-of-war is 23¾ inches in diameter and 33 long, and
the bowsprit is 36 inches in diameter, and the mainmast 38. The
house of the Commissioner, who is the head officer of the Dock and
of all the other officers, are on the east side of the Dock. The
Academy is a handsom building for fifty youths to be instructed in
the theory and practice of Navigation, where they are lodged, dieted,
and wear the sea officers uniform, blue turn'd up with white; here
they remain three years, and then are made midshipmen; and this,
or serving under captains of men-of-war three years, is the only way

of being advanced in the Navy. They go out once a week and work a yatch, which is full rigg'd as a man-of-war, in order to be well versed in the practice. In the Academy they have a fine orrery which cost £200, and a model of a first rate man of war rig'd. Tho' they have several advantages in education, yet they cannot live here under £50 or £60 a year, and those who cannot afford it send their sons into the Navy in the other way. From the Commissioner there goes up an account every week to the Navy Board of all the work that is done in the Dock. On the Gosport side is lately built of brick part of a very noble hospital for the sick and wounded sailors; it is to make four sides of a square court, one of which only as yet is finished, which is 574 long and 100 deep. There is a fine alto relievo in the pediment relating to the subject.

Gosport.

It consists of four floors above ground and one under ground for certain offices, but what is most curious, the whole is built on arches in such manner that the highest tyde does not come to the top of them, and there are passages by the galleries under the arches exactly in the manner of the Temple of Diana at Ephesus, so that the tide comes in and out without being any way offensive to the buildings or apartments. It is divided into several wards, with many beds in them, as other hospitals, and there is a kitchen at each end.

Winchester, Sept. 26th, 1754.

From Portsmouth I went by water on the 24th to Portchester, situated on the north-west part of the harbour and to the east of the river which comes from Fareham. It is the Μέγας λιμὴν (the great harbour) of Ptolemy, said also to be call'd Port peris now Portchester, where it is supposed Vespasian landed. It is now an enclosure about a furlong square encompassed with a wall, and tho' very litle if any part of the wall be so old as the time of the Romans, yet one sees much Roman brick in it. At the north-west corner are large remains of a castle of a more modern date than the

Portchester.

walls. A litle way from it to the north and west is a large ram-

part which I take to be the Roman work, and there is somthing of
it to the south. Within the walls is a church, the most perfect
building of the Roman architecture corrupted, which we call Saxon,
that I have seen, without any alteration, except that the south part
of the cross Isle is demolished. Over the west door is a round
window with two arches that are lower on each side adorn'd with
carvings like mosaick in a very good taste, appearing something
like the Venetian window used in Venice. There are very
particular stalls work'd into the stone work of the wall, four
on each side of the chancel in this manner
and some of them also in the North Isle, where
their priests might say their matins and vespers.
There is an old Font in the church, adorned
with grotesque figures, running scrolls, and arches intersecting each
other, like that I saw at St. Martins in Carterbury. There is a
monument here for Sr Thomas Cornwallis Groom porter to Queen
Elizabeth and King James. In this place there were kept between
2 or 3000 French prisoners, the town is now dwindled into a
village of houses scatter'd on each side of a street half a mile long.

I had formerly been at Tichfield near the river which rises
towards Petersfield, and passes by Wickham; here was a monastery
founded by Peter de rupibus Bishop of Winchester, which has
passed through the hands of several noble families and now belongs
to the Duke of Beaufort. Wickham is famous for the birth of
William of Wickham whose name was   He was Wickham.
patronized by the Uvedales of this place, whom he mentions with
much gratitude in his statutes. Further on is Hamble, a litle port
where they build ships, it is on the river Hamble, which rises near
Bishops Waltham, that derives its name from a castle the Bishops
of Winchester formerly had there. In 1723 a Gang of Deer Waltham.
Stealers, who black'd their faces and resorted much to this place,
were call'd Waltham Blacks, and were soon suppressed by Act of
Parliament.

From Portsmouth I went on the 25th over Portsdown to Southwick, the seat formerly of the Nortons, now of Mr. Thistlethwaite, a relation of the last of the name of Norton ; it is on the river on which Fareham stands, which is a small town a litle above Portchester. It is a good old house which the present proprietor is improveing with great expence and laying out the ground in the Park style. We went through the forest to Soberton, late the seat of Mr. Lewis, now the estate of Lord Anson; it is on the river that runs to Tichfield ; going near the river we came to Droxford, the seat of the Morleys of the family of the Bishop of Winchester of that name, who are buryed in the church, in which there is a very ancient Saxon door. Leaving this river and going near Corhampton, we saw the villages of Exton and Warnford on the river; at the latter the Earl of Clanrickaid has a seat ; Cambden saies, Adam de portu rebuilt the church and quotes a distich in relation to it in the walls, and verses puting forth that Wilfrid was the founder of it. We saw Westmean above the rise of the river. Over Warnford to the east is old Winchester, a large camp on a hill, of which the people of the country have a tradition, that it was an ancient city. But as Wulphur king of the Mercians gave Edilwalch king of the South Saxons the country of the Meanvari, which is now divided into three hundreds, Eastmean, Westhean and Meansborow, together with the Isle of Wight, it is probable that this place was the stronghold of that people. I crossed the down to Kingston where a rivlet rises that falls into the Itching near Alresford. To the right of it is Hinton, the seat of Lord Stawel, and passing near Cheriton and Tichburne the seat of the Baronets of that name, I came to Alresford a small neat town very pleasantly situated on a rising ground, near the source of the river Itchin, this river rises about a mile from the town at Sutton, and forms a large pond near a mile round at the head of which is an old Roman road which goes to Alton. Another rivlet joyns these two about Itching, where I suppose it took the name of Itching, and that the branch which rises near Alresford was called the Alre, and there being a passage across by that Roman road, gave the town the name of Alresford. This town has been burnt several times. It is a great thoroughfare from London to Winchester and Southampton. At the first planting of Christianity King Kinewall gave this place to the church of Winchester and in 1220 Bishop Lucas restored the market to the town. On a rising ground half a mile beyond the river is a church called old Alresford, which has been lately rebuilt. Here Mr. Rodley, captain of a man-of-war has built a fine house near the parsonage, which would make a very good figure if it had not so near a neighbour. I left Alresford and did not go in the high road to Winchester over the hill, but went by the river and crossed the stream which falls in above Itchin and rises near Chilton Candover, the late Sr Robert Worseley's, Grange, Mr. Henley's, and Abbotston, the Duke of Bolton's. I had an exceeding pleasant ride by Itchin and the Worthies passing by the seat of Mr. Pawlet and of Lord Kingston late Mr. Evelings at Martyr Worthy, and at Headbourn Worthy saw in the churchyard the tomb of Mr. Bingham late Rector of that parish and of Havant, the author of Origines Ecclesiasticae, who married my Father's sister. He dyed in 1723.

Rumsey, Sept. 28th, 1754.

I came to Hide Abbey, near Winchester. King Alfred built a new minster or abbey near that of the cathedral, but the monks not agreeing, and the new monastery being incommoded by the water, they removed to Hide on the river, in the time of Henry I., and built a magnificient monastery, the foundations of which are only seen near the river; but it is not easy to determine the site of the church, one building indeed remains near the parish church of St. Bartholomew and adjoyning to an old gateway, which I take to have been the apartment for strangers, in the outer court of the convent. This monastery was burnt down soon after it was finished, as it is said by the contrivance of Henry de Blois, Bishop of Winchester, in which fire King Canute's cross was burnt, said to have cost a year revenue of the kingdom. Winchester is situated on the Winchester. river Itchin, and is the old Venta Belgarum, call'd in British

Caer Gwent or Guen, that is, the white city, from the chalky soil. Camden thinks the Roman Emperors had their imperial weaving shops here, mention being made in the notitia of Cynegium Ventense, which is interpreted Gynaetium—that is, it is supposed, a company of all sorts of weavers for the army. Others think it was the place where the Emperor's dogs were kept, as Britain was famous for dogs. Constans, who set up to be Emperor against Honorius, depending on the good fortune of his name, was of this place. It was the capital of the West Saxon kings. King Ethelstan granted them the privilege of six money mints. Edward III. settled here the staple for cloth and wool.

The cathedral is a very grand building. Kingie King of the West Saxons, being converted to the Christian faith by the preaching Binnus in 635, he began to prepare to build a church, but dying he left that work to his son Kenelwalch, who began to build the church here in 649, as it is said, after the college of monks of the Roman times was destroyed, on the site of which a more magnificent cathedral was erected. The Bishop Walkelin enlarged and improved it about 1052. Bishop Fox greatly improved the east part and the Quire. Much of the Saxon architecture is seen in this, and two arches beneath the Quire, which might be the utmost extent of the old building to the west. Bishop Fox collected the bones of the Saxon kings, and deposited them in chests placed on each side of the choir. The Gothick work over the altar is very fine, and so are the stalls. Bishop Fox's monument and chapel was built by himself, where he had a litle closet in which he kept some books, the presses for which still remain, and here he spent a great part of the latter end of his life.

In the choir is the plain tomb of William Rufus. The soldiers in the civil wars opened it and found on his thumb a gold ring with a ruby in it. There are many fine monuments to the east of the choir, as of Henry Blois, brother to King Stephen, William Wainsfleet, and many others. The body of the church was built by William of Wickham, as well as his own monument, under which his body is deposited. It was begun by Bishop Edindon, and the two Saxon arches possibly might be built by him. Near the west end of the church is a thick wall, thought to be part of the old monastery. Both the old and new monastery were at one time for married priests untill St. Dunstan declar'd against 'em. In the south coast isle is the library, and at the east end is a chapel for early prayers. The ascent to the choir by several steps adds much to the grandeur of the church, and there is a skreen at the lower end of the Quire of the Roman architecture of Inigo Jones, said to be the gift of King Charles I. His statue and King James in bronze are set up in the front of it in two niches. We have now come into a better taste of not mingling Roman architecture with Gothick. There were 45 churches in the city and suburbs, now about twenty-four, and all of them but indifferent buildings except the cathedral. In the close, which is walled round, the dean and prebendaries have their houses and gardens, and the river runs thorough some of them. D^r. Wishart, a French refugee, having the deanery conferr'd on him, as he was not very expert in the English language, and could not render himself as serviceable in other respects as he might desire to the people, laid out his gardens in a very elegant manner, and made them publick in order to promote society and conversation, and give a polite turn to the young people. On the other side of the river is the Bishop's house called Woolvesey, which has its name from an old house, on the site of part of which it was erected by Bishop Morley. The ancient fabrick was the work of Henry du Blois, Bishop of Winchester, in 1137, which was pulled down in the civil wars to make money of the materials; what remains of it is a very strong building. Within the close is a college founded by Bishop Morley in 1672 for ten clergymens widows of the diocese, who have each of them five shillings a week.

The College of St. Maries, near Winchester, built by William of Wickham, is a noble foundation for a warden, ten fellows, school-master, usher, three chaplains, seventy boys, fourteen choristers, *St. Maries College.*

and three clerks. It consists of four courts, in one of which is the handsom school, built in the last century, and the beautiful chapel is between another and the cloysters, the windows of which are finely painted. The library is in the middle of the cloyster, and behind it is a meadow for the boys to divert themselves in, and there is an infirmary at the further end of it.

Over the door of the school is a statue of the founder, by Cibber, father of the poet, who made the statues at the gates of Bedlam.

William of Wickham, Henry de Beaufort, and William Wainfleet, sat in this See successively 120 years.

The walls of the town are defended by a deep fossee, and at the south corner of the town are some remains of an old castle, which was likewise encompassed by a deep fossè. The county hall was the chapel of the castle, which is a fine Gothic building as it appears within. It is 110 feet long and 55½ broad. This, with the castle is said to have been built by King Arthur, and at the west end of the outside of the chapel I saw some very old pillars. For King Arthur lived at this place. They have a table hung up at the west end of this room, which they call King Arthur's round table, but it is supposed to be a table of much later date, used in the time of justs and turnaments, being convenient to sit at in order to avoid disputes in relation to precedency. The names of the twenty-four knights are round it: Sr Galahallt, Sr Lancelot Duelake, Sr Gavey, Sr Pribald, Sir Lyonell, Sir Tristram Delyens, Sir Gavetbe, Sir Bedewere, Sr B. Bibrys, Sir Lametemale Tayte, Sir Bicane, Sir Oplomyds, Sir Lamorak, Sir Boro de Ganys, Sir Sater, Sir Pellens, Sir Kay, Sir Edorde Marys, Sir Degonet, Sir Degare, Sir Brumear, Sir Lybyns Dillong, Sir Allymore, Sir Mordrede.

At the top is the figure of a king, sitting, with these words— "King Arthur." In the middle a rose is painted, with these words round it: "This is the round table of King Arthur and twenty-four of his Knights."

Within this castle King Charles II. built a very fine palace of the architecture of Sr Christopher Wren. In digging they found a brick pavement, and coins of Constantine the Great and others. This palace was begun March 23ᵈ, 1683, and the roof was raised and leaded over when the king dyed. It consists of the grand body, and two wings on each side, all joyning together, and of three floors and vaults under. In the inner front, towards the house, was to have been a pediment supported by five composit pillars, and by composit pilasters in the back part of the building. It is built of brick, the window frames and door cases are of stone. In the center of the building is a cupola, which was to have been high enough to have been seen from the sea. On each side is a chapel, one for the king, the other for the queen, with a Dorick colonade between the chapel and inner court leading to the colonade in front of the building. There is a grand entrance on each side, adorn'd with pillars, and over each entrance there was to have been a cupola. The grand string of rooms on each side is very fine. Water was to have been conveyed so as to have made canals ; and there was to have been a grand street from the house to the west end of the cathedral, which would probably have consisted of the houses of the great officers and nobility ; and a park was to have been made, for all which they had actually agreed for the ground, and what is done cost £250,000,

To the west of the palace, where St. James's Church stood, the Roman Catholics bury, and that way it was designed to lower the ground, so as to have opened a view to the south. When King George I. came here, he made a present to the Duke of Bolton of the fine pillars of Italian marble, which were to have supported the grand staircase. Queen Anne had settled it as an apennage for life on the Prince of Denmark.

There is a fine market cross in the town adorn'd with statues. Near the east gate is St. John's house, founded about 1554 by John Lamb, Esqre., in which the mayors give their entertainments. A county hospital has been founded here by subscription, set on foot by Dr. Alured Clark, prebend of Winchester. King Arthur, son of Pendragon in the year 523, enlarged Winchester. ·Egbert was crowned in this city the first monarch of England. St. Swithin, Bishop here, and who was tutor to his son, is buryed in the churchyard of the cathedral. The Danes destroyed the city in his reign, Edward the Confessor was crown'd in the city, and William the Conqueror sometimes resided in it.

The Empress Maud being besieged here by King Stephen, caused to be reported that she was dead, and so made her escape in a coffin. Henry II. held a Parliament in this city, and as they took part with King John, he resided here, and his son Henry III. was born in this city, and William Duke of Saxony, from whom our present royal family is descended.

Near the town is St. Catherine's hill, on which there is an old camp, and a mile below the city on the river is the hospital of St. Cross, said to be first founded by William Rufus, and then enlarged by Henry De Blois, out of the riches he took from Hide Abbey, and was enlarged by Cardinal Beaufort for a master, chaplain, and 35 decayed gentlemen. They are now reduced to 14, and are commonly poor tradesmen. The mastership is £800 a year. They wear black gowns. The church of it is a grand old building.

Southampton,   , 1754.

On the   I left Winchester and went across the downs in the Salisbury road, and in about four miles had to the left Launston, Mr. Meril's, a very pleasant situation on an eminence, formerly Sr Philip Meadows. About two miles further we had Crowly, Lord Egmont's, to the right, and Rookly, late Lord Gallway's, now Mr. Spencer's. We ascended the hill and came to a camp called Dunbury, a very fine situation, commanding a view of all the country. I saw Quarley hill to the west north west, and the camp near Andover, and that town about north north west. This camp is about a thousand single paces round. We descended from it to Stockbridge, a small town and borough, remarkable for nothing but their elections to Parliament. I turned out of the Salisbury

road to the left, and went about two miles to litle Samborne. I
found a petrified echinus in the road. Here lives Mr. Worseley,
heir to Sr Robert and Sr James, who married Lord Orrery's daughter,
by his first lady of the Orkney family. It was formerly the hunting
seat of the Duke of Marlborough and afterwards of Duke Hamilton.
I went by the Test ten miles to Rumsey, passing by *Motson*, Sr Mottesfont.
Richard Milles's, on the other side of the river. It is a pretty large Rumsey.
town. King Edgar founded a nunnery here. The old church now
standing is of a singular Saxon architecture ; the three arches of the
west end are Gothick. King Stephen's only daughter was abbess of
this nunnery ; they lately found a tomb in the corner of the garden
on the side where the cloyster was, which is supposed to be her
monument, being a couchant figure in alto relievo. They say she
was secretly taken from the monastery by Mathew of Flanders,
younger son of Theodorick of Alsatia, Earl of Flanders. After the
death of William, her brother, she was Countess of Bologne and Mor-
taigne, and had two daughters, Ida and Maud. She was afterwards
by the censure of the church separated from her husband, and sent
back to her monastery ; but her children were legitimated by Parliament in 1189, and she left the earldom of Bologne to her
daughters. Sandford's Genealogical History.

On the south wall of the church on the outside are some remains
of a large crucifix in relief. In the south isle is a tomb of the
daughter of King Edgar. There is an old square font in the church
on five pillars. It is said that King Edward and his son Alfred
were buryed here. Sr William Petty, father of the late Lord
Shelburn, was born in this town, and the annual income of a small
estate of the family was given by him to the poor of the town,
and is continued by the present Earl. I came eight miles from
Rumsey to Southampton, passing by Broadlands, Lord Palmerston's,
late Sr John St. Barb's, within a mile of Rumsey. About three
miles from Southampton I went by Shirley Mill, a small stream,
which, as I take it, falls in at Milbrook, and then by four posts, a
litle above which is a publick house much frequented upon excur-

sions from Southampton, to which place I came, and shall take another opportunity to give an account of it.

I went from Southampton northward near St. Denis, where I had formerly been, and where there are some remains, particularly of a chapel of a convent, and came to South Stoneham, where Commissioner Dummer built a good house, Mr. Nicholas liv'd there, and then it was Mr. Sloan's. A litle further is Swatheland, in the same parish, a handsom house built by Mr. Edmond Dummer, being the place of his birth ; he rebuilt the very house he was born in, like a cottage just by it. A mile further is North Stoneham, where Col. Flemming had a fine seat, now Mr. Willis's, son of Dr. Brown Willis, which estate came to him by his mother, after the death of Sr Seymour Pyles' widow, whose joynture it was by Mr. Flemming. The litle beautifull summer house on the common I formerly mentioned belongs to this house. Near this are paper milles, and here they cross the river, as they do at South Stoneham.

Near South Stoneham is Beauvoise Hill. Bogo or Beavoise, a Saxon, at the time of the Conquest was Earl of Southampton, much renowned for his valour and conduct. He engag'd the Normans at Cardiff, in Wales. Whether this mount was erected by him, or he was buried in it, or it might be made to his honour, is not easy to determine. Near it is the seat of the late Earl of Peterborough, now of his Dowager; it is taken into the gardens, and the top of it commands a most beautiful view of the harbour, which is very fine when the tyde is in. After we had crossed the river on a bridge at

Bittern.

S. Stoneham, we went a mile down the river to Bittern, where it winds so as to make a peninsula. It is defended by two fossees; the water seems formerly to have passed through the inner fossee and to have made it an island; this is 300 paces long, the other 630. The remains of a wall appear on the north side, and of a rampart all round, and of towers at certain distances, as may be judg'd from the rising ground, particularly a large one at the west end. Beyond the first fossee, about 20 yards, are seen on the shore on the east side foundations so strong that they look like a rock, and something resemble the pavement of the Via Appia, and fifty yards further is such another. This I take to have been a place for laying up small shipping; it is not in the least to be doubted but that this is the ancient Clausentum, made by the Romans to shut up the mouth of the river of this harbour, as it is said by Gildas that they erected many such forts on the southern coast to prevent the inroads and piracies of the Saxons, and there are no marks of antiquity in any other place here of a tower or castle; within it are ruins of a building, with a Saxon pillar or two. Part of the building to the east is very old, as I imagin'd, older than those Saxon pillars.

The Editor of Camden sayes that a golden coin was lately found at Bittern, but that the place where coins were formerly dug is now a dock for building ships. This is Northam, and on observing the situation, it is just such another point further to the south, that is nearer to the town on the other side, which I imagin'd was a proper place for another fort; but on enquiring, I could not find that there were any marks of building or fortifications.

From Bittern I crossed Botteley Common, passing by Milan Pond, where there is a spaw water, and half a mile further by Titchfield Pond, both which are sources of small streams. We then turn'd to the right, through a wood, and came to Nettley, an ancient monastery. Some think this place had its name from Natan Leod, a King of the Britains, who had a country call'd Natan Leod, mentioned in the Saxon Annal, whose country is said to have extended to Cerdick's Ford, now Charlford, where the Avon enters Hampshire, which had its name from Cerdick, who there vanquished the Britains, and before that had conquered Natan Leod in 508. It is possible the country of Hampton, or Hampshire, might have its name from Natan, and some places in particular about the rise of the Test bear that name, as Southampton or Hamton, and it may be Overton from Over Antan, and from thence the river might have the name of Anton, afterwards changed to the Test, and I should conjecture that Natan Leod comprehended Hampshire, and that all that chain of camps—one over Stockbridge, another over Wontson, near Sutton,

Nettley.

Woodcot, Beaconhill, Ladle Hill, and Old Winchester—might be
the barrier fortresses of this country, as the camps beyond the Avon
near Andover, Dunbury, Quarley, &c., might be the enemies' camps.
Possibly also this monastery might be founded by Natan, as some
imagine his name was, and that Leod, British for country, was
added to it. . There is a large pond near the convent which might
have been moated round.   The body of the church is of a Gothick
architecture of great simplicity, but the east end is very fine, and
the flat arch of that, and of the cross isle, is beautifully adorned with
arms and devices, among which I saw the Pelican, the Nails of our
Saviour's sufferings, and a W.   To the south of the cross isle is a
pile of building, which seemed to consist of a chapter house, a refectory kitchin, a cellar, and the dormitory.   To the east of the church,
about half a furlong, is a building which might be some office belonging to the convent.   A quarter of a mile from the convent is a
heavy, strong platform for guns, built of stone, with a parapet wall.
I came back near Woolston, late Lord Carberry's, a very fine situation, and so by Itchin Ferry to Southampton.   I left that town and
came by Milbrook and to Redbridge, the old Vadum Arundinis,
call'd by some author who has writ in Latin, translated by Bede,
Redford.   Here was a monastery in the early Saxon times; Cym-
bert, abbot of it, baptized two sons of Avandus, King of the Isle of
Wight, just as they were about to be murdered by the command
of Cedwalla the Saxon, who invading the island, the young sons
escaped and were betrayed *Ad Lapidem* (Stoneham).   At this place
they have frequently built ships, and the timber of the New Forest
is sent from it to the King's Dock at Portsmouth.   And of late years
they import coal, deal boards, and other goods, and have shops well
stored for the supply of the country that way, to the great prejudice
of the trade at Southampton; and at Eling, on the other side of the
water, the Salisbury merchants have their coalyards.   A mile above
this place on the river is a large old house, at Testwood, belonging
to Mr. Serle, with a salmon wear.
I went by Eling throrough the new forest to Beaulieu, a very small

town on the river which rises between Lindhurst and Dibden, but, as the tyde comes up to it, ships of burthen can sail to the town. King John founded an abbey here of Cistertians to attone for the murther of some abbots of that order whom he caused to be trodden under his horses' feet. The chapel and some parts of the monastery remain. The estate belongs to the heirs of the Duke of Montagu, Beaulieu. who have a house here; and the late Duke endeavoured to make it a place of trade. This monastery had a great demesne. At St. Leonards was the farm, where they had a very large barn, still in use. There was also a chapel here. Another estate was called the Boverie, where it is supposed they had their kine, and another the park for the deer, which is near the mouth of the river call'd which runs by Beaulieu, where ships often take in their loading. I came to Sowley, where there is a fine lake four miles round, and great iron works. Two miles from it is Pilewell, Sr James Worse-ley's, a very fine situation; and from the house one sees the Isle of Wight through an avenue, and the sea appears only like a great river. Near this place I formerly saw the elm call'd the groaning tree.

I came to Lemington on the   a small town most delight-fully situated on a high ground, which commands a fine view from the gardens to the south of the sea, of the Isle of Wight and the Needles. The street is broad, extending up the hill, and to the top of it for about half a mile; on the flat below they make great great quantity of salt with sea water. I think the duty here at 3s. a bushel comes to fifty thousand pounds a year. It is esteemed the best for salting meat. From Lemington I went by Milford to at the beginning of that point on which Hurst Castle stands, which is the shortest passage to the Isle of Wight, and commands the Streight, it not being two miles over. This and Calshot, and many other castles along the coast, were built by Henry VIII.; the latter is to defend the passage up to Southampton. The place we went to is a creek at the mouth of a rivlet. I went there in order to go to the Needles, to see the curious manner of diveing which they lately began, in order to raise what they could of the wreck of the   man-of-war, which was lately cast away. They are let down in a machine made of leather, strengthened at the knees and shoulders, and if I mistake not on the head with brass. There are two leathern tubes to it—one for the air to go down and to speak by, the other to pump out the air. They stay down five minutes. As soon as the man is let down they ask him how he does? and he answers, and they speak to him every minute, and if he does not answer they draw him up; and sometimes, not attending to answer, they have drawn up the man when he had been laying hold of some valuable thing. Sometimes, as it is imagined, when they have gone too far down, they have bled at the nose and eyes. It is undertaken, if I mistake not, by a company. And whatever is found belonging to that man-of-war is taken by the king on paying salvage. They go out from Yarmouth every fine day in summer at a proper time of the tyde. I went four miles further beyond Milton into the road to Christ Church, and then turning off to the right over the heath came to   , Lady Mews, and then to Ringwood on the River Avon. It is a long town of manufacturers of narrow cloths, serges, druggets, and stockins. There is a free school here, with an old inscription over it. At Horton in Dorsetshire, about six miles from this place, the Duke of Monmouth was taken, by one Perkins, in some bushes, where he had hid himself after his defeat at Sedgmore. He was brought here to the vicar's house, near Blackford. I saw, on the other side of the river, the seat of S^r   Pile, and then saw Ibsley to the right, Mr. Cary's, and Moyle's Court, Mr. Lisle's, now inhabited by Lord Windsor. We came to Fordingbridge, where we cross'd the river; went through Bremmer, where Sr Edward Hulse has a good old house which the late and passing Charlford before mentioned, as famous for the defeat of the Britains under Cerdick the Saxon, we came into Wiltshire and to Dunkton, a poor long town, where I crossed the river. Adjoyning to the town is Mr. Cole's house and garden. The latter

is very prettily laid out and improved, being on a large old fortification with a double fossee improved into terraces above and walks
below, with buildings on two mounts ; the old keeps of the castle,
and the river runs at the foot of it. This was probably the Castle
of Beauvois, Earl of Southampton, who lived here. Below this, I
was informed, there is a pretty place belonging to Commissioner
Eyres. I passed by Barford, Lord Feversham's, on that side of
the river, the high road being on the west side. We went by
Mr. Young's, finely situated on an eminence, and saw Langford at
a litle distance, Lord Folkstone's, where a small river falls into the
Avon. We went near Clarendon Park. King John built two
palaces here, King's Manor and Queen's Manor, where a parlia-
ment was held in the time of Henry II , and also under Edward II.
in 1317. But as the divisions were great between the King and the
Barons no business was done. This place gave title to Edward
Hyde, Earl of Clarendon. There is a camp near it, said to be
Roman, and between this and the park is the Roman road between
Winchester and Sarum. I came to the city of Salisbury, of which
I shall give you an account in my next.

Wilton, October   , 1754.

I had formerly been at Old Sarum, which is about a mile from
Salisbury ; it is the old for Vio (?) Dunum of the Itinerary, which is
thought to have had its name from the Emperor Severus, for the
country was call'd Severnia and Provincia Severonum. Many
coins of Constans Magnentuis and Constantine have been found
here. The situation is very fine and elevated; it is defended by a
double rampart and two deep ditches, and was walled round ; great
pieces of the wall are still to be seen. Kennil the Saxon took it in
553. King Egbert frequently resided in this place, and King
Edgar called a Parliament here in 960. Swane the Dane burnt it
in 1003. It began to flourish again after the Synod of 1076, when
it was decreed that all Bishops should live in towns; and Hernam,

Bishop of Shirbourne and Sunning, encouraged by William the Conqueror, removed his See to this place, and the next Bishop, Osmund, built the cathedral: The Conqueror, after he had made a survey of England, summoned to this place the States of the kingdom to swear allegiance to him. And the Norman kings often liv'd and sometimes held their parliaments here. The insolence of the soldiers, and scarcity of water, occasioned the inhabitants to begin to move down to the river, and the castle which belonged to the Bishop, being seized by King Stephen, who put a garrison into it, was looked on as a violation of the rights of the Church, so that the Church thought of removing also in the reign of Richard the first. But King John succeeding, the turbulency of the times was the reason why it was deferred to the time of Henry III. when Richard Poor, the Bishop, effected it; and in May, 1228, began this beautiful cathedral in Merrifield; it was finished in 43 years, and consecrated in the presence of King Henry III. The steeple of the church is 400 feet high, and is a most beautiful piece of architecture, and so is the whole church, inside and out, except the upper part, which to me seems heavy, consisting of three small arches under a broad flat arch, which has not a good effect. It is not so in the cross isle, and it is probable these were made to strengthen the building, and that too great weight might not bear on the pillars of the windows. The walls of the spire itself are but nine inches thick, tho' it is 150 feet high; it inclines in some places both the south and west, supposed to be an original settlement. It was strengthened with iron hoops in the building, and also by Sr Christopher Wren. In 1741 it was set on fire by lightening, but the fire was happily extinguished. The manner how the central piece of the timber frame hangs to and is fixed by the standard of the vane, is described in Mr. Prile's account of this cathedral, in which and Sr Christopher Wren's are many curious observations on this beautiful fabrick. They had a strange way of diverting themselves, which Bishop Sherlock put a stop to, as really prejudicial to the building, which was to go out of the window of this tower, near the top by the knobs to the weathercock, and also of going about the leads and doing much mischief.

The church is 480 feet long, the cross isle 232 long, the west end is 115 broad and 130 high, and the three isles 102, the heigth of the walls of the nave is 90 feet, the top of the rooffing 115 and within 84. The ceiling of the quire is painted with the representation of persons mentioned in sacred writ, and the sides in scrolls. It is arch'd with chalk, and the church is built of the stone of Chilmarsh, twelve miles distant. The inner pillars are of Purbeck marble laid as in the quarry, and the outer are of the same polished, not as laid in the quarry, which is the cause of its splitting.

St. Mary's Chapel, at the east end, is a wonderful piece of architecture, the vault of which seems to be supported by six very slender pillars of polished Purbeck marble. It is supposed they were supported by frames of timber, till the arch was finish'd ; this is reckoned a very bold piece of architecture, to make these small pillars support such arches. The cloyster and chapter house are supposed to be of the execution of the first architect. The latter is an octagon, the arch of which is supported by one pillar in the middle. There are fifty-two stalls in it, the old number of the monks of the chapter, and over them is cut, in small alt relief, pieces of sacred history.

The belfry on the north side of the west end is of the same architecture as the cloyster and chapter house ; in the center of it a single pillar of Purbeck stone, set as it lay in the quary, supports the floors, bells, timber, tower, and spire, covered with lead. This building is so solid, that I should think it originally designed for a high tower after the old way. As to things remarkable in the church :—in St. Mary's chapel is the monument of the Stouretons, and a wire hung up in remembrance of the execution, as mentioned before. On the north side of St. Mary's Chapel is the chapel and burial place of the Hungerfords; an additional building, as on the south side is that of   . In the nave is the tomb of a boy with a mitre; 'tis said a bishop was chosen annually on St. Nich⁸ Day out of the choristers for the twelve days, and that the child died for joy.   I rather imagine that in their processions at that time, one of them represented some particular bishop, as they frequently represented saints and angels in those processions.   Lord Chancellor Windham's monument is at the lower end of the church, with an epitaph (as it is said) writ by himself.   There are two or three old monuments of bishops brought from Old Sarum, and many monuments of the bishops of this church.   Bishop Sherlock took care with great assiduity to get the church put in thorough repair; part is at his own expence, the rest was done by the chapter, and by voluntary subscriptions to the amount of above £1,200.   Bishop Ward procured the Chancellorship of the Noble Order of the Garter, to be restored to the bishops of Salisbury, after it had been in lay hands 130 years.   The close, which is the south west part of the city, is encompassed with a high wall, not much less than a mile in circumference.   The bishop's house, with a chapel belonging to it, is at the south east part of it.   The house was sold in the great rebellion to Venting, a taylor, who pull'd it down and sold the materials.   The deanery is opposite to the west end, and most of the members of the chapter have houses on that side.   The north side is mostly let out, and there are very good buildings on it.   Bishop Ward founded a college here for clergymen's widows who are ten or twelve, and, if I mistake not, have twenty pounds a year.   In the time of Henry VII. Old Sarum was entirely deserted ; New Sarum being at the confluence of the Willey and the Avon is happy in a great command of water.   Tho' the Earls of Salisbury had their seat in the castle for some time after the town was diserted, which had been disputed with the Bishop, and was to have been decided by combat, but King Edward III. forbid it, least he should loose his right, and the matter being compounded, the Bishop paid a sum of money for it.   The streets are laid out regularly, and streams of water brought through all of them.   In the square, the first old townhouse, built of frames of wood, is still standing, and the citizens, having obtained leave of the Bishop, fortifyed the town on the east side with a large rampart, great part of which is still remaining and is called   .   There are a great number of gentlemen's houses in the town, especially about the Close, and I saw in the garden of one of them, through which the river passes, very large fish, if I mistake not both carp and trout, the running water being fenced in such a manner as to keep 'em in.

This town is famous for cutlery ware, bone lace, and for a manufacture of linsey woolsey.   They also make flannels, druggets, and cloths called Salisbury whites for the Turkey trade, but these are all much decay'd.   What has greatly contributed to make the town flourish was a liberty a Bishop obtained, when the church was first built, to have the western road turn'd this way, which before went through Wilton, the decay of which town is dated from that time. A navigation of the Avon was begun some years ago, but was brought only within two miles of it.   Bishop Ward was a great benefactor to it.   To the east of the Close is a suburb called Harn-hambridge.   Here was the College de Vaulx, built by Bishop Bridport in 1260, for scholars who, as it is said, retired to this place on some disturbance at Oxford.   But whatever gave rise to it, I take it to have been in the nature of a seminary for young persons to be educated under the Bishop's eye, who were to be ordained by him; on a certificate from their Chancellor they took degrees at Oxford. And this continued to Leland's time.

From Salisbury I went to Wilton, and from that place to Litle Dunford, Mr. Young's, a very pleasant place on the Avon, having a great command of water.   There are some statues here at the angles of a piece of water.   They were given him by Thomas Earl of Pembroke, and, it is said, were the design of Inigo Jones, executed at Florence.   They are naked figures in lead, and painted. They relate to some uncommon water diversions, particularly of the bever, the swan, &c., and were in the grotto at Wilton.   He has built a litle room in which there are some good landscapes.   On the down over it, Mr. Young has planted some clumps of trees.   In one of them is a curious hermitage, adorned with Gothic grotesque figures.   Opposite to the entrance are these verses:

> Ie me retire
> En tems jespere.

To the right under an urn is this inscription—

> If you would rest in peace bury these bones.
> Here lye interr'd a skeleton found in this place in 1754.

Near this spot also were found in 1734 two urns with bones in them.   There were two low barrows at this place in which these antiquities were found.   From this place there is a fine view of the large village of Wooford, which abounds in trees.

                                            Blandford, Oct.   , 1754.
I left Wilton on the 5th, and ascended the downs to the south, pass'd by the 4th and 5th stone in the way from Salisbury to Shaftsbury, and cross'd the down passing by a barrow, and descended to Bishops town on that river which falls into the Avon at Langeford, Ld Folkestone's.   There is a mount at the entrance to the village, and great remains of an old convent, as I was informed it was.   We ascended up to   Chase, belonging to the Earl of Pembroke, and descended to a valley, which is the bounds between Wiltshire and Dorsetshire, and came up to Fenditch Wood. I observed here an old Roman road, which seemed to be in the direction as from Winchester to Dorchester, and coming to Cran·bourn Chase I cross'd it and observed a great trench brought down the hill and carried about a mile along the plain northward, within it are some barrows and a long one that is about half a furlong round, and coming up to the top of the hill saw Pentridge Hill Camp, over a village of that name ; then descending .and going to the south-west passed near Bowridge, a pleasant well wooded village on a hill, the seat of Mr. Hooper, and crossing a vale went by Napper's Barrow and descended to a poor small town,

call'd Cranborne, consisting chiefly of farmers, a few shops, and Cranborne.
publick houses; it belongs to the Earl of Salisbury, who has a
good old seat here of hewn stone, which seems to have been built
about the beginning of the last century. Robert Cecil, who had
been Secretary of State to Queen Elizabeth, was created by King
James Viscount Cranborne, and afterwards Earl of Salisbury. It
was said there was a monastery here, built by King Edward the
Elder. The river in winter rises near Bowridge, but in summer
they have no water, nor less than half a mile below it where the
springs always flow, and the river falls into the Stour near Christchurch. This place is 12 miles from Salisbury, 14 from Shaftesbury, ten from Blandford, eight from Winborn Minster, and consequently but six from Badbury Hill, where I had been in my
journey to the Land's End in 1750. I saw in the church here
some old monuments of the Hawle's, of Mount Town. Cranborne
is in the high road from Poole, Wareham, and Wimborn Minster
to Salisbury. On the 6th I went two miles to St. Giles Wimborn,
commonly called St. Giles, where Lord Shaftesbury has a seat.
In a saloon are pictures of the family. In another large room lately
finished in a very elegant manner are some fine pictures of Gaspar
Poussin, Claud Lorain, and others, and one of Nicholas Poussin, the
story of the Levite and the Harlot. In another large room are
family pictures, as that of the first Lord Shaftesbury, who was
Chancellor, and four daughters of the present Lord's grandfather, each
having the emblems of one of the four elements, with Latin poetry
under them, relating to those subjects. There is a sleeping apart- St. Giles.
ment on this floor, and I observed some Chinese figures made with
shells in China. The gardens are very beautifully laid out, in a
serpentine river, pieces of water, lawns, &c., and very gracefully
adorn'd with wood. One first comes to an island in which there
is a castle, then near the water is a gateway, with a tower on each
side, and passing between two waters there is a fine cascade from
the one to the other, a thatch'd house, a round pavilion on a mount,
Shake Spear's house, in which is a small statue of him, and his

works in a glass case ; and in all the houses and seats are books in hanging glass cases. There is a pavilion between the waters, and both a Chinese and stone bridge over them. I saw here a sea duck which lays in rabbits' burrows, from which they are call'd burrow ducks, and are something like the shell drake. There is a most beautifull grotto finished by Mr. Castles of Marybone; it consists of a winding walk and an anti-room. These are mostly made of rock spar, &c., adorn'd with moss. In the inner room is a great profusion of most beautiful shells, petrifications, and fine polished pebbles, and there is a chimney to it which is shut up with doors covered with shells, in such a manner as that it does not appear. The park also is very delightful, and there is a building in it. The present Lord has no children.

Middleton, Oct.   1754.

In two miles from St. Giles I passed Lower Glisset, where Mr. Daimour, brother to Lord Milton, has a seat. About two miles further I went near Chettle, where there is a very large house, the seat of Mr. Chaffin, and in a mile came to Gunfield, near which village is Eastbury, the seat of Mr. Dodington, built on a rising **Eastbury.** ground on the design of Vanbrugh, consisting of the main body, with a square tower at each corner, and two wings on each side; the wings next to the middle court are faced with a colonade of twenty-two arches; in one is the kitchen and offices belonging to it; over it are about twelve lodging rooms, on the other side are the stables; over them a billiard room and three or four bed-chambers, the other offices are divided by a narrow court, and joyned at one end by an octagon tower, one of which is a sort of a steward's dining room, the others is designed for a chapel. It is built chiefly of Melbury stone, six miles to the north; the ornaments are of Portland stone. It is said the carriag of the materials of this house cost £20,000, and the whole not less than £200,000. It was begun to be built by Mr. Dodington's uncle, and by him was entailed on a nephew, one Mr. Bubb, who assum'd his uncle's

name, and then on Lord Cobham and his lordship's heir, Earl
Temple; with this condition, that so much should be laid out
yearly to finish the design, as he had only built the offices. The
other offices on one side are laundry, &c., and maid servants' apartments, and, on the other, stables and men's rooms. The grand
building consists of eleven windows on a floor in front, and is
adorned with a pediment supported by six rustick pillars, and before
them on the basement, one each side of the stairs, is a large statue
of a sphinx; one first enters a great hall, and then a most magnificent saloon, the whole in stucco, the walls adorn'd with flowers,
&c., gilt, the pediments of the doors supported by pillars all carv'd
and gilt, &c., with a Cupid on each side of each pediment, and a
bust in the middle where the pediment opens, except at the sides,
where in one is the groupe of Cupid and Psyche saluting; and that
to the garden is an entire pediment, with a recumbent angel on each
side. The top is painted from antique paintings, mostly, I believe,
taken from the illuminations of the old manuscript of Virgil. On
one side of it are two rooms, one a dining-room, in which is a most
beautiful table of Fineered Iallo of Siena, with pieces chosen out so
as to have a very fine appearance; and a picture over the chimney
of Lord Strafford and his secretary. The next is the drawing-
room, in which on consoles are the twelve Caesars, the heads in
bronze, the bust in a kind of agate. The walls of both these
rooms, and the cielings of all of them, are stucco, beautifully
adorn'd with flowers and architectonick ornaments gilt, the ceilings
being in compartments; to each of these are closets in the towers.
On the other side are three rooms. The first is the best drawing-
room, hung with flowered uncutt velvet of Genoua; and there are
several very fine pictures in it; to this room there is a closet; the
next is a dressing-room, hung with green sattin, on each side of
which large flower vases are painted in oyl colours. The room
beyond it is the best chamber, all furnished with crimson velvet,
and on each compartment a gilt eagle holds in his mouth a golden
horn, the arms of the family; they are in bas relief either of thick

paper or past board. There are several fine tables of the green Sicilian marble and oriental flowered alabaster, &c. Above are very handsome lodging rooms ; in one is the picture of the Farrier of Antwerp, promising to make himself a compleat limner, with the pencil, &c., in his hand, addressing himself to his mistress ; he is a very fine figure and has but litle drapery on him, whether it was his own performance I could not certainly learn. There are good bedchambers over these apartments, and the chimney-pieces are mostly rustick, with the spar fixed on between the stones, which is found at Benson, about five miles off, and has a good effect. To the saloon and hall there are as mezaninis above the windows ; and the low rooms over them lighted by the arch'd tops of those windows, and they appear as one window on the outside. The gentleman who amassed this wealth together was paymaster to the navy in Queen Anne's wars. The gardens are well laid out, lawns, clumps, and some walks of trees in the old way, and there is an open pavilion at the further end of the garden, with a pediment in front supported by columns.

Dorchester, Octr. 1754.

From Gunfield I came four miles to Blandford, passing by Pimpern Barrow on the down over Pimpern, which may be a hundred yards long and about ten broad ; near half a mile to the east is, as I was informed, such another call'd Hinketon Barrow, being near a village of that name; this I saw plainly, Mr. Dodington having planted a clump of trees on it. From Pimpern we went over another down to Blandford, and at the descent two piers are very judiciously placed, opposite to Mr. Portman's house, which I shall have occasion to mention, and is in a bottom on the other side of the river, and would not otherwise be observed from the road, tho' it is famous for one of the most beautiful terraces in the world.

Blandford.   Blandford is pleasantly situated on the river Stoure, consists cheifly of a street about half a mile long and another which meets it at right angles. The town is well-built having been burnt down in Queen Elizabeth's time, and again in 1731. There are many good inns and shops in the town, and they have a considerable trade in malt; it is a great thorough fare to the west. They have a very handsome church of hewn stone, built by the contributions after the fire, and the roof is supported by Ionick pillars. In it is buried Mr. Creech, who is mentioned as the father of the learned, much admired, and much envied Mr. Creech, Fellow of All Souls College, Oxon.

There is also a monument here with this inscription on it:—" In memory of Christopher Pitt, Clerk, A.M. very eminent for his talents in Poetry and yet more for the universal Candor of his mind and the primitive simplicity of his manners. He lived innocent and died beloved, April 13th 1748, aged 48." The town house is a very handsom building on a good style of architecture. It has not sent members to Parliament since the reign of Edward III. On the 7th I went a mile to Brianstown, Mr. Portman's, originally a Berkeley, but has estates by inheritance with the Portmans and Seymours from the present Duke of Somerset's family, which two names he bears. It is a large building in this shape ⌐. The right side is a good pile of two stories handsomly adorned, with round pillars of the Dorick and Ionick order; the other part is lately new cased in the modern way. It is situated on the river, which by art is made to form an island, near which is a delightfull lawn and plantations; Brianston. from this there is a gentle ascent for a quarter of a mile, to a high natural terrace which extends near to Blandford, and is almost three-quarters of a measured mile long, being a beautiful hanging ground. About three quarters of it towards the house is so broad as to have clumps of evergreen and flowering plants on the side which is towards the road, with winding and cross walks through them. That end is very steep, and the whole hanging ground is planted with trees and shrubs and is most charming. From this place four or five miles off, about Hatton near Sherminster Newtown, they find in a wood a fine shining sparr. King Edgar gave Sherminster to the Abbey of Glastonbury as did Edmond Ironside Newtown Castle on the other side of the river Stoure.

I went on three miles to the south-west to Strickland at the rise of the rivlet which falls into the Stoure a litle above Winborn, and we ascended a high hill which commands an extensive view. I saw from it Shaftsbury, the hill over Mere and Stourton, Mr. Hoare's, Pool, the Isles of Wight and Purbeck &c.: from this hill we descended to Middleton, commonly call'd Milton, which place gives the title of Baron to Mr. Daymour who married Lady   Sackvile, only daughter to the Duke of Dorset, who has a seat here, which was the old Abbey. This place is situated on a rivlet which falls into the Puddle, Bere being on the same water about four miles below it. An Abbey was first built here by King Athelstan, which was afterwards very much improved. The cross isle and the east part remain, and show that it was a very grand building, the arch under the tower is lofty and noble ; some fine Gothic work remains, which seems to have been over two altars in the south part of the cross isle and a kind of a model of a Gothick steeple fixed to the wall, probably over some statue, or it may be over a font. The high altar seems at first to have been Isolee, but has been raised and a door placed on each side: on it I saw the following imperfect inscription—

Orate pro bono Statu et animabus Willelmi Middleton Abbat hujus almi monasterii, ac etiam Magistri Thomas . . . . Sumptibus anno incarnationis Doมิ nŝi Ihũ Xti millesimo Quadringentessimo nonagesimo sexto.

In another place under a ton which supports a water mill, the arms of the Abbey, is this date 1418.

In the north isle is this inscription on a monument with the person kneeling, in brass, and this label coming out of his mouth:—

Milton.

Nos autem gloriari oportet in Cruce Dñi nostri Jesu Christi. Here lyeth buried Sʳ John Tregonnil, Knight, Doctor of the Civil Laws, and one of the Masters of the Chanceries, who died xiiᵗʰ day of January in the year of our Lord 1565, whose Soule God save, Amen.

This is I suppose is the Tregonnel who was Proctor for Henry

VIII. in suing a divorce from Queen Catherine, to whom he gave the site and demesne of the Abbey. Sr James Banks, a Swede, marrying an heiress of this family about the latter end of the last century, came to the estate. It is said afterward to have come to the Strachans, and is lately purchased by Mr. Daymour, now Lord Milton. There are great remains of the Abbey, as a hall with a fine carved skreen, a date on it of about 1428; a room called the Starchamber, from the wooden cieling in compartments adorn'd with gilt stars; most of the other rooms are alter'd, but some of the old building which was very fine remains. Lord Milton is casing it all round in a beautiful modern taste. The town is a very poor small place.

Sherborn, October 1754.

From Milton we went over a hill and came to a rivlet which falls into the river Puddle near Puddleton, and crossed over another hill to Chiselborn, and over another to a third water at Collier's Piddle, a fine village, to the north of which is Atton, the late Mr. Hescot's; and traversing another high hill we came to Cerne town and abbey on the Cerne, which rises at Upcerne. This is a large poor town, being near a mile in circumference. They make malt, and are now more famous for beer than in any other place in this country; they also spin for the Devonshire clothiers. This town owes its rise to the Abbey, which tradition saies was founded by Austin the Monk; but some think that it is more probable that St. Bertinus was the founder of it. In the scite of which and near the churchyard is his well, for there are no marks of the church, tho' probably it was where the churchyard is; it may be to the east of a peice of a cross now remaining. There are ruins round Cerne. the well. To the east of the churchyard are signs of great foundations, and particularly of buildings round of two courts, and there are three or four ruins which seem to have been of round towers. A low ridge of hills ends to the north of the abbey, on the west side of which is a figure cut in lines by taking out the turf and showing the white chalk. It is called the Giant and Hele, is about 150 feet long, a naked figure in a genteel posture, with his left foot set out; it is a sort of a Pantheon figure. In the right hand he holds a knotted club; the left hand is held out and open, there being a bend in the elbow, so that it seems to be Hercules, or Strength and Fidelity, but it is with such indecent circumstances as to make one conclude it was also a Priapus. It is to be supposed that this was an ancient figure of worship, and one would imagine that the people would not permit the monks to destroy it. The lord of the mannor gives some thing once in seven or eight years to have the lines clear'd and kept open. I came mostly along the valley in which the Cerne runs to Charminster, where in the church some of the Trenchard family are buryed. The east window is the ancient Saxon arch, which led to the chancel. I went a quarter of a mile further to Wotton in this parish, the seat of Mr. Trenchard, a very ancient house built at different several times. One part next to the garden is handsomly built, with large windows such as were in use in Queen Elizabeth's time and King James I., with fine entablatures and ornaments. They speak of it as Inigo Jones's design, but I rather take it to be of the architect of Somerset House. There are fine chimney pieces and carved door frames and wainscoat in the house all of wood; the skreen of the old hall is finely carv'd, and the kings of England, small and at full length, are round this wanscoat. There are a great number of arms in painted glass all over the house, some of the family, and many of the abbeys, nunneries, and monasteries in Dorsetshire, which the family collected at the dissolution of them. There is a pile of hewn stone building which is for very grand stables. This house married into the Russel family of Kingston Russel in the time of Henry VII. In that reign Ferdinand, coming from Germany to take possession of the Kingdom of Castile, was drove into Weymouth. Sr Thomas Trenchard, being the principal gentleman of the country, waited on him and conducted him to his house, and acquainted the king of it, who invited him to London.

Philip.
Spain.

Sr Thomas Trenchard, not understanding foreign languages, had
sent for Mr. Russel, a younger brother of the family he had married
into, a very fine young gentleman, who had travelled abroad, and
understood the languages. The king asked Sr Thomas Trenchard
if he could serve him, who, declining any thing for himself, said
if he had an opportunity to recommend Mr. Russel to the king he
would be obliged to him ; and when he mentioned him to King
Henry VII. he said he had taken particular notice of him, and had
him in his thoughts to serve him. He took him into his court,
made him a peer, and this is the ancestor of the Duke of Bedford;
and the elder branch failing, the estate of Kingston now belongs
to the duke. *See* Eckard's History, p. 618.

Wine Caunton, Octr 1754.

From Wotton I went a mile to Dorchester. About half way I
observed signs of foundations and remains of a trench drawn down
to the river near Burton farm house, and passed by a hamlet called
Frome Whitfield, where they say the old parish church of Dorchester
was, and it is now in one of the parishes, the church of which is in
the town. They have a tradition that the town was anciently about
these places, and, if so, it is probable that it was before the time of
the Romans. Dorchester is very finely situated on an eminence
over the Froome. It was certainly a Roman town by the name of
Durnovaria, Durnium, and Duniceni. It was one of the two winter
stations of the Legion Vindo gladia; Wimborne is supposed to be
the other. It is said it had two mints in the time of the Saxons.
The square entrenchment round the town is remaining, on which
probably the Roman walls were built, of which there are not the
least remains, for the Danes are said to have demolished the castle,
and probably they demolished the walls of the town also. The
Saxons are said to have a castle here, too, which might be that of
the Romans. What is called the Castle is on the north side of the
town over the river, but there are no remains of the walls. The Dorchester.
Normans are said to have rebuilt the Castle, and the litle ruins of

old walls on the west side of the town are probably those of the Normans, for they are of bad masonry. Forthampton is a village and church just at the north-east corner of the town, the high part of which seems also to have been in some measure fortifyed. The town consists chiefly of one long street, another which meets it at right angles, and one that runs paralel with the first. It is well built, and there are several good old houses in it. The principal street commands a view of Mr Pitt's house and plantations at Kingston, near a mile from the town. In St. Peter's Church is the monument of Sr Denzill Holles, Lord Ifled, who died in 1699, to whom the Duke of Newcastle of that time was heir. Here is also a monument to the memory of Sr John Williams of 1628. In the garden of the Free School they lately found a rough mosaick pavement. This school is a good building, and there is a library to it. It was founded by the Nappers, a considerable family in these parts. They show some very litle remains of a fryery on the river. I could not be informed whether this is Ashby le Frieri mentioned in the map. They have a manufacture of linsey woolsey at about fourteen pence a yard, they make malt, and are famous for beer; but the chief support of the town is the thoroughfare to Exeter, and the nobility and gentry who live near it. There are two Roman roads go from this town, one to Weymouth, the other to Bridport, and it's thought to Exeter, and is supposed to be Ikeneld Street. From the town I went about a quarter of a mile to the ancient amphitheatre called Mernesbury. It seems to remain in its ancient state, and is neither circular nor oval, but something of the shape of two Gothick flat arches joyned together in its length; it consists of a rampart about sixteen yards broad at bottom, and thirty-six feet high; it is about fifty-four paces broad and sixty-six long. The entrance is ten yards wide, and opposite to it at the other end is a gentle ascent. On the right hand at the entrance is a hollow a litle way up, as if the place of some particular officer. From these sort of entrances at each end there is a terrace, which is form'd in an ascent on each side from the ends, and widens to the middle, where it is three yards in breadth and six yards high, or half the heigth of the whole; this seems to have been for spectators to stand on. At top there rises a narrow rim, I think all round, on the outside, and is only about a yard broad, and may be about eighteen inches high, the whole breadth at top being about 9 feet, if I do not mistake. In the middle on each side the ground is a litle raised for about six yards as in a semicircle, but higher on each side than in the middle. This is a singular work, and seems to have been raised by skooping out the ground within, and taking it all round in such a manner as no hollow or unevenness appears. Near the town to the west is a Roman camp, which may be a quarter of a mile square; it is continued to the hanging ground over the river, and is a fine situation; there is a narrow terrace below it, and the approaches to the west of the rising ground seem to have been helped by art, so as to make it stronger. This is call'd Pomeroy, probably from the Latin Pomærium. I went about a mile to an ancient British camp on a hill that is not high, called Maiden Castle; it is a very strong entrenchment with three deep fossees round it, and a fourth at each end to defend the entrance. From this camp I saw to the east, came Mr. Daymore's new house which is now building. This continued probably to be the head camp of some empire in this island for a considerable time; I should think rather of some ancient British kingdom than of the Saxons. And that chain of camps to the east might be sort of fortresses against this power, as Badbury, and, as I was informed, Woodbury, near Wareham, Hamilton Hill, four miles west of Blandford, and, it may be, Bulbarrow, which I saw when I went to Sherborn, and is on the Piddle, above Colliers Piddle, and the camp of   , near Cranborne, and the great lines I saw drawn from the hills near it, tho' I did not observe on which side they were a defence, tho' if I mistake not were to defend the country from the eastern people. I saw a great number of barrows along the hills to the south which I had observed in the way to Weymouth in 1750. I pass'd by a large barrow in the bottom to the north-west with a small one near it, and one made in a circle with a small fossee round it. This probably was the tomb of the monarch.

Bruton, Octr. 1754.

On the 9th I set forward for Sherborn, the road being on the Downs between the Puddle and the river Cerne, and saw those places I had passed two days before, and about the rise of the Cerne saw Lady Abington's seat of Minterne. We descended the hill into that valley which they call Blakemore, and the vale of White hart, through which the several rivlets run that fall into the Stoure and into the Parrot that runs into the Severne near Huntspill. We came to Sherbourn, which is pleasantly situated on one of those streams, great part of it being on the side of a hill over the river. It was made an episcopal see in 704 by Ina, King of the West Saxons. In King Ethelred's time Herman, Bishop of Sunning, being advanced to this see, united Sunning to it, and transfer'd the see to this place, which in the time of the Conqueror was removed to Sarum, the bishop keeping his house here for a place of retirement. But when Henry VIII. erected a new see at Bristol, Dorsetshire was made part of that see. Soon after the translation of this see to Salisbury, the Cathedral was turn'd into an Abbey Church. There are great remains of old buildings about the Church, and one that seems to have been the refectory. In the Church the arches on which the steeple stands, those at the end of the isles and the south porch are of Saxon architecture, and there is some remains of that style at the west end, before which I judg'd there had been a grand portico; and they have a notion that the church extended to the west as far as the houses, as they find foundations in digging graves, which is a proof that some buildings were formerly there. This old building is probably of the time of Herman, who translated the see of Sunning to this place. It is mentioned that at the entrance of the church, probably in the portico, two Saxon kings, Ethelbald and Ethelbert lye buryed, but I met with no account of it here. In the time of Henry VI., in a quarrel between the people of the town and the monks, the church was burnt and the townsmen were obliged to rebuild it, probably in the form it is now in, which is very beau-

Sherborn.

tiful both in the arch and windows, and what is particular, the whole
church is adorned with the same kind of carv'd ornaments as the
windows. In a chapel of the church is a fine costly monument
ornamented with pillars and statues of Lord Digby in 1698 ; there
are also monuments of others of the family, and in the same chapel
is the monument of an abbot. In another chapel to the west there
is one of the Fitz James's in Queen Elizabeth's days ; there are also
monuments here of the Chichesters and of Sᵣ John Hausy. As this
church was built by the town, they were very desirous to get it into
their possession at the Reformation, and they keep it in great order.
And to enable them to purchase it, it is said they destroyed three
churches and four chapels. Adjoyning to the church is a very good
freeschool founded by King Edward VI., in which there is a statue
of him. And there is also an almshouse founded by Robert Nevil,
Bishop of Salisbury, in 1448. They have an old cross in the lower
town, and another, which appeared to me to have the statue of St.
Andrew on it. Adjoyning to Sherborn is Castletown, with a new
built church to it, and it is said they have a distinct market. Roger,
the third Bishop of Salisbury, built a castle here, but King Stephen
was so offended at it that he took possession of it, and it was kept
by the Crown till in 1330 Bishop Wivil recovered it. Some part
of this building seems to be older than King Stephen's time, there
being one window of very ancient Saxon architecture in a tower; it
may be built before the rest of the castle. There are ornaments of
arches intersecting each other in one part, and an old Saxon pillar
remains as if it had been the supporter of an arch. In some of the
walls is the Roman style of building, two or three tiers of common
stones, and two tiers of flat stones to bind them. The inner gate
consists of a regular Roman architrave, and the whole is well
defended by a deep fossee. Near it is a good old house call'd the
lodge, belonging to Lord Digby, who is improving the place. On
May 16th, 1709, a hail storm so fill'd a torrent which came
down the hill that the water was two feet ten inches high in the
church. Mr. Seymour has a very good house and offices on the

high part of the town.   Sherborn is in the high road to the west, by
the way of Shaftsbury, as well as a passage from Bath to Dorchester and Weymouth.   They have a manufacture of buttons and
bone lace, and it is computed there are 20,000 souls in the town.
The Prince of Orange was met here by the Prince of Denmark, the
Dukes of Ormond and Grafton, and Lord Marlborough, who left
King James at Salisbury, and thereby contributed to make it a most
peaceable revolution.

Devizes, Oct.   1754.

On the tenth I left Sherborn, and coming into Somersetshire had
a fine view of the vale in which the Parret runs, on which river
below Sherborn stand Ilchester, Langport, and Weston, and on
another branch Queen Camell.   We descended into the vale having
a view to the east of the hills on which stand Pen and Stoureton,
from which we were not above two or three miles.   We ascended
to Wine Caunton, situated in a romantic manner on the side of a
hill, being but a poor place; they have a manufacture of spinning
thread and woollen yarn.   It is said an urn was found here lately
full of Roman money.   We went on two miles to Redlinch, the seat
of Lord Ilchester, eldest son of Sr Stephen Fox; he is married to an
heiress, the only daughter of Mrs. Horner.   It is a handsom pile of
building, with two grand offices on one side of it, all built of the
freestone of the country, with window frames of freestone.   The
house is well finished within, and there are many good pictures in
it.   The ground of the park is very fine, and there is a large piece
of water before the house.   I went on two miles to a pretty good
town called Bruton, situated on the side of a hill over that river, on

Bruton.   which Glassenbury stands.   The church is an handsom light
Gothick building, and the chancel has been rebuilt, and is kept in
great order by Mr. Berkley, younger son of the late Lord Berkley
of Stratton, whose plain neat monument, in the Roman taste, is put
up in the chancel, and near it one in the same manner to his second
son, Captain William Berkley, who died in 1733, commander of the

Tyger, in a voyage from Guinea; here is also an old monument of this family, with couchant statues on it without any inscription, and another to the memory of Sr William Godolphin, of the county of Cornwall. There is an old chapel under ground, the arch over which is supported by three rows of pillars, three or four in a row, and is about ten feet high, and extends farther to the west than the chancel; this is the burial place of the Berkley family. In the churchyard is a monument with this inscription:

Pulvis et ossa Sumus
Cadavera ante bac jacentia
In Ossuario
Sub Aditu
Hujusce Ecclesiæ
Sub hoc Marmore Condita
Jussu Honorabilis C. Berkley
Anno 17-3.

The monastery, with its demesne, was given by Henry VIII. to Sr Maurice Berkley, ancestor of the present lord, this family having been fixed in this place ever since the time of Edward II. I uid not see the free school, said to be founded by Edward the VI.

There is an alms house for twelve boys and twenty-two men and women. Under the founder's bust is this inscription:

Henry Saxey, Esqr,
Founder of this Almshouse,
Auditor to Queen Elizabeth
And King James.

I saw several stones here full of shells, which are dug at Kineton, near Somerton, and all the stones of these valleys are of the shelly kind. From Bruton I rid twelve measur'd miles to Froome, passing by Nunney Castle, on a rivlet which falls into the Froome, and saw Marston, the seat of Lord Orrery, within half a mile from the road, of which places I have before given an account. I came by Philips Norton to Bath.

Bath, Oct.   1754.

On the 14th I went by Mr. Allen's house, turn'd off at the Quarries to the left, descended to Comb, and from that village came into the turnpike road to a bridge over Comb brook, and by Bradford into Wiltshire, and coming near Stoke, crossed over the Avon and went by Winsley to Bradford, seven miles from Bath, which is a place I have formerly mentioned, and crossing the Avon I came by   three miles, and cross'd the river Froome into Somersetshire at Farley Castle, of which the old enclosure remains over the river defended by round towers, but the castle it self has been destroyed.   Mr. Camden seems to be mistaken in saying, that Humphrey Bohun built a monastery here; for that I apprehend was at Monkton Farley, near Clarendon Park, not far from Salisbury.   But what the place is famous for is the monuments of the great family of the Hungerfords in a chapel in the castle belonging to them.   One is cut out in lines, being a figure at full length, with a defaced inscription round it of Walter Hungerford, said to be of the thirteenth century.   At the south-east corner of the church is a tomb, with this inscription on it :

Farley.

Tyme tryeth truth. Walter Hungerford, Knight, who lyeth here, and Edward his son. To God's mercy in whom we trust for ever. Anno D° 1585, the vi. of Desb.

The motto, they say, relates to his having forfeited the estate and its being restored to him again.

On the opposite side, between the chapel and their particular burial place, is the monument of Sr Thomas Hungerford, and of John Hungerford, with their couchant statues.   They have a tradition that the former was Speaker of the House of Commons. In the middle of the Chapel, to the north, is the fine monument of Sir Edward, Knight of the Bath, son of Antony of Black Courton, in Oxfordshire, and of his wife Lucia, daughter of Thomas Ash; he dyed in 1648, aged 52.   Near it is a plain tomb of Sr Edward, of 1607, who was uncle of the above Lucia, and from whom she had the estate. On the fine monument also is a memorial of Margaret, daughter of Holyday and his wife Susanna, who was afterwards Countess of Warwick. The two marble couchant statues on the monument are fine statuary, highly polished, as is the white tomb; they lye on a black marble polished slab, eight feet long, five wide, and seven inches thick; the ornaments of foliage and flowers at the angles and the arms of white marble are finely polished. In another part is a small monument set in the wall to Mrs. Mary Shaa, of 1613, daughter of Walter Lord Hungerford, who 'tis said was beheaded by Henry VIII., and heyre general to S[r] Edward Hungerford. The last of the family, who died about   years ago, spent an estate of £14,000 a year and 80 thousand pounds, and died in Spring Garden supported by charity.

The top of the Communion-table is a piece of fine marble, not well polished; they call it Egyptian, but it seems to be one of our pieces of marble, which consists of several pebbles cemented together. I came home by Charterhouse Hinton, in the turnpike road from Froome, and by Midford, where the two brookes meet of Combhay and Twiney; and going near Southstone came to Bath.

On the 15th I saw Mr. Allen's gardens, which are laid out in wilderness, with a piece of water in the middle, from which there is a descent, on each side of which are beautiful meadows arising up the hill; on one side is a new Gothick building, higher up is a statue of Moses with his hand striking the rock, and below it a beautifull cascade falls down about twenty feet; a little higher is the building of the Cold Bath. The center of the gardens commands a fine view of Bath. I took a ride round by Combe to Hampton Down, where I observed great remains of foundations of Mr. Allen's walls, which made me conjecture that this heigth might be inhabited, in times of danger, as a place of security. Part of this ride was in the walks and woods which Mr. Allen has made for ten or twelve miles round, taking in Hampton and Claverton downs. Another day I went by Bathwick to Bathampton, where, having rebuilt the west part of the church, the old belfery I formerly mentioned was destroyed ; but I observed at the east end of the church a very particular mezzo-relievo set in the wall, cut within the surface of the stone ; the drapery and every part of it very uncommon. I saw also, in the churchyard, as taken out of the church, the tomb

Quaere, if not a common cross-leg'd figure ?

of a Knight of St. John of Jerusalem, with a shield and dagger; there is also the statue of a woman with a remarkable dress, and a large bead, if I mistake not, in her hand.

Great Bedwin, Octr. 1754.

On the 18th of October I left Bath and went five miles and a half in the London road, coming into Wiltshire a litle beyond Bathford. In two miles we came to Alford, where at Mr. Claiden's house I observed an old building like the remains of a convent. We crossed the Avon three miles further at Milsom, a small clothing town in

Melksham

which there are several good houses. I saw Bromham steeple to the left, Spree Park and Boden Hill over which they go to London, and Lacock near it. Milsom is four miles from Troubridge, five from Bradford, seven from the Devizes and from Calne. In about two miles we came to Seen, another wealthy village, with several good houses in it, and a churchyard most delightfully situated, commanding a view of the vale towards Troubridge to the west, and Lavington to the south-east. Five miles more brought us to the Devizes, 88 miles from London, from Salisbury, 18 from Bath, and about six from Lavington. A low hill extends from east to west, and here dividing into three parts ; the old town and castle are on the middle part, the new town to the north, and part of the

Devizes.

old town extends to the southern part of the hill. The town consists chiefly of two streets in length stretching along the northern part of the hill, and one street of communication; the principal street to the west is broad, and there are several good houses in it. There are two good churches, St. Marie's to the north and St. John's to the south ; the former is a good Gothick building. In the latter are some remains of a very ancient church, that is, the tower and east end with ornaments within of arches intersecting each other.

On the outside is a Saxon corniche; there are capitals of pillars adorned with triangles four rows one over another, two above and two below the swell of the capital, and placed in the Quincunx order. In the churchyard an obelisk was erected in 1751, with an inscription on it to this purpose :—That a man, his wife, sister, and another man were drowned in the flower of their youth in a pond near the town called Drew's pond, on Sunday, June 3d, 1751. On another side is this inscription :

"This monument, as a useful monitor to young people to remember their Creator in the days of their youth, was erected by subscription."

On another part—

"Remember the Sabbath day to keep it holy."

The castle is said, but 'tis thought without foundation, to have been built by Dunwallo, King of the Britains, and there was a tradition it was built by King Alfred; but the last founder of it was Roger Bishop of Salisbury, who, falling into disgrace with King Stephen, the king seiz'd on this and the castle of Sherborn, belonging also to the bishop. It was esteemed one of the strongest in Europe. Sr William (Ralph?) Hopton was shut up in it by Sr William Waller, which occasioned the battle called Roundway Down fight, from the hills near the town, on July 13th, 1640. The castle is now entirely demolished; there are two windmills on the keep or inner part; it is defended by two very strong fossees; the rampart of the inner one and the fossee of it extends into the gardens to the east, and houses are built that way on the outermost rampart; the rest is all an orchard. They have a handsom town-house and wool-hall for the weekly wool-market. On the old market-house they have an inscription to this purpose :—that in January last year a woman joyned with two others in buying a sack of wheat, and each, as supposed, had paid their proportion. Money was wanting, every one said she had paid her due, the innocent in such a manner as made them fix on the other, who wished if she had not paid it she might immediately drop down dead! which she

Quaere. if not of a common cross-leg'd figure?

tioned was de......
a very particula.. .
face of the sto..
I saw also, in th..
of a Knight ..
there is al.. th..
large head. .. ..

On the ...
in the Lo.. ..
In two ....
observed ....
the Av.. ..

Melksham

which th..
the left, S..
and Lav.. ..
from P.. ..
two m..
good ....
commu.. ..
Laving.. ..
Deviz..
and ....

Devizes

West, ...
are m ..
old to.. ..
sists ch..
part ..
street ..
Their ..
to the ..
are .. ..
east ....

.... of the crowded multitude,
.... sum that was wanting.
.... and some corn. They
.... ms here, and particularly
.... iree flat stones, and cover'd
.... .. about England, and are
.... on them, and they say on
.... overlooks the town, there is a
.... a Roman; and I saw a hill to
.... fortified and in that situation.
.... miles I ascended Roundway
.... ds Shord, is Wansdike, which
.... Mercury, the God of bounds.
.... ds between the kingdom of the
.... Crossing this whole county the
.... older than the Mercian king-
.... edie, the first king of the West
.... slight enclosure, like a field,
.... several on the others, which, if
.... for the tent only of some great
.... in honour than for any defence.
.... ws all the way from this place to
.... conclude that this had been the
.... And there are many dikes at
.... and it is supposed they were only
.... We came to Beckington, near
.... Bath, where there is a great inn,
.... Minal. On the 19th, I went into
.... rough Savernac Forest, going near
.... ds not far from Lord Bruce's, and
.... rise of a small river, which joynes
.... and makes that river on which
.... falls into the Kennet. Bedwin was
.... of Cissa, who was Viceroy of Wilt-

shire and Barkshire. Mr. Camden saies he built a castle to the
south of the town, and less than a mile to the south of it is Castle _{Great Bedwin.}
Cops and mead on a heigth, where I found some litle remains of a
rampart, and to the west of it a deep fossee, with a rampart on each
side of it for about a quarter of a mile, at the place where there is at
present a gibbet. But I imagine the chief place of Cissa's residence
was at a castle a mile to the north-east, called Cisbury. In 675, a ^{Qu.}
bloody battle was fought here between Wulfere and Esewin. It is
a poor town of farmers, malsters, and publicans. It is a borough,
but all the parishioners do not vote, and those who do not are said
to be of the Privent. The famous physician, Dr. Thomas Willis,
the father of Dr. Brown Willis, was a native of this place.

P.S.—I went about two miles to Shawborn, under Buttermore
Hills, the seat formerly of the Burdetts. Dr. Edward Pococke, the
famous Orientalist and my great-grandfather, of Hawkley, auditor
of the Duchy Court of Lancaster, married two sisters of this family,
and Archbishop Lamplough's son married a daughter of the other
sister, married to the Rev. Mr. Boham, in this county. I passed
through Ham and Inkpen, and near Mr. Sloper's, of Westwoodhay,
and came by Enbourn to Newtown.

London, November 28th, 1754.

After I left Newtown on the 25th, I went by Sidmounton, the
seat of Mr. Kingsmill, which has been lately much improved. Near
the east end of the house they have built a handsome summer-house,
which commands a view of a piece of water below that appears like
a serpentine river, near which also there is a building, and another
towards the park. I observed, a litle below the camp at Ladle Hill,
a circular tomb.

I crossed the road from Whitchurch to Kingscleer and Basingstoke, and came in five miles to Overton. To confirm a conjecture
I made, that the Test, on which this town stands, is the old Anton,
I found there was a place call'd Quilhampton, and another Seventon,
probably Seven Anton, for all these names are pronounced short, as

Southington for Southampton. This place is 54 miles from London, eight from Basingstoke, three from Whitchurch, and eleven from Andover. About a mile below it is Laverstoke, formerly

now Mr. Dawkins's, who travelled into the East with Mr. Bovery, and the drawings lately published of Palmyra were executed under his direction. He is making a very fine serpentine river here, as I suppose, by enlarging the Test. Overton is a small town; about 3 miles from it is Mr. Horwood's, of Dean, and over that late Mr. Withers, now Mr. Bramston's; it is situated on an advanc'd ground. I came through Church Okely and Worting to Basingstoke, situated on a rivlet near its rise, which falls into that river I formerly men-

Basingstoke. tioned at Sherfield. It is a large town on the side of a rising ground, with many good shops in it; they have a litle manufacture of serges, horse-cloths, and blankets, but the chief support of the town is a trade in malt, and it is a great thorough fare from London to the West.   Henry III. in 1261, founded an hospital here, at the instance and on the estate of Walter de Merton, for the maintenance of superannuated priests, and after Merton College was founded the incurable scholars or fellows of it were to be sent to it. Above the town, to the north, are the remains of a Chapel of the Holy Ghost, built by William, the first Lord Sandys, who was buryed in it. It appears to have been a beautiful Gothick building of freestone, lined with brick; there are fine niches between the windows and at the angles of an octagon tower at the west end. The burial place seems to have been to the north, where some building has joyned, and there are several hewn stones which may be the remains of a monument.   On this spot are tombs of the Cufaudes, of Cufaude, in this county. One of the ladies of the family is mentioned as grandchild to S[r] Richard Rook, Knight of the Garter, and cosin-german to the Countess of Salisbury, daughter of George, Duke of Clarence; this was a Roman Catholick family. Close to this chapel is a free school, which seems to be the remains of an old building, and there are some foundations from it, near the chapel, as if some fabrick had extended to the full length of the chapel. A hospital is men-

tioned as founded at Basingstoke by Henry III. for the maintenance
of altar priests.

A mile from this town is Hackwood, a beautifull seat of the Duke Hackwood.
of Bolton's, which I have often seen. The walks, wood, and lawn in
the garden are very fine, and it is adorn'd with statues, particularly
an equestrian statue of

I have formerly been at Alton, ten miles from this town; it is
famous for a manufacture of baragons, and King Alfred left this
town by will to the keeper of Leodore, and the mannor did afterwards belong to Hide Abbey, near Winchester.

On the 26th, after going a mile in the London road, I turn'd to
the left, and in half a mile came to Basing Castle, which is a round
enclosure encompassed with a double ditch ; the inner fossee is very
deep; the area within is above an acre, the circumference a quarter Basing Castle.
of a mile, and it was made a vineyard in the last century, which has
been destroyed. It stood several sieges against the Parliament
army, and at last was taken under Oliver by storm in 1645, and
the Marquise of Winchester was made a prisoner. He called it
Love Loyalty, and Aymè Loyaltè has since that time been the
motto of the family. To the east of it is an enclosure in which they
say were the offices, and they show some vaults which probably
serv'd as well for salleying out as for conveying provisions in time
of a siege. After the Restoration a house was built below the farm
house, which has been since pull'd down, and many of the materials
carried to build the house at Canom Heath. Below the castle is a
bowling green, and a large garden with turrets to it. The east end
of the church is the burial place of the Duke of Bolton's family ; it
is divided in very good taste from the isles by arches, under which
are plain tombs. Over the arch at entrance to the north isle is this
inscription :

Ad laudem Xti et Mariae Matris hic per Johem Poulett Winton haec erecta
con - - tat Anno Dni 1519.

On the first arch to the north, which they call old Joram's monument, is this inscription :

·Hic jacet Johes Poulett miles et Elinor ux - - ej.   Qui obierunt mense Septembris Anno Dni, 1488, 111.

On the next arch is this inscription :

Hic jacet Johes Poulett et Alicia ux. ej.   Qui obierunt mense

This seems to have been erected whilst they were living, and that the date was not put in after their death.

The first to the south appears to have been a Knight of the Garter, and tho' no coronet on the arms, there are coronets on two arms in the angles.   Over the arch to the west of it are arms with on it of an heiress.

In the church is a monument of Charles Duke of Bolton who died in 1698, and left some benefactions to the parish.

At Basing, Ethelred and Alfred fought the Danes and were beaten. In half a mile from Basing I crossed the London road, at the Bell, two miles from Basingstoke ; in half a mile passed by Maplederwell, where there is a small stream ; in a mile came to Neatley ; here the hop country begins.   I observed a Saxon door to the church, and an arch at the east end, which probably led to a chancel.   One mile more brought me to Gruelt, where Mr. Toll has a house, and I saw to the south Mr. Jervais's of Herriards, which seemed to be a fine plantation.   Here I passed the river Ditford, and in half a mile came to Warnborow on the same river, where there is a small manufacture of barge clothes at 3s. 6d., and Medleys at five shillings, both a yard wide.   This river seems to be the bounds between the gravelly chalky and the sand country beyond it.   I went to see Warnborow Castle on this river, which is an octagon with   at the angles from bottom to top ; the walls are twelve feet thick, built of flint, and seem to have been cased with hewn stone inside and out.   The sides within are eighteen feet long ; it consisted of a ground floor, the grand floor over it, and a sort of attick over that, each floor having a window or door in each side ; except the side of the chimney, which was only to the middle floor, the area it stands in is an oblong square of about an acre, encompassed with a wet fossee ; to the east is another area of about half an acre, with such a fossee round it, and there is a double fossee to the south and north, tho' the river runs near the south side ; but on the west side the river and morass serve as a defence instead of a second fossee. It was defended fifteen days Warnborough by thirteen men against the Barons, in King John's time, and in the reign of Edward III., David King of Scots was kept prisoner here. This is called by historians the Castle of Odiham, tho' it is a mile from the town, and is mentioned as a royal seat and palace, and Warnborow may be a new name to this hamlet, it being in the parish of Odiham.

At this town Mr. Kenton has a house, which seems to be on the site of the old monastery   and some other ruins still remaining.

In the church are monuments of the Mores, formerly of this place, Odiham. Handikes and Wolverdales, one of which, a knight, was a master in Chancery; there is also a monument of Mr. May, Founder of the Free-School, and a memorial of Mr. Pit, Founder of an Hospital or two, there being three in the Town, one of which was founded by one of the Mores. There is an ancient inscription on the Font. Lily the Grammarian was a native of this place.

London, Novr. 29th, 1754.

A long mile from Odiham is Dogmansfield, Mr. St. John's, an estate which came to the family from the Goodiers by his mother, the family estate being at Farley between Winchester and Rumsey. Dogmansfield. The ground, water, the park and plantations, are very beautiful. A fine apartment has been lately added to the house of two large rooms highly finished ; in which I saw two marble tables of pebbles cemented together, which I was told came from Mr. Bridges's estate at Keinsam in Somersetshire, they are very beautiful, tho' they do not take a high polish.

From the house there is a view of seven ponds, which appear like a serpentine river and of a Gothick arch on an advanced ground half a mile further, it is built of brick and flints in squares. There is an imitation of a British or Druid avenue to it of large stones set up on end for half a mile, which are found on the sandy heaths. On the other side of the house is a small round hill well planted, with a colonade in the front of it, call'd the Temple; beyond this on a more advanced ground is another plantation and an octagon turret, on the summit which commands a fine view of the country, as of Tilney Hall near Sherfield, which I passed through in the way to Oakingham, further was Bramshot, Sr Maurice Cope's, they call it the Belvidere. Below this in a wood is a thatch'd house, further down a large piece of water of thirty acres, in the middle of which is a small low turret on four Gothick arches, called the Chinese building, but is rather defective in the execution, and near the water is a cottage built to resemble a Gothick chapel.

Going from the arch I passed a stream, and came to Crodham in about a mile, passed through part of the parish of Crundal and came to the heathy hills, at the end of which is a small hill called Upshot, which seems to have been separated by art from the hills, as a sort of pyramidal monument. Over this is a hill, where there is a tree, which they call the beacon, and this hill is known by the name of Renan Roan, which has a British sound, and may relate to some ancient history. Further on the left hand, on the point of the hill, is an old camp, which some have judg'd to be Roman because it is square, but I believe they seldom had camps on high hills. It has the name of Brigborough. A litle beyond it is a publick house call'd the Lady House, where all the Bishop of Winchester's courts for this mannor must be opened. I came down to Farnham, a large town situated at the foot of a hill on the river Wey, which rises above Alton. Farnham is supposed by some to be the Caleva Attrebatum of the Itinerary, 22 miles from Ad Pontes, it may be Stanes, 22 from Venta Belgarum. It was given by Æthelbald, King of the West Saxons, to the bishop and congregation of the Church of Winchester. Alfred beat the Danes here in 893. When King Stephen gave his friends leave to build castles, his brother, Henry de Blois, Bishop of Winchester, built a castle here. Henry III. demolished it, but in time the bishop rebuilt it. It is a fine situation on a high ground over the town ; there are Farnham. some remains of the old castle, and a good house is built on part of the site of it ; there is a park belonging to the house, with an avenue of trees three-quarters of a mile long. In the old wooden town are some remains, of which Fuller tells a story. The chief support of the town is the hop trade, a market for oates and wheat, and the thorough fare to Winchester and Southampton.

On the 27th I went three miles and passed near More Park, Mr. Temple's, which place I did not view. but 'am well inform'd that in the house and garden are several small statues, busts, reliefs, &c., of the Arundel Collection, and under the dial in the garden was interr'd the heart of Sr Wm Temple, according to his will. The cave in the park cut out of the sandy rock near Waverley Abbey is singularly beautifull. In about half a mile I came to Waverley Abbey, on the River Wey. It was founded in 1128 by William Gifford, Bishop of Winchester, for Cistercian Monks, being the first in England of that order. The estate was Mr. Aislabie's, who built the house and made the plantations and other improvements; it was Waverley. then Mr. Child's, and now belongs to Mr. Hunter, son of the Governor. The house is a fine piece of architecture of Campbell's, on one of Palladio's designs ; Mr. Hunter has added wings to it, joyn'd by a Gallery adorned on the outside with Pilasters, the grand front of the house is to the garden, which is laid out in lawn, wood, and winding walks near the river. The ruins of the monastery add no small beauty to it; the church is much destroy'd. A building which seems to have been the refectory is pretty entire, except that one end is down.

From this place I went over the hills by Crookbury hill, and pass'd by Shackleford Mr. Gathwait's, a bad situation, and by Eshen and Paper Harrow, Lord Middleton's, and adjoyning to Godalmin, General Oglethorpe's, where there is a vineyard, out of which they make a wine like Rhenish. And I was informed that there are in the house some good drawings of Albani's which serve for hangings.

Godalming is a considerable town; Alfred gave it by will to his brother's son Ethelwald.   It was said, but I know not on what authority, that it was the see of a Bishop before the Conquest; and that the Dean and Canons had their houses on the spot now called Church Street; that the Bishoprick was dissolved in the time of Henry II. and the estates of it conferr'd on the Deanery of Sarum; and it is certain the Dean of Sarum has an estate here, and is patron of the Living.   But this is on no good authority, for Tanner, in his Notitia Monastica is wholly silent in relation to it. The tower of the Church is very ancient, I judge from the old cornice that it was built before the Conquest, and there are some remains of the old church in the cross isle, the pillars in the church also seem to be old.   The Oglethorp family are buryed here, originally of Yorkshire they are descended from Ligulp of the time of Ed. Confess^r.

Godalmin.

Oxensend is mention'd in this neighbourhood as a place where old English money and rings have been found.

And the mannor of Catteshull is said to have been held by Hana de Catton to be marshal of the king's meretrices, when he came into these parts, which in another place are mentioned under the name of Lotrices.

This town is a great thoroughfare to Portsmouth.   They have a manufacture of kerzeys for the Canary Islands, and of stockins and paper, particularly the white brown, and they have a great plantation of liquorice.   Here that vile imposture was carryed on of a woman bringing forth rabbits, which was a contrivance of the woman and her mother, and she was prosecuted for an imposture.

In the road, towards London, I saw to the left on a hill St. Martha's Chapel, and to the right   Sr More Molineux's, a fine situation and a good old house, and in about three miles came to St. Catherine's Chapel, on a hill very near Guilford. It has been a handsome Gothick fabrick with turrets, and is built entirely of stone; 'tis said it was erected to say masses for the safe journey of travellors.

Guilford is very pleasantly situated on the side of a steep hill over the Wey; it consists chiefly of one street about half a mile long. It was a villa of the English Saxon kings, and given to Guilford Athelwald by his uncle. The old castle, in the style of the Tower of London, is remaining, and was the house of the kings, in which they passed some time every year. King Aelfred was betrayed here by the Danes.

Queen Eleanor, wife of Henry III., founded a house of Friers Preachers near this town, called Langley, which, if I mistake not, now belongs to Speaker Onslow; it is at the foot of the hill to the west. A house of Crouched Friers is also mentioned here.

They have a free school, a handsom building, founded by King Edward VI. Archbishop Abbot and Sᵣ Maurice Abbot, Lord Mayor of London, and Robert, Bishop of Salisbury, were the sons of clothiers of this town. Archbishop Abbot founded a large almshouse here, and there is a fine monument in it to his memory, on which his couchant statue, in white marble, is well executed. The clothing trade is entirely decayed in this place, and it chiefly subsists by the navigation of the Wey, and by the great thorough fare to Chichester and Portsmouth. The road from this place to Farnham, on St. Catherine's hill, like a grand terrace, is very fine, and so is the bridle road either by Letherhead or Epsom over Banstead cowns to London. In about two miles I passed the road which leads to Clandon, Lord Onslow's, where I have formerly been; it is a fine new house, and there are some beautiful chimney-pieces in it, adorned with fine reliefs in white marble.

I left Guilford on the 28th; in about five miles I came to Ripley, and just beyond it passed by Lord King's house and park in Oakham parish, if I do not mistake. I went over the heath in which is the camp on the rising ground, which I had formerly viewed, and is thought by some to be Julius Cæsar's, where he encamped his army before he cross'd the Thames. This is the camp which is mentioned in the parish of Walton. As I remember, it is an irregular camp, and might be made by the Britains and used by Julius Cæsar as a camp.

We came to Painshill, near Cobham, Mr. Hamilton's, which is a most beautifull farm improvement. One first enters a lawn in which sheep are fed; there are plantations towards the south to hide the heath, and a walk within it with clumps and knots of trees on the side to the field, scatter'd up and down without order; going to the left is a walk to a small lawn encompassed with evergreens, and leading to the greenhouse; then returning, there is a valley, mostly near the hanging ground, from which there is a fine prospect, and turning more to the right is the Botanical walk, in which there are evergreens of almost all kinds; from this one descends to a piece of winding water, in which there are four or five small islands and a large one. A narrow walk leads from this part over the river, which conducts to a wheel for raising water, an invention of Mr. Hamilton's; it consists of four spiral square pipes from the radius to the center, the mouth being open; it conveys the water to the axel where 'tis emptied, and the water is convey'd by pipes to the piece of water I have mentioned. From this place the walks are through the wild wood, and leads to an old farm house, where the great lawn first mentioned begins. The whole circuit is four miles, and there are a great variety of fine prospects from the different parts of it. The whole to be improved consists of 300 acres. They have all sorts of pines and firr trees in this place, particularly the Jerzey firr or pine, and they have much of the Virginia acacia as well as cedar. There is one good room in the house in which there are some fine pictures, particularly two of Paulo Panini. There are ten acres of vineyard here in two places; the grape gently press'd makes an excellent champaign, and pressed out, and left on the husk, produces a very good Burgundy; five or six hogsheads have been made in a year, and it sells at the inns here at 7s. 6d. a bottle.

Cobham is a very small town full of inns.

About a mile from it is   , late Mr. Bridges's, now
Sr John Ligoniere's. It is a beautiful house, and there is something
very curious in the contrivance of having two stories in some part
of the house to one in another part.

This I have also formerly seen, and most of the following places
in this country, taking the course of the Mole. This river rises
about Leth Hill, to the top of which there is a gentle ascent from
Wotton. Towards the bottom I observed a brown kind of alabaster
in veins of different shades, a specimen of which I brought away.
There is also a gentle descent on the other side almost to Horsham
in Sussex, eight miles from the top. From this hill one sees the
South downs of Sussex, all that county and all Surrey, part of
Hampshire, Berkshire, Oxfordshire, Buckinghamshire, Hertfordshire, Middlesex, Kent, Essex, and 'tis said part of Wiltshire, as
'tis thought a circumference in the whole of two hundred miles.
'Tis said that one part of the brow of the hill has fallen down,
occasioned by digging stones below, and the soil being red that it
is seen forty miles off. At the foot of this hill is Wotton, Sr John
Evelyn's, on a stream which falls into the Mole at Darking.
They found here in the churchyard a skeleton nine feet long, which
fell to pieces when they touch'd it. Mr. Jacobs also has built a
very pretty small box near this hill, in which there is great variety
of architecture; it is called   '   . The Mole for a
considerable way is the bounds between Surrey and Sussex. At
Gatton also, near the rise of the Mole, said formerly to have been
a town, Roman coins have been found.

Reygate stands in Holmsdale on a rivlet which falls into the Reygate.
Mole. The east side of the river is a sandy soil, and the west
is chalk, where it has been observed that young women are apt to
have swell'd throats, occasioned by some peculiar property in the
chalk there communicated to the water.

It is a large town. The Earls of Warren and Surrey built a
small monastery here of regular canons. It did belong to the
Mordaunts; at present it is in Alderman Parson's family. The

same Earls built a castle now in ruins, a vault of it remaining. Near Okewood, not far from the rise of the Mole, are pits, in which they say jett has been found.

A small house and garden here, to which the famous Lord Shaftsbury used to retire, has been greatly improved of late years.

Returning to the Mole towards Darking is Deepden, which, it is said, is a most curious situation and fine improvement of Mr. Howard's, encompassed as an amphitheatre with beautiful hills. Mr. Evelyn mentions a wild cherry here, that makes a wine like French claret.

Darking.

A little lower is Darking, a small town; it is said to have been destroyed by the Danes, and rebuilt by Canute. They dig cellars in the soft stone here.

Here the youngest son succeeds to copyholds of tenants dying without will. They have good markets, especially for lambs. The heath near is esteemed by some as the best air in England. The Roman road called Stone Street passes through the churchyard; and there is a large camp not far from the town, near Homebury hill, in the road to Arundel; it is a double trench, and contains ten acres.

Below Darking, I saw the place where the Mole runs under Box hill, the same I suppose as White hill, where there grows much box, and where they make box ware. I went up the hill, having first seen Mr. Fryor's park. I then took a view of Epsom, famous for its allom waters, which were formerly much frequented. Near it on a hill is Wood cote, abounding in trees, where they say there are signs of an old town supposed by some to be Noviomages of the Itinerary, ten miles from London and eighteen from   ,

Qu.

supposed to be Maidstone, tho' I think it must be much further. I returned by Leatherhead, where I saw the water come out from under the hill, about two miles from the place where it went first under.

I came by Mr. Reading's and by Effingham, Lord Howard's, who is distinguished by the name of this place. The Mole falls into the

Thames at Moseley. On the down near this the Roman road is seen from Darking to London. A Roman way also is seen between Guilford and Ripley, and between Richmond and Putney.

Between the Mole and the Wey, Mr. Fox, who has taken the name of Lane, has a good house, in which there is a fine room ; it is at East Horsley. Farther west, if I mistake not, in the parish of West Horsley, is Sheep Lees, the seat of the late Mr. Nicholas, whose grandfather was secretary to King James the First. He lately left it to Mr. Weston, pursebearer to Lord Chancellor King. This place is much admired for the beech wood which grows round the fields, and the great beauty is said by connoisseurs to consist in the outline of the woods. To the south east rises a small river that falls into the Wey, a litle above Guilford. On it is Albury, the seat of the famous Earl of Arundel, who collected the Oxford marbles. His grandson, the Duke of Norfolk, built a grand house here. But what it is most remarkable for is a passage under a hill, which was to have been a way to the house, but a rock at one end was the reason why it was not brought to perfection. Albury.

Heneage Finch, Lord Aylesford, bought it of this family. The famous mathematician, Oughtred, was rector of this place.

There was a round Roman building here, supposed to be a temple. and old bricks and tiles have been found on the heath, where there were marks of great buildings. St. Martha's Chapel, mentioned before as on a hill, is not far from this river. And at Chilworth were famous powder mills, but I do not know whether they remain at present.

At Bagshot I saw Lord Arran's great plantations and gardens. I have been also at most of the places on the Vandal which rises near Cashalton where Mr.   had an elegant house and garden.

Then it runs by Merton where Kenulph, King of the West Saxons, being murdered by Prince Kinehard in a harlot's house, that Prince was also immediately kill'd on the spot. Here was a monastery founded by Henry I., it was of Canons regular of St. Austin, in which a Parliament was held under Henry III. Litle remains of it but the large enclosure of flint and brick.

At Croyden rises a rivlet which falls into the Vandal. 'Tis said a royal palace stood to the west of the town near Haling, where **Croyden.** foundations are discovered by the husbandmen. It was given to the Archbishops of Canterbury.

The Archbishop's palace is near several ponds, out of which I suppose the rivlet rises; and there is a story of a torrent rising as a presage of dearth and pestilence.

The coals mentioned as a trade here was I suppose charcoal, a great quantity of which is made yearly out of the neighbouring woods, and vended at London.

I saw in the church Archbishop Sheldon's monument which is very fine, the carving of Deaths heads, the several bones of a skeleton, and other marks of mortality, are judg'd to be extremely well executed. To Archbishop Grindal also there is a monument in this church. The present Archbishop has much improved the palace. Archbishop Whitgift founded here an Hospital for decayed House keepers, and a free school. An old Hospital is mentioned here founded in the time of Henry VI. by Elias Davy, mercer of London.

Beddington near adjacent is the seat of the Carews, Baronets, where I saw the orange trees said to be planted in the time of Queen Elizabeth by Sᵣ Wal. Raleigh, are shelter'd in winter by a moveable cover, and were the first that were brought into England.

At Bottle Hill is a square rampart and a single ditch, and another on a hill near Katheram, which place is directly west of Westram, and is I believe the same camp I mention'd before.

Over the Vandal at some litle distance is Wimbledon, where the Saxons fell out among themselves. Ethelbert King of Kent was engaged in a civil war, and Ceaulin, King of the West Saxons, **Wimbleton.** defeated him here and killed his two Generals Oslan and Cneben; 'tis conjectured that a round fort call'd Bensbury may be a corruption from Cnebensbury. Here was a house built by S[r] Thomas Cecil, son of the great Lord Burleigh. A new house is built there, which Mr. Spencer inherits from the Dutchess of Marlborough.

On another branch of this river stands Towting, where there are several seats of the nobility, gentlemen, and citizens, and a hospital was founded here by the Bateman family. Here was a Priory of Black Monks, dependant on the Abbey of Bec in Normandy.

The Vandal passes through Wandsworth and falls into the Thames. **Wandsworth.** It is a disagreeable town. They have a manufacture here of brass plates for making vessels. To the east of the town where the roads part, one leading to Lambeth, the other to Chatham, from the fields over the river is an exceeding fine prospect, as it takes in a view of London, of Putney and Fulham, and of the country between.

A small river rises at Ewell out of a very fine spring, near it is **Nonesuch.** Nonesuch, which was a most magnificent palace, built by Henry VIII. The front of it in Speed's maps is hereunto annex'd, it was called before Cudlington; Queen Mary I. exchanged it with Henry Fitz Alan, Earl of Arundel, for other lands. He left it to Baron Lumley, who gave it up to the Crown. It was much damaged in the Civil wars; but Charles II. gave it the Dutchess of Cleveland, who sold the materials, with which the Earl of Berkley built Durdans now the house of Lord North and Guilford; which the late Prince of Wales took of him ; so that at Nonesuch there is only a farm house.

At the mouth of the rivlet is Kingston, first called Moreford, but in the time of the Danish wars the kings, Athelstan, Edwin and Ethelred, were crown'd here, and then it was called Kingstone. It was famous for the castle of the Clares, Earl of Glocester. And Hircombs Place here was the house of the king.

In the church are the pictures of the kings crown'd here, and of King John who incorporated the town. At the town house there is a statue of Queen Anne set up. There is a wooden bridge here over the Thames of twenty arches. To the east of it on a gravelly hill was a burial-place of the Romans, where the urns are often found.   At Combnevil also, a seat of the   , old coins have been found.

On the Thames, below Kingston, is Ham House, the Duke of Lauderdale's in King Charles II. time, and afterward Lord Disert's, his Dutchesses son, and brother to General Talmash.   Lower is Petersham, in a corner of the New Park, a most charming place of Lord Harrington's.   The house is built on the spot of Lord Rochester's house, which was burnt down in 1720.

Richmond,   •.

Below Richmond is Shene.   Here the kings of England had a royal palace, which, on account of the wholesomness of the air, was made choice of for the nursery place of their children.   And here many of the kings of England, particularly Edward III., died.   It was burnt down in the time of Henry VII., and rebuilt by him, and called Richmond, as he had been long Earl of Richmond.   The gardens here were much improv'd by Queen Caroline in plantations, buildings, and particularly with a hermitage and Merlin's cave. Henry VII. founded a convent for observant friars near the place. The rich prospect from Richmond Hill is very fine, and hardly to be exceeded by any inland prospect whatsoever.   The part now

Shene.   called Shene, a litle lower, is a very pleasant place.   Henry Vth, in 1404, founded here the house of Jesus of Bethlehem for forty Carthusians, and Edward II. founded a convent of 24 Carmelite Friars.   Sr William Temple had a house and garden in this place.

Lower down is Putney, where many citizens have houses. Thomas Cromwell, Earl of Essex, and Cardinal Wolsey's favourite, was born here, where his father was a blacksmith.

At a distance from the river at Dulwich, William Allen built an hospital.   Near this place   are Sidenam medicinal waters, as there are also at Stretham.   Near this place is Norwood, which used to be a famous resort for gypsies, 'tis a vast wood of the Archbp. of Cant.

Lower is Battersea, mentioned before; it extends to Lambeth, a very large parish that stretches to the Burrough. It is said to derive its name from Lome hills—that is, dirty station or harbour, and is divided into several parts:—the Deans precinct, Stockwell, Lambeth. Kennington. This last is, I suppose, the place of a royal seat, of which at present there are no remains, nor is the exact site of it known. Vauxhall is in the Prince's precinct, and the Archbishop of Canterbury's. In the Marsh and St. George's Fields the ditches are seen which Canute made when he besieged London and turned the course of the Thames from the King's Barge House (I suppose at the creek by the Spring Gardens) to a place below the bridge, probably the creek at Redriffe. And here he dyed of the excesses in which he lived.

Baldwin, Archbishop of Canterbury about 1183, made an exchange for this place with the Bishop of Rochester, and when his successors began to build a collegiate church here it was opposed by the members of the Chapter of Canterbury, who feared it might deprive them of electing the Archbishop.

The Archbishop's palace is a large precinct, with a church. library and grand hall. It is said that a Roman road was visible in St. George's Fields, where there is a medicinal water, commonly called the Dog or Duck Water, which is much esteem'd as a remedy for all scorbutick humours. I have been informed it is a mixture of allum and some other minerals.

Lambeth Wells, not far from it, is a purging water, as the other is of a binding nature. A litle further is Westminster Bridge, which, without all doubt, is the grandest that ever was built.

WALES.

Pulhelly, Aug. 15th, 1756.

I landed from Dublin at Holyhead on the 12th. I here saw, in a collection of Mr. Morris the surveyor, two different kinds of those bags which appear like a vegetable substance, and have a string at each corner as I described on the riff of Portland; the large black sort, he said, were those which contain'd the young of the ray; the long narrow yellow kind he hād found in the bellies of the dog-fish.

This gentleman is son of a farmer; first took delight in botany and now in the whole natural collection, and draws well; he has a brother, who has surveyed and published the Ports of North and West Wales. A third is a genius in some other way, particularly in finding mines, and is collector of Aberdour.

On the 13th I went 17 miles on the south of the Isle of Angle-sea, and observed at the north-west corner of the bay, to the west of a village call'd   being, as I believe, the bay of Aberffraw, in the sea coast, a curious green stone with shells in it; the whole bay abounds in this stone, but in the other parts it is without such petrifications. I observed a mineral water on both sides of the large bay of Maudraeth. We came to Abernai ferry, about two miles west of Carnarvon. This is called the Menay, being that channel which divides Anglesey from North Wales; there are four other ferries over it, Carnarvon, Moer-y-Clon, two miles to the east, Bangor, and Beaumorris. We left Carnarvon to the east, where I had formerly been, and went two miles along a marsh near the sea, and came to a natural small hill, which seemed to have been improved into a fortification, and is called Dinas Dinla. Some Roman coins have not long agoe been found there; and it is remarkable that one of the fords near is called Reedeh Equestre, another Redell Pedestre; so that it is supposed that the Romans used this place as a fortress. We then turned up from the sea, going near west in that fine country which lies between

Snowdon and the mountains of this promontory, which extends near to the Isle of Bardsey. Snowdon is a chain of hills, anciently call'd the Lordship of Snowdon, but one mountain higher than the rest is particularly known by that name by the English, and is the highest in Wales, but the inhabitants call it Mount Guedvà.

We passed by Sr John Wynne's, and in 4 miles came to Clinok near the sea, just at the approach of the mountains; it is also called Clinok Vaur, the great Clinok; it is a poor village, and is remarkable for nothing but a fine Gothick church, which seems to have been owing to an ancient devotion here to St. Baino, whose plain tomb is in a large handsome chapel, built seperate from the church, with a passage of communication, in which and the church are remains of some very good painted glass. The ancient rood-loft is standing, and they have a wooden branch to illuminate their church at their early devotions on Christmas day, which is a custom that prevails in most parts of North Wales. The church is built of several kinds of freestone, which was brought from some distant places. On the south side of the Communion rail is a chest cut out of one piece of wood, into which the people, who at this time come here out of devotion, put their offerings, and it is called Keif Beuon, as Dr. Willis calls it, but is pronounced Beino. As there was, probably, a sort of shrine here, so this fabrick might be built out of their offerings, which now go to the repair of the church. The people come to bathe in St. Beuon's Well, and children are left to sleep on the tomb after bathing for the rickets, which is part of the cure. The reading desk is within the skreen, and the minister comes out to an elevated seat in the body of the church to read the lesson. A friery was founded here in 616 by Guifluin or Guiddaunt, related to the Princes of North Wales; afterwards there were White Monks here; at Lincoln taxation it was a collegiate church of six prebends. In the mountains near they have very large flag stones. I saw a small room covered with two of them, and at the inn is a cellar in which the flags are placed on each side at top, so as to be the rests on which they have laid the flags which cover the whole,

extending about ten feet from side to side, and they are the floor
of the room over it. I here also first saw a sort of small pancake,
made with the addition of barm, and eat like butter'd oat cakes,
are served up with tea and very good, being call'd light cakes. On
the 14th we went about four miles through a very pleasant romantick
country, having the high rocky mountains to the left, and the sea
at about the distance of half a mile to the right. There is a foot
way over the mountains near the sea to Nefyn, but we turned
up between the mountains, and pass'd again between 'em towards
the sea, and in four miles came to Nefyn, leaving Pulhelly road
to the left. There are grous in all these mountains, and the
black game in Denbighshire; neither of them could ever be kept
confined so as to breed, but I have seen the black game confin'd.
Nefin or Nevin is a large village near a small bay, which is within
a larger called Porthdillyn, both very good harbours, and the Irish
packet often puts into the latter when the wind is strong from the
north and they can't reach the head. Here I met with two clergymen, who in an obliging manner offered to accompany me four miles
to Carne Madrin. We immediately came into a very fine country,
in the middle of which stands that high rocky hill call'd Carne
Madrin. At the foot of it we came to Madrin, the seat of Mr.
Bodvil, who divided the county interest with Sr John Wynne, but
proving the weaker, Ld Powis brought him in for Montgomery.
He has here a very fine demesne. We went half round the mountain in a beautiful valley, which almost encompasses it, and ascended
on the south-west side, there being an artificial ascent, so that one
rides all the way, it having been formerly a place of strength, of
which there are marks, several bulwarks being made of loose stones
in different places. On the top of all is the Carne, which seems
to have been in a circular figure, but very small, and so much
defaced as hardly to be discerned. This hill consists of a dark grey
granite in very small grains. From this spot is a most glorious
prospect of the fine country to the south-west, with only one hill,
and a few barrier rocks against the sea. Bardsay Island, the fine

country all the way to Pulhelly, Festiniog, and Harleigh, the coast all along to St. David's head, the mountains of Cadir Edris and Plinlimmon, on which I saw two years agoe the rise of the Severn, the Wye and the Ridal : on the other side Snowdon mountains towards Bala, the Isle of Anglesea, and the mountains of Wicklow in Ireland. I was shown a bay called Hell's mouth, by reason of the danger of coming into it which ships often did in stress of weather before St. Tudwal's road was known. I observed a church near it with a tower call'd San Ennyan Brenan, which they say is dedicated to a Saxon king of the name of Ennyan, which they pronounce Ennyan. Between this bay and St. Tudwall's road is a fine broad head of land most beautifully improved. This road has not been long known : it is shelter'd from the south by two small islands, and on every other side by the land. Tho' Bardsey Island appears from the hill to be joyn'd to the land, yet they affirm it to be two leagues distant, tho' by Norris's sea cart it is not a mile, which I believe is the truth ; it is about three miles round. There was an abbey founded here in 516 ; it has been called the Isle of Bards or Poets, or Aberdaron, and had the name of Insula Sanctorum, from the many holy men it produced. It has also had the name of Healy and Ynikalley. Didricus, Archbishop of Caerleon, resign'd his archbishoprick and retired to this abbey.

From this mountain, taking leave of my friends, I came five miles to Pulhelle, a small neat town consisting chiefly of one street about a quarter of a mile long, most beautifully situated between two rivlets that run along the strand when the tyde is out, which leaves the town a considerable distance, and 2 or 3 isles are form'd before the town, on one of which is a beautiful rock ; the houses have gardens towards the sea, and over the town is a beautiful hanging ground diversifyed with gardens and wood, so as altogether to make it a most delightful place ; they have some trade in supplying this part of Wales as far as Bala, and also southward, with matting, made of a grass that grows on the marshes, and they import lime stone from Anglesea, near St. Nicholas Bay, and make lime of it ;

they supply also this country and the south with the conveniencies of life brought by land from Chester. Irish boats come into the Bay and lay pots for lobsters and carry 'em off. The rocks about this place are of a yellowish stone, with small grains of a white spar quite through it. They have in this country a great growth of hemp, chiefly used for making fishing nets, and some of the poorest people make cloth of it, but they most commonly use flannell instead of linnen; they wear stockins without feet or shoes, being made so as to cover the upper part of the foot, with a hole to go over the toe. Their bread is chiefly made of a mixture of rye and barley; bread, cheese, potatoes, and fish is their principal food; they have the latter in great plenty, as well as fowls; their mutton is very small and excellent. They sheer their lambs and mix the wool with a coarser kind, and use it also to make felts. There are none of the Romish religion in Carnarvonshire.

1756, Aug. 18th, Machinleth in Montgomeryshire.

On the 16th I set out and rid six miles near the shoar to Criketh, where, directly opposite to H rleigh, is a multangular castle with two round towers at the entrance. They have a notion that all the strand between this and Harleigh was once dry land, and that a sort of a riff of stones (as I take it to be), a litle beyond a point towards Barmuth, call'd Sarn Badrig, was a causeway over to Bardsey, and is represented in Morris's Cart as dry at low water.

We went on five miles to Penmauvra, coming into a most beautiful romantick country, a fine vale of pleasant meadows, and most extraordinary high rocks on each side, in such figures as one would imagine gave rise to many Gothick ornaments. From this place we came down towards the strand call'd Traethmaur, and coming upon it, the most extraordinary scenes opened to us I ever beheld. On the strand some beautifull rocks, all round is a mixture of woods, rocks, high vales up between the hills diversifyed with meadows, corn-fields, and woods, and over them rise the high mountains and make a most aweful appearance. We travers'd the strand to the

north end, and passed two miles over some of these fine hills, and
descending to Tanibulch we had a view of the finest verdant
meadows I ever beheld, with a serpentine river running through it,
and such an charming variety on each side, as has been allready
describ'd.   I was here within two miles of Festiniog, where I lay,
1751, and went 14 miles from it to Carnarvon.   I observed coming
down the hills an accidental formation of a slaty-stone that exactly
resembled rotten wood, and the hills abound in a sort of ash-colour'd
granite, in very small grains, as far as Dolgelle.

On the 17th we proceeded over very disagreeable mountains for
seven miles, and descended to a narrow vale, on each side of which
on the mountain is an agreeable variety of rocks, wood, fields, and
meadows, much resembling the lower part of the Alps towards
Chambery.   We saw several curious bridges of one arch built on
the rocks, and many fine cascades, one in particular, call'd Afon
Gamblas, which tumbles down from high hills through the rocks
and trees, and makes a most agreable appearance as one walks up
the side of it.   We soon turn'd into another valley, much resembling
those in Ireland, which have high, bare rocky mountains on each
side, and crossing over the river on a bridge we came within half a
mile of Dolgelle to Fenner Abbey, call'd in the map and in the
Monasticon, Kimmer; they were Cistertians and founded by Lluellen,
son of Gervase, about 1204; nothing remains of it but the church,
with three narrow Gothic windows at the east end, and some pillars
in the church; both show it to be a building of the time the abbey
was founded.   There is a beautiful vale, which extends to the sea,
at Barmuth.   At Dolgelle they have a handsom new-built church
of hewn stone, and a manufacture of Welch webbs.   This town is Dolgelle.
pleasantly situated between the hills at the foot of Cader Edris,
which is 1,000 yards high, Snowdon being 1,200.   The road was
very rough in crossing the skirt of the mountain for three miles, and
we descended to a naked valley and in two miles came to a beautiful
lake with a good country beyond it, in the middle of which a green
hill has a very particular effect; this is some thing like the 7 churches

in the county of Wicklow, but the hills on each side are finer. We then descended to a most beautiful valley, the hills on each side adorned with woods and fields and some houses, exactly like Swisserland; we went round into it, and came, as I believe, into the high road from Flint, Ruthen, and Bala, and from Merionethshire into Montgomeryshire. Here, as in Carnarvonshire, we found the miles short, but in Merionethshire they are very long. This river falls into the Douy, which falls into the sea at Aberdouy.

We saw on the other side of the river an old seat, called Dolgeog, where they say is the house from which the Powis family came, and the estate belonging to it about £100 a year, lately sold by the Marquis. We cross'd this river on a bridge of many arches, and soon came to Machonlleth on a stream, which falls into it under a ridge of hills which divides the plain; it is an ordinary town, but full of inns, there being a considerable manufacture of Welch webbs and in tanning of leather. In the church here the rood loft remains, and many Gothick skreens to the different parts of the church, all adorn'd with beautiful carvings in wood. This place is thought to be Maglona of the Romans, where in the time of the Emperor Honorius, as Mr. Cambden observes, the Præfect of the Solensians lay in garrison under the Dux Britanniae, in order to keep in subjection the people of the mountains. And two miles off, near Penasht, is a place call'd Keon-Kaer, are remains of a round fortification, and Roman coins are found there.

Cardigan, Aug. 20th, 1756.

On the 18th we left Machontleth, and ascending the hills we went over some vales finely adorn'd with wood on each side, and observed one most singular riseing vale on one side in the form of the inside of a ship, like the Carinae at Rome, the whole being covered with wood. We came over the river Cyfnant into Cardiganshire, and began to ascend most dismal mountains, like those between Dungarvan and Youghall, in the county of Waterford. We travelled on them for three hours, and came into a fine uneven

country like Sussex, five miles of Aberistwith. This was not the
direct road, but we came into that from Llanidlos by Plinlimmon,
and were only 15 miles from that town, where I had formerly been.
Within a mile of Aberistwith we came to Llanbadan Faur, thought
to be Mauritania, where St. Paternus in the middle of the sixth
century founded a monastery and established an episcopal see,
which continued untill they murder'd their bishop, when it was
united to St. David's. In 1111 it was given to St. Peter's,
Glocester, and afterwards appropriated to the abbey of Vale Royal
in Cheshire. The church is in the shape of a cross, with a tower
in the middle. There are no marks of very great antiquity about
it. There are stalls in the east part, which is a common thing in
Wales. And on the each side of the east window is a common
monument shut up in a cupboard, as to preserve it from the dust.
This is the parish church of Aberistwith, and near it, towards the
river on a litle rising, are some old buildings, called Place Craig,
which they speak of as the spot of the bishop's house. We came to Aberistwith.
Aberistwith, which is situated on a rising ground to the north of the
river, and the ruin'd castle is on a promontory exactly like old Tyre
in miniature. On the south side of the river is a high, round hill,
the top of which is work'd into a strong fortification, with three
ramparts towards the land and a considerable outwork towards the
town. We saw another in our road this way, about three miles
from the town. This place is a good harbour for small boats, of
which they have several employed, chiefly in the herring fishery,
and in bringing lime stone from Milford Haven to make lime for
manuring the land. They are here a most profligate, lawless sort
of people, and do justice themselves on all strangers, and even on
gentlemen of the country who have difference with any persons in
this place, and often send 'em off with severe chastisements. I saw
an instance of it myself; they were assembled about the inn, and
ready to redress a pretended grievance, untill they saw it was
without foundation, there being no justice of peace residing in their
town.

On the 19th I went on and observed, on the other side of the river opposite to the old fort, a small hill with a barrow on the top of it, which seemed to be made into a circular bank, and probably it is the burial place of some chief. In about a mile we passed over the lstaith, the other river at the town being the Rydal, at the rise of which I had formerly been. Five miles more brought us near Lannistyt, which by mistake we left to the right. I saw the large church supposed to have belonged to a nunnery. A mile further is Lansanfride, another nunnery. We came into the road at Landoui; before we came to it we passed by a stone ten feet high and about five broad; there are many stones of this kind in the country, but not so large, all which I look on to have been burial places of some great people, or heads of clans.* In a mile more we came to Aberayron, on the river Ayron, which runs through a pleasant narrow vale, and at the mouth of it is a harbour for small boats. We went on three miles to Lanerth, on a hill near the sea, with a beautiful glyn or valley on three sides of it covered with wood, in one of which near the sea Mr. Lloyd has a house, which seems to be a beautiful and uncommon situation. We had a pleasant ride through a fine uneven country to Cardigan, situated between low hills on the river Tivy, which runs on the south and west of it, and a rill and rivlet on the north side make it a peninsula. Before we came down to the common near the town we passed between small hills, some of which seem to have been improv'd into a fortification, and near one of them is a large stone set on end within a sort of enclosure. At the south-west corner of the town is the old castle on a rock, with two semi-circular towers towards the river. The situation of this town is pleasant; it consists chiefly of two streets, for the most part very indifferently built. The church did belong to the priory, of which there are very litle remains; they were black nuns, and a cell to Chertsey, in Surrey. The town is situated about two miles from the mouth of the river, to which there is a bar. The country round is a very fine uneven country. A hill a litle above the town, the river on one side and the rivlet or rill on the

* Quære it not a Meny Cerw? See Rowland's Mona Illustrata

Cardigan

other, is something like the situation of three very noted places, Veii, Jerusalem, and Old Troy, where the Simois and Scamander meet, and I think most like the last, except that the ground of Troy is higher and more pointed towards the sea.   It is certainly a most beautiful spot of ground.   They have a small key here, but no great trade.   There was such a plenty of fish that salmon sold for a peny a pound.   Cardiganshire is a great corn country, for oats, barley, and some rye.   The soil is very shallow, and they manure it with lime; the fences are made of sod, on which they sow furze, for they want depth of ground to make other ditches.   The river Tivy rises near Rose Favre, and passes by Strata Florida, call'd also Strathur, Strat Flour or Istrad Street, where there was a Cistertian abbey, founded by Rhesun, son of Griffith, Prince of Wales, in 1164.   It was burnt in 1294, in the wars of Edward 1st with the Welsh, and was afterwards rebuilt.   Lower down is Tregavon, and below that the town of Llanbeder; the vale all the way from Cardigan to that town, as they say, is exceeding fine.

St. David's, Aug. 23d, 1756.

On the 20th we cross'd over the bridge at Cardigan into Pembroke shire, the same kind of fine country and the same shallow soil; they improve it here by mixing lime with sods and earth dug up in waste places, and thrown over the fields; this way the lime goes further than when it is thrown on the ground.   Near College we passed by a large stone, on which this figure was cut $\oplus$ and descending to Nevern, on the river Nevern, I saw the old church; they have in this country wooden latticies before the glass windows of churches, which have a very mean appearance.   This vale is very fine, the beauty of it consisting in hanging ground adorn'd with wood; two miles brought us to Newport.   Near the strand at the mouth of the river Nevern 1 went to see the church, which I suppose belong'd to the Augustinian friery here, tho' there are no remains of a convent.   There is a rood loft in it, and a chapel with the old altar remaining.   There are ruins here of a very grand castle. The entrance is a large pile of building, defended by two semicircular towers; on the left was a large building, to the south-east a tower multangular within; to the north-west another tower, entirely destroyed. There is a fine bay at the mouth of the river, and a litle further a small bay with a beautiful glyn leading to it and a few houses; this place is call'd Dinas. Three miles brought us to Fiscard. There is a bay here with a creek in it at the mouth of the river, which forms an excellent harbor for small boats, the bay it self being exposed to the north wind. Over this creek is the poor village of Fiscard, inhabited by fishermen and lime burners, there being a great demand here for manure; they bring the stone from Milford Haven. In five miles we passed under Mathus, a very fine summer situation on the top of an agreable round hill. After travelling six long miles we came to St. David's. This poor village is situated on a rising ground on the east of a rivulet, called the Alan; it is said that St. Patrick founded a monastery here to St. Andrew in 470. St. David translated the Archbishoprick of Wales from Caerleon to this place. Dubritius, his predecessor, being the first Archbishop of Wales, and tho' after 930 they were not archbishops, yet they continued to consecrate the Welch bishops to the time of Henry 1st, when it became entirely subject to Canterbury. Giraldus Cambrensis, archdeacon of Brecknock, was elected Bishop of this see, and went to Rome to solicite the Pall, by which he offended the King and Archbishop of Canterbury to the degree that he was outlawed, lost the bishp^k, and was obliged to desist. The 7 suffragans of St. David's met St. Austin, that is Worcester, Hereford, Llandaff, Llendonor, St. Asaph, Llanbellam, and Maryam, at an oak near Petbury in Gloc:shire.

.St. David's.

At the bottom of this hill is the cathedral and palace within a large enclosure which takes in part of the rising ground on each side, the gateway being on the side of a hill built to a fine octagon tower, which they say was formerly a belfrey, and is, according to the old custom; but others, and more knowing, say it was the courthouse, and that the jayl was in the gatehouse adjoyning.

Dr Willis has published an account of this cathedral, the architecture of which is of a very mixt nature, tho' originally it seems to have been of the fine Saxon architecture.   But the tradition is that the tower has faln and probably beat down a great part of the church, particularly almost all the quire, for at the east end three old windows remain, and the middle one, being probably damaged, appears now a Gothick arch; over them is a Gothick window of about 5 feet in length, only below the spring of the arch all the ancient pillars of the quire remain, the arches being all Gothic.   In the chancel are the three seats for the priest and attendants, who celebrated pontifically, and the Bishop's seat is singular, consisting of three stalls, probably for the Archbishop and two of his suffragans, in case they should happen at any time to come.*   There is a fine Gothic ornament over them, something like that at Exeter.   The under part of the seats of the stalls are carv'd in many odd figures. The skreen at the west end of the quire is highly ornamented in the Gothick taste; the Saxon arches are double turned after the old way towards the isle, but to the body they are partly Gothic workmanship, partly Saxon.   The present quire is in the tower, the lower part of the west side of which is old; all the rest is of Gothick architecture, except a few windows.   The south end of the Cross isle is ancient, with more modern windows built in it; all the pillars of the body of the church are old, covered with 4 semicircular pilasters over the large arches, but they seem to have been rebuilt, with the addition of Gothick arches in front of the passage under them along the wall; all the great arches on the pillars are old, except the two western arches.   The west end is all old, and the upper window is most singular in this manner, being as two quarters of a circle, or half windows on each side of the arch'd window. What they call the Bishop's door is narrow.   All the arches are finely adorn'd with Saxon ornaments, and most of them and the pillars with different ornaments.   The destruction of the church is

* The like at Hereford, which is said to be for the Archdⁿ and Chancellor; they are somewhat lower than where the Bp. sits, and the same at Durham.—*Note in MS.*

threatened by the same means as before, for the tower is split and the pillars have given way, so as to drive the arches of the body of the church much out of the perpendicular. Archbishop Peter de Leia, about 1176, rebuilt the cathedral; this was probably the Saxon building. In 1220 the tower fell down; in 1248 great part of the church was thrown down by an earthquake. There are tombs of many bishops and canons about the church. There is a remarkable monument in the midle of the chancel, which I judge was the old quire. It is of Edmund, Earl of Richmond, father to Henry 7th, and, it's said, this saved the church when Henry VIII. thought of removing the episcopal see to Carmarthen. The College is to the south of the Cathedral, with its cloyster and refectory. This is, it may be, the College for a master and seven priests, founded by William, Duke of Lancaster, and Blanche, his wife, and Adam Houghton, Bishop of St. David's, in 1365.

On the other side of the river is what they call the Palace, a very grand building, and what adds to its magnificence are the handsome small arches at top with battlements over them ; these arches were made for the water to run from the top of the buildings. They are adorn'd with pillars and grotesque figures ; they might be design'd to defend the roof against the weather.

The east side consists of the Bishop's hall with his bedchamber, at the end which might be afterwards converted into a chapel. There being a building of another kind built to the hall, which seem'd to serve as a bedchamber, with a closet to it; the hall has been divided to make a sort of withdrawing room. At the other end of the hall is the kitchen with a small chimney in it, but it is crown'd at top with a funnel to draw up the smoak, and from the walls and from 4 arches across 4 chimneys are built in a curious manner; there might be four grates which might serve as eight fires to roast the provisions. Part of the large oven also remains. The door to this building is singular. Pilasters of 5 sides of an octagon support a Corinthian cornice in the form of four sides as of a hexagon. The door to the grand building on the other side of the court is arch'd in this shape ⌐‾‾‾‾⌐, with an handsom cornice to it, and is finely adorned; over it are the statues, as they say, of King John and his Queen. For this building, they have a tradition, was erected to receive King John on his landing from Ireland; it consists of a very grand hall, a presence chamber, and the King's bedchamber on one side, and a room on the other, as for the officer in waiting. There is a fine round window at the end of the hall, divided into sixteen parts by carved work, and the frame is adorned with roses and flowers. This building is in the same taste as the other, and there is an ascent of some steps to both, there being a great number of arch'd rooms under them.

Within the great enclosure the dignitaries seem to have had their houses, one of the Treasurer's remains, and is built like a tower to the north of the palace. Bp. Barlow, in the time of H. 8th and Ed. 6th, began to destroy these buildings for the sake of the lead. The Bishops have formerly resided at Brecknock, but now live at Aberguilly, near Carmarthen. He was probably, in ancient times, the head of the Chapter, and he has a prebend or   out of the Chapter revenue, but no vote, and his vicar seems to have presided over the musick on his side, as the sub-precentor on the other, in the absence of their principals. I went a mile to a litle bay, made by the head of St. David's, across which is a bulwark of loose stones, and there are some signs of outworks, probably made by some piratical people who infested the road. This is the shortest passage from England, being about eighteen leagues from Wexford.

In these rocks are veins of small chrystal, said to be harder than those of Bristol; some say they are of an amethyst colour, but that it wears off with handling. On the north side of the bay is a quarry of very good slate. A mile east of St. David's at Carn-oehr is a sort of ore which looks like copper, and is, I suppose, mundik. Ramsey Island belongs to the Bishop, the rocks near it being called the Bishop and his Clerks; some of them have the names of some of the dignitaries, but there is no property in them.

Tenby, Aug. 25th, 1756.

On the 23rd we left St. David's, and in about three miles came to Solbay Harbour, a creek into which a small river runs, and a vessel of about 100 tuns may come into it at high water.   In about 3 more we came to some old coal pits near Roch Castle, which is thought to have serv'd as a beacon.   Six miles more brought us to Haverford West, situated on a hill over the river Kiog (?) which falls into Milford Haven ; it is the principal port town of this harbour, and chiefly consists of one street up the hill and the houses by the river.

Haverford
West.

There is a stone bridge and a draw-bridge across the water. There is a church on the hill built to a high tower, which seems to have been originally design'd for a watch-tower and for a place of defence, of which there are others toward the seaside.   There are two more churches in the town.   The castle to the north on another hill over the town is a very grand building in ruins.   At the lower end of the town on the river are the remains of the Priory of Black Canons founded in the twelfth century by Robert de Haverford, lord of the place.   There are remains of a large church in the form of a Greek cross very strongly built with narrow windows, part of it seems to have been blown up.   The trade of this town seems chiefly to consist of collieries.   The coals here seem very much to run into culm which they work up with clay and make it into balls, it is very good fuel, and they have good shops to supply the country. Some merchants of other places import wine.   Leaving this place we soon came to Frotorp collieries.   We saw an old ruined mansion-house to the left called Harrison, which now belongs to Sr John Packington ; and in five miles came to Pembroke Ferry which we cross'd, and in a mile and half arrived at Pembroke, a walled town pleasantly situated on a rising ground.   There is a vale to the south in which a small stream runs, and a creek to the north ; there is a bridge over the stream which runs into the creek and tyde falls in a cascade through the small arch.   The town consists chiefly of one street.   The grand castle in ruins is at the north-west part of

the town, it is large of a circular form and was defended by circular
towers, some of which seem to have been blown up. On the north Pembroke.
side are the remains of a hall and chapel and a very fine round
tower entire, the walls of it at bottom are 18 feet thick, a litle
higher 15 feet, the diameter within is 24 feet, there being a pillar
built in the middle, 6 feet in diameter, up to the first floor, which
is about 15 feet from the ground, the other three might be about
the same heigth ; the fine arch at top remains entire. There seem
to have been battlements round it which are now gone; it was
built with a very coarse gravelly mortar, and I think it is the finest
round tower I have seen. There is very litle trade in the town
except shops to supply the adjacent country. To the west of the
town is the Priory. Arnulph, Earl of Pembroke, gave St. Nicholas's
Church in the castle and some lands in 1098 to the Abbey of St.
Martin at Sayes in Normandy, who founded here a Benedictine
priory as a cell to it. It was afterwards given to Humphrey, Duke
of Glocester, who made it a cell to St. Alban's. There is a high
tower to the church and several ruins near it. On the 24th I went
five miles to the end of Pulcrahan parish to take a view of Milford
Haven, which is esteemed the finest in England. In the way I had
a view of a bed of oysters called Pannermouth on which I saw the
women picking them up; they are a litle larger and almost as much
esteemed as those of Colchester ; from this hill I had a view of a
litle seaport called Hubberston, to the north of Deale on the same
side further south in the beautifull bason near the mouth, which I
suppose is ten miles in circumference ; I saw the lighthouses on that
side on the point at the mouth of the harbour, and the litle village
of Nangle near opposite to Deal. The situations on this harbour
are very fine, and they say it is sufficient to hold all the shipping of
whatever kind in the King's dominions. The whole country here Milford haven.
is marvelously fine and abounds in wheat. By manuring with lime
they raise wheat, barley, pease, barley, and then oats; but they
reckon this is rather a crop too much. They have in this country
great plenty of limestone on this side of the harbour, only one patch

or two on the other. If they tryed they would without doubt find a great variety of marbles in these quarries. They have a black marble exactly like that of Kilkenny, which is full of shells, and is called the half-moon marble, with a mixture of coral in it; this is found at Templeton three miles north-east of Pembroke, and also at Mr Campbell's near Stakpole. The burning of lime for manure, and exporting the stone to be burnt, and corn to Ireland and other parts, and coal, is the general trade of this country. The coal does not cake but flames and may be burnt twice over. They have at Pembroke a club of the clergy and gentry, who meet once a month and have an annual subscription for buying the best books that come out, which are kept in presses, and circulate among them for reading.

Caermarthen, Aug 27th, 1756.

We left Pembroke on the 25th, and in about two miles came to Lanphy and saw to the left Lanphy Court which was a place of residence of the Bishops of St. David's; it was alienated by Bishop   and is now the estate of Sr Wm Owen. The grand hall built to the house is in the same taste as that of St. David's, with arches for the water to run through from the roof. In four miles we came to Tenby, beautifully situated on a promontory about half a mile in length, on the top of which there is a street extending the whole length of it; there are some good houses in it, but in general

Tenby.

it is ill-built. It depends chiefly on the coal trade, and vessels put in by contrary winds especially the south-east. The walls were built by Jaspar, Earl of Pembroke, uncle to Henry 7th, and repaired by Queen Elizabeth. This town with Pembroke sends one member to Parliament. To the south-east of the town is a promontory on which the Castle was built, and under it is the harbor which is defended by a mole on the south side on which alone it is exposed. Near the Castle Hill is the Island of St. Margaret, a high rock with a chapel on it, it is left dry at low water   From this I went under the cliffs below the tower, and at low water cross'd the river to the cliffs on the other side passing by some deep holes made by the falling in of the earth, and the tyde comes into them; here the rocks run in strata near perpendicular but inclining a litle to the north. We came to a bay on the other side of which we found in the rocks strata of oyster shells and also of other shells, and at top I saw a stratum of small shells. I returned by Finall, a romantick situation under a hill and crossed over to a ford to the end of Tenby next the land. On the 26th I went a league to the Island of Caldee, which Caldee. is about two miles long and half a mile broad; there are high cliffs round it with some few bays, the strata are likewise near perpendicular and run from the west and by north to the east and by south; a litle north of it is St. Margaret's Island to which there is a passage at spring tides, it consists of the same kind of rocks. Among these rocks are strata of different kinds. As going from the eastern bay to the north we came first to the stratum of coral then to one of St. Margaret's shells, and saw a variety of welks sticking to the walls. I went all Island. round the island and to the south-east saw some belemnites and asteriæ. The north part is marble, the south they told me is not. It is a fine island for pasturage, for corn, and for rabbits, and they have a spring of excellent water. Here are the remains of the cell which belong'd to St. Dogmael, and was given to that abbey by Robert Fitz Martin's mother. Tenby is famous for the largest Tenby oysters. oysters in the world, they are about seven inches over; in drudging for them we found the Echini, twelve fingers and fourteen fingers of the five fingers (sic); we saw a great number with the oysters sticking to them. I found a spungy sort of a fish full of water, and on pressing it a great number of cylindrical bodies came out like mamillæ and returned in when relax'd, which I suppose to be all so many different animals like the Polypus. They have also the Pecten which they call hens about two inches long, growing not much longer; both the shells are convex, whereas one of the shells of the scollop is flat. They also find in the sands at spring tides the echinus call'd   which is covered with a sort of hair; they are full of spawn, and the very thin shells are often found on the north coast of Wales as well as here. From Caldie we saw Lundy very plain and the land to the south-east of it about Ilfracombe in Devonshire.

On the 27th I left Tenby and in two miles came to the collieries of Sanderfoot, from this place they go on the strand to Larne, the collieries continue for about three miles eastward and sloops come on the strand and the carts go to them and load. They separate the large coal from the culm; the latter sells at 35*s*., the former at £5 a hundred, which is ten cart loads, of six barrels to a cart. In two miles we came to Erivare, Mrs. Elliot's, a handsom new large house built with battlements. We came into Carmarthenshire, keeping on the strand, and turning off from it about four miles farther; in two we came to Larne, situated near the rive Tavè on a creek, and on each side of two valleys water'd by rivlets; the situation is very beautifull and romantick. They have a well-built castle; a view of the front is here seen. It is remarkable for a bow in the middle, in which is the door, and the windows over it; the upper one was, it may be, the first of the kind of our Venetian windows. There is a tradition that it was built by Sr Jno Perrot. They have an export here of oats, barley, wheat, butter and beans. We here cross'd the ferry, and in two miles came to Llanstephan, where there is a good inn, and to this place travellors use to come who can pass at low water and avoid a troublesome ferry. On the hill over Llanstephan are ruins of a large castle. Here we came to the river Tavy, and travelled near it for about two miles; the country on each side is very fine, consisting chiefly of small hills well cultivated, and then we went about four miles at some distance from the river to Carmarthen.

Llandillo in Caermarthenshire,
Aug. 30th, 1756.

Carmarthen is situated on a rising ground, on the north west side of the river, which winds beautifully through the fine meadows; on each side of which are low hills, highly improved, which altogether form a most delightful scene, and the same all up the river with the addition of a fine cultivated vale opening on each side. The town consists chiefly of three short streets and a very large suburb; the old gates and some ruins of the walls remain, and very Carmarthen. litle of a large castle, which is turn'd into a jayl. There is a good key to which ships of 150 tuns can come up, as they have eleven feet of water. They have a great trade in butter for London, and of wheat, barley, and beans to all parts, mostly coast wise; and they are famous for pickled salmon. In the church is an old monument of Sr Risan Odoly or Risan Dowdal, with the couchant statue of a man and woman; and there is a very old one of one figure on the ground, with the right hand on the breast; this is the ancestor of Mr. Rice, of Newtown. Just without the town is the Northern road, and some litle remains of the priory of Black Canons, founded in 1148. Merlin, the prophet of the 5th century, was of this place. There is an ill built round tower to the town house.

On the 28th I went on by the river, and in a mile passed by Aberguilly, where the river Guilley fall into the Touy. Here the Bishop of St. David's has a house, and usually resides when he comes into the diocese. In this place Bishop Beck founded a collegiate church for 22 prebendaries, 4 priests, 4 choristers, 2 clerks, annexed by King Henry 8th to the collegiate church of Brecknock. Three miles further I passed a large bridge over the river Leffy, which falls into the Touy; a litle further we had a view of Treslane Castle, a singular situation on a high hill near the river, it belongs to Mr. Vaughan. Further on are several gentlemen's seats, gloriously situated and adorn'd with fine plantations, and coming towards Llandello-vaure, commonly called Llandillo, a spacious and extensive amphitheatre of low hills appears. This litle town is Llandillo.' situated under a hill on the Toui, and as it is the high road from many parts to Brecknock, Hereford, and many great towns on the Severne, there are good inns in it. Having a desire to see the furthest town this way I set out in the afternoon, and in three miles passed near Tarryaron, Mr. Gwyn's, on the foot of this hill, a large house, fine situation, and most beautiful plantations. In two more miles I came by Abermarlas, an old mansion house, belonging to Lady Maud, with a park ; and rideing five more arrived at Landovery, a small town near the conflux of two or three mountain torrents, one of which runs thorough the town, and between them both it is often terribly overflowed. It is supported by being a thorough fare from Brecknock, 14 miles off, to all these parts, being distant from Tregavon 14 miles, from Lanidlos 31, from Cardigan 28 ; to all the southern parts they go by the towns on this river. There is but one gentleman's house beyond to this place, which is to the north-west on the Brairè. There are ruins of a small old castle here on a litle hill, with outworks and 4 fossees round it. A litle above this place the mountains are not much cultivated, and make a very different appearance from the beautiful hills below. I saw in the church a very particular red and green marble, which they told me was of this country. We return'd by Langadoc, a very poor sort of a village, tho' a market kept at it. They call it 18 miles from Swansey, the road being in part by the river Southy, a branch of which rises near the river on which Swansey stands, but the greater part of the road is on the mountain to the north-east of the river. The fatigue of this ride was sufficiently recompenced by the beauty and variety of the prospects ; and descending to Llangadoc, we saw the fine cultivated hills which form an amphitheatre round the litle plain. One hill, in particular, to the north of Llandillo, affords the most delightful and rich prospect I ever beheld, especially as it is seen in the street going out of the town. At Llangadoc, otherwise Llancadane, the Monasticon mentions a collegiate church with a precentor and 21 canons, of which seven were priests, seven deacons, and seven subdeacons, as founded by Beck, Bishop of St. David's, in 1263, but doubts whether it was carried into execution ; near the church yard is an old building call'd, if I mistake not, Manner Court, and probably belongs to the impropriator, and might be the habitation only of the common priests who attended the service of the church. From Llandillo I walk'd a mile to Denver Castle, within half a mile of Mr. Rice's

house of Newton, belonging to his estate, and just over the river ;
it is a large ruin, with a fine round tower in it of much the same
size as that at Pembroke, but not so high. From the top of it is the
most glorious and richest prospect I ever beheld; below the river
winds through most beautiful meadows, and by Golden Grove on
the other side, the estate of the late Dutchess of Bolton, whose body
is deposited within the parish church ; there are fine plantations
about this place; we saw most delightful hills almost as far as Carmarthen, and the prospect up the river of all those hills and vales I
have already described in the way to Llandevery, and a view of the
upper part of the valley through which the river Southey runs near
to Llangadoc. I return'd by Mr. Rice's house, lately fitted up with
an addition of a turret at each corner and battlements at top. This
gentleman is lately married to Lord Talbot's daughter, and his
grandfather and Mr. Stanley of Hampshire and another gentleman
married the co-heiresses, daughters of Mr. Hoby, of Neath Abbey,
in Glamorganshire. This river abounds in pike, salmon, eels, and
seuin, rather bigger than herrings, which some say are young
salmon, others that they are a particular species of fish. The
country people fish in corricles, made of a few wattles in the shape
of a half oval, about five feet long and a yard broad, with a seat
across the middle and a hoop like a handle by which they carry it;
'tis cover'd over with tarr'd flannel, and in these they fish for
salmon, two of them holding a sort of a sceine net and draw it to
when they fish. They pitch night hooks with worms on the banks
for pyke and eels. I enquired here for the Ichthyomorphi Lluidii,
and found 'em to be what was called the Anthropo Morphe, but is
since found to be the Pediculus Marinus, of which I have seen preserved in spirits, and are a sort of a sea grub; they are found about
Anglesea and North Wales. They are here all flat, and are found
in two quarries of stone, which they say is not a limestone, one in a
field to the north of the town, where they are rather small, from one
inch to two inches long; the other, which I suspect to be a sort of
tortoise, in a quarry near the river and towards Denever Castle;

they are from 3 to 5 inches broad. I saw none of the whole length, and all of the other quarry are more compress'd; these are rather more convex, however. I do not imagine that the former were so much of the crustaceous kind as those of Dudley. They cover their houses here with a thin stone, which they bring from Pen Arthur, near Kilywen Lluid. They manufacture Welsh webs in this country only for their own use, and they make some very good blanketing of two breadths, being the same kind of manufacture, only a litle thicker and well knap'd.

Swansey, Septr. 1st, 1756.

I set out for Llanelthy, and went thorough the park of Golden Grove, which is very well timber'd, and from the heigths in it had several fine prospects. We soon came to the mountains, which are soft, but not deep. We had a view of the fine vale in which the river runs to Llangadock, and in it of Carigkennen Castle on a rock, and further to the north of it the hills call'd Kilimen Lloyd, beyond which is Pen Arthur towards Llangadock, and this must be the hill on which, it is said, there is a circle of stones called Bruarth Arthur (King Arthur's throne), like those at Role Rich. At the first entrance on the mountains are rocks of marble, of which they make lime on the spot; and coming on the other side of the mountain, I saw Chalybeat waters all the way to Llanelthè. We had a view of the vale in which the river runs to Kidweley, where I formerly was; it is a poor litle town. There was a Benedictine priory here subordinate to Shirbourne, and founded by Roger, Bishop of Sarum, about 1130. We had also a view of that fine vale in which the river runs which falls into the bay to the east of Llanelthi. Coming from the mountains we arrived at a small village call'd Llannon, said to be seven miles from Llandillo, which it took us up three hours to ride, and 4 from Llanelthè two hours more. We mistook our road, and going by an house of Sr Thomas Stepney's we came to Llanganoe, near the marsh which is cross'd to Langhor Castle, two miles further, which place is only 4 miles from Swansey;

but we in a manner came back 3 miles to Llanelthè for accommo- Lanelthè.
dation, a very poor town, where Sr Thomas Stepney has a good
house in which he lives. The chief support of this town are the
neighbouring collieries, which are very near it. There is nothing
remarkable about the church, but a small square tower to the east
of the chancel, with a very litle octagon spire on it. On the 1st of
September we went four miles to Llanghor ferry, but the tyde
being not come in, we went a litle higher and forded over after a
guide. This litle town, which depends also on the coal trade, is Llanghor.
prettily situated on a promontory, which is in the sea at high water.
There is a very pleasing valley in prospect to the north, through
which the small river runs that falls in at this place, which is but
four miles from Swansey across that neck of land which joyns that
promontory to the land, most part of which is called the land of
Gower, interpreted to be the Land of Men or Giants. If the tyde
had not been too far in, we should have had a very pleasant ride to
Penclah Burn, two miles to the south, but we were obliged to go
round by the marsh, to cross over a bridge, and then by a very bad
road 4 long miles to Penclaharn, known by the sailors by the name
of Burry Harbour, which is esteem'd a very fine one, the vessels
when the tyde is out lying on a soft bottom; and when the tyde is
out it is but two miles to cross over to that point of land which is
nearest to it at Llanelthy; here they load coal and bark. We went
three miles further on this head to Webley Castle, belonging to Mr.
Talbot of Margam; it is finely situated, commanding a view of the
country about Llanelthy, and of what they call'd Penbranhead, to
the east of Kidwelly, which I suppose is the same as Penbraye in Penbranhead.
my map, commonly call'd the quarter master's map, made by the
direction of Oliver Cromwell and engraved by Holler. We had
also a view of the fine rocky sea cliffs to the south west on this
point, and ascending the hill to the south east we had a fine view of
a vale between the hills which are the barriers against the sea at the
end and both sides of this head, being bounded on the east by a fine
bay, on which is a small town call'd Penrice at the south west angle

of it, and a litle to the south a church and house, a most romantic situation on the side of the rocks, adorned with wood and over the bay; to the north west the large castle of Penrice.   I stop'd and dined with Mr. Walker, minister of Penmahen (top of the rock), and going on we first pass'd through a most delightful uneven country and near Pennent Castle, then over a heath and soon came to the strand, over which we went 3 miles to Swansey, in all six from Penmahen.   We saw on the west side Oyster mouth, built near the sea and up the sea cliff, and the houses whited (as is the custom in this country) make a very pretty appearance.

Penmahen.

Llandaff [September, 1756].

Swansey is very pleasantly situated in the bottom of a large bay at the mouth of a river, which runs near the town through a very pleasant narrow valley, but higher up as well as that of Neath they say is rough and full of collieries.   I observed on the bay the stumps of large trees and also a boggy ground, that seem'd to have produced good turf, which shows that the sea has gain'd on the land.   They have built an handsome new church to an old chancel; it is supported by Dorick pillars with galleries.   In the chancel is an old tomb with a couchant statue, and a hatchment of Hugh Gore, Bishop of Waterford and Lismore, who dyed here in 1691.   When he lost his understanding, he was hurryed away by his Welsh relations, who made a new will, which after many tryals was set aside, and is quoted in the law books as a point of law.   In a chapel to the north of the chancel is a tomb of Mathew Cradoc's, deputy to Charles, Earl of Worcester, Steward of Gower.   There is also a tomb of the Hobby's of Neath Abbey.   There are remains here of a grand castle belonging to the Duke of Beaufort; it is in the style of that of St. David's, and it appears plainly that those arches and battlements were design'd as a shelter to the roof in an exposed situation.   The Herbert palace, also, was a fine house of about the time of King James the First; it is built round a court.   Over the entrance are the Herbert arms quartered with three boars' heads, and this motto often repeated round it, ILEƏKYMEROF, the English of which, I was told, is, " Where I take." This house, and a considerable estate in the town, descended with an heiress to the family of the name of Powel, near Cardiffe. There is a good key here and it is a large town. They have had great business in building ships, timber being plenty, but now in time of war they have litle business in that way. They have also a considerable coal trade, but the great support of the town are the smelting houses near it up the river, and a work for making iron plates, at a litle distance from the town, and dipping them in tin to make vessels of different kinds. On the 1st of September we cross'd over the ferry and went about two miles by the strand, on which I observed some very beautiful compositions of pebbles, that probably would be very fine if polished. We turned towards Neath, and passed between fine low hills cover'd with wood and corn, and commanding a view of the remarkable ruins of Neath Abbey and of the copper works on both sides of the river of Neath, of some villages on each side of the river above it, as well as of the valley and beautiful hills on each side of it, and especially of Mr. Mackworth's house and plantations, just over Neath, which also commands a very fine view. We descended to Neath Abbey, as it is now call'd, but it is in the parish of Cadveston, and I suppose was call'd by that name. Litle remains of the Abbey is left, except some arches, which seem to have been the ancient refectory. The church is much ruined, but appears to have been very grand, it is in the shape of a cross, there were seven arches in the lower part on each side, and seven windows, and as many over the great arches, and there were three on each side of the ends of the cross isle and of the chancel. It seems to have been in the finest and highest Gothick taste. Richard de Grainville (one of the twelve Norman lords to whom this country was granted) and Constance his wife gave this church in their castle and the tythes belonging to it to the convent of Savigney near Lyons, who founded an abbey and put into it the order of Savigney or Fratres Grisei, who became Cistercians. A large house in the manner of building of the time of King James 1st was built on the spot of this abbey, and now it is inhabited by labourers in the neighbouring works and mines. It belongs as mentioned before to the families of Rice, Stanley, and   who married the three co-heiresses. I went a small mile to Cadvestone and returned and went over the bridge to Neath, a small town which depends on the collieries, copper works, and great markets for cattle, which are bought up here by English graziers. They have built a handsome new church to the old tower. And there are remains of an old castle defended at the angles by circular towers. At a colliery near this town, belonging to Mr. Powel, and if I mistake not called Melinanthen, they find a slate near the coals in which there are impressions of fern and other plants of which I procured a specimen.

I set out on the east side of the river and passed near Briton ferry, where Bushey Mansell, the last Lord Mansell, had a very pleasant house, in a most shelter'd situation, with fine plantations about it, it now belongs to his only daughter. He was third son of the first Lord Mansell, was succeeded by his grandson, who soon dyed; then the title came to the second son . . . . . his sister was married to Mr. Talbot of Laycock in Wiltshire, to whose son the estate was left: he is Mr. Talbot, late Minister of Coling-born in Wilts, who at present lives at Margam, to which place we went six miles, having steep low hills to the north all abounding in coals. I omitted seeing the mountain Mynydh Drymmee to the left of the road in which I came to Neath over the Abbey, where a stone is mentioned call'd Gistvain (the stone chest), another Maen-hire (the great stone), near which are two circles of stones, and south of them a smaller stone set up at end. At Burton ferry a chapel is mention'd supposed to have belonged to an hermitage.

[September, 1756]

Margam is pleasantly situated at the foot of the hills, about a mile from the sea. In 1147 Robert, Earl of Glocester, founded an abbey here: they were Cistercians. In 1210 they entertained

King John and his whole army in their way to Ireland, and on his return he excused them paying a tax laid on the Cistercians. It became the estate of the Mansells, who were enobled in 1711. The second lord was grandson of the first; he was succeeded by his uncle, who was succeeded by the youngest son of the first lord, and was the last of the family. The second son cut off the entail and left the estate to a sister's son as above, the Rev⁴ M˙ Talbot. A very large house seems to have been built out of the old abbey, great part of which has been taken down by the present possessor and by the last Lord. The chapter house remains, and is a very fine building, covered with an arch rising from the middle pillar, which was composed of eight round pilasters, from each of which spring three ribs of arches, 24 in all; it consists of twelve sides. There was one grand entrance from the cloyster under 2 arches, with a small one on each side, on each side of which were two large arches. There seems to have been another entrance from the north by a fine Gothick porch. The body of the church remains, the arches of which are of the most simple Saxon architecture, the pillars square and quite plain, corresponding with the double arch; some of the old windows of the north isle seem to remain which are very plain; on the south side are some remains of the inside wall of a Gothick cloyster. In a chapel to the south are four grand monuments with couchant statues, probably the four generations from the Reformation, there being a grand table monument to the father of the first Lord in the chancel. To the north of the church is a Gothic building called the infirmary, and in the street there is a Gothic peculiar cross of one stone, and on the side of the hill in the wood a large ruined chapel. In the garden they have fourscore large trees, mostly oranges and lemons and some citrons and bergamots, which usually supply the family with fruit; the first Lord used to send of the fruit every year to Queen Anne. They say that the original of them were some taken out of a shipwreck and that they have kept them up ever since by graffing. The park and estate is finely timber'd, and a rivlet runs down the hills through the park and by the house, which might be improved into a very beautiful thing. There are very fine stables here built by Sr Edward, father of the first Lord. The ceilings are adorn'd with stucco fretwork, and the stalls are carv'd: some of the best rooms of the house are over the stables. To the east, on a rising ground, is a very fine summer house of two floors, and built of hewn-stone and cover'd with lead, the stair case is very grand, fineered with walnut, and the balusters carv'd in Corinthian pillars, the floors are inlaid, the wanscoat carved and gilt, with marble slaps to the windows, and the entrance paved with marble of different sorts, some of which are very beautiful, and all from the quarries of Gower. On the hill of Neath I saw the English land, about the bounds between Devonshire and Somersetshire, between Mynhead and Ilfracombe, which is computed seven leagues over. On the 2nd I went on and soon came to Eglwys Nunny, said to be a nunnery to Margam Abbey. The present house seems to have been an old chapel, the west end, with a cross on it, remaining. A litle farther in the road we saw on a rough long stone this inscription:—

P: MPEIVS

CARANTO PᴊIVS

We then pass'd in sight of the ruins of Kentig Castle among the sand banks, which belonged to Robert Fitzhammon; the town was on the sea, but was burnt in the wars, and it is said there are hardly any signs of it. The Lord of Margam puts in annually the Constable of the Castle. I went two miles further to Newton to see a spring, to which there is a descent by several steps, it flows and ebbs contrary to the tyde; this has been accounted for by supposing that there is a natural syphon in the earth. In the church is a stone pulpit, on which there is a barbarous relief, of one standing, and a person on each side holding his legs with a cord, and having a flagellum in the other hand lift up to strike with it: whether this is designed to represent the scourging of our Saviour, I cannot say. The people have lately put up a very bad picture of the Ascension. We travelled about a mile round by the strand to the mouth of the river Ogmore, and soon passed near Ogmore Castle, which belonged to William de Londres. We went a litle higher and came to two passages under the rock, through which a rivlet falls into the Ogmore, and near that on an eminence is the small covered chapel cal'd St. Roch, with a remarkable open belfry for a very small bell. We crossed the Ogmore on a bridge, and came to Wenny on the river Wenny. Here was a Priory of Benedictines, Wenny. founded by S[r] John Londres, Lord of Ogmore Castle, and given by Maurice de Londres as a cell to Glocester Abbey. The cross isle and east end of the church remain entire, but of the church only one row of pillars, which are four feet diameter, the capitals of which are very plain. There is some very singular architecture in this church, as every other turning of the arch from the pilasters is circular, which is something of the Gothick; and the pilasters are Attick and supported by consoles, this order being rather in a barbarous taste. The tower is very large and ·entirely in the simple Saxon taste. Wenny is a large scatter'd village, and they have a pottery in it. There is a very good mansion house adjoyning to the church in which M[r] Turberville lives, the last of the descendants of the twelve Norman chiefs; but the estate of Corfy has been for some time out of the family.

[September, 1756.]

From Wenny I went a mile to St. Bride's, where, in the church, is a stately Gothick monument of the Butlers, two couchant statues, and the ornaments round the figures are very fine Gothic workmanship. We went a mile to Nashe, which was the grange, as is commonly said, of Netley Abbey, but I should think more probably of Wenny. The shell of the barn, almost entire, is, they said, 215 feet long. The point here on the sea has its name from this place, and near this point, two miles farther, just on the sea, is St. Donat's Castle, the seat of the Easterlings or Stradlings, one of the twelve Normans; it is a very noble pile of old building round a court, and kept in fine order. There is a grand old hall, with the arms of the

S. Donats
Castle.

twelve Normans, and an account of the estates which fell to the share of each of them; from the top of it is a glorious view (which we had mostly in our ride) of the sea and of the coast of Devonshire and Somersetshire, and that so plain that we could distinguish the fields.   The court is adorned with busts set into round niches; and there are hanging gardens down towards the sea.   The descent to the church, in a hollow on one side through groves of trees, is very beautiful and romantic.   In a chapel on one side was the family burial place, in which the oldest monuments are some pictures of the 16th century.   In the middle is a fine marble tomb to the memory of the last baronet and of his elder brother; the latter had a great character, and dyed, if I mistake not, at two or three and twenty; the other dyed at Montpelier, at 28, in 1738, neither of them having been married.   The estate came to Lord Mansell, and is now by Chancery divided into four parts; this castle and about 700 a year belonging to Sr John Tyrwhit.   Some bad paintings are mentioned in a house below the castle, which I could not see as it was lock'd up.   About a mile to the west is Lantwich Major, or Llan S^{ti} Ittuti. I was too late to go to it.   Germanus and Lupus, who were to extirpate the Pelagian heresie, form'd a University here, and it is said there is an old church there, and an older west of it, and a remarkable stone in the church yard.   It is not settled whether Bovium was at Cowbridge, or at Boverton, near this place; a gentleman, who is of opinion that it was the latter, saies that there are some remains there.   The ride from this place by the seaside to Cardiffe

Cowbridge.

is, they say, extremely fine.   I went five miles to Cowbridge, situated in a fine country on a small rivlet which falls into the sea.   There are remains of the walls and gates.   There is a well endowed free school founded here by Sr Lionel Jenkins, who was of mean parentage near this place; there are exhibitions from it to Jesus College, to which foundation he left £800 a year, and some annuities to relations to be paid out of it.   On the other side of the rivlet is Llanblethien Castle, which belong'd to Robert St. Quintin, one of the 12 Normans.   The grand gateway is Gothick, but the building within

it seems to be very ancient, was probably British; the walls are
eight feet thick, the outside for about eighteen inches is built with
lime, but all the rest with a coarse clay. On the other side of the
road is a large ruin, as of some office. On a hill to the west is a
parish church, and near is a ruin as of an old church. From
Lanblethiean I had a very distinct view of Lantiscent (Church of
three Saints), near which place is Lord Talbot's estate, which came
by his wife, an heiress of the family of Jenkins, of Hensol. About
two miles west of Cowbridge is Golden Mile, where Robert Fitz-
hammond beat and slew Justin ap Gwrgant, the last British prince
of this country. From Cowbridge we went on and came to a heigth
near to S' Edmond Thomas's, which commands a very fine view of
Bristol Channel, the Holmes, Somersetshire, and King Road, and of
the beautiful country of Glamorganshire; and after travelling a few
miles we came to Llandaff, on the river Taaf. This church was
founded by St. Dobritius in 520. There is a grand Gothic entrance
to the church, but nothing of the old Saxon building, except two
fine Saxon doors on the north and south sides very highly adorned.
The Gothick windowes of the isles remain, and they have finished
it above with sash windows like a play house, and made a modern
front of Roman architecture, and the east end in the same style
with a Venetian window, so that altogether it is the most absurd
improvement that ever was made. Another particular I observed
in this church is monuments erected to children of a few weeks old,
which I am told is common in Wales. This church lost its great
estates soon after the Conquest, when the first church was destroyed,
and it was rebuilt in 1147. The north-west tower of the church
was built by Jaspar, Duke of Bedford, which probably is that of
the later Gothic front. The Bishops did live in the castle. It is
said there were Roman remains in the Bishop's garden, on which
spot Admiral Mathews built a large house. Coming to Llandaff we
saw to the left St. Tegan's, the estate of the late Mr. Lewis, now
Lord Plymouth's, where, in May, 1648, 3,000 of the Parliament
army beat 8,000 Loyalists, having had a skirmish the day before at

Ely Bridge, which we passed a mile before we came to Llandaff. In two miles from this ancient see we arrived at Cardiffe.

[September, 1756.]

The town of Cardiffe is pleasantly situated on the river Taaf, about two miles from the sea, the river running through a dead flat, something inclining to the marshy, which makes the air of this place rather unhealthy. The walls of the town are above a mile in circumference; the principal streets are pretty well built, but there are many indifferent houses towards the outskirts within the walls. There is a fine tower to the church, adorn'd with beautiful Gothic pinacles. Without the town, to the north-east, is a very fine old house in ruins, built with beautiful bow windows of the architecture of Queen Elizabeth's time; it is on the spot of the Black Fryars, and belonged to the Herberts, as did the great house at Swansey, and it is now the property of Mr. Powel. To the north-west are some litle remains of the White Friars. At the north-west part of the town is the castle, near a measured mile in circumference, encompassed with a wall and deep fossee. The entrance of the castle seems to have been built about the time of the Conquest; in it they show the small room, in which they say Robert, the elder son of Henry 1st, died after 26 years' imprisonment. At the north part of the castle is a large mount, on which there is a building of ten sides, and vaults under it; this I should think the oldest part of the castle. On the west side is a fine Gothic building with beautiful bow windows, in a singular style, with coats of arms in each of them; this building consists of two stories over the grand floor. In this part I have been inform'd are the arms of Richard Beauchamp, Earl of Worcester, with a scutcheon of pretence of Isabella le Dispenser, his wife, the heiress of that family in the time of Henry 4th. This castle did belong to Robert Fitzhammon, leader of the 12 Norman knights who conquered Glamorganshire, and held their castles of him. The Red house, the principal inn of the town, was built by the ancestor of Mathews of Thomas town, in Ireland; it is a fine old house, with old wainscoat, &c., and some old furniture remains in it. This town subsists chiefly by being a thorough fare, and by its shops and markets, and some iron manufacture. From Cardiffe we went northward, ascended the hills and came to some collieries; they find a stony stratum for 5 or 6 feet before they come to the coal, and on the outside of this they meet with a vein of iron about a foot thick. We descended the hill to the famous castle of Caer Philley, situated on a rivlet in a bottom encompassed Caer Philley. with hills, five computed miles from Cardiffe. This castle which, without the least doubt, is British, consists of three kinds of architecture; one rather simple, and seems to be an imitation of the Roman walls round their towns, and consists of 3 solid towers or rather upright buttresses nine feet broad, seven feet and a half deep; the wall on each side is built in a strait line for one foot eleven inches, and then in about a quarter of a circle for seventeen feet six inches; these arches in the wall are strengthened at bottom by buttresses, which come out so as to be even with the wall, and rise with an inclin'd plane to the heigth of twelve feet and end in a point. These buttresses seem to be an imitation of the Roman architecture, but the circular part is caprice, contrary to all the rules of architecture, by which a building, erected for strength, was weakened on the south side; adjoyning to this wall is a fourth tower, which is semi circular, and seems to have been on one side of a gateway over the rivlet, there being another on the other side, which was a way leading to this part of the castle, there being a large semicircular building to the south of the rivlet, defended by two other such towers, one at the bottom of it, the other on the other side. The first building mention'd seems to have been a simple square enclosure, of which there are some plain marks within, tho' every thing there is destroyed. To this most singular wall, which I have described, there joyns on another building of as singular a kind. First, a very large tower ending in a semicircle, which may be 30 yards in diameter; at some distance from this, but joyn'd by a wall, is a very grand gate-way, defended by towers

of five sides, near this is a smaller entrance, and then at equal
distances are four large towers of five sides; but to the sides
on each side of the middle part, as well as to those on each
side of the gate are buttresses rising up, it may be, fifteen feet
in the shape of a half pyramid, which shows the odd humour of
the architect in making those towers of five sides, which would have
been stronger, if they had been only of three. The third kind of
architecture is Gothic, and is in a manner a very grand castle within these with a magnificent entrance and a very fine round tower at
each corner, the walls of which are about ten feet thick, and the
diameter within about twenty. They all of them appear to have
been destroyed by force except one, and one of them is a very great
curiosity: it seems as if they had undermined it, so as that one side
sunk down and broke off from the other part and overhangs eleven
feet, a drawing of which may be here seen. There is a grand hall
on the south side, and the consoles from which the arches rose are
adorn'd each with three heads not ill done. It is observable this
extraordinary building is not mention'd before the time of Edward
2nd, before which time probably this great addition was made, and
caused it to be look'd on as a very strong fortress, which without
doubt belonged to some of the most powerful Princes of this country.
It was afterwards in the possession of the Clares, Earls of Glocester.
Mr. Watkins is of opinion that this was the Bulæum Silurum, and
that he found a farm house near it call'd Caer Vace (the Royal City)
and refers to Baxter on Bulæum. A litle beyond this place is a
manor in which the lands gavel and divided into many small farms;
the country is exceeding populous. Leaving Caerfily we soon came
to the river Romney which divides Glamorganshire from Monmouthshire, aud travelled by it in a most beautiful hilly country,
coming into Monmouthshire. In the road I was shown Ruperra
summer house, where Mr. Watkins told me he was inform'd by
Mrs. Morgan the proprietor that a skeleton was found upright but
soon fell to dust.

We went on to Tredegar Park and to an old British camp on an eminence in it, defended by three fossees. From this place we had a fine view of the country, and saw under us Mr. Morgan's large house where there is a very grand greenhouse. From this place we came to Newport.

[September 1756.]

Newport is finely situated on the side of a hill and on the river Usk. Near the church on the hill is a Celtic tumulus, with a large tree on the top of it. To the castle on the river are two grand Newport. entrances, one of which was to the water, where the tower on each side is of five sides, and strengthened with such buttresses as at Caerphily. They have a way of collecting coals on the slub on each side of the river, when the tyde is out, and have boats for that purpose; among it there is a great deal of charcoal. When a tax was imposed on this coal they left off collecting it, and took it up again when it was taken off. This is a poor town, but as it is a great thoroughfare there are two or three good inns. From Newport I went three miles by Christ Church on a high hill to Caer Leon. This was the Archbishoprick over the seven Bishops in Britain, independent of any Patriarch before the coming of Austin the Monk. This was Isca Legionis. The second Augustan Legion was stationed here, and they find on the bricks LLG · II · AVG. It is situated on the river Uske. One may trace the old fosse round the walls, and many Roman bricks are found about the place. The hollow of an amphitheatre appears about 25 paces from the walls. There were eight vomitoria to it about six yards wide, at the distance of about 22 yards. There are some stones round an old cross in the churchyard which I thought might be remains of the seats. I went five miles to Pontepool in a very romantic situation between the hills on a rivlet which falls into the Uske at Caerleon. Here Major Hanbury, father of the present possessor and of Sr Charles Hanbury Williams, ambassador in Russia, set on foot great iron works of many kinds, which occasioned a litle compact town to be built here. The houses and buildings belonging to this manufacture are scatter'd, and extend for above a mile along the river. Here they work iron from the ore into several sorts of utensils. They make wire, nails, and plates of iron for tin. This latter secret was learnt in Saxony, but immediately improved, for they did it by hammers; but Mr.

Pontepool.

Hanbury invented 2 iron rollers, which can be scrued together at any distance. They take a piece of red hot iron about four inches broad and five long and put it between the rollers, which roll it thinner; then they double it and heat it, and so continue doubling and putting it between the rollers untill it is thin enough for the purpose; the thinnest they make is for tags to Manchester laces used by the ladies, 450 of them go into a box 5 inches and $\frac{3}{4}$ deep; these plates being soak'd in a composition of thin sal armoniac, and some other things are dip'd into fire, which, especially in the thin plates, incorporates with the iron. What they call double block tin is done with a finer tin, and is less apt to rust, as well as the very thin sort. Of a thicker kind of plate they make salvers and candlesticks and many other things which they japan; I am told the light parts of this in imitation of tortoise shell is done with silver leaf. They adorn them with Chinese landscapes and figures in gold only, and not with colouring, as at Birmingham. This ware is much better than the Birmingham, but is dear, there being only two brothers and their children, who make it and keep it as a secret. They will also japan copper boxes, or anything made in copper which they cannot well work in iron. Mr. Hanbury has a good house and gardens and a fine park here, and it is a most delightful summer retirement. They have a particular way of procuring iron ore; they make holes in the mountains for rivlets to run into, which bring down iron ore when there are floods, and when the waters fall they pick it up; some time agoe the rock open'd in the bed of a river, and the water took its course down the hole, but this carrying off the water, the country people fill'd up the hole, and the rivlet took its usual course. The manufacturers and miners all over the country wear crimson flannel shirts and no other garment over them, which looks very well, and is proper to dry up the sweat of those who work at the fire, which it is said would otherwise prejudice their health. From this place having been most generously entertain'd by Mr. Hanbury, I went five long miles to Uske. This is supposed to be the Burium of the Romans; there are remains of a large town, most of which seem to have been built about the time of Henry 7th and before. It was a flourishing town, for they had the iron manufacture here, particularly of nails, till within these fifty years, that it has been moved to Pontepool; there are several good Uske. old houses in the town. There was a religious house here; the church is now the parish church. The old tower is the only remains of the Saxon building. In the house near which seems to have been the site of the convent are no remains, except an old square tower. The castle on the side of the hill over the town seems to have been mostly of the British architecture.

[September 1756.]

From Uske I went four miles to the south east up to the point of that hill which is known by the name of Wentwood, and extends a good way to the north, being a forest, which belongs to the Duke of Beaufort; on this point is a ruin'd building call'd Kemys's folly. We went up to it to enjoy the fine prospect, which takes in the British Channel, Somersetshire, King road, King's Weston, the mouth of the Bristol River and the Severn and Gloucestershire, Wentwood every way indeed a most glorious view. We descended and passed by a chapel in the middle of a clump of yew trees, and came to Penhow Castle, a small private fortress on an eminence, most of which is destroyed, to make room for a modern house; this was the seat of the St. Maurs. Near this place we lay. About three miles to the north is Strigol Castle, from which place the Clares, Strigol Castle. Earls of Pembroke, had the title of Earls of Strigol; it was built by William Fitz Osborn, Earl of Hereford.

On the 7th we went on two miles to Llanvour Castle, which seems to have been a litle fortifyed town on an eminence with a castle at one corner of it, and probably some people retir'd to it after the destruction of Caerwent; there is a low wall remaining in one part with a semi-circular water table, and there are remains in another part of a round tower and an apartment like one of the old halls; the walls extend near a mile in circumference. I copy'd out this extraordinary inscription on the style to the church yard—

> Whoever hear on Sonday
> Will practis Playing at Ball
> it may Be before Monday
> The Devil will have you All.

We went a mile further to Caerwent, the Venta Silurum of the Romans, situated on a flat ground near a rivlet which falls into the sea near Caldecot Castle, and it's said there was navigation to this town; the walls are built with towers of five sides, as I suppose, at about thirty paces distance, for I found two of them to be so far apart; there are some remaining on the south side, and a sign of a tower built with the walls at the south-east corner. They have found a Mosaick pavement here with a beautiful border round it and in different compartments; I saw the figures of a stag and a bird, so that probably it was a temple to Diana the goddess of the neighbouring Wood of Went. They find a great number of Roman coins here, mostly of the Lower Empire. We went on another mile to Caldecot Castle, which did belong to the Constables of England, and gives the title of Baron to the Duke of Beaufort. On this spot Harold might have built his fort against the Welsh in 1066, which it is said they destroyed; it is a most noble building, about half a mile from the sea. There is a grand entrance to it, from which to the east there was a large hall and other apartments adjoyning; there is a round tower in the front of the entrance, and a square one opposite to it on the north side; and at the north-west corner a very noble round tower on a mount, with a semicircular tower adjoyning to it for a staircase, as I suppose, for we could not get into the tower; this seem'd to be the stronghold, to retire into in case of distress. Very near this is Port Sheath, and a litle beyond

Caerwent.

Caldecot Castle.

it at Sudbrook is a very strong semicircular camp with a triple ditch, it is on the sea-cliff; the bow measured within 330 paces, the string about 240, but it was not in a strait line. Near it is the small parish church call'd Trinity Chapel in ruins. There is a Roman road from it, and this seems to have been originally a British camp, yet it was probably made use of by the Romans. Mr Watkins makes this observation, on this road; speaking of the present passage, he saies, " higher on the Severn stands Aventon, the Abone of the Romans, which was the Trajectus into Britannia Secunda. It is ix. miles from Caerwent." He supposes the Julia via began there, and lead to Venta Silurum, and that the road we saw near the camp at Trinity Chapel was that road. He imagines that when the Romans landed at Aventon their ships coasted the Severn, and that this camp was thrown up in order to secure a retreat for their ships, and conjectures that after that they built Caerwent. This parish consists only of 400 acres belonging to Mr Vaughan, and is farm'd by one man. We went about two miles farther to Matharne, an ancient house of residence of the Bishops of Llandaff; it is but a mean building. Over the gateway are the King's arms and Bishop's, with an inscription under them; the Bishop's arms is the pall with an inscription in it and round it. We went near the new passage across the mouth of the Severn, about two miles below the old Aust passage, and in three miles came to Chepstow. We had seen the tower of Dundrey church on the heigth in Somersetshire towards Glassen bury, which is seen at so great a distance from many parts.

Chepstow is situated upon the side of a hill, on the west side of the Wye, which rises at the bridge fifty-two feet, and sometimes has risen to   feet, as may be seen in the Philosophical Transactions. The church did belong to the religious house of
founded

It is a very ancient Saxon building, the west part of the tower Chepstow. being made the east window; all eastward is entirely destroyed. The castle is a most noble structure, on a point over the river which is separated by a fossee cut through the rock. There is a very grand gateway, with round holes down through the arch to annoy the enemy. At the entrance to the left, at some litle distance, is a very fine large tower; on the outside round, and of six sides within. There is a private small chapel in it. On the right hand were the apartments of the castle. At the further end of the court is the gateway to another court, which is closed at the further end by the grandest building for a single room I have ever seen in any castle. It is about 90 feet long and 30 broad. The lower part is of Saxon architecture, but it has been rais'd, I believe, to the heigth of 60 feet in a Gothic taste. On one side is a bold piece of work— half an arch turn'd with Gothic members, so as to appear in the grand hall; it was for stairs to go up to the top. There are pilasters on the side of the building next the river, and four rows of Roman brick at the further end of the hall, about ten feet from the ground, which extend for about ten feet on the side next the river. There was a room under the ground room, and the great saloon was divided by a fine Gothic arch, within which it is probable was the bed of state. Beyond this is another court, leading to a gateway with a tower on each side of it; beyond it is a draw bridge, where the point is cut off from land. This castle belongs to the Duke of Beaufort; it formerly belong'd to the Earles of Pembroke, the last of whom was Richard Strongbow, who conquer'd Ireland, and by his daughter it descended to the Bigots. This town is in a flourishing condition, several branches of trade beginning to thrive in it, and it is a great thoroughfare into Wales.

[September, 1756.]

From Chepstow I went a mile to Persfield, Mr. Morris's, situated over the west side of the Wye; it chiefly consists of a long walk over the brow of the hill near the river, which in many parts ends in rocky cliffs cover'd with wood, and some of them are perpendicular; the furthest above a mile beyond the house is an eminence which commands not only a view of the Wye, but of the Severn, Bristol

Channel, and most of those places I have already mentioned. The next is at an iron rail over a perpendicular rock from which one sees below the wood, river, &c. The gardiner told us Mr. Morris was standing on the projecting rock and that soon after it fell down, on which he had this rail put up. The cliff must be between 2 and 300 feet high. We were then conducted to a seat, which is the most beautiful I ever beheld; the river winds so as to make a penin- Persfield. sula on the other side, which is a piece of ground gently rising to a point, on which there are two or three houses, and all this ground is diversifyed with an agreable mixture of corn fields, meadow, wood. This seat commands a view of all I have mentioned to the south, and moreover of Bristol Channel, in three or four different parts divided by the land. The walk then winds, and there are several seats of view; in one part where there are large stones they are making a small Druid Temple like Roltrich. On one eminence towards the house are several grass walks and a shrubery of a variety of plants, and beyond that the house, lawn, and plantations disposed in a very fine taste. This is one of the most beautifull places I ever saw. On the 8th I went ten miles to Ragland Castle situated on a small eminence, and the seat formerly of the Marquis of Worcester, and now belongs to his descendant the Duke of Beaufort; it is a noble ruin of fine hewn stone, I could not be inform'd from what place it was brought. At the entrance to the court are remains of a gateway of modern architecture. The entrance to the castle it self is very grand, there being a large tower on each side, with projecting battlements and holes all round to annoy the enemy. Adjoyning to these are several apartments with fine Gothic windows towards the court. On the right hand, at the north-west corner, was the Ragland kitchen in a tower, and the offices belonging to it take up all that Castle. side of the court. On the other side is a grand hall with a most magnificent bow window; the funnels of the chimney on the sides of a window over it. Adjoyning to this, towards the next court, were some fine apartments now destroyed; one chimney still remains adorned with two fine freizes, the entablature being supported by two Cariatides on each side; but what is grander than all, is a multangular tower of an irregular figure in the front, with a deep fossee round it, and a draw bridge to it which on the inside is defended by a tower on each side rising to the heigth of the parapet, for there is a terrace round this tower; the front part of it appears to have been destroyed by force, and we could find no way of approaching to it. To the south of all is a very grand platform as to walk on, and there is a view from it of a very fine uneven country highly cultivated. This place was, they say, destroyed by Oliver Cromwell. I met with a piece of an extraordinary stone in the village, which they say was in a jetteau of the court of the castle; it looks something like the ore of antimony, when rubbed it has a bituminous smell; I have a piece of it, in which there is a petrifyed cockle. From Ragland I went about six miles to Gethly, Mr. Watkins', which is three miles to the east of Abergavenny; and on the 9th we went a mile to the top of a high hill called Skirret Vawr, on the top of which are the foundations of a small chapel, dedicated to St. Michael; about half way down the hill is a litle valley to the west and a summit to the west of that, which the Roman Catholicks say was divided by the earthquake at the time of our Saviour's Crucifixion; and they come to this place and to the chapel in great numbers on Michaelmas day. This hill commands a very fine view. Two miles from it is Abergavenny, which I passed through in 1754. We went down and dined there, and rid up to the top of Blavons to the south of it; the prospect from it is very fine and extensive, as it takes in the whole country to the Bristol Channel, the Malvern hills in Worcestershire, as well as the hills of Gloucester and Herefordshire, and the fine vale up to Brecknock by Crickhowel which we saw very plainly, and the litle beautiful valley to the north of it. This hill abounds in limestone, and there are great numbers of lime kilns to burn for manure; in this limestone they find the Siliquastra or palates of fish, and Glosso petrae; and somewhere in these parts Lloyd gives an account which may be seen in the Philosophical

Skirret Vaur.

Transactions, of what they call fairy causeways, being litle masses about three feet long, like the Giant's Causeway, such as I saw with Mr. Mendez de Costa, the pillars of which were about 3 inches long, and the whole not a foot in length, between two binds found in Derbyshire. At the foot of this hill the youngest of the Hanburys has a seat; and opposite to it S‍ʳ Charles Hanbury Williams, our ambassador at Russia, has a house on the estate left him by Mr. Williams, which is entail'd on the younger brother.

[September, 1756.]

On the 10th I went to see White Castle, four miles from Abergavenny and a mile from Gethly; it seems to be an old British building; the strong part is defended with round towers, and it was considerably enlarged by an enclosure, defended also in the same manner. The cement is nothing more than clay like the castle of Llanblethian near Cowbridge, which with the openings of narrow spike holes circular at each end I esteem a mark of its antiquity. I return'd to Gethly, and went 3 miles to Llanbyhangon, a seat of Lord Oxford's, at present belonging to the Countess Dowager, and soon came into that valley in which the river Hodny runs, which falls into the Morury. It is a narrow winding vale, with a pleasant hill on each side. The bird-cherry as well as the quicken and yew grow here in great abundance. Near the extremity of the county we came to Lantoni, where the vale appears as enclosed in an Lantoni. amphitheater of high hills. This abbey was founded by Walter Lacy (from whom the Lacies mentioned among the conquerors of Ireland are descended) in the place where one of them and his companion, both hermits, built a monastery. The body of the church and the tower at the east end of it are exceeding grand and stately with a mixture of Saxon and Gothic architecture, but in such a manner as show that it was all built at once; the cross isle is Saxon, and the east end is Gothick; neither of them in any wise suitable either as to extent or architecture to the body of the church. On the hills to the west are some stone kerns as I was informed. We

went on from this place and soon cross'd the river into Brecknockshire, and in two miles came to Chapel Fine, encompassed with old
yew trees ; a mile further we came to the hills, at the top of which
are the foundations of an old chapel, with the remains of an enclosure of stones set an end.   Here a most noble view opened of the
maeandring Wye, and of the delightful vale in which it runs.   Out
of these Hatterel hills rises the Munnow, near the rise of which, Old
Town, is supposed to be the Blestinna of Antonine.   We descended
to the Hay, and saw in the way the autumnal red crocus growing in
the meadows, which I have been inform'd is very common in these
parts.   Hay is a long town of one street, most delightfully situated
over the Wye.   A private house is built on the site of the old
castle, and at the other end of the town is an ancient tumulus.
They some time ago were stopt in building a bridge, the piers of
which were begun, but now they have obtain'd an Act of Parliament for it.   There is a family of the name of   which
they have always kept, at a place call'd   who have
liv'd there ever since the time of   the estate having
descended constantly from father to son.

[September, 1756.]

On the 11th we crossed over the ferry into Radnorshire and soon
ascended the heathy hills, two or three of which we cross'd and as
many narrow well cultivated vales and came to that valley in which
the village of Glastre is situated, on each side of which are small
hills under corn ; and towards Burshop and Old Radnor they are
mostly under wood ; we ascended to Old Radnor, on the hill which
is between this vale and that in which New Radnor stands ; the
latter is an exceeding pleasant vale, New Radnor being situated at
the neck of it between the hills.   We could hear of no remains of an
old town here, but were inform'd that General Gwyn had caused
the ground to be dug between 4 stones set up an end under the hill
and found some bones.   Mr. Cambden supposes this place to have
been Magos or Magnos of the Itinerary.   We ascended a hill and

cross'd Offa's Dike, commonly call'd Off Dike, which Offa made
from the mouth of the Wye to that of the river Dee near Holy
Well, between his kingdom of Mercia and the Britains. And
Harold made a law, that if a Welsh man appear'd without the
Dyke his right hand should be cut off. The ditch is on the Welsh
side. We descended to Presteign situated on the river Lug, a town
of two streets, consisting chiefly of wooden projecting houses; and
rose by the favour of Martin, Bishop of St. David's. As Mr.
Cambden saies in the time of their grandfathers, tho' the wooden Presteign.
houses with the upper floor projecting, in which style most of the
houses of the town are built, seem to be of an older date. This town
consisting mostly of inns and shops is in decay, as the markets fail
very much. From this place I went near Kenson, another seat of
Lady Oxford's, which with an estate of about £700 a year was left
to the family by a relation, Mr. Thomas Harlay, who was ambassador in Holland. Two miles more brought me to Shobden, the
seat of Lord Bateman, built on a rising ground from which there is
a fine view of the country. The house is finished and furnished in
a very grand manner. There are many good pictures in it, and a
fine statue of Mercury of Grecian workmanship, brought from Naples.
There is a fine lawn at the back of the house, adorn'd with clumps
and single trees; terminated with a portico, which appears like a
small temple. Up the side of the hill to the north also is a lawn
and plantations, and on it is a building, consisting of a large arch
and one smaller on each side; they are made out of three Saxon
arches of the old church very highly adorned, and over them are
two reliefs in a very bad taste, taken out of the same building, and
beyond it is the old font which is Gothick and was adorned with
ancient reliefs; further to the west clumps of trees form a sort of
avenue up the hill, and lead to very fine rideings through the top
and sides of an agreable hill, which commands a most glorious view
of a rich country. Near the house an old mount of a fortress
is improved into a bowling green with a summer-house. To the
south of the house is a piece of water and a wood below it, through

which are several walks, and a piece of water appears through them like a river. The greatest part of this beautiful place has been laid out by this present Lord; near the house was the church of St. Julian which belonged to an old cell; this was the parish church, and about fifty years ago was removed to the spot of the present. This church Ld Bateman has rebuilt (the tower of the old church remaining) in the Gothic style, and it is very finely finished within all in the same style, every part being embellished with Gothic ornaments; the east window is all painted glass in very elegant taste, and the other windows are ornamented with colour'd glass: on each side next the chancel a closet is taken off, which is open to the church, one is built with a chimney, for Lord Bateman's family; the other is to be a burial place and a seat for the servants. They have a good freestone here with a greenish cast.

[September, 1756.]

I made several excursions from Shobden. To the west of it, about three miles, is a very strong British camp, on Wapley Hill, which commands a most extensive view, I think to Snowdon, or very near it, in the north-west part of Wales, near as far as Chepstow to the south-east. This camp, which may be about half a mile in circumference, is defended by strong fossees, in most parts three, and in some four. Another day I made an excursion along the river Lug, and first past by the camp, call'd Arnbry, on a high hill in the park belonging to Croft Castle. We then came to Wigmore Castle, near the village of that name; it is very strongly situated, the keep is very high, and there is a wall below which encloseres about two acres of ground that surrounds it on every side, except to the north.

Wigmore
Castle.

There are great remains of this castle, tho' much of it has been carryed away for buildings within these 50 years. This castle was repaired by King Edward the Elder, came to the Mortimers, and now belongs to the Earl of Oxford. Going on, we passed by what they call the Abbey of Grange, but it is the old Abbey of Wigmore, which was founded by the Mortimers; there are some remains of it in the old house. A litle beyond this is Brandon Camp, situated near the Teine; it is a fine Roman camp, on a rising ground, of such a nature that on two sides one may see that the ascent has been render'd more difficult ; on the other two a rampart has been raised within to strengthen the natural situation, and is broad enough at top for four or five ranks of men to stand on it; in one part, where it is entirely defended by this rampart, it is at bottom twenty paces broad. There is no way out on the west side, because it is very steep, but there seems to have been a port at the north-west angle. It is of an irregular shape as the ground runs, and about 800 yards in circumference. A mile to the west of it is Coxal Knowle, a high hill cover'd with wood; this was the British camp, and the fosses round it remain. A litle to the west of this I went to Brampton Brian, an old castle, which, to the time of Edward the First, belonged to the Brians, when it came by the female line to the Harleys. Litle remains of the old castle, except the gateway and one side of Brampton an old hall, adjoyning to which there was a good mansion house, Brian. built about the time of Charles the First, for it was destroyed in the Civil wars. In an old wooden house near it Treasurer Harley lived, which has been lately new fronted by the present earl before he came to the title, and here he passes most of his time in the summer, keeping his publick daies at Haywood. From Coxal I had a view up the valley in which Knighton stands, about 3 miles off, on the Teine. It is a small market town, in which the Welsh sell oates and tares, and buy wheat. I was told that two miles (I think) on this side Knighton is an old camp, call'd Gard Ledger. I came to Lanterdin, and went down by the Tein for two miles and cross'd over the hills to Richard's Castle, on the side of a hill; it was a large enclosure with a keep, only a very litle part of one wall remains, built of bad mortar, which I look on as a mark of British antiquity. We were here within two miles of Ludlow, which I had formerly seen, and the remains of the old castle built by Roger of Montgomery, but Henry 1st took it to himself, in whose time it was besieg'd by King Stephen, when Henry, son of the King of Scots, had like to have

been drawn up into the castle by a hook. Dr. Gale supposes Rush-
bury near it to be Bramonium of Antonine. I omitted to see the
Bone Well near Richard's Castle, in which the bones of frogs, as it
is supposed, are sometimes found. We returned to Shobden by
Mortimer's Cross, on the Lug, where there is a paper mill in a
large plain. Near this Cross, in Henry 6th's time, Earl Mortimer
defeated the Earl of Pembroke. Before I came to this place I
passed by Lutton School, a good building, founded by one of the
name of Purpous, for teaching the children of the neighbourhood.

Another day I went to the south-west, along the Arro, and first
saw Staunton, under Wapley Hill, where there seemed to be some
old fortification with a keep. We then passed by Haywood, where
Ld Oxford has a large house and a fine lawn, with a beautiful peice
of water and great woods on the hill over it. l came to Kyneton,
a small town full of inns and shops, chiefly supported by its markets
for oats, wheat, and fowls, and they have a small manufacture of
coarse woollen clothes. In the east part of the church are narrow
windows in a singular style, and in the church is an ancient tomb
of the Vaughans, on which are couchant statues of a man and
woman, in white English marble. We then crossed the hill to
Walton, by which we had passed before near Old Radnor, and went
across that fine plain to New Radnor, a very poor town. The
castle, and especially the keep, was strong; there are no remains,
except a wall on the keep. This part is separated from the rest of
the castle by two deep fossees. I should rather think that this was
Magnos or Magos of Antonine, where the commander of the Pacen-
tian regiment lay in garrison, in the time of Theodosius the Younger.
Two measured miles beyond it is a romantick waterfall, the approach
to it is between winding rocky cliffs, beautifyed with trees growing
out of them; the rivlet runs down about fifty feet in breaks, and
then about as many more in a sheet gliding down the rock. We
return'd six miles by the way of Presteign and crossed Offa's Ditch,
and beyond Presteign passed by Stapleton's Castle, which was
situated on a rock covered with wood, but now a modern house is

built in the place of it.   At this waterfall we were but four short
miles from Llandrindod Wells, which I went to see in the road from Llandridod
Rhyader, going to Bealt, in 1754.   The following account of them Wells.
has since been published by Dr. Linden, a German: " What they
call the rock water consists of much ætherial, elastic volatile mineral
spirits, of mineral balsam of the amber kind ; a volatile vitriolic acid
much of the chalybeat; a perfect sulphur, a nitrous purging salt,
participating of the nature of borax, and is good for weak nerves,
scorbutic eruptions, palsies, agues, &c.   The pump water consists of
sal enixum boracis nativi, of a like opaque bituminous earthy parts,
etherial, elastic volatile mineral spirits, of the nature of ambergreece
and a mineral oyl, and is good for scurvy, ulcers, hypochondriac
disorders, the morphew, fevers, leprosy, and gravel.   The sulphur
water contains ætherial volatile mineral spirits, a litle vitriolic acid,
a mineral unctious mucus, a fine mineral oil, a subtile crocus of
marcasites, soluble in spirits of wine, a perfect sulphur and a neutral
salt, whose texture is a briny alkaly, and is used both for batheing
and is drank with the batheing."   I went also four miles to Leominster, a market town on the Lugg, a great thorough fare, and they Leominster.
have a manufacture of coarse woollen cloth.   Merwald, King of
Mercia, and his successors, according to tradition, had a palace here,
on a hill to the east of the town, now call'd Comfer Castle, where
there are no remains that I could see, except some ramparts ; these
were probably thrown up round it.   This king founded a nunnery
here, which was destroy'd by the Danes ; but Henry 1st gave the
lands to the Abbey of Reading, to which it became a cell.   The old
church, of Saxon architecture, is most of it standing, adjoyning to
the north side of the present church ; the pillars are six feet in
diameter ; the lower part of the tower is also Saxon ; but the addition of a new Gothic church to it is very fine, the windows are of a
light architecture, and three members round are adorned with roses,
and a single member in every part of the window, as well as within;
there is a very large Gothic window to the west, the members of
which are so fine that I suppose, on their finding they began to give

way outwards, they practiced two very light buttresses up against the pillars of it, in order to strengthen it, which is a singular thing. They talk much of a passage underground from this place to Evington Camp. The street near the church is paved with a stone composed of pebbles, of a lighter colour than those of Hertfordshire.

I went also to see Lingebrook, or, as it is call'd, Limebrook Abbey, near the Lug, to the north of Kynsham. In an inquisition mentioned in Dugdale it is call'd the Convent, and the donation was made to the Prioress; it is the poorest ruin I ever saw, and seems to have been a very small convent under a hill cover'd with wood.

[September, 1756.]

mbridge.   On the 20th I left Shobden and came three miles to Pembridge, a living which belongs to Corpus Christi College in Oxford. There is a good church with an isle on each side and a singular belfry near the church. It was formerly a market town, but is now a poor place. In about 5 measured miles I came to Webly, a very poor market town tho' a Parl' borough. There is a good church here with a fine tower and steeple; the south door is Saxon. In the chancel is a monument of a man and another of a man and woman, all couchant statues, the men in coats of mail, and the woman with the head dress rising on each side like two horns. There is a monument of Colonel Birch with his statue standing upright, whose estate now belongs to Mr. Peploe, son of the late Bishop of Chester, and he is Chancellor of that Diocese, by marrying the sole heiress of Mr. Birch. From this place I went two miles to Mr. Price's, one of our party to the glaciers in Savoy, and married to Lord Barrington's sister. The house is in a bottom on one side of the vale, which is form'd by a chain of hills in form of a circus, and covered with wood. He is practising a rideing all round the inside and outside of the hills, which within is at least six miles, and making sheep walks down from the wood, and corn fields are to be in the middle. From the house there are winding walks through woods of fine young oaks, up to the top of a little hill, which commands a view of the country to the south-east and north-east, and of the city of Hereford. The same view (except of Hereford) is seen on the south side of the hills which I have mentioned, as well as of the Skiret Vaur and Blarens, over Abergavenny; also of Radnorshire, and a great way farther into Wales. The north side commands as far as the north part of Worcestershire, and the north-east a view of the opening between the hills and of the two Butts in that vale, through which opening Hereford is seen from some heigth about Shobden. Altogether the greatest variety of prospects I ever saw without going two miles from the house. They have a quarry here of the most beautiful freestone; it has a green cast, and works extremely well. I left Foxley on the 21st, and went three miles to Kenchester, the old Ariconium, near a rivlet call'd Einbrook. The old ramparts on which the walls were built remain. It was of an irregular Kenchester. figure of six sides, probably following the natural situation of the ground. It is about thirteen hundred yards in circumstance. There are marks of many buildings, especially on the north side, where they show'd an arch'd nich turn'd with Roman brick, which are about a foot square and three inches thick, and probably was a nich in a temple, for they describ'd some pavement found here which I conclude was Mosaick. They find much coin of the Lower Empire on ploughed ground after rain, and frequently in fresh earth thrown up by the moles. About a mile to the north of it is Credenhil Camp, a high situation, and might be the Æstiva of the Roman town. Two miles brought us to the turnpike road between the Hay and Hereford, 14 miles apart, and in two more we came to Hereford, passing by the ruins of a fine old cross, the lower part of which remains, with several arms round it.

[September 1756.]

Hereford is situated on the River Wye and was encompassed with walls above a mile in circumference, great part of which are still standing. At the north gate I observ'd in two niches two statues as sitting. This town was fortifyed by Harold, and the Normans built the castle; the ramparts, part of the wet fossee and the keep, are still remaining, but all the building is entirely destroyed; it is situated on the river, and a rivlet fills the fossee and falls into the river; they have made a fine gravel walk on the rampart and another below round the court of the castle, which is a small meadow.

Hereford. This town is said to have owed its increase to the devotion which was paid to Ethelbert, King of the East Angles, who was to be marryed to the daughter of Offa, King of the Mercians; but King Offa's wife got him assassinated, some say out of jealousie, for fear he should conquer this kingdom; others, that Offa might seize on the kingdom of the East Angles; and some say that a compunction of heart induced him to found the Church of Hereford. But a manuscript in the possession of the minister of Marden mentions that King Offa's palace was there, and that the Pope advised him to give the site of it for building the Church of Marden, and also to found the Church of Hereford to expiate his crime. In the Church of Marden is a well, of which there is a tradition, that it is on the spot on which Ethelbert's head fell, and I was inform'd that they have Ethelbert's well in Hereford. I should think that the Saxon work in the quire of the cathedral was the old church, and that the body and front was built in the time of Henry 1st as mentioned by historians, of which the lower part and towers on each side remain, but the middle part is of another kind of building in the Gothic taste; they have practised Gothic windows above within the Saxon frames. I do not recollect whether there is any Saxon work in the Cross Isle; if not, I suppose that there was one isle the whole length of the church, which is now all Gothic. I imagine what Saxon work remains in the quire is part of Offa's building, being in a very heavy and particular style. To the south of the church are remains of a very fine light Gothic chapter house, which I conjecture might be of twelve sides; they say there was a chapel adjoyning to it, which has been lately entirely destroyed, and was very fine. There is also a large cloyster with a singular old cross in the middle, but so as to have an opening four ways, out of which, it is said, they used formerly to preach. To the Gothic quire Bishop Biss put up an altar piece of Dantzick oak and Roman architecture, and on one side is his monument and that of the Countess of Plymouth, his lady. To the east of the quire is the library, a very elegant Gothic building, and on one side of it a singular chapel, which we could not see. Here they have laid King Ethelbert's couchant statue, which they say was in the quire, on the south side, probably on his tomb or shrine. There are many old monuments of Bishops round the cathedral (viz.), 5 or 6 in a row, each of them under an arched recess of the wall of the south isle, which were all made at one time, many years after some of the Bishops died whose monuments here occur. A fine monument, two couchant statues of the ancestor of Judge Denton, and of the Lingens, of Sutten, great partisans for King Charles 1st, and their old mansion house is there in ruins, belonging to the co-heiresses, but some of the family are at Ladbrook, in Yorkshire. It seem'd to me as if a great part of the church had been destroy'd by some accident. To the south-east of the cathedral is the vicar's college, a building and cloyster round a large court, where the twelve vicars and their custos live. There were probably many more formerly. They have a hall in which they eat, which is fitted up in modern taste, and they have public music in it at the triennial meeting of the three quires. Hereford is supported intirely by the thoroug fare, the shops to supply the country, the markets and fairs, and a manufacture of gloves. There is a navigation to this city and up the Wey to the Hay, tho' they seldom go more than six miles above the city; there are many old wooden houses in the town.

[September, 1756.]

I went from Hereford 4 miles to Sutton, and a mile further to Marden Church, where I saw the well, what they call the Mercian arms painted on the west end, but in place of the East Angles 3 crowns, and on the north side the red and white rose. It is close to the Wye; if this was the habitation of the kings of Mercia it is probable Sutton hill was the place they retir'd to in time of danger, · which is very strong in its natural situation, a litle help'd in some places by raising a terrace on the inside near 4 feet high ; on the outside it appears all round, like an artificial rampart, but within, excepting the terrace, it is all even ; it is consequently irregular as the hill runs, which is not high, but commands a very fine prospect every way. There is a pond on the hill, which probably is never dry. I imagined I saw to the south below a fossee and rampart made as to defend that part.

I had formerly been at Hampton Court, which did belong to Rowland Lenthal, Master of the Wardrobe to Henry 4th. He built this house and married a daughter of the Earl of Flanders. The only original of Henry IV. is said to be there. The place now belongs to the Coningsby's, enobled by the title of Earls. I went from Sutton to Willington, near which place a tradesman of Hereford has a house, and a summer house on the top of a hill, on each side of which are some oaks extending over the top of the hill, and being cut up, and only some small boughs growing out, they have a most singular and beautiful effect. I came to Bromyard, 14 measured miles from Hereford, situated over a stream which falls into the Lugg ; a poor town, without any manufacture, chiefly subsisting by the thorough fare. I went to see the church, on the north side of which are two Saxon doors, and to the tower is a round turret for a staircase, which in size and make comes nearest to those in Ireland of any I have seen. All the old houses in Herefordshire are built with frames of wood and cage work between call'd pargiting ; their barns and outhouses are generally built in this manner, but with what they call lath walls, which are broad laths twisted in between four upright styles fixed on the frames. There is one thing remarkable in Herefordshire, that from many places you see the whole extent of the county, which is most exceedingly beautiful ; and I do not remember that I saw one heathy common in it, being all rich profitable land ; but the roads are generally exceeding bad, which takes off much from the pleasure the country would

otherwise afford.   The common people have a custom, in all these
parts, of kneeling down and saying a short prayer when they go
occasionally into a church.   All South Wales and Herefordshire
abound in stones for covering houses, and also in a larger kind for
tombs and chimney pieces.

On the 22nd I went seven computed miles, about 14 measur'd, to
Witley, Lord Foley's, and before I came to Clifton I pass'd a small
stream into Worcestershire.   We came at Clifton to the turnpike
road 14 miles from Ludlow and ten from Worcester, and soon
descended by Holm Castle, Sr Edward Winington's, near the river Holm Castle.
Teine, and a litle farther are Shelsely ironworks for making iron
bars.   We cross'd the Teine to Selsley, and came to a quarry, the
joynts of which are perpendicular, and it consists of a stone which
is brown for about two or three inches on the outside and blew
within ; in it I saw cockles and the chamey petrified, and, what I
never found before, the razor fish, one of which I brought away.
This is Woodbury Hill, on which they say is a camp, which, by
tradition, was Owen Glendour's, but was originally a Roman fortification.   I saw to the left on a hill, Aberley Lodge, Mr Bromley's,
a very fine situation, and below it a publick house in the turnpike
road call'd Hundred House, leading from Tenbury and Ludlow to
Bewdley.   Witley, Lord Foley's, is nine miles from Worcester and
121 from London; it is pleasantly situated between agreable hills,
mostly cover'd with wood; there is a park and a piece of water on
each side of the road leading to the house, which is built in a half
H, and consists of a handsom gallery and a great number of good Witley.
apartments elegantly furnished, and one sees in the different rooms
several things relating to foreign customs, especially the Chinese.
But what is most curious is some presses made of fineer'd oak of a
tree which grew on my Lord's estate, which exceeds in beauty the
finest root of walnut or any other tree ; and I was told there is
enough of it to fineer the wainscoat of a small room.   But the
greatest curiosity of this place is the church adjoyning to the house,
built of brick, with a baluster at top, window frames, and a Dorick

open portal, all of free stone.   Lord Foley bought the painted
windows of Canons to adorn this church, eleven of them; there are
four on each side, which are lengthened out by a running foliage in
the original design; there were five windows, but two of them were
stop'd up to make an organ loft, probably before this treasure was
acquired; this seems greatly to have hurt the uniform beauty of
the church, which I think would have been much greater if there
had been five windows on each side and none in the front, and
terminated at the west end by a copy of some good picture, or
otherwise properly embellish'd ; whereas now there are two
arch'd windows in the west end above, and two sash'd windows
below.   But the west end is well adorn'd on the outside by a
handsom cupola.   There is a painted window at the east end of the
Resurrection; in the ceiling also are pictures of the Nativity,
Ascension, and taking down from the Cross, with angels on each
side, holding several emblems relating to the history of our Saviour,
brought also from Canons.   The whole church above and on the
sides is richly adorn'd with papier maché gilt in imitation of the
finest carvings.   On the south side is a very fine monument to the
memory of the late Lord, by Rysbrach, erected by the dowager, in
which are the statues of Lord Foley and the Lady with a child in
her lap, of the eldest son and eldest daughter on each side, and two
other children, all deceased.   Leaving this place, I observ'd we soon
came on the sandy red stone, and got into the turnpike road from
Ludlow to Bewdley, and came to the banks of the Severn, about a
mile before we came to Bewdley.   This town is well situated on a
declivity to the Severn.   Henry 7th built a place of retirement for
his son Arthur, here call'd Tikhenhall, destroy'd in the civil wars.
They have a handsom new built church of hewn free stone.   I
crossed the Severn on the bridge, and went two miles further to
Kedderminster, where the church is a very handsome Gothic building.   I came four miles to Hagley, Sr George Lyttelton's.   On the
23rd I went to Lord Stamford's; we passed through Sturbridge,
formerly describ'd, and a mile further over the Stour to Stourton,

where there is a good old mansion house built to a square tower of the castle. We had pass'd by old Swinford before we came to Stourbridge, where an ancestor of Lord Foley's founded a handsome well regulated school for the maintenance, teaching, and apprentice-ing of sixty boys out of some neighbouring parishes. I passed in sight of Kenver Edge, on which there is a camp, and came to Enfield, the Earl of Stamford's, who married the only daughter and heire of the Earl of Warrington, by whom he has three sons, the eldest Lord Grey, and one daughter ; the house built like a castle, with many additions to it, is at the foot of a hill ; on one side is a piece of water, and in an island is a Chinese octagon building with a square at each end, to which there is a long bridge ; the building stands on three arches. Behind the house is a gravel and lawn on each side of it, and from the end of it is a walk up to an elegant Gothick summer house of Mr. Miller's design; from this there is a winding walk through shrubberies, which leads to a lawn, at the upper end of which is a Gothic seat which commands a fine view of the vale towards Bridgenorth, of the country beyond Woolverhamp-ton, of Lord Ward's house, of Dudley Castle, Hagley, and of the country to the south. We then went along the top of the hill to a gateway that appears like a castle, and to a string of ponds which extend down to the lawn behind the house. Near these ponds is a pheasantry and hermitage for the keeper of the fowl. We then went in the same direction to another valley about a furlong wide, and is a hanging level for half a mile up the hill to a seat, having a pleasant wood all along on each side of it. There are such a number of hares in this part, we saw several of them feeding in the lawn. Near the wood on the hill lives Lady Dorothy Grey, the Earl's sister, who not far from the front of the house has built a handsom schoolhouse for the education of girls, whom she maintains there.

On the 24th I went to Halesowen, in Shropshire ; in the church here some of the Lyttelton family are buryed, and at the Cathedral at Worcester and at Over Arley. The father of Adam Lyttelton, Halesowen. who writ the Dictionary, was minister of Halesowen. Half a mile from it I view'd the ruins of Halesowen Abbey, commonly call'd the Manor. There remains of the large church only one of the north windows of the chancel, and two of the south cross isle, all plain narrow windows with the mitred arch. To the south are six narrow windows with the same kind of arch, but of a finer Gothick workmanship. This might be part of the refectory. I return'd from this place to Halesowen, and observ'd on each side of a rivlet a rocky bed, which produces a blew kind of fire stone, as I take it to be. I went a mile to Mr. Shenston's, situated on the side of a rising ground facing to the south. We were led first towards the bottom of the west side, and going into a shady walk we saw a cascade, the water of which passes through a narrow bed into a pond below, which might be improv'd to great advantage. We then came round to the south, and after passing some seats we came through an arcade made of roots, which opened surprizingly on a water that falls down in many breaks, and is seen through the wood, which has a most charming effect. Ascending up the hill, still round the skirts of the farm, which is all meadow, we came to a seat, which commands a fine view, and coming on the north side we descended to a fine piece of water ; and ascending again we came to a shady walk in a strait line, but uneven at bottom ; it is about a furlong in length, with a building at the end ; we then went into an open walk commanding a glorious view of the country and of Dudley, as well as the town of Halesowen. We return'd and descended to a wood and came to a steep descent, and were all of a sudden surpriz'd with a beautiful cascade, tumbling down a precipice, and two or three more as the river winds round, a bridge, and different views of water, as of the same river, all down to the large piece of water before described, which appears as part of it. From this the descent is through a lawn to the house. There are urns in several parts, on which and on most of the seats are inscriptions, mostly of the Latin poets, and some inscrib'd to the memory of his friends, as an urn to Somerville, who writ the Chace, and a seat to Thompson, the poet.

Abbey.

[September, 1756.]

Hagley is greatly improved since I saw it. A very fine house with four fronts of freestone, and a tour on each angle, rising higher than the rest of the building, have a fine effect, and as it is seen through the trees from different parts, appears like what we may imagine one of the Greek and Roman palaces to have been. There is a grand gallery and saloon in it. The offices are like a litle town to the left or north, with meadows, kitchen garden, &c., all hid from the sight by plantations. On the right the meadows are taken into the park, so as that the house stands on an eminence, and commands very extensive and beautiful prospects to the west, Hagley. north-west, and south-west. The ground to the left beyond the house, where the garden was, is likewise now within the park, and so will be the scite of the old house when it is taken down. There are some alterations in the park. As on the left, up the side of the hill, the woods form three irregular theaters, in the largest of which, to the right, the Prince of Wales's pillar is now placed, which I formerly mentioned. In a half octogon building on an eminence to the north of the waters is this inscription :

Ingenio Immortali
Jacobi Thompson
Poetae Sublimis
Vivi Boni.
Ædiculam hanc, in secessu, quem vivus dilexit
Post mortem ejus constructam
Dicat dedicatque
Georgius Lyttelton.

In the seat at the bottom of the water, which is the most beautiful in the park, is this inscription :

Viridantia Tempe,
Tempe, quae silvae cingunt super impendentes.

In the part of the hermitage, on a seat adorn'd with bones, is this inscription, made in thin snail shells split in two :

Sedes Contemplationis
Omnia Vanitas.

On the seat, which commands a very extensive view of the country and hills to the west and south, are these lines :

These are Thy glorious Works, Parent of Good.
Almighty ! Thine this Universal Frame
Thus wondrous fair ! Thy self how wondrous then !
Unspeakable, who sit'st above the Heav'n
To us invisible, or dimly seen
In these Thy lowest works. Yet these
Declare Thy goodness beyond thought,
And Power Divine.

—Milton.

Between the park and kitchen garden, and a meadow adjoyning to it, is a beautiful shrubbery, full of curious plants and shrubs. The entrance is near the end of the new house.   There is a winding walk which leads to a lawn in front of the dairy, over which is a single room with a rough Dorick portico to the lawn, and to the meadow on the other side.   From this, after going a few yards, is a strait cover'd walk, with a winding walk on each side between shrubs and flowers, at the end of which are orange trees and other exoticks.   There are plantations and nurseries on the other three sides of the kitchen garden, and altogether it is a most delightful improvement, and so is the approach to it across the meadows from the Birmingham road.   Clent Hills, which run near north and south paralell to the park, and close to it on the east side, are a great beauty to the place.   The turf on these hills is remarkably fine; they rise gradually from the lower end of the park in a long spine or ridge, on which and on the hill itself clumps of firrs are planted, with seats to almost every one of them ; and there is a gentle ascent made to the great heigth, which is over St. Kenelm's Chapel, whose figure in relief I formerly discover'd on the south wall.   Here is a double seat which commands a glorious view every way, for, I believe, 40 or 50 miles round.

About a mile from the house to the north-west is Wichbery Hill, formerly a Roman camp, now covered with wood, and cut into walks with seats that command very fine views, especially of

Stourbridge, Dudley, and the villages adjacent. And in one part, looking towards the house, is a very well designed sylvan hexagon temple; the sides are open, and it is built on pillars made of the trunks of oaks, between which lathes are fix'd, to which the rods of ivy are nail'd on the inside and outside. Before the ends of the rafters litle clumps of wood are fix'd, which resemble a rustick freize, and above it is a projection as for the base of the cornish, all made in like manner with rods of ivie. In digging in a quarry in the park they found, in a different kind of stone from the rest of the quarry, one of the pediculus marinus stretch'd out, now in the possession of the Rev. Dr Lyttelton, Dean of Exeter, as well as a teraphim or icunculus found in the very body of a stone, which must have been dropt and the earth petrifyed round it many ages past. It is of a white freestone, but has taken the colour of the stone in which it was buryed, and is about two inches long, a drawing of which may be seen on the other side.

Sr George Lyttelton has adorn'd the church in a most exquisite Gothic taste, Mr. Miller's design. The chancel is entirely new ; the windows are adorn'd on the sides and every part with Gothic ornaments in hewn stone, and all the other parts of it is in stucco. On the cieling and at each end are the arms of the paternal ancestors of the Lytteltons, in a direct line from Thomas de Luttelton, *temp.* Hen. III., to Sr George Lyttelton, impaling their respective wives, each coat in a seperate compartment, and in the corniche are single shields of arms, being the same which constitute the great shield over the north door. These were all done at the expence of the Dean of Exeter, who has also given a Persian carpet as a covering for the communion table. The east window is entirely of rich painted glass, viz., four large shields made in 1569 of *Lyttelton* with his quarterings impaling *Pakynton,* and *Willoughby of Wollaton* with quarterings impaling *Lyttelton,* with quarterings ; also the portrait of Lord Lyttelton, Keeper of the Great Seal, *temp.* Charles I., some Scripture peices, likewise in Flemish glass, &c., the whole border'd with blue, purple, and green glass, lately made at Stourbridge. The three windows on each side are in Gothic style, adorn'd likewise with bordering of colour'd glass thrown into pretty Gothic figures. The windows in the church are of the same style, but plain, and the seats are in the Gothic taste. The gallery is very beautifuly adorn'd with roses, &c., carved in the wood, and the Communion rail is of a Gothic design. And I must not omit that the monuments to Mrs. Lyttelton on the north side, and of Sr Thomas and Lady Lyttelton on the south, are no small ornaments to the church, both which I have formerly describ'd.

About five miles from Hagley is Frankley, the old seat of the Lytteltons, which Prince Rupert made a garrison of in the Civil Wars, and burnt it when he left it, that the Parliament army might not avail themselves of it. The family after this liv'd at Arley above Bewdley, and latterly in this place, which before was only their hunting seat.

Since I left Hagley Sr George Lyttelton, Chancellor of the Exchequer, has been made a peer by the title of Lord Lyttelton of Frankley.

Buckingham, Sept. 30th, 1756.

On the 28th I left Hagley and passed by Hewell Grange, Lord Plymouth's, a large handsom house with fine lawn and water near it. We came into Warwickshire, and avoided the ridge way, which is called Ikenil Street, a Roman way, and is a very bad road. We came to Studley, on the river Arrow. I went to see the church; the north door is of Saxon architecture. Adjoyning to it is the wet mote that was round the castle, in which is an old mansion-house, inhabited by a younger branch of the Lyttelton family. We passed at the entrance of the village by the site of the Priory, founded in the time of King Stephen. I saw a small piece of old wall, probably the enclosure of it. Another mile brought us to Coughton, where Sr Robert Throgmorton has a house. The gate way is of hewn stone, and one of the finest Gothic buildings of the kind in England, having an octagon tower at each corner. A grand building, round a court of brick, with stone window frames, seems to have been begun about Queen Elizabeth's time; a very litle part of it is finished; on the rest there is raised a wooden building. In this house they say the Gunpowder Plot was contrived.

In less than two miles we came to Aulcester; they have a very handsom church, of light plain Gothic architecture, which I was inform'd has been lately built. Edward the 4th appropriated the Priory here to Evesham Abbey. It is supposed that this was a Roman town, and gold coins have been found in some fields, call'd Blacklands, to the left going to Ragley, which are in possession of Lord Brook. I went a mile to Ragley, which is a grand seat of the Earl of Hertford's, situated on an eminence that commands a fine view of the country. It is a very large house, and seems to have been built about the time of King Charles II. The hall is 67 feet long, 41 broad, and 38 high, and has been just new modell'd and embellished with ornaments of stucco; there are several good apartments in it. There is a fine lawn, woods, and water like a serpentine river, behind the house, and it commands a view of small hills from the front, either finely cultivated or diversifyed with wood. From this place we cross'd to Wigesford, upon the sluggish Avon, towards Stratford-on-Avon. I observed that the waters of this river appear like a stagnating pond, so that one cannot discern which way it runs. I came to a fine quarry, call'd Cranelees, in the parish of Grafton. The first I came to was of a yellowish colour (as I observ'd) towards the surface, and pale blew within; this is mostly used for lime. Just beyond it is another, in which they have sunk down about six beds; they told me the second was the best marble, and it polishes a grey with white streakes; where the shells are, there are some beds full of cockle shells. They raise also fine flags and stones for tombs. This is 4 computed and 5 measured miles from Stratford. Going on, I observed in the road some stones, brought to mend the walls, which were full of the small gryphites, and I suppose came from Wyncot Quarry, about three miles from Stratford, near the road to Alcester, and I saw some of it polish'd, which confirmed me in the opinion of this kind of shells which are in this marble, both which stones are known at a distance by the name of Stratford marble, of which there are several chimney pieces at Stow. I came to Stratford-on-Avon, a town formerly belonging to the Bishops of Worcester, but in the time of Edward 6th Bishop Heath gave it up to Dudley, Earl of Warwick, afterwards Duke of Northumberland. They have here great markets for corn, are famous for malt, and have a great cheese fair. The parish church was formerly collegiate ; it is a fine light Gothic building ; in it are the grand old

Stratford. monuments of the Cloptons, also of Carew, Earl of Totness, and his Lady, an heiress, with their couchant statues. That family being extinct, she left the estate to her nephew Clopton, son of her sister. But what it is most remarkable for is the monument of Shakespear, who was born and buryed in this town ; it is a half figure under a corniche, supported by Corinthian pillars, with an inscription under it, and on his tombstone a copy of verses, all which are to be seen in his Life. The comedians who were here some years ago repair'd and adorn'd it, and added a canopy over it. In the middle of the town is the handsom Gothic chapel, built by the same Hugh Clopton, who was Lord Mayor of London in the time of Henry 7th. The bridge, as appears by an inscription on it, was built at the expence of the above mentioned Hugh Clopton.

From Stratford I came, on the 29th, to Kyneton, a very bad road; here is a new Gothic church, built to a good old tower by the care of the worthy minister, Mr. Talbot, nephew to the late Ld Chancellor, with the help of some subscriptions, but chiefly, as I have been inform'd, at his own expence, on a very small living, not so good as a curacy. I went two miles further through the field of battle of Edghill, which was in the grounds under the hill, where they find many bullets, and came to Mr. Miller's house at Radway. This gentleman, who lives on his estate, has a great genius for architecture, especially the Gothic, and I waited on him

Edghill. to consult about the adorning the Cathedral of Kilkenny, the design of which he had been so kind as to undertake. He has embellish'd his own house with Gothic architecture, and has made a fine lawn up the hill, with shady walks round it, up to the ruined castle on Edgehill, which he has built adjoyning to the houses of some tenants. But he has erected a very noble round tower, which is entire, with a drawbridge, to which there is an assent as by a ruine, and there is a very fine octagon Gothic room in it, with four windows and 4 niches, and some old painted glass in the windows. In one of these niches is to be placed Caractacus in chains, modeled, under Mr. Miller's direction, by a countryman of great genius, now settled in London; it is executed in the yellow free stone. This gentleman design'd the County House in Warwick, with great contrivance and taste, in the Corinthian order. From this town we saw what they call King Charles Camp. They have a yellow freestone, and between it they find a brown stone of a smooth and soft surface, but it does not polish; they make chimney pieces and coving stones of it. At Horton, a little beyond the castle, they find a freestone, some of which is full of shells, mostly a white cockle, many of which may be taken whole out of the soft earth. On the 30th I went to see Farnborough, Mr. Holbeche's, a good house in a narrow valley; there is in it several ancient busts and very beautiful fineer'd ancient marble tables; he has made a very grand grass terrace, winding round the hill for half a mile; there is an obelisk at the end which may be 80 feet high, and in another part an oval open summer house, with a room over the colonade. This terrace commands a fine view of the rich country, which is called the Vale of Red Horse, from a red horse, near Tysoe, cut in the hill.

London, Oct. 5th, 1756.

I went from Radway to Lord Guilford's, called Wroxton, an estate which Sr Thomas Pope left to Trinity College, Oxford, of which he was the founder. His son had a lease of it, built the house, and it has been ever since in the family. There are several good portraits in the house, many of them Cornelius Johnson's, and a very remarkable one of Prince Henry, King James's eldest son, by a foreigner, who did not stay long in England. But this place is more to be admir'd without doors. There is a green house, with a lawn and large piece of water. This leads to a wood through which there is a view of the Prince of Wales's pillar, erected when he was here in 1749. We then descended to a serpentine river, which is supplyed from the large pieces of water ; and going up by it we came to the Gothic open rotundo of Mr. Miller's design, in which he has practis'd curtains, that by turning screws let down so as to afford shelter which ever way you please. This commands a most delightful view of the head that supports the great body of water I have mentioned cover'd with shrubs, and a cascade falls down twenty feet from it, and forms the serpentine river which runs by a Chinese summer house ; and there is another stream and small cascade to the left, which leads to a Chinese seat at a gate of this fine place that leads to Banbury.

Roxton.

I came to Banbury, a very indifferent town, but has a great trade in cheese. Here the Earl of Warwick surprized the Earl of Pembroke and his brother of the party of Edward 4th, and beheaded them. The church is a fine Gothic building ; what is uncommon, one half of the cross isle is rais'd in its length much higher than the other, and so is the west part of the chancel, and is made very light, probably for the sake of the rood loft. There is a fine old Gothic monument in the church, but it is not known to whom it was erected. There is also one to Judge Chamberlayne and his lady, with two kneeling statues.

On the 1st of October I went on in the road to Buckingham. At Fenmere, four miles from Buckingham and Stow, we turn'd off to the latter, and took a walk in the garden, and saw in the house the new Brussels tapestry, and in the garden the Grecian temple entirely finished. I observed the columna rostrata, with Neptune on it, to the honour of Captain Greenville, who died in a sea-fight in 1747, and the Dorick pillar to the memory of Lord Cobham, erected by his Lady in his life time. It is an octagon, with a large flute on each side, a sort of a cupola at top of it, on which is Lord

Cobham's statue. There is a stair case up to it ; it is built of the freestone of Thornborough, which looks very well ; it is 120 feet high, and the statue is eleven feet. On one side of the pedestal is this inscription : " To preserve the memory of her husband, Anne Viscountess Cobham caused this pillar to be erected, in the year 1748." On another side is this inscription: " Quoniam nobis denegatur diu vivere, relinquimus aliquid quo nos vixisse testamur."

From Stow I went through Buckingham, 57 miles from London, and came to the small town of Winslow, given by King Offa to the monastery of St. Alban's, in a council held at Verulam in 794. We found ourselves in a country which abounds with freestone, that is found 4 or 5 feet below the surface, and in it cockles, hearts, and the Cornu Ammonis very large. We came to Aylsbury, where I went to see the church, which is a common Gothic building, except that to the chancel there are long narrow windows with pointed arches, but the cornice seems to be of a much older date. A mile from Aylsbury Sr Wm. Lee has built a most beautiful small chapel, which place I formerly saw. I came on the 2nd through Wendover and Missenden Litle, and in about a mile by Windsor Lane, over some commons and through woods, to Beaconsfield, where the poet Waller is buryed. I cross'd by Farnham, Salt Hill, Eton, and Windsor to Old Windsor, where, not meeting with my friend, I din'd at Staines, so call'd from a stone formerly set up there as a mark that the jurisdiction of London on the Thames extended so far. From this place to Brentford was the forest or warren of Stanes, disforrested by Henry IIId. I came to London in the evening.

I went from London to Wilton, and so to Newtown. The whole route I have set down on the other side.

Dunkton, March 24th, 1757.

I left Newtown on the 18th, and paced round the camp over near Sutton ; it is of an irregular figure paces in circumference, and commands a very fine view. I went to see

St. Cross, a mile beyond Winchester. The east end and the cross isle were built by Cardinal du Blois, King Stephen's brother, and is of Saxon architecture; the body is mix'd, but mostly Gothick, and was built by   .

This was a foundation for   , who wear black gowns. There are   poor men; the master ship is £700 a year. They have a custom of giving a piece of bread and a cup of beer to all travellors.

The Corporation of Southampton have intentions of making it a free port, and of carrying a wooden pier two hundred feet from the quay to defend the shipping in stormy weather, when they are often dammag'd by beating against the quay. The town have given £500, and several of the Corporation have subscrib'd. For there is but litle trade at this town, and if it had not of late been much frequented for bathing and drinking the salt waters they would have had very litle commerce, except among themselves. And this is a dissadvantage to those who are not in trade, or do not lett lodgings, as it has greatly rais'd the markets.

I left Southampton on the 21st, and passing thorough Eling came to the turnpike in Salisbury road, in which we went for some time, and left it to the right to go in the road to Ringwood, which is made very good near as far if not quite to the Castle of Malwood;[a] towards the end of it we saw the boundary stone between Eling and Minsted parishes. Ascending the hill, we pass'd through the Castle of Malwood without knowing it, which is describ'd as consisting of many acres, and that large oaks grow on the banks round it. But a litle beyond it, half a mile to the right of the road, at the summit of the hill, we were directed to the site of the famous oak which it is said blew on Christmas day and wither'd before night; pales were put up round it by K. Charles 2^d, and the tree being quite decayed and the wood taken away, a triangular pillar was set up, about sixteen feet high, a drawing of which may be seen on the other side. These inscriptions on the three sides of it :

[a] So call'd, but is only a large Roman camp.—*Note in MS.*

I.

Here stood the oak
on which an arrow shot by Sr Walter Tyrrel
At a Stag glanc'd
And struck William the 2^d
Surnam'd Rufus
In the breast of which he instantly dyed
on the 2^d of August A.D. 1100.

II.

King William the 2^d
Surnamed Rufus
Being slain as before related
Was laid on a Cart belonging to one Purchess
And drawn from thence to Winchester   ·
And buryed in the Cathedral Church of that City.

III.

A.D. 1745.
That where an event so
memorable had happened
might not be
hereafter unknown
This stone was set up by
John Lord De la War, who
has seen the tree growing in
this place.

On the top of this hill I saw some barrows, and particularly one which is flat, with a circle round it. Somewhere near the Castle of Malwood, as I was told, near a publick house call'd the Coach and Horses, not long ago was found two urns of brass coins of the Lower Empire, a cart wheel striking on an urn.

We cross'd this hill and another and two rivlets, and had the Lord Warden's house to the left, belonging to Lord De la War; we should have struck out of this road to the right to go to Moyles Court, but we went on within two or three miles of Ringwood, and went out to the right into the road from Limington to Fordingbridge and came to Moyles Court. This place is situated in a bottom, just without the Forest; it was the estate of that Lisle whose lady was beheaded, in King James' time, at Winchester. From her descendant this estate, being entail'd, came to Mr. Lisle's son, who dyed abroad, and after him to his brother, whom I knew at Constantinople.

It is a large convenient house, and on one side is a wing which was Lady Lisle's meeting house for Divine worship. There are very good gardens, woods, groves, and fish ponds, and Mr. Lisle is greatly improving the place. In the evening I went four miles to Fordingbridge and six more to Dunckton, which place I have formerly describ'd. I saw Mr. Hull's house, and Mr. Archer's on the other side of the river opposite to it, formerly mentioned.

On the 23d of March I went to Minat, on the 25th to Ld Feversham's ; and saw the house in which there is a good hall, but rather too high for its dimensions. We passed by Mr.   and came into the turnpike from Southampton at Alderbury, about two miles from Salisbury, and went from it to the left to Clarendon Park, Mr. Bathurst's seat, which gave title to the Earls of Clarendon. Here, att the south end of the park, the Kings and Queens of England had each their house, call'd now the King's and Queen's Manor ; but there are no remains of them. Two Parliaments were held here, temp. Henry 2^d.

From this place I went about two miles to Farley, where Sr Stephen Fox founded an almshouse for six men and six women opposite to the church, it being his native place. On it is this inscription—

> Deo opt. Max. Omnium Largitori
> Istud Quantulumcq' Grati Animi
> Monumentum acceptum refert
> Scholæ hujus et Ptochotrophi
> Fundator Humilis Gratabundus
> Anno Salutis reparatæ
> MDCLXXXI
> Quid tibi Divitiæ prosunt quas congeris ?
> Solas quas dederis semper habebis opes.

The church also was built by Sir Stephen Fox. It is the family's burial place, which is under an isle, in which are several monuments; on one of them to Sr Stephen and his second wife—

Cy Gist le tres Honourable	Cy Gist le tres Honourable Dame
Et tres Ancien Chevalier	Christina Hope Epousé en second Noces
S^r. Stephen Fox	Du tres honourable Chevalier Etiene Fox
Fondateur de Ceans	Elle Trepassa agé de 39 Ans
Qui Trespassa agè de 90 Ans	Le dix septiene de Fevrier
Le Vingt troisieme de Septembre	1718.
1716.	Dieu ayè Merci de Leur Ames.

There is also a monument to Elizabeth, first wife of Sr Stephen, who dyed in 1696, and left two sons.

Another of Charles, the second son of the first wife, who married the daughter and heir of Sr William Trollop; was Paymaster of the forces to King James, King William, and Queen Anne, and dyed at the age of 53.

Also of two daughters of Ld Ilchester and Staverdale—

Juliana Judith, who dyed in 1749.

Charlotte Elizabeth, in 1753.

From this place I went mostly through woods 3 miles to Titherley, and then to Winterslow, where the Rev^d Mr. Thistlewaite has a house, and is minister of the parish; and to the south his brother has a seat, not far from the statue of Mercury on a pillar in the London road to Salisbury, at the 77th mile stone. Crossing to the London road we saw fine downs planted with clumps of trees to the east, and going through Winterslow we came to the inn on the London road, call'd Winterslow [Hut?], about 76 miles from London. There are several barrows near it, and on the heigth to the north a work that looks very much like a Roman camp; we saw on a hill, a litle to the east, three small arches, but forgot on what occasion they were erected, and soon cross'd a Roman road, which seems to be that from Winchester to Sorbiodunum. I pass'd a dyke, which I imagin'd might be an ancient boundary, and came to East Tedworth, the seat of Mr. Smith, whose father was Speaker of the House of Commons. Land

springs rise here and as far as Colingborn, and sometimes run down
to Shipton and Newtowntoney, near which Mr. Greathed has a seat
improv'd in good taste, and so they fall into that river which runs
under the bridge a mile or two from Salisbury in the London road,
up part of which river I went when I came from Ireland in 1754.
From Tedworth I cross'd that low hill which is called Hampstein
Gap.   I saw some fossees here that were probably boundaries, for I
did not hear of any camp.   In three miles from Tedworth I came
to Lurgishal, formerly a market town, but now a poor thatch'd
village, in the road from Andover to the Devizes.   There is a
tradition among the common people that King Lud built the castle,
and lived in this good air as he was infirm.   It is 6 miles from
Andover, 4 from Weyhill, 16 from Salisbury, 8 from Ambresbury,
18 from Newbury, by Oxendon, Linkenholt, and Woodhay, 12
from Marlborough, and 14 from the Devizes.   It is at the north
end of the town; is defended by double fossees of an irregular
multangular figure, and is about 800 paces in circumference measured in the inner fossee; part of it is taken into a gentleman's
garden, and work'd into a mount.   On the north side are the
remains of an oblong square tower, about 25 by 30; 'tis built of
flint, with the angles   of hewn stone; the entrance
seems to have been on the north side, and the walls are ten feet
thick.   Near it are   foundations of the mannor house, and
here the mannor courts are open'd.   This castle did belong to
Jeffrey Fitz Peters, Earl of Essex.   The estate then came to the ·
Brydges's, and now belongs to Mr. Selwin, and is a borough town.
In the church is a monument of a good design, ill executed, of the
Corinthian order, open on both sides, with two couchant statues
under it, and over the arch the relief of the woman   on the
man's side, and of the man's on the woman, with several ornaments.
On one side is this imperfect inscription —

Hear lyeth the Body of Sir Richard Brydges Knyght whose Şoule
Jeşu take to his mercy he deceas'd the fyfth of August Anno

On the other side—

Heare lyeth the Lady Jane wife to Sr Richard Brydgys Knyght
And Daughter to Sr William Spenser Knyght.

His medalion is exactly in the dress of Henry the 8th.

In the street are curious remains of the pedestal of a cross, with a relief on each side of it much defaced ; on one side is our Saviour taken down from the Cross, on the other side are sketches of what remains of those reliefs.

This town consists mostly of farmers, and a great number of labourers, who are much employed in Ld Bruce's wood.

I could get no information of Escourt, near which is a   road mentioned by Mr. Cambden, where a large urn, supposed to be   was found with two urns in it, one of which was full of ashes and bones.

On the 25th I was going to Everley, where I had formerly been, a camp on Sudbury hill, suppos'd to be the highest in Wiltshire, and to have been the place of residence of King Ina ; it is defended by a double ditch and a trench is made for it, supposed to have been design'd to secure a passage to water ; there are many barrows near it, and it is conjectured that some battle had been fought here ; tho' I suppose the chiefs who tended in these camps had the honour to have such barrows made over their bodies by their people where they were buryed.   A hare warren, I have it mentioned as near this place, which I was told is still in being.

I went two miles to Collingborn Ducis, that is, it was the estate of the Duke of Somerset, now Lord Bruce's, to whom the advowson of the living of £400 a year belongs.   It is a village a mile long in which several farmers live.   A mile from it is Collingborn Regis of the King's patronage ; here Mr. Delme has a country seat.   From the other Collingborn a stream runs down to Tedworth, which is dry in summer.   I went on three miles to Burbiche, where there was a religious house.   It is six miles from Marlborough, and from this large village we struck out to the right into Savernake Forrest, and went near Ld Bruce's house and through the forest and came into the London road, from which we cross'd to Minal to Mr Pococke's, where I was inform'd by the clergyman that an urn was found at Ogmore with the mouth turn'd down, and it appear'd that some bones and coals had been in it.   I was also inform'd that in wood, three or four miles from Marlborough towards Martinshall Hill to the south-west, are larger stones than any of the Grey Weathers, which probably might afford the materials for Stone-henge.

Highworth, April 12th, 1757.

On the 11th I left Newtown, and going through Newbury and near Bagnor, I came to Wood Speen, where there is a paper mill. Three miles more brought us to Boxford, a large village on both sides of the river, and two more to Welford, Lady Archer's, a large house in the bottom, and a great command of water improved into canals, and a piece of water with an island in it.   Going through Weston 1 mile, litle Shelford ½ a mile, where I saw a small ruin like some religious house.   Great Shelford ½ a mile, East Garston two miles, where the church is cover'd with lead. Eastbury, ½ a mile in Lamborn parish ; here are remains of an old cross, and here I saw the stones call'd the Grey Weathers; I came a mile and half to Lamborn.   I do not know whether I formerly observ'd that there is a handsom Saxon door to the west of the church, and a round window in same style over it, and one of the Saxon windows in the body.   There is also an almshouse for ten people well endowed, and one for five ; the former, I think, was founded by Sr Wm Ishbury, if I do not mistake the name.   This is the road from London to Auburn, and from Marlborough to Oxford.   About Auburn, and other parts of this country, they spin cotten for can-dles, for cotten clothes and stockins; and the carriers go with cotten backward and forward through this place to and from London.   A mile further is the hamlet of Up Lamborn, which is a pretty place where this river rises.   We went up the down to the right of it, and in three miles came to the camp over the White

Horse at the end of these hills, which commands a glorious prospect into Wiltshire, Berkshire, Oxfordshire, and Gloucestershire. We passed a line to the east of it ; the camp itself is defended by one deep fossee, it is of an irregular form of four sides, about 800 paces in circumference ; to the north-east of it is a small hill like a barrow, which was cut of from it: it is call'd Dragon hill; on the side of the hill over it, just under the camp, is the White Horse, cut in turf, as in a trot, the green sod remains to form the body; it may be 100 yards in length, and is well designed. On Dragon hill, the common people say, St. George kill'd the dragon, and show a spot on it which they affirm is never cover'd with grass, and there they say the dragon was killed, and I think buryed, and that the white horse was St. George's steed, tho' all this history was acted in Syria, as I believe may be seen according to the tradition in the Description of the East. At the foot of the hill is a spring call'd   out of which the river Ock rises, which falls into the Thames at Abington.

We went to the west   and came four miles by very bad road to Becket, in the parish of Shrivenham, Lord Barrington's, where there is a great command of water, and the whole is well laid out, very fine lawns and clumps of trees, all in the farm way ; and near the house are walks round some of the lawn, with trees and shrubs and evergreens on each side of them. On one side is the water, which is very broad near the house, with a summer house built in it, and is continued on in a serpentine river for a considerable way, with walks near it adorn'd in like manner with trees, &c., and this is to be carried on further, and to be divided into two branches; in the church here, which is a very modern structure, there is a singular Saxon belfrey, and the litle old windows remain. From this place I went three miles to Colleshill, where Sr Mark Pleydwell has an exceeding well built house of hewn free stone, brought from Barrington, near Burford. There is a wilderness garden behind the house. But the great curiosity of this place is the water, which Sr Mark has brought to his house, and the garden.

There was a well on the side of the hill, 63 feet above the basin in the garden, from which the water being drawn up was conveyed by pipes to the house; but the pipes being out of order, he thought of bringing it under ground from the bottom of the well, which was 63 feet below the surface; in order to make the springs more plentiful he dug forty yards from the bottom of the well higher up the hill, and arches it from the level of the bottom of the well; here it is 70 feet below the surface. He then carried the canal under ground to the road and under some offices, about half a furlong, springs rising plentifully for 40 yards below the well, the earth was brought up by windlaces to the mouth of the well; it then made a turn down the yard for half a furlong more; here another well was dug down in order to bring up the earth; it was then carried into the garden, where they open'd a trench and carried it about 100 yards in the same direction, and then making a turn brought it to the basin, and arching the whole over with bricks this part was cover'd over; they reckoned the whole about two furlongs. From the basin it is carryed back under ground, and passes down a wall on two sides of a garden, from which it falls down through stone pipes into litle basins, and forms another basin in a garden below. This underground work is exactly like that mentioned between Damascus and Palmyra in the Description of the East, and as it was done about 8 years agoe it is probable he took his hint from that.

From this place I went two miles across a marshy common, in which a river rises, which falls into the Thames near Lechlade, and came to Highworth, finely situated on a heigth much like Dudley, in Worcestershire. It is a market town, and in the turnpike road from London to Farington and to Badminster by the places I shall mention. This place is six miles from Farington and 12 from Wootton Basset. The town subsists by the thoroughfare and markets of cheese, of cattle, and corn, being but four miles from Lechlade; from this place there is navigation to London; there is an old cross in the market place. In the church there are light round pillars, with octagon   a ceiling of boards in compart-

ments, adorn'd with stars over the rood loft ; in one isle are monuments of the Warnefords, and of the great travellor of 1724, who
marryed into the Dorset family, with a very elegant epitaph. In
the chancel is the monument of Mr. Derham, the minister, erected
by his son, T. Derham, who I conjecture was the writer of the
phisico-theological lectures. There are grotesque figures on the
four pinnacles of the tower.

Wallingford, April 13th, 1757.

The turnpike road goes 7 miles to Crikelade, ten to Malmsbury,
and   to   the town and the parish, if I mistake
not, in which Badminton is, the Duke of Beaufort's, is situated, where
it comes into the Bath road from Glocester, &c. I went to Cricklade, which is a small town with several publick houses in it; 'tis
situated on the branch of the Thames, as I was inform'd, call'd the
Isis ; the country people have a notion that it has its name from its
being a very cold water ; as that branch at Fairford has the name of
Caldow, as they say, tho' it is Coln, from being a warm water.
This river rises near Minchin Hampton, which is look'd on as the
source of the Thames, as the Caldow does near Cheltenham.
Another river falls in here from the north west, call'd the Churn.
From the south, according to Speed's maps, falls in the river Rye,
and a smaller stream from the south-west, which seems to be most
convenient for navigation from the branch of the   near
Wotten Basset. There is navigation to this place in boats that hold
about six tons, but 'tis only for the market of Cricklade. It is said
that this branch of the Thames could be most easily made navigable
to Bath by the branch of the Avon above mention'd, by which there
would be a communication between the Severn and the Thames, and
'tis thought that the expence would come under £100,000. They
have a manufacture here in spinning of wool and yarn; I suppose of
cotten.

The tower of the church is on the outside adorned with Gothick
arches; the arch and ornaments within are a very fine piece of
architecture. The man who show'd it me mentioned but imper-

fectly that the Hungerfords were the founders of it. I observed
the bear holding a club, and another a cross, with a pidgeon in each
of the four divisions. There are in the church some few Saxon
pillars remaining. The Jenners of the neighbourhood have a
chapel here for a burial place ; there is another small parish church
just on the river called Cricklade St. Mary's. I rid five miles to
Fairford, most of it is very bad road ; it is in Glocestershire, and on
the high turnpike road from London to Glocester, which we went
in as far as Dorchester by Farington and Abington; it goes through
Cirencester to Glocester, and from Cirencester the road from these
parts to Bristol turns off by Tetbury. It is a small market town
for cheese and corn, and abounds in publick houses ; when I cross'd
the river at Cricklade we came into the free stone country, all
before is something of the nature of the grey weathers, it is at the
distance of from 5 to ten feet under ground, and the beds are often
of great thickness. This brought to my mind a conjecture that, as
all the moisture is drawn from the higher parts towards the principal
rivers, that there are peculiar juices to particular countries that
hardens the earth, and turns into limestone, freestone or firestone ; the
grey weathers is, I believe, of the latter kind, and the large lumps
which are seen I believe are commonly found on the sides of hills or
rising grounds, or in bottoms having slid down from the sides of the
hills or rising grounds, and that they have been left bare by the
continual washing away of the earth from all hills down to the
valleys. Towards the top both the one and the other are commonly
in small rubble, and here the freestone does not rise large, but it
does at Barington, near Burford, and at Barnesby, about four miles
towards Cirencester, from which place they are now supplyed. I
was told that this mannor did belong to the Traceys, afterwards to
the Tames, that then it came to the Barkers, and now to Mr. Lamb
by marriage of one who proved a sole heiress. Near the town he
has a very good house with a fine lawn before it, in which the trees
indeed are planted as three avenues ; behind this house the gardens
are laid out in the wilderness way, and there is a small park beau-

tifully adorned with clumps of trees. But what is very fine is a
terrace on an eminence over the river, which is form'd into a very
fine serpentine for near a mile in length; towards the north end is
a round basin, from which a cascade opens to a walk of the garden;
this at some distance is encompassed as with a square form'd by
canals that spoils the beauty of the thing, which, if the angles were
broke, would form a beautiful island, as made by the division of
the waters. But the great curiosity of Fairford is the church. In
1493 John Tame, Esq., took a ship in which there was painted
glass, designed for a chapel of the Popes; it was the work of
Albert Durell, said to be an Italian, tho' it is a French name. Mr.
Tame being or coming to be Lord of this Mannor, built the fine
church here on purpose for the glass. It is said to be 125 feet long
and 55 broad. The tower is in the middle, and the whole is of
good Gothic architecture. The windows· are divided into four
compartments, but sometimes one subject takes up two, and over
every compartment are two small ones, as in Gothic windows, with
each a figure in it of a single person. In the first window which is
shown in the north side of the cross isle is Eve and the tree of
knowledge, Moses and the burning bush, Joshua, the Queen of
Sheba, and Solomon, each in its separate compartment. In the
next window, going to the east, Zacharias and Elizabeth, the birth
of St. John, Joseph and Mary contracted, married. In another
window, going on in the same direction, the Salutation, the birth of
Christ, offering of the Wise Men, the Presentation. At the east end
of this north isle, Joseph and Mary going into Egypt, in two compartments, Christ disputing with the doctors, and the Assumption
of the Virgin Mary. In the east window of the chancel, Christ
taken, praying in the garden, before Pilate, scourging, bearing the
cross, crucified, with soldiers on each side. There is a window only
on the south side of the chancel, the vestry being to the north. In
that window Christ taken down from the Cross, and put into the
Sepulchre. At the east end of the south isle is Christ anointing for the
Sepulchre, appearing to Mary, and then to the other Mary, as a

gardiner, the Transfiguration with Moses and Elias, Peter, James and John. These and some others below seem to be wrong placed, and that it should have been where the Assumption of the Virgin Mary is, which should have been last before the 12 Apostles. On the south side, Christ going to Emmaus, 12 Apostles see him when breaking bread, Thomas putting his finger in his side. This is in two compartments. The next is the Draught of Fishes, the Ascension, the Descent of the Holy Ghost. In the three following windows are the Twelve Apostles, and in the last the four Doctors of the Church. Opposite to these, on the north side, are the 4 greater Prophets and the twelve minor Prophets. In the four windows over the body of the church are twelve persecuting Emperors, and in small compartments over them a devil figured, all with different appearances. Opposite are twelve Saints, the supporters of the church, probably each of them martyr'd by the opposite Emperor. In the chancel is the monument of a Lady Tracy,* and of Oldisworth, minister of the place, and several others of that family to whom the rectory did belong.

I went four miles in the London road to Lechlade, where there is a church with a small spire, and light Gothick pillars ; here the River Lech runs into the Thames. The great navigation for London begins ; they have two wharfs within a basin on each side for the barges to lye in, which are from 60 to 80 tons. I went on six miles to Farington, prettily situated on the back and side of a hill, which commands a view into Glocestershire and Berkshire, for when we passed the river at Fairford we came into Berkshire. There is a Saxon door and pillars to the church, in which are buryed the   knights, to whom there is a monument with two good couchant statues, in the dress of about the time of Henry the 7th. Sr Henry Purefoy and the l'ages the present lords.

Farington is 9 miles from Wantage, Starford being about the middle way. Wantage is in the road to Oxford from Marlborough

* A daughter of John Lyttelton of Frankley, in Worcestershire, Esq., who appears by her epitaph to have been skill'd in all the learned languages.—*Note in MS.*

by Highworth, and the road from Wantage to London is by
Wallingford and Henley, and a stage coach goes from that town to
London. In three miles from Farington I pass'd by Sr Willoughby
Aston's house, two miles further by Buckland; opposite to this
place is a very good house, Mr Brotherton's, called Pusey; two
miles and a half further is M^r call'd Longworth Lodge,
and in a mile and half we came to Kingston, where I lay at Kingston
Inn, a very good house.

London, April 14th, 1757.

On the 13th I went on from Kingston, and in a mile pass'd
through Fifield, and in half a mile more by Tubney, Captain Stone-
house's. In three miles came to Shippon, where I observed in the
free stone, coraline petrifications, and those very large. On this side
Farington I first observ'd the free stone which extends, I suppose,
beyond Shotover hill near Oxford, and as I recollect, all along
towards Aylesbury, and so across the country on the high ground
through Oxfordshire, Buckinghamshire, Bedfordshire, opposite to
the Chiltorn chalky hills, which are to the south-east, and extend
from Cambridgeshire to the Isle of Purbeck, there being another
chain of chalky hills from Dover through Kent and Sussex. A mile
more brought us to Abington, of which place I have formerly given
you an account. I observed an old gate, I believe the east gate.
with a statue over it, and the town house is a fine building of hewn
stone of the composite order above, with two arches at each end and
four on each side. The, arch'd windows are no advantage to it.
From this place I went through an exceeding fine country mostly
near the Thames, six miles to Dorchester, passing by a ferry which
is a short way to Wallingford. I went to see the church at Dorchester, and shall add my observations to a former account. The
old north wall of the church is standing with one Saxon window
remaining in it, to which the ancient tower is built, the old cornice,
the south wall was probably where the middle row of pillars within
now stand, and the two true arches of the cross isle remain; all the
rest seem to be new Gothick work. Round one of the pillars, as for

a sort of shelf, is a stone work, on which is cut the parable of the
Foolish Virgins. The east window and the north window are so
divided by mullions in a Gothic taste that at the joyning of them
our Saviour's history seems to have been cut in relief, part of which
remains; but on the north window the genealogy of Christ from
Jesse, as in a tree, is represented. On the south side are the three
seats for the officiating persons. and an arcade for the elements with
two basons, and holes at the bottom for pouring out the water that
might be left. The lower part or pedestal of the font is talk'd of as
a very old thing, tho' I think I am sure it is not so old as the Conquest, being Gothic ; the bason cast in lead has greater marks of
antiquity, there being reliefs round it very much in the Greek taste.
They show a monument of Segur, Earl of Cornwal ; I observ'd an
old camp on the hill on the other side of the water. I went from
Dorchester five miles to Wallingford, there being a shorter way over
a ferry.

Wallingford is a fine situation on the Thames, and a very pretty
town. It was a place of note in the time of the Saxons, and in 1006
'tis said 'twas destroyed by the Danes; it was a borough in the
time of Edward the Confessor, and the castle was surrendred to the
Conqueror. It was often besieged by King Stephen, but a peace
was concluded here between him and Henry 2d. The Glocester
road went through it till bridges were built at Abington and Dorchester. There are remains of the old castle and of the keep, which
was encompass'd with a wet ditch. The old fossee and rampart are
remaining ; the south part is call'd Cliny Craff and the west side
Bull Craff. There were formerly twelve parish churches here; at
present there is only one very indifferent church in service. There
was a priory here of Black friers. Trinity Church near the west
gate belongs to the Abbey of St. Alban's ; Wolsey got a grant of it
for his College, and on his disgrace coming to the king, it was, if I
mistake not, given back again to Christ Church College. I went to
Nettlebed, where I have been since inform'd there is a spring which
never fails in the driest summers. And from that high ground we

descended to Henley, most delightfully situated on the Thames ; there is one church in the town, in which there is a handsom monument of the Dorick order with this inscription on it—

Memoriæ Sacrum D   Dominæ Dominæ Eliz* Periam viduæ Quondam uxoris Domini Roberti Doyley denuo Henrici Neville, ultimo Gulielmi Periam Militis Quæ in hoc oppido Scholam fundavit educandis pauperium filiis viginti : E. F. Balliolense Collegium in inclyta Academia Oxon unius socii et duorum scholarium ditavit obiit antem Anno Domini Millessimo Sexcentessimo Vicessimo primo Maij Sexto.

Near the town Mr. Cooper, a banker of London, has a very good house ; has adorn'd the opposite hill, and made a beautiful entrance into the wood, and erected a building in the island below. Lower Mr. Freeman has a fine house. But the most beautiful situation is Park place, which belongs to General Conway. The house is situated on the hill a mile above the town, being shelter'd on each side two fine points on the hill, which commands a most glorious prospect.

On the 14th I crossed to Maidenhead, and came by Braywick to Lord Harry *Pawlet's* in the forest,* and near Cranborn Lodge to Beanclerck Sunning hill, and from that place in the evening to London, having quere ? given an account before [of] all the places I pass'd through.

Richmond, April 30th, 1757.

On the 23rd I went from London to Aldersbrook in Essex, and going to Marybone passed that fine New way which from Padington communicates with all the northern roads, so that going over the ferry at Stepney one may now go all round London by Westminster Bridge and by Petty France.

Aldersbrook is greatly improv'd, a walk being made all round it, and a gate at the angle nearest London, which way leads to the nearest piece of water, on the north side of which is the beautiful hanging kitchen garden and a greenhouse, which makes a very

---

* Mr. Bulkely's a litle beyond is an exceeding good new built house and fine offices, and by Colonel Clayton's.—*Note in MS.*

good room.　Clumps of trees are planted before the house as well as behind it, so that altogether it is become a very fine place.　I went to see a house call'd Valentines, near Ilford.　It did belong to Archbishop Tillotson, and is now in the possession of Captain Raymond of the East India Company.　The house is very finely furnished with India goods, particularly there are the several building of a Bramin's house cut in ivory, in which he receives people nearer or further from the entrance according to their quality.　A unicorn's horn of a light colour and greenish cast about eighteen inches and much larger at the buts than the horn of the rhinoceros, it is in a neat irregular figure, probably by art.　'Tis said this horn grows in the forehead of this animal which lives in the kingdom of Assam.　I also saw in the canal a Chinese duck with the wings rising up on each side as represented in the Chinese pictures.　I pass'd through London on the 28th, and at Hamersmith saw Mr. Dodington's house, lately belonging to the Duke of Athol; he has new model'd it in a very elegant taste, and 'tis finely furnish'd; but the gallery, which is the length of the house, is a very beautiful piece of architecture of the Ionic order; there is a Venetian window at each end and two windows on each side of an arcade supported by two fine pillars of Italian marble; in this arcade is a colossal statue of Flora, and in a nich on each side a statue with bronze groups over them.　On each side of the arcade and the Venetian windows are busts on terms with bronze groups likewise over. The heads of those at the ends of the room are of porphiry. Between the windows are statues, as well as between the looking glass opposite to the windows.　At each end is a column with a vase on them of Oriental alabaster, and one of the pillars is of the same fineer'd, the other of some very fine marble.　The pillars of this door at entrance are of lapis lazuli fineer'd, which cost four shillings an ounce.　'Tis said they were made for the late Prince of Wales.　The cov'd ceiling seem'd to be of the Caterani form. The whole is paved with fine marbles in beautiful figures.　The back part of the house consists of a fine large room, highly adorned with gilt carv'd work, and a small room at each end of it. Behind the house is a lawn and plantations to the river, and there is a walk some way by the water side.

From this place I went to the Duke of Argyle's, a small mile from Hounslow, where the duke began a plantation mostly of evergreens and American plants about 28 years ago, built a green house and a menagerie for different kinds of forreign fowls. The whole is laid out much in the wilderness way, with a broad walk of grass all round The Duke has lately built a small house, cover'd with a single roof like Lord Westmorland's, and long narrow offices are built on each side, to which there are passages at each end from the house, as to communicate with every one of the four rooms, of which I take it the house consists.

From Hounslow I went in the road to Bath to Cranford bridge, which is over a stream that rises towards Uxbridge, and leaving that road to the left I had Heston, Lady Bulkeley's, to the right, then passed through Harlington, and by Ld Uxbridge's seat at Drayton came into the Uxbridge road at Hellingdon. Pass'd through Uxbridge, seeing the late judge Talbot's, a very pretty place to the right, and going in the Oxford road we had Mr. Way's to the right, near the road to Chesham and Rickmansworth, pass'd by the Aylesbury road and came four miles to Gerard's Cross, at the park wall of Bulstrode, the Duke of Portland's, which I came to see. This was the seat of the first Earl of Portland. The ground and plantations of the park are very fine ; on an eminence to the left is a British camp. There was a long avenue to the house which was taken away and a kitchen garden near it is removed; to the left was a lawn to which there was a steep descent of several feet, all which is now forming into grass with a gentle descent, behind the house is a wood with walks through it and round it ; and a parterre is forming in one part and in another a shrubbery. At the further end of it is a canal covered with wild ducks ; from this there is a descent to the left to the dairy and menagerie, in which several sorts of birds and fowls are kept and breed, particularly Chinese pheasants

of both kinds.   The dairy is adorn'd with a Chinese front, as a
sort of open summer-house, and about it are some pieces of water
for the different water poultry.   In the same vale is the kitchen
garden lately wall'd in and planted, in which are all sorts of con-
trivances for ripening fruits.

On the 29th I went from Bulstrode by Fulmere and then by
Langley Park, where the Duke of Marlborough has built a very
handsome new house of hewn stone, with four fronts and five windows in the principal fronts and seven on each side.   We came into
the Bath road a mile to the west of Colnbrook, and going through
that place turn'd to the right and came to Stanes, where the Coln
falls into the Thames; we went to Chertsey, and then about two
miles further to Mr. Southcote's within a mile of Weybridge.   This
is the first improvement in the farm kind, and is esteem'd the most
elegant, in England.   It consists of walks to the left, first round two
meadows on rather high ground and then round another on low
ground, on the right side of them, through the further side of which
a canal is made from the poultry house, which is in form of a
temple, and extends towards the Thames.   These walks are adorn'd
not only with plantations of wood but with spots and beds of
flowering shrubs and other flowers to fill up angles, and other shrubs
to diversifie the scene ; from the end next the house and behind it is
a piece of water form'd like a river, over which there is a bridge
that leads to several small fields mostly of corn and some meadows
with walks and plantations round them.   This was the first beginning of the farm.   From this place I pass'd through Weybridge to
Oatlands, Lord Lincoln's, famous for a terrace, lengthened by the
present Earl; it is over a hanging ground, at the foot of which is a
meadow bounded by a serpentine river, which with the Thames
seems to form a large island; the only objection to it is that the
banks appearing to be made with art it looks litle in comparison of
the Thames; but this might be alter'd by making the banks a litle
broken, and by planting them in an irregular manner with withy
and other trees.   At first entrance strangers are lead into a winding

walk to the left through shrubberies, and so down the hills to a nursery, laid out like an elegant parterre, in which there is a basin for Chinese fish. And near it there is lately made another enclosure for all sorts of exotic plants that will thrive abroad, with boards plac'd over them on which their names are cut. In the lawns sheep are grazeing; and at the end of the terrace is one of Inigo Jones's gates with this inscription on it :—

Henricus Comes de Lincoln
Hunc Arcum
Opus Ignatii Jones
Vetustati Corruptum
Restituit
Anno Georgio 1¹
XXI.

There are several acres of ground at the entrance laid out in fine lawn, and planted with clumps of trees in a very beautiful manner. I went through Walton to Hampton Court, passing by the large enclosure of Abscourt, and then near Moulsey; I saw the Palace here, and besides, Raphael's cartoons. I took notice of the of Cæsar, painted by Andrea Mainteino, which, if I mistake not, are engraved   . And in another room the Battles, &c. of Alexander, by Le Brun, executed in very fine tapestry. I went through Kingston by the river to Ham, and to Richmond Hill.

On the 30th I went to see Petersham, the Lord Harrington's; the house is of good architecture, Lord Burlington's design. The back front is the grandest, in which there is a room at each end of a peculiar form, joyn'd to the main body of the house in front by a colonade, but the communication with it is from the house it self. There is a fine lawn before it, and an ascent to a green terrace, above which is a wood with walks through it up to Richmond Hill, and there is a shady walk to it on the side and by the end of the lawn from the entrance. I went by Roehampton and Wimbleton, the park being shut up, and passed near Merton, and came into the turnpike road to Guilford by Epsom, and going near Mitcham I came to the part

of the road near Cheme, and turning to the right came to None Such
Park, and to the site of the Royal Palace of that name, the history
of which I have given in the travels of 1754 and 1755. From the
Dutchess of Cleveland it came to the Duke of Grafton, who sold it
near thirty years ago. This park consisted of above 500 acres.
On the other side of the high road to Epsom was Worcester Park
of 1000 acres, which Ld Leicester bought of the Duke of Grafton
for Sr George Walton, who was steward to them both, and it has
been since sold in several parcels. I examined the foundations of
the Palace, which appear to have been built round a court. I saw
signs of the foundations of towers to the north, which I suppose to
be those represented in Speed's maps of Surrey; the grand front
seems to have been to the south, as there represented, and there are
ruins of offices for twenty acres to the south; they said also that
there was a avenue to the east, and there are remains of a large
canal. The way to go to it is to keep on in the road to Epsom till
one comes within half a mile of Ewell, and then one furlong further to
the left out of the road there is a farm house built close to it. I went
on to Ewell and so to Epsom. This place was a famous resort on
account of mineral waters that are near it, of which the best salts are
made, but they are not now frequented. There are many gentlemen's seats near it. We went from it to Leatherhead, where the
waters of the Mole come from under the hill, which looses it self on
the other side, near Darking; this river runs through Esher Park,
and falls into the Thames at Moulsey, opposite to Hampton Court.
We went toward Cobham, and had   house to the left, and
afterwards Ld Effingham's, and then Ld Carpenter's to the right;
we cross'd the Thames at S^r   Vincent's, passing first by a
large mill and building belonging to it, the property of a College in
Oxford; and coming to Cobham we left the town to the right, and
came by Sr John Ligoneer's, and so to Ripley, and leaving the
Guilford road we came in a mile to the ruins of the Abbey of
Newark, of which what seems to have been the church and refectory
in part standing. We went round by a heath about 3 miles to

Woking, a market town, but a very inconsiderable place. Here was a royal seat inhabited by the Countess of Richmond, mother to Henry 7th, where she died. This place belongs to the Zouches, to Sr Edward, knight marshal in the time of King James the First, and then to his son James, one of the Lords of the Treasury. The last of them built a high tower like a pillar, which seem'd to be octagon, in order to keep a light on it as a watch when he came from London at night, to find his way across the heath. There is a good mansion house built of brick, with a large enclosure, probably round part of the Old Park. It was afterwards sold to one Mr. Walters. The ancient house of the Countess of Richmond (as I was inform'd afterward) was where a farm house now stands in a meadow. I rid three miles mostly near the Wey, through a beautiful country to the high road from London to Guilford, to which place I came in three miles more.

I observed at the castle remains of Saxon windows, but most of the windows have been new made ; and the entrance, probably a later work than the castle, is Gothic. Mention is made of this castle before the Conquest. There are two churches in the town belonging to the same minister. One of them is a handsome new brick building not yet open'd. There are some marks of Saxon antiquity in the other. The Grey Friers had an old house and large enclosure out of the town, [which] belongs to Speaker Onslow. I left Guilford on the 2nd of May, and after riding about three miles came to the Heath, and in five more cross'd over a stream at Farnborough into Hampshire, the seat of the Earl of Anglesey, and immediately cross'd at Cove, the high road to Farnham from Bagshot and those parts, and coming to Mindley Warren we cross'd the high road to Basingstoke, and came to Yately and Eversley, where the Windhams have houses; and here we were in another high road, if I mistake not, from Ockingham into the great western road, and we were near Finchamstead, which I had formerly passed in the way to Ockingham. We cross'd another stream which falls into the Lodden, and came near Heckfield that belonged to the

Sturts, but is lately purchased by Mr. Pitt as a fine addition to his estate at Stratford Sea⁷, where we passed, as I take it, the main branch of the Lodden, and came to Mortimer in Berkshire, a populous parish of great extent. We had also gone through a spot of Wiltshire which is entirely inclosed between Hampshire and Berkshire. We came to the heaths near Silchester, and passing down to Aldermaston we struck off the commons to the left, and came through Brimpton, having first observed a fossee, which seemed to have been some ancient boundary, and so came by Greenham Common to Newtown.

Malmesbury, May 23rd, 1757.

I left Newtown on the 21st, and going through Newbury came to Chively, and turning out of the Oxford road about half a mile to Prior's Court, belonging to Dr. Barton, Canon of Christchurch, where he has built a very handsom house. It is said to have been the house of the Prior of the Abbey of Abington. I left this place, and came by the north end of Cheveley. This place is inhabited much by the family of the Pococks; and as the family of the famous Orientalist came from this family and place, so there is a tradition too that our family of Hawkley in Hampshire, and my great grandfather, who was auditor of the Dutchy Court of Lancaster, were nearly related, and liv'd there ever since Henry VII.'s reign. The family are at this time the lay impropriators of the rectory here. From this place I went to the right of Peysmore and Bright Walton, came into the Newbury road to Wantage at Lilly, and went to the left of Farnborowe, a fine situation, commanding a view into the vale, as well as to the south, and coming on the downs left the Wantage road on the right and came to Letcombe Castle, a strong camp near a mile in circumference and something of a round figure, defended by a strong ditch, with a rampart about twenty feet high on the outside and ten within. This probably was the camp of the enemy against the camp of the hill of White Horse, which I have describ'd in one of my letters in my last tour. About two miles further I saw a barrow, probably on the field of battle that had been between them. This camp had its name from Letcombe in the vale at the foot of the hill. We pass'd by the camp of the hill of the White Horse, having first seen Kingston at the foot of the hill, where Mr. Atkins has a house and fine water, at the rise of a stream, that soon falls into the Ol , and afterward saw Uffington, I have mentioned before. About two miles from this hill in the way to Swindon I observ'd to the right some stones on an artificial heigth, and going to it found it to be an oblong mount. Near the south end is a stone laid on three stones, which, with two stones at the entrance, form a room which is about five feet long and four feet wide and four feet high. About it are several stones, which seem originally to have been plac'd in order. This is probably some Druid superstition, and is call'd Old Waylam or Waylam's Stone. The stones are of the kind of the grey weathers, which I did not see anywhere in these parts in this journey. We went on and pass'd near Warnborow, where there is a church with a tower at one end, and a steeple, as I conjecture, in the middle, probably at the west end of the old church, now the chancel. We turn'd to the right to Leddenton, and coming to the bottom pass'd over two streams, which, according to Speed, run into that river which falls into the Thames at Inglesham, a litle above Lechlade. As soon as I had pass'd the last I found the soil alter'd from a chalkey to a yellow sand and clay, first without stone, and then we came to the stone, which I shall describe at Swindon, to which place we assended three miles from Leddinton.

Swindon is pleasantly situated on an eminence, and commands a delightfull view of the villages which are at the side and foot of the hills to the east. It does not lye in any high road, but they have a great market every Monday for fat black cattle. The common people work very much in the quarries. The lime stone is at the top, about 3 feet thick and four from the surface, and in it there are hearts, cockles, charmæ, serues, ammons, horns, trochi, and entrochi. Then there is four feet of flag, 8 feet of sand, 5 feet main rock, which is the best sort, and then what they call hard rock, which is under water; this, when cut into flag stones, never sweats; the main rock is most proper for hewn stone. They do not call it a freestone, tho' it is very much like it, especially the limestone. I observed some small shells in some of the hard stone, and I think in the main rock also. They raise these flag stone very large, 8 or 9 feet long and five broad, and make very handsom tomb stones of it, which they colour black, and the letters being white have a very good effect, and if well done the colour lasts. This place is ten miles from Farington, Lamborn, and Marlborough, 6 from Highworth,. 7 from Cricklade, and 5 from Wootten Basset, tho' we made it 7 by North Lediard, where Mr. Askough has a seat, whereas we ought to have gone to the left of Ld Bolingbroke's.

Stroud, May 24th, 1757.

I have formerly given an account of Wootten Basset. Lord Hyde has an estate here, and the late Lord's father, Ld Clarendon, is buried in the church, without any monument. Mr. Brinsden and Mr. Long have the influence to return Members to Parliament opposed by Lord Hyde.

From this place I went 3 miles to Lediard Tragose, the seat of Ld Bolingbroke; it belong'd to the late Ld Bolingbroke's father, and tho' by his patent the title was to run up to his father, in case he dyed without children, yet, when he was attainted, the father would not take the title, but was created by King George the first St. John, which title descended to his son, the late Lord, by another mother, and his son, on the death of Ld Bolingbroke, has taken the title; it is a pretty park, with a serpentine river in sight of the house, which is a good piece of architecture, built with square turrets at the corners, from a design of Campbelle's; there is a handsom hall and apartments, and an elegant library, in which there is a genealogical history of the family. In the church are some monuments of the family, one of Queen Elizabeth's time, in which the name is spelt Seyntjhon. There is a fine monument of St. John with couchant statues; he put up the genealogical table of the family opposite to the monument, from the time of the Conqueror, with whom they came over; they have been doubly allied to the Royal family, one of the alliance being by the Countess of Richmond, mother to Henry VII. Another monument is to   who was kill'd, if I mistake not, in the Parliament army. In the east window are the two St. Johns, in painted glass, as the patrons of the family; and there are some litle remains of painted glass in the other windows. This estate came by the Tregoes and Beauchamps by marriage with the St. Johns. In the church yard is buryed   who dyed Dean of Down in Ireland. About 1000 acres in this parish pay a very triffling modus; among 'em is Priorsfield, and as the living pays something to the Chapter of Glocester, 'tis probable this estate did formerly belong to the Abbey. All this country abounds in stone in which there are shells. On the 23d we went 7 computed and ten measur'd miles to Malmsbury, which is 89 from London, passing mid-way the living of Brinckworth of £400 a year in the gift of Mrs. Horner. It is a fine summer scituation, but the roads in all this country are so bad in winter that it breaks off all neighbourhood in that season. At the point of the hill to the south are some remains of the Abbey of Broadstock near unto the road from Wotten Basset to Chipenham and 4 miles from the former.

Malmsbury is finely situated on an eminence where two rivlets meet and fall into the Avon, two of them bounding it on two sides; it is a fine hanging ground on these two sides down to the river, in which respect it somewhat resembles the scituation of Jerusalem. The most eastern branch, which in the map is made to rise at Hanberton and passes by Chadleton, is that which comes nearest to the branch of the Thames which rises near Okesey, and according to the map are not above 3 miles apart. This seems to be the most convenient place for joyning the navigation. It is said that Dunwallo

King of the Britains, first built this place, and call'd it Caer Bladon
from the name of the river. This town was destroyed in the wars;
there a castle was built call'd Ingelborne. 'Tis said the Saxon
petty kings had a palace at Caer Lurburge, now Broken Bridge,
not a mile from the castle of Ingelburne; it belong'd to the
Bishops of the West Saxons. It is said that Madulphus, a Scot,
taught here, and prevail'd on King Athelstan and a Bishop of
Winchester, or rather of the West Saxons, to found an Abbey here,
and thus from him was call'd Madulphusburi. Aldhelm, the King's
great favourite, was the first abbot, who afterwards got him
canonized; and the Charter from Eleutherius to Aldhelm is supposed to be dated at Caer Cleerburge, being mention'd in this
manner: "Achem publice juxta flumen Badon." Great part of
the Abbey church is very old Saxon building, but Gothick windows
have been made in it. It is all down above the transept, of which
only two very high arches remain; that to the north about twenty
feet wide, that to the east 30; they are flat arches. It is said they
supported a very fine spire, and they then were four towers, one at
each end of the transept and two at the west end. King Athelstan's
monument, with his couchant statue, remains on the south side of
the upper end of the body of the church; it is in the style of the
statue at Ramsey Abbey of the person who is styled Aldermannus
totius Angliæ; but they have added above the head a fine Gothick
ornament over the porch, where there is a very fine Saxon door of
seven or eight numbers adorn'd with historical sculpture, they say
was Don Scotus's study; and there are remains of a church to the
north in the churchyard, where 'tis said his scholar murder'd him
in King Alfred's time. There is a steeple to the west of it, which
seems to have been detach'd from this building, tho' some low
fabrick joyn'd to it. In the garden of Mr. Wilkins, apothecary, is
a couchant statue of a monk with the tonsure, which does not seem
to be very old; it was found in the church or churchyard, buryed
in the ground. A meadow near the town still retains the name of
Aldhelm. In the time of Hen. 8th Wm. Stump, a great clothier,

bought the site of the Abbey and church for £1500, and gave the church to the parish. The corporation consists of a lord steward, who is now Mr. Fox, and of twelve capital burgesses, who are called aldermen, and must be dwellers in the town and have had an acre of land for twenty years, and they choose the Members of Parliament. William Somerset, commonly call'd W^m of Malmsbury, and Hobbes, were natives of this place. The former writ an abrigdment of the History of the Kings of England, from the Saxons to the time of Henry 1st. Aldhelm, a monk of this Abbey in the 8th century, writ very fine Latin. They have small markets here, and are a thoroughfare by a turnpike road, as mentioned before, to   near Badminton.

From this place I went two miles to Charleton house belonging to the Earl of Berkshire and Suffolk. It is a fine regular old house, built round a court in the style of Burleigh house but much smaller, middle part of the front is built on a Dorick colonade; and there being a court before it and a porter's lodge at the entrance it appears as if it was built round two courts and has a fine effect; there is a handsom gallery in the house and the park is fine. The late Lord has been dead about 2 months and was succeeded by his grandson. I went 3 miles to Tetbury, in Gloucestershire, situated on an eminence at the rise of a branch of the river Avon. There is a steeple to the church in which are monuments of the Gastrels, and, if I mistake not, of a Lord Bruce. There are some marks of old foundations near the church, which I take to have been of the castle. Here the cloathing trade begins, and it is a great thoroughfare from Cirencester to Bath and Bristol. After I left it I was inform'd that there is a spring near it, which incrusts sticks with stone. I went 2 miles to Beverston Castle, belonging to Sr Baptist Hickes; it has been large, but turn'd into a farmhouse. An old chapel remains entire in it. I went on two miles to Horsely on a branch of the river Stroude. This is the first of the cloathing villages, which opens to a most delightfull narrow vale with houses all up the hills on each side, and a great mixture of wood, that renders it one of the most delightful scenes that can be imagin'd.

Gloucester, May 25th, 1757.

From Horseley I went through the fine valley near as far as Woodchester, to which it was not convenient for me to go; a mosaic pavement was found there some years ago, and in pulling down the chapel of St. Blaire they met with some Roman coin. Earl Godwin's wife built a monastery here to expiate her husband's treachery in relation to the Nunnery of Berkeley. This place belongs to Ld Ducey Moreton.

I turn'd up from this place and cross'd to that branch of the river which rises near Ld Ducey's house and runs down this vale, and by means of heads, which have been thrown up, makes several ponds, which have a beautiful effect, between the hills on each side, which are cover'd with wood, there being a very good road made on each side. From Ld Ducey's we ascended up to Forceter Hill, when of a sudden a most surprizing beautiful prospect presented to the view of the fine vale in which Glocester stands, of the hills to the east and to the Severn, the Forest of Dean, and of the mountains of Wales to the west, and of the wood and country to the south-west as far as Chepstow. At Ld Ducy's seat, at Wickwar, I saw the chesnut tree formerly, which is said to have been planted in 1216. It is fenced round and much decay'd, and, if I remember, almost all broken down, but is alive; I forgot the measure, but have been inform'd that it is fifty-seven feet in circumference.

We descended to Froceter Inn, and on the 24th we went through such another beautiful vale, being the lower part of the river Stroud, into which that which runs by Woodchester empties it self, and in four miles came to Stroud, having first pass'd the turnpike at Cainscross, 104 miles from London, 14 from Cirencester, 10 from Glocester, and 8 from Framicode. Stroud is a sort of capital to the clothing villages, and is a neat town well situated on the foot of the hill; the water is look'd on as very good for dying. The clothing trade is in the hands of such clothiers who employ the poor, and have been known to make 1000 pieces a year. We ascended the hill and came in three miles to Bysley, a very small town, where they have a litle market; there is a good church with a steeple, and remains of a handsom octagon cross in the churchyard. In a window of the church is a couchant statue, cross leggd, with a coat of mail, the feet on a dog, a shield on the arm, a long sword girt round the body. This is the mother church to Stroud; half way between is Minchenhampton; at Toadsmore Fryar Bacon was born, and they pretend to show some building for his study. From this place we went west and descended to that rivlet that runs from Painswick to Stroud. I saw a petrifyed scollop shell on this hill, and crossing over another heigth we came to Painswick, a market town prettily situated and on the side of the hill, and esteem'd an exceeding good air; just above it Mr. Hyatt built an house of hewn stone, in a fine situation, and made a very pretty garden; before it is a court with statues and sphynxes, and beyond that a lawn for the grand entrance; the garden is on an hanging ground from the house in the vale, and on a rising ground on the other side and at the end; all are cut into walks through wood and adorn'd with water and buildings, and in one part is the kitchen garden. We ascended the hill between several quarries, and going out of the road to the right came to the summit of it, which is worked into a very strong fortification by deep double ditches, and is call'd Kingsborough. A litle turret is built on the south side. This summit commands a glorious view of (what besides I have mentioned already) the country to the north and the hills to the east, especially of the beautiful hill towards Glocester, call'd Robin-hood, and another to the north, near the road to Cheltenham, which has the name of Cloven Hill. I descended, and was told at the quarries that they find oyster shells and something like hearts, and they gave me a piece of a rib'd cockle. In about three miles from this hill we came to Glocester, situated on the Severn; here is the bridge on this river. Ships come up to the key, the tyde going but a very litle further;

large barges go up the river, they are supplied by them with coal, which are brought from about Kidderminster to Bewdley.* It is a large town, consisting of two broad streets that cross, and of several others; there are an equal number of inns and good shops in it, and several market places with open colonades cover'd with lead, and they have erected statues to the honour of some Kings, particularly King Charles 2d and one of Queen Anne. This city was call'd by the Britains Caer-Glow (the fine city), and Glecum by the Romans. Edol, a British nobleman, who came with King Vortigern to the Congress here, was Earl of Glocester.

Edmund Ironside and Canute the Dane engag'd in single combat for the kingdom in sight of their armies. William the Conqueror gave this city and castle to Robert Fitz Harman, who was afterwards Lord of Glamorganshire. A large building remains of the old castle and the keep, near which Mr. Hyatt has made a pretty garden in the wilderness way, and has built a very small lodge, in which he lives at present. The town was wall'd round, but the fort were destroyed since in the civil wars, when it held out for the King. At the north-west part of this town is the large enclosure of the Abbey, now called the College, being erected into a Bishoprick by Henry 8th, with a Dean and six prebendaries. Bishop Hooper, who was burnt in the church yard of this cathedral, was the first Bishop of it. The body of the cathedral, except the upper windows and the isle, is the old Saxon building, except the two western arches, which are new, the west end of the church having faln down, and they say the church has been more than once damag'd by fire. King Osric is said to be first founder of it; his tomb is on the north side of the quire, in which is his couchant statue, with the model of the cathedral in his hand. The Saxon pillars also remain on one side of this isle, and on each side of the choir. The skreen, which is a gallery supported by a Gothic colonade, the benefaction of the late Bishop Benson. The choir was

---

* Quere if Glocester be not serv'd with pitt coal from Broseley which lies above Bridgenorth on the Severn ?—*Note in MS.*

casd within, and the tower built by Abbot   , whose tomb
is on one side of the quire. It is an exquisite, fine, light, Gothic
building, finished about 300 years ago. The fine tower is singular,
in that it is built over the west end of the choir, and there is no
appearance in the choir, as I could observe, either of the tower or
of any support of it. It is a fine building of it self, entirely adorn'd
with carv'd work, litle windows, and the battlements and four
pinacles are most beautiful open work, like that of the tower of
Strasburgh. The stalls of the cathedral are carv'd in oak, and are
light and beautiful; to the east of them the sides are open, adorn'd
with several Gothic ornaments. The east window is grand and
beautiful beyond description, taking in the whole east end, and is
all painted glass; under it is an opening, through which one sees the
east window of St. Mary's Church, which has a wonderfull fine
effect. That chapel was built by Abbot   ·   ; it is all window,
in the style of King's College Chapel, in Cambridge, and is exceeding fine. In the north isle, besides King Osric and the last Abbot,
are the monuments of two very unfortunate persons. Robert, the
eldest son of the Conqueror, who was confined about twenty years
in the Castle of Cardiff, where he dyed; his couchant statue is of
oak painted. The other is of King Edward 2d, who was murder'd
at Berkley; 'tis said, that out of the offerings to his shrine the
choir was built. I have been inform'd since I left the place the
famous Strongbow is buryed in the chapter house. The isle south
of the quire is very shamefully turn'd into a library. In the south
part of the old transept a very magnificent monument is erected, by
Mr. Hanger, to the late Bishop. It is fineer'd within a frame with
fine Italian marble, I believe that which is call'd Jaspar of Barga.
The long inscription is in English, very high encomium, and over
it is a medalion profile of his head, not in the least like him.

The cloyster is esteem'd a very fine Gothic building.

Winchcomb, May 26th, 1757.

I left Glocester on the 25th and came 7 computed and 10 measured miles to Cheltenham. A litle below the surface of the ground which is a clay is a blueish hard stone in small pieces, which they call a clay stone, and say it will not make lime: it seems to be very hard. Cheltenham is a small market town, famous of late on account of the resort to it for the mineral waters, which purge and are very good, especially where the habit is too full. There is a tolerable room built for the company to meet in, lodgings near it, and a pleasant walk planted through a meadow and a way to the well. There is a fine wheel window in the church about ten feet in diameter. Dr. Tomlinson has a very good collection of pictures in his house, about twenty in number. We came near two miles to Presbury, and came over that chain of hills which go by the name of Cleve; they are steep and pretty high, and are of a sort of stone which appears to me to be a free stone, much of the same kind as that over Painswick; descending I saw a fine piece of scollop shell and a piece of a large ammonis horn. At the foot of the hill we came to Portle where there is a large house and a chapel, the door of which is Saxon; here rises a branch of the river Iston, another rising near Charleton Abbey two miles south of Winchcomb, and a little way beyond that the river Colne rises which falls into the Thames, those two rivlets unite at Winchcomb and fall into the Avon at Evesham. On the first-mentioned rivlet very near the town is a paper mill. Winchcomb is a pretty summer situation on the side of the hill as in an amphitheatre, also encompassed with beautiful hills. It is said to have been formerly a county granted by King Ethelred to the Abbey of Glocester. It was a borough in the time of Edward the Confessor. Here was an Abbey under a mitred abbot, part of the enclosure remains, of large hewn stone with a basement, and a small part of the Abbey, probably the dormitory, and a house has been built on the spot out of the ruins of it. No part of the church is remaining, but about the site of it they have found some stone coffins. On the dissolution it was granted to Sr Thomas Seymour, and then to William Parr Marquis of Northampton, was forfeited, and 'tis said the site of the abbey and I suppose the estate was granted by Queen Mary first to John Ld Chandois. It afterward belonged to Dr Lloyd, Chancellor of Worcester; and lastly descended to two co-heiresses, and is just now purchased by Mr Pitt of Hampshire, being about £1000 a-year. Sudley Castle, half a mile from the town, is on this estate; whether the same as was call'd formerly Ivy Castle, I cannot say. But what remains of the house was probably built by Lord Chandos, for it is most of it in the style of the time of Queen Elizabeth,[a] and is a fine building. The remain[in]g apartments are a single house on three sides of a court, which led to another, there being at present no building between them, but remains of a grand entrance on one side; in the other court on one side was a very grand hall, now in ruins, with a fine bow-window, at one corner a tower with some apartments in it; and at the other a turret from which they say water was convey'd to the house. All is of fine hewn stone, which they have here in great plenty. To the east of the buildings is the shell of a beautiful chapel, of five windows on each side; and on the side of the chancel are the three seats for the persons administring, with niches between them as for statues. A singular tower is practiced at the west and which projects a litle over the wall to the west, and to the east rests on two pilasters projecting likewise about a foot beyond them. In the front also are two niches for statues, of which statues there are some remains, they are a white free stone. To the north of this chapel is a building joyning to it, about ten feet wide and 30 long, probably built over the vault in which Lord Chandos is buryed; here service is now perform'd once in a fortnight. The parish church is a very handsom Gothic building with a tower to it, with an isle on each side, all cover'd with lead, except the chancel; the rood loft remains in the church which they call an organ loft. The Vicaridge is worth only £30 a year, but has commonly two schools here of different foundations. This place is

---

[a] Chiefly built in King Edward 6th's time. See *Sel. Itin.—Note in MS.*

out of all roads, they have markets and it is a Corporation consisting of five bailiffs and small number of burgesses, a few of which
are only just kept up in order to collect the tolls, for they do not
send members to Parliament. They have a trade in spinning, and
weave coarse woollen cloths for their own use. I saw in the town a
large ancient Saxon capital, which probably belong to the abbey
church. In some of the quarries they raise such large stone as to
make cisterns of any size they please.

Evesham, May 26th, 1757.

On the 26th I went 3 miles to Halls Abbey, to the north-east, at
the rise of a small stream which falls into the Isbon. This abbey
is in Ld Tracey's family, and was one of their seats about sixty
years ago, but very litle now remains of the old buildings, except a
part in the front, with a handsom bow window call'd the Abbot's
Chamber, some fine arches, which they say was the cellar, one
entire side of the fine cloyster, and the outer wall is all round, several
large barns and a pidgeon house near 40 feet square with buttresses
at each corner, and a chapel now in service all of hewn stone. From
this place we came by Didbrook and Stanway, Mr. Tracey's, an
exceeding good old house built of hewn-stone, and a very pleasant
place. A sort of Saxon cornice round the church is remarkable;
they have cut some Gothic figures on it. We came by Staunton
and Childeswickam to the great turnpike road from London to
Worcester just three miles from Evesham, in which we went to that
town, which is most pleasantly situated on an eminence over the
river Avon, navigable from Stratford to the Severn at Tewkesbury:
here is a bridge over the river, which winds so as to make the town
and some fields a peninsula. At the south-west part of the town
was the Abbey, of which there are very litle remains; the oldest
part is the ruins of a very old Saxon gateway to the north. To the
south-west are some litle remains of the cloyster, but they say the
Abbey church was to the north of two churches now standing and is
entirely destroy'd. These churches within 50 yards of each other

are two parish churches; in that to the north is a very fine chapel, at the entrance of which Abbot Litchfield was buryed, who built the chapel, and over it are these letters ⌞ ⌐ the initial of the Christian name escap'd me; the two letters stand for Litchfield Prior. There is a singular   in this church. In the other is such another chapel in the north side also, and the chancel, which is much narrower than the breadth of the church, is an exquisite piece of Gothic workmanship on the outside, and was doubtless well adorn'd within. There is a vault in the church in which they found nothing but a large chest, and which is supposed to have contain'd some valuable things of the church; there is a tower and small steeple as well as to the other. To the east of this court is a very fine tower 30 yards high built by Abbot Litchfield for a belfery; it is something in the style of that of Glocester. I went to see Dr. Bailie's garden, which is prettily laid out in wilderness, &c., with a hermitage. In one part is the abbot's chair of oak, the covering of which is very well executed, Sphynxes make the arms, a running foliage of vines make the back, on one side of which a monk in a bending posture holds a cross, on the other side another figure answers to it, and 'tis a fine piece of antiquity, which was kept in an alehouse till the D^r rescued it. He has also made a turret two stories high with stairs round the outside of it, and the lower room is adorn'd with several carvings in wood taken from the church. I walk'd near a measured mile to Battle Wells in the northern road, famous for the battle in which Prince Edward, afterward Edward 1st, beat Simon Mounfort and the Barons, and restored liberty to his father. They say the battle was in the road and in Upton lane, but possibly there might then be no enclosures. They say also that there was such a slaughter that the blood ran down to the Avon, and they frequently dig up bones, and they told me that they found in the road a vault full of bones, which formerly might be under some chapel. The great support of this place is the navigation, a great manufacture of yarn, stockins from 8d. to 2s. 6d. a pair; flax prepar'd for spinning;

and above all, gardens and orchards, which supply all the country round for a great way, and they have all things very forward. I went in the turnpike road to Worcester 6 miles to Pershore, situated on a flat on the same river, 10 miles from Worcester and 106 from London.   There was an Abbey here, said to be founded by King Edgar; litle remains of the very ancient church except the middle and north part of the transept, which is very ancient Saxon, and they have built a Gothic tower on it, which has given way, and is supported by a modern very curious buttress, as well as by one of an older date; the semicircular pilasters remain to the west of it, which are nearer the ancient Doric than any I have seen, and there must have been an uncommon grandeur and simplicity in the body of the church.   That which was the quire part is not large and in the Gothic style, with a passage over the arches in front like windows, divided by slender pillars into three parts, and the same at the east end, which consists of three sides, like three sides of an octagon; there was an opening from it, I suppose, into a chapel, one of the side windows of which remain of a singular kind with arches more joynted than ever I saw; the cornice round the church on the outside is of the Saxon kind, and altogether it must have been formerly a magnificent edifice.   Near it is a small church of another parish, which they call the Mother Church, but there is no marks of antiquity in it but an old font, adorn'd with arches intersecting each other.

Banbury, May 28th, 1757.

On the 29th I left Evesham and came in the same road back 3 miles, and then further in it to Broadway, near 6 miles, and a litle beyond it turn'd out of the London road to the left, and came three miles to Combden.   I had seen to the left, under the hill faceing. Evesham Norton, the late Sr Thomas Keyt's, purchas'd by the late Sr Dudley Reider; it is a pleasant place, and there are fine plantations about it, but the inside was burn't.   The first post from Evesham is Morton Hennerske, twelve miles, the next is Chipping Norton, 8

miles, Woodstock more, and so to Oxford. I came to Camden to
see the ruins of Camden house, and the monuments in the church.
The church it self is a fine Gothic building, with isles and a chapel
on each side, as a cross isle. The tower is lofty and beautiful. In
the south chapel are the monuments of the Camden family. First
of Sr Baptist Hickes, Londoner, and his wife, whose fine couchant
statues are under a canopy supported by ten Dorick pillars of black
and yellow marble; they are in robes. It was this gentleman who
built Hickes Hall, as I was told; he dyed in 1629. Lady Juliana,
their only daughter and heir, married Sr Edward Noel, who was
created Viscount Camden Baron Noel of Ridlington and Hicks of
Hemington. He was made a knight bannaret in Ireland in 1611,
and died at Oxford in 1642. His lady died in 1664. The second
son Henry died a prisoner, I suppose, to the Parliament army. A
daughter, married to Lord   , by whom, I suppose, the
estate has descended to Lord Gainsborough. Their monument, the
work of Marshal, consists of two statues of white marble, well
executed, standing as in their shirts, with a flowing garment tyed in
an open knott on the head and finely flowing as to represent the
shroud dress, but has a very good effect and is altogether a fine
piece of sculpture; a leaf of black marble opens on each side, which
are two inscriptions. There are two or three other monuments, and
one of a daughter of the Earl of Denbigh, who was married to a
second son. Near the church are the ruins of Camden House, the
architecture of Inigo Jones, but with the old windows of King
James 1st's time. Near the church is a gate, with a porter's lodge
on each side; going down to the town and entering a court are two
piles of offices with handsom offices, with handsom door cases; then
we came to the terrace which was behind the house, at each end of
which there was a banqueting house built with three clos'd arches
and a basement and rooms above, the chimnies are as twisted fluted
pillars, with a stone in appearance laid on them, and a rose cut at
each corner. Here seems to have been a terrace round a grass
plat. The house fac'd to the church; there is not one stone of it

left. They have here a manufacture of spinning thread. I went a mile farther to Ebrington, where the Lord Fortescue has a seat. In the church is the monument of the famous Lord Chancellor Fortescue of the reign of Henry 6th. His couchant statue is supported at the feet by a lyon and an angel on each side of his head. There are arms round the tomb, over it is an inscription put up by his descendant. In the inscription he is call'd Legum Angliæ Hyperos-pistis fortissimi. Going on I saw Foxcot, Mr. Canon's, a Roman Catholick; it is a large house. I just saw Stow on the Would, on the point of a hill, which is but seven miles from Barford, and a hill over Monto Henmarsh, in the way to London, a litle beyond which is Northwich, Sr John Rushout's. I saw also Stratford on Avon to the north-west, and came to Shipton on the Stour in Worcester-shire, a small market town, said to have had its name from being a sheep market. They knit stockins, mostly white, from 8d. to 6s. a pair, and they weave hair or worsted shag, from 5s. to 15s. a yard; a coach goes through this place in a day from Birmingham, by Euston to Oxford, 28 measur'd miles from this place, and in another day to London. We came 9 computed, and 15 measur'd miles, to Banbury. They have a manufacture here in combing wool and weaving hair or worsted shag. On the 25th I went 3 miles in the London road to Adderbury; here is a good church with a steeple, and, what appear'd to me at a distance, a fine light Gothic cross isle and chancel. Here the Duke of Argyle had a house, now Lady Dalkeith's, with large offices, built of a large sand stone, in some of which are small holes with diamond shoots, as about Redway, but it is a dark colour'd looking stone; lower down Sr George Cobb has a very good old house. Here I left the London road and went in the Oxford way to Dedington, where there is a good Gothic church, but no marks of great antiquity, as I expected, having some idea that it was the see of an ancient bishoprick.

Warwick, May 30th, 1757.

On the 28th I came from Banbury to Redway. When I was last here I did not see the walks up the side of the hill through the woods. I went also to see the Red Horse, which is not above 30 yards long. It is represented with the tayl held up; 'tis not so good a figure as the White Horse. 'Tis said the lands of Tysoe are held on condition of cleaning this Horse, which is distinguished by the red soil. About two miles from it is Compton, the Earl of Northamton's; near it also the road comes up the hill from Stratford to Banbury. I went a mile to Red Chiffe Church, where are remains of painted glass and a variety of Gothic windows. The situation of Redway Hill is so chearful that Burton on Melancholy mentions it with Beauvoir Castle as a place that inspires with chearfulness. On the 30th I came 9 computed and 14 measur'd miles to Warwick, seeing by the way   Mr. Newton's, whose mother is married to Mr. Nugent of the Treasury. I observed also this way a lime stone, much like what they call the clay stone towards Glocester. Warwick is most delightfully situated on an eminence on the Avon, over which there is a bridge. It is 88 measured miles from London. The hill it stands on is a fine free stone with a blueish cast. The best part of the town consists of two cross streets. It is supposed to have been the Præsidium, where the præfect of the Dalmatian horse was posted. 'Tis said that the Picts and Scots destroy'd this place; that it was rebuilt by Caractacus, who was general of the Silures, but taken by Osorius. Ethelfleda, a Lady of the Mercians, put it again into a flourishing condition about 911. Dubricius is said to have founded a Bishoprick here in the church of the saints before he founded Llandaff. Some say it had its name from Warremund, an ancestor of the Mercian kings, who rebuilt it. Roger, the 2d Earl of Warwick, built that part of the church called the quire, which is a fine Gothic structure, whose monument is in the middle of it. The Beauchamps became Earls of Warwick, who built a chapel to the south of the quire, in which is a fine old monument of the founder of it, with brass hoops over it. Here are also the monuments of Robert Dudley, Earl of Leicester, fifth son of the Duke of   and also of a younger son. The frame of the east window is finely adorn'd with reliefs of Scripture history, and the window is painted glass. To the north of the chapel is a confessionary, with a hole from it into the church, which I first thought was to view the exposition of the host, but they said it was for confession. Before the confession seat are three or four seats for the penitents, one behind the other, from which they say they went by a door into the quire to confess. In the front of the quire is set up the brass plates gilt of the monument of   .

The town was burnt in 1694; the body of this church was consum'd and rebuilt with a tower near 150 feet high. The church and the tower are a mixture of Gothic and Roman architecture. The cathedral is said to have been in the castle and removed to St. Mary's Church, which was collegiate. In the new square of the town was an Abbey destroy'd by Canute in 1016. There was a Priory to the north of the town of Canons Regular of the holy sepulchre, on the site of the parish church of St. Helen's; 'twas begun by Henry de Newburgh, Earl of Warwick, and finished by his son, Hen. 1st. There were some hospitals likewise founded by the Earl of Warwick. The castle is finely situated and a noble building. Richard the 2d began a strong fortification here, probably the keep at the corner of the castle, which is finely planted. Roger de Belle Monte removed the college to St. Mary's. The castle was made the county goal, and granted by King James 1st to Sr Fulk Greville, who made it very fine at a great expence, and it now belongs to Earl Brook his descendant, who has greatly beautifyed the park and the whole place by plantations. The castle is situated on the rock, which is not very high over the river. To the right of the entrance is a tower, a fine old one of twelve sides. The chief building is over the river, which consists of very handsom apartments. One of the rooms is wainscoated with cedar, and there are several pieces in the house of Vandike and Lilly,

Mary Queen of Scots, and Anne of Bullen, said to be Johnson's. There is very beautiful tapestry in one room, the drawing of which are exceeding fine. They represent gardens, buildings, and landscapes. 'Tis doubted whether they are needlework. I should think they are, because I never saw such tapestry in any other place, and when tapestry is wove they commonly make many setts of the same sort or pattern. There are some beautiful marble tables in the castle brought from Italy by the present Earl. His private apartments are very neat, and his study is adorn'd with drawings of the capital statues in Rome and Florence, and also of several views of buildings. In an out-office are some things preserv'd, which they say belong'd to Guy Earl of Warwick, as his armor, all of immense size, and his sword ; they pretend to say he was nine feet high, and show the   he used in turnaments, his iron shield, the helmet, and part of the coat of mail, and the head-piece of his horse, and a pot of bell-mettle which holds 92 gallons. He is drawn on the walls as encountring another giant. All which seems to have had some foundation in his being a man of great size, and possibly on some extraordinary tryal of skill might wear this weighty armour ; tho' others think the whole is fabulous. They also show the rib of the Dun Cow, and one of the vertebre of the wild boar, which he kill'd, which seem'd to be of the size of the largest ox. They told me that to Henry the eight's time two pence a day was allow'd for cleaning the sword, and another mentions that Henry 8th granted 2^d a day to William Hoggeson for showing these acoutrements. There was also some tapestry of the actions of Earl Guy, which were left as heir looms. I have been inform'd since I left that place that a mile from the castle on the Avon is Guy or Gib Cliff, where there is a cave with trees and water rising about it : to which place they say Guy retir'd after all his conquests. On Blakelow hill Peter de Gaviston, Earl of Cornwall, was beheaded by the Barons. There is a handsom town house of hewn stone. But the county house is an exceeding fine piece of architecture, of the design of Smierson Miller, Esqre. It is in the Corinthian order, with three windows crown'd with circular pediments at each side of the entrance, with pillars between them, there are stones left in the frieze for carv'd ornaments : how this will succeed I cannot say, but I fear they must be too heavy. They are also left within for the same purpose. You enter an oblong square saloon, the whole length of the building ; two pillars on each side of the two middle pilasters open into two courts, which are made octagon, by six more detach'd pillars, and this is done only by the addition of about half a square at the back of each, in which the judge sits between the two pillars; between these courts is a room for the grand jury. All these publick buildings are of the Warwick stone already described. The support of the town are the inns and shops which supply the neighbouring country. They say they have several vaults cut into the rocks for cellars.

Woolverhampton, May 31st, 1757.

Coventry is eight measur'd miles from Warwick. I went three miles in that road, and then turning to the left came a mile further to Kenelworth Castle, near a large village of that name. It was built by Geoffry de Clinton, Lord Chamberlain to Henry 1st, who afterwards founded a monastery for Canons Regular, of which I saw some small ruins, as they told me it was toward the village which appear'd like a gate way. The castle stood a siege six months, and Edward 2d was made a prisoner here. It came to the Earl of Leicester, who entertain'd Queen Elizabeth here, and they say exhibited on some water a sea-fight. Before I came to it I saw a small fortification made by a deep trench, probably the work of the enemy when it was besieg'd; the enclosure large, defended by semicircular towers. The entrance seems to have been on the north side, where there is a handsom pile of building of about four rooms on a floor, which they call the Lodge, with a tower at each corner, which, if I do not mistake, are octagons. There is a handsom door case to it, and some good carved chimney pieces and wainscoat. This probably serv'd for the steward and upper servants. Coming on to the building of the castle, which is something in this form *⌐ ⌐*, to the right is the strong building of the castle it self ; the walls are very thick, I think 30 feet, built with openings of true arches, with a broad foundation, every tier of stone setting in for about ten feet. It consists of a large room below, probably the magazine and another above. This seems to be the building of the time of Henry 1st; close to this was the entrance. To the left was a grand building, which was the habitable part, and is a double house of about six rooms of a floor, and three stories high, with the large windows of Queen Elizabeth's time, adorn'd with fine mouldings and water tables and most excellent masonry in hewn stone ; some of the fine chimney pieces remain, but most of them are taken away. There is a square tower at one corner, which served for the stair case ; from this there seem'd to have been a Gothic building, chiefly as of communication with a grand Gothic hall on the other side of the court opposite to the entrance. This building I have described seems to have been executed under the Earl of Leicester, for there is a date of 1500 and odd. The grand hall was a fine room ; on one side is an open apartment, which might serve for the side-board ; opposite to it is a small room with a chimney to retire to ; there was a large chimney on each side of the hall, and a grand portal of entrance, towards the other end of the room, with a rich Gothic frame of a door, directly opposite to the entrance ; between this building and the strong part of the castle is a small space without buildings. The whole is one of the most magnificent sumptuous structures in England, and I do not recollect any that exceeds, except Ragland, the Duke of Beaufort's, in Monmouthshire. From this place we went eight computed miles and twelve measured to Sullihill, a pretty small neat town ; there was a fine high spire to the church, which was blown down by the high wind last winter, and broke down the roof of the church every way, there being a cross isle over which the tower is built. In five computed and eight measured miles we came to Birmingham, a fine large town of manufacture, of all sorts of toys and implements in the iron way, and some in brass, and they japan also and enamel in great perfection, and cheap. The town is built of brick, and there are several good houses in the High Street, in New Street, and round the fine square, in which the church stands, which is a grand building of hewn stone, and there is a beautiful new built free-school, of the foundation of Edward the 6th. From Birmingham I went   computed and   measured miles to Walsall, 113 measured miles from London, and 5 computed from Litchfield. It is finely situated on a hill, the church being on the summit of it, in which is an old monument of one of the Hilary's, a knight of Edward III^{ds} time. The face is almost entirely cover'd by the armour. I was inform'd after I left it that there are iron mills near, and of the iron ore call'd   mentioned by Dr. Plot, which I suppose by steeping it in water makes a cool agreeable liquor. We went 5 miles to Woolverhampton, passing by a litle manufacturing town, about half way, call'd Wellinghall.

Ellesmere in Shropshire, June   , 1757.

Woolverhampton is a large town, pleasantly situated on a gentle rising ground; it is a great manufacturing town in all sorts of toys, and particularly of locks, in the greatest perfection. This place was first call'd Hampton, and had the name of Vulfrunes Hampton, from Vulfruna, King Edgar's sister, who built a monastery here. King Edgar built founded a chapel here, with eight   , the head of whom had sole jurisdiction over them. Edward the 4th united the deanery of this church to the deanery of Windsor. They have, as I have [been] inform'd, quire service on Sundays, but forgot to enquire. It is a very good Gothic church, but no marks of great antiquity in it. 'Tis commonly fill'd with between 3 and 4000 people. There is a fine stone pulpit. The following inscription is in the church :—" In the year of our Lord 991, in the reign of King Ethelred, Ulfrun, or Wulfrun, widow to Athelane, Duke of North-ampton, founded this church." In the quire is a fine bronze statue in armour, with an angel on each side all gilt, of Admiral Richard Leveson, who married Margaret, daughter of Charles Howard, Earl

of Nottingham; he commanded against Spain in 1588, was knighted
at the Siege of Cales in 1590, obtain'd a victory at the Azores in
1597, and in 1598 he was made Admiral to defend the Channel.
He beat the Spaniard at Kingsale and Castle Haven in 1601. In
1602 he took their East India fleet. He was made High Admiral
by King James 1603, and sent Ambassador to make a peace with
Spain, and died in 1605. In the north transept is an old altar
monument, with statues of the family of the Lanes, and near is
the monument of Col. John Lane, who assisted in the escape of
King Charles II. after the battle of Worcester; he dyed in 1667.
There is an elegant inscription on it relating to the history, and a
fine relief of the Royal Oak and a Crown on it, and the back of an
horse on one side and of the forepart of a horse on the other, with
trophies in the middle, very well executed. From the church yard
I saw Tettenal, about two miles off in a valley to the west, where the
Danes were cut off in 911, by Edward the Elder; and on the hill
about a mile beyond is Wrottesher, where I find there is mention
made of an old town near four miles in circumference, of which I
could not get an account, and the weather did not favour in making
enquiry on the spot. A baronet of the name married the late Lord
Gore's daughter, lives there, and is lately gone into orders. I went
five miles to the small town of Brewood. The windows of the
church are all narrow and more pointed than any I have seen.
Here are several fine old monuments of the Giffords. Two miles
more brought us to Boscobel, famous in history for being the place
where King Charles 2d lay hid after the battle of Worcester.
Richard Peverel, a wealthy farmer, who liv'd at Hubal, a mile to
the east of Tongal, the greatest hand in the transaction of this affair;
in the house they show, up in the garret, the trap door by which the
king went down and sat in an enclosed place, to which there was no
other entrance, being separated from a closet below by a plaister
partition, and the whole room was matted over so that the trap door
could not be seen. In a parlor below is the bed he lay in, to which
the wainscoat opens, and I suppose the landlord, Fitz Herbert, a

Roman Catholic, has hung up over it a print of a young person
with the ornament of a cross and this motto, " Misero succumbere
sæclo"; opposite is another closet where the king used to sit. We
were then conducted to the site of the Oak.   Close to it is an oak
about 70 or 80 years old, which they rose up from an acorn of the
tree ; up on a bough of that tree the king was hid, or in the hollow
of it the king was hid, when they were searching for him in the
house.   The tree is enclosed with a wall, and over it is this inscription :

Feliciss. Arborem quam in Assylum Potentiss. Regis Car. 2ᵈˡ D. Op. Max. per
quem Reges regnant hic crescere voluit tam in perpet. rei tantæ memoriam quam
in Specimen firma in Regis fidei Muro cinctam posteris commendans Basilius et
Iana Fitz Herbert.

Quercus amica Iovi.

Mrs. Jane Lane, who had so large share in this transaction,
liv'd at Bentley, near Walsal.   From Boscobel I came in about half
a mile to White Lewies, where the old Saxon church is almost
entire; the door in the middle on the north side and one towards
the end are adorn'd with semicircular members round the arch,
which is singular ; there are two or three other doors ; the whole
building of the church seeming to be entire, and is an oblong square
about three times as long as it is broad.   On the other side of
Boscobel we saw a large wooden house to the right, with a large
piece of water near it ; this is call'd Black Ladies.   In about
two miles we came from Staffordshire into Shropshire, near Tong,
where we lay.

Wrexham, June, 1757.

Tong is a small village, but is remarkable for its church and for
the monuments in it.   This place having belong'd to the family of
Morcar, earls of Northumberland, in the Saxon times, it was given
from them by the Conqueror, came to the Zouches of Ashby, then
to the Badlesmeres, and by the female line to the Veres, earls of
Oxford, and as they told me here, to Sʳ Fulke Pembroke, from him

by the female to the Vernons, then to the Stoners and Harvy, to
Lord Pierpont, and, by the marriage of his daughter, to the Duke
of Kingston. In the north isle of the church is the monument of
Sr Folk Pembroke and his lady, with their couchant statues, as are
all the others, except one; he has on the chain armour, and his head
rests on the helmet, the crest of which is the head of a woman with
her hair plaited behind, after the Eastern manner, and a Turkish
head dress, of which they tell this story:—That when he was in the
East he fought in single combat for the Grand Signior's daughter,
and overcame; that she was offer'd to him, but that he could not
accept her, as he was marryed; and therefore she desir'd she might
lye with him on his tomb. Under the pulpit is the tomb of S^r
Richard Vernon and his lady, who they say married Sr Folke's
daughter; round the tomb are arms and saints in alternate compartments, adorn'd with beautiful Gothic ornaments, as are all the
other tombs. Opposite to the pulpit is the tomb of Sr William
Vernon, of 1419. The figures of him and his lady are in brass
plates, and of twelve children at nine births, there having been three
births of twins. In the south isle is the monument of Sr George
Vernon and lady, and the arms born by angels and compartments
are alternate; beyond this an arch is turned, finely adorn'd, and
three Gothic niches over it. Under this arch is the tomb of Sir
Henry, of 1515; within it, at one end of the chapel, is a memorial
of Sr Arthur Vernon, priest, and on a brass plate on the floor he
is called Master of Arts of Cambridge; and at the other end he is
represented in a pulpit with a short inscription; he died in 1517.
And Sr George is mentioned as the founder of the chapel. S^r
Henry Vernon is mention'd as the donor of the great bell in 1518,
who seems to have been the last of the family; for in the chancel
is a very magnificent monument of Sr Thomas Stanley, second son
of the Earl of Derby, who married the co-heiress of Sr George
Vernon, who had two sons, Edward surviv'd, whose couchant
statue is under those of his father and mother. They are on a
marble slab, supported by sixteen pillars; the outer row are round,

and within them are square pillars finely adorn'd with sculpture. In this chancel is a small monument, against the wall, of one of the Harris's, who had this estate, and probably married a daughter of the Stanleys, as Ld Pierpoint might ally with one of the Harris's. The great bell is very fine, and weighs two ton and a half; they only toll it. There are stalls in the quire, handsomely carv'd. To the south of the church are some remains of what they call the college, which was for priests, if I mistake not, to serve the church; it was built round a court, founded, as they say, by the lady of Sr Folke Pembroke, when she thought he was made a slave by the Turks. There is an almshouse near the church. I went to the castle, which is a building of no great antiquity, most of it having been built within these two hundred years. There are apartments in it, with door cases of Derbyshire marble set up by Ld Pierpoint, who inhabited the house, and has been dead about forty years. We went from Tong, and passed by Lydeat forges for making bars of iron, the ore being found and smelted at Dauly, and in about two miles came into the high road from London to Shrewsbury. We saw to the right Weston Hall, Ld Bradford's, and in seven miles from Tong came to Penslarn, where the collieries begin. It is a large coal, burns swift, and is very cheap, and from this colliery they are supplyed very much down the Severn. We soon came to Watling Street Collieries, being on each side of the road. This place has its name from the old Watling Street, which is the Roman way from Dover to Cardigan; goes by St. Alban's, Dunstable, Towcester, Atherton, enters Shropshire at   ; goes by Wroxeter, Aston, Bornel, the Strettons, and to Lanterelen in Herefordshire; it is commonly call'd the   , and in different parts goes by the name of High Dike, High Ridge, Forty Foot Way, and Ridge Way; this name continues near to Wellington, where our turnpike goes to Shrewsbury, and the other towards Wem, in which road we went, and immediately came to the end of the poor town of Wellington, on the foot of the Wrekin, which on this side appears a very beautiful hill, with shrubs, and something like Sidon Hill in Hampshire, but it is steeper and the ground more uneven; on the south side it appears more rough and steep, as I remember. I went to see the church, in which there is one remarkable Saxon window, of which I have given a drawing.

There is also an old monument of the Charletons, with two couchant statues on it, and it is adorn'd with arms supported by angels and compartments of saints alternately. From Wellington we [came] in three miles to Arthur's Court, a fine old mansion house, which did belong to S^r   , and is now the estate of L^d   ; there are some additions to the old house of very good architecture, with fine door cases, windows and entablatures, and the date of 1514, and that it was built by   . .

We came to the river Rodon, and near it, in 4 miles from Arthur's Court, to a most noble house, never finesh'd, called Moreton Corbett, adjoyning to a strong built old castle, of which there now remains very litle; it anciently belong'd to a family of the name of Turet. Robert Corbet began this magnificent building in the time, if I mistake not, of King James the First; the windows are adorn'd with the different orders, something in the style of Somerset House, tho' much grander; but he dyed before it was finished. The church is near the house, in which are monuments of the family of Sr Robert of 1514, Sr Richard of 1688, and Sr Vincent of 1680. Two or three miles more brought us to Wem, a very poor town, 121 computed and 148 measur'd miles from London. It was a barony in the families of the   Butlers, Ferrers, and Dacres, and of King James 2d his Jefferies, and is now in his son. Wicherley, the poet, was born here. There is a remarkable statue in a nich in the tower of the church, and another, if I mistake not, at the west end, and to the west of the church (there was a garrison here for the Parliament, of which Mr. Baxter was chaplain) are some signs of fossees and ramparts of an old castle.

On the 2d of June we came 10 measur'd [and] 6 computed miles to Ellesmere, very pleasantly situated between two lakes abounding in fish, from which it takes his name, the church being on the side of a hill just over the fine eminence, which was the site of an old castle. It was settled on Llewellin, Prince of North Wales, by King John, on his marriage with his natural daughter Joan. It was in the Estampes, and now gives the title of Baron to the Duke of Bridgwater's family.

I came ten computed and fifteen measur'd miles to Wrexham, passing by Oreton, famous for a church yard encompass'd with fine yew trees, and passing over the Dee into Derbyshire, not far from Bangor, the site of the famous Abby I have formerly gave an account of, and came to Wrexham.

Llanrust [June,] 1757.

Wrexham is pleasantly situated on a small stream that falls into the Dee. There is a good town house and market place, but it is most famous for the church and tower, which is indeed very fine; a prospect-of it, and some account of this building, is here inserted. Near Wrexham, at a place call'd Stort on the Dee, Cambden supposes was Leonis Castrum, so call'd from Legio Vicessima Victrix. It belong'd to S^r Wm. Stanley, who was beheaded by Henry 7th on his reproaching him for not being sufficiently rewarded for his good services. We went on the third over the hills which are between the Dee and Cluyd, on which there are lead mines, and had a view of the fine vale of Cluyd, and came ten computed and fifteen measur'd miles to Ruthen, a pleasant situation on a rising ground near the Cluyd. There are great remains of a large castle, which seem to have been very strong. The church is rebuilt close to the ruins of an old monastery, and there is a free school adjoyning to it, founded, if I mistake not, by Dr Goodman, Dean of St. Paul's, in 1598. We came along the edge of the vale, 5 long miles to Denbigh, now situated on the side of a hill, but formerly on the top within old walls which now remain. There are ruins of a large church in it, and of a castle, with a very grand gate way, over which there is a remarkable statue much decay'd. The stones of this hill abound in petrifyed cockles. I went on over the hills eight miles to a small village call'd Bettles, and on the 4th as many more to Llanrust, six miles above Conway, and on the river of that name. This place and a neighbouring seat belong to the Duke of Ancaster, and came to him, as I apprehend, by marrying an heiress of the Wynne family baronets, who are buryed in the church, where there are several monuments over them. In one they are mentioned as descended from Owen Guynean, Prince of Wales, who marryed Emma Plantagenet, sister to Henry 2d. Leolin, the last Prince of Wales of this house, is also mentioned, who liv'd in the time of Edward the First, and over an old coffin of stone, if I mistake not, is this inscription: " This is the coffin of Leoline Magnus, Prince of Wales, who was buryed in the Abbey of Conway, and, upon the dissolution, removed thence." The seat is most beautifully plac'd on the side opposite to the town on a flat, a quarter of a mile up the hill, and commands a most beautiful prospect of the fine narrow vale down to Conway and up the river, the hills being very beautifully adorn'd with trees and fine fields. The small house is embellish'd in several parts. Near the house is a very handsome chapel. They show'd us also below Llanrust the remains of an old monastery; and, three miles above Conway, they told me was the Abbey of Caerlyn (the old city), where the old town Cono of Antonine is supposed to have been. Out of this town Edward 1st built Aberconway, very pleasantly situated at the mouth of the river. The land call'd Orrus Head I take to be Gogarth, mentioned by Cambden, where, he saies, stood the ancient city of Diganwy, which was consumed by lightening; he supposes it was the city Dictum. According to the editor of Cambden, there were [found?] fifty brass instruments, such, I take, as have the name of celts given to them, with stems to have been fixt to a handle, but what is more extraordinary, brass cases are found to fit them. This river is famous for a black muscle, in which they find large well-colour'd pearls ; and so also, if I mistake not, in the River Aberavon, which falls into the sea to the east of Bangor.

Holyhead, [June,] 1757.

I went about three miles down by the Conway, and cross'd over the mountain to this river, and went over the strand to Beaumorris ferry, which we cross'd, to the town pleasantly situated on the sea and side of the hills.   Its ancient name is said to be Banover.   The town was rebuilt by Edward I., who call'd it Beau-marish, its said from its situation, the ground near the sea, I suppose, having been marshy.   He built also the large castle, which remains very entire. In the church is a fine old monument of white marble, with couchant statues on it and arms round, said to be remov'd from a monastery near.   Here also are inscriptions to Sr Henry Sydney and Sr Anthony St Leger, Mr Thwaites and another person, who were shipwreck'd near in their return from Ireland in 1560, the two former having successively been in the Government of that Kingdom.   I walk'd about a mile to the Priory, if I mistake not call'd Penan Preston, where there are remains of the church and some other buildings, and on the Head to the north I was shown the site of a famous Monastery, I think of Lanover of Minorites, where several personages were buryed, who dyed in the wars between England and Wales, to one of whom the monument in the church at Beaumorris might probably belong.   Lord Bulkeley's situation over the town is very delightfull.   On the fifth we went on towards Holyhead, and hence out of this way to the left to the church of   where I saw a fine monument of the same kind as that at Beaumorris, which they say is that of Owen Tudor.   The couchant statue is in chain armour, with long spurs, and there are some particular ornaments on the garments both of the man and woman.   I came to Holyhead and embark'd immediately for Dublin, where we arriv'd the next morning.

INDEX.

WESTMINSTER:
PRINTED BY NICHOLS AND SONS,
25, PARLIAMENT STREET.

Lightning Source UK Ltd.
Milton Keynes UK
04 February 2011

166919UK00005B/85/P